Praise for *THE SECOND ASSASSIN*

"This is different . . . a standout thriller combining real period charm with brutal up-to-the-minute suspense."—Lee Child

International Praise for the Novels of CHRISTOPHER HYDE

"Hyde's storytelling is pure genius."
—*New York Daily News*

"Draws tension with the skill of a surgeon."
—*New York Times* bestselling author Michael Connelly

"A writer to watch."
—*The New Orleans Times–Picayune*

"Powerful, stunning." —*Publishers Weekly*

"A model of plotting so dazzling it makes other page-turners look positively anemic."
—*Kirkus Reviews* (starred review)

"Mr. Hyde spins a great yarn with a likable hero."
—*London Spectator*

"Not a dull page, not a false note." —*Ottawa Citizen*

"The best-written, best-plotted heist novel ever published—bar none." —*Los Angeles Times*

continued . . .

More Praise for the Novels of CHRISTOPHER HYDE

"A whizzer of a story." —*Library Journal*

"Brilliantly realized and compulsively readable." —*Macleans*

"What a read! Hyde's ability to describe people and places is fantastic!" —*Herald American*

"Sophisticated, intelligent, and wonderfully literate suspense. A unique and masterful work of historical fiction." —*Los Angeles Rapport*

"A superior piece of work." —*Houston Chronicle*

THE SECOND ASSASSIN

Christopher Hyde

AN ONYX BOOK

ONYX
Published by New American Library, a division of
Penguin Putnam Inc., 375 Hudson Street,
New York, New York 10014, U.S.A.
Penguin Books Ltd, 80 Strand,
London WC2R 0RL, England
Penguin Books Australia Ltd, Ringwood,
Victoria, Australia
Penguin Books Canada Ltd, 10 Alcorn Avenue,
Toronto, Ontario, Canada M4V 3B2
Penguin Books (N.Z.) Ltd, 182–190 Wairau Road,
Auckland 10, New Zealand

Penguin Books Ltd, Registered Offices:
Harmondsworth, Middlesex, England

First published by Onyx, an imprint of New American Library,
a division of Penguin Putnam Inc.

First Printing, March 2002
10 9 8 7 6 5 4 3 2 1

Printed in the United States of America

PUBLISHER'S NOTE
This novel is a work of fiction. Names, characters, places, and incidents either are the product of the author's imagination or are used fictitiously. Except for obvious historical figures, any resemblance to actual persons, living or dead, businesses, companies, events, or locales is entirely coincidental.

For my grandson
Gabriel,
with love and hope.

Treason doth never prosper: What's the reason?
For if it prosper, none dare call it treason.

—Sir John Harrington, seventeenth-century poet

Prologue:
Tuesday, October 9, 1934

The man sat at the window of the darkened room on the fifth floor of the Hotel Louvre et Paix in Marseille, patiently watching the broad avenue below through a narrow gap in the heavy pea-green drapes. He brought his arm up into the light and checked his wristwatch. It was almost 4:00 P.M. The crowds had been gathering on the wide sidewalks of rue Canabière since noon, waiting for the Yugoslavian king, Alexander Karageorgevic, who was making his first state visit to France.

According to the front-page stories in *Le Petit Provençal,* the king was scheduled to arrive in Marseille on the cruiser *Dubrovnik,* then drive along the Canabière in regal procession, continuing up the steep hill to the Gare St. Charles. At the railway station, a lavishly outfitted train was waiting to take him to Paris for a grand fete later that evening in Versailles.

Standing, the patient man took a step forward and unlatched the tall windows, pushing the right side open several inches. He could hear the excited chatter of the crowds below him on the sidewalks. In the distance, he could hear the faint sound of martial music coming from the bottom of the hill. Alexander had arrived at last; there wasn't much time left. He turned away from the window and went to the freestanding armoire beside his bed.

He opened the heavily varnished cupboard and took out a small valise and his leather golf bag. From the golf bag he removed his chosen weapon for the work at hand, a Swiss M1931 Schmidt-Rubin carbine fitted with an eight-power Zeiss prismatic sight, also Swiss. The Schmidt-Rubin, minus the optics, was standard issue for the Swiss army and also the Papal Guard at the Vatican.

He'd purchased the weapon from a discreet gunsmith in Paris, complete with the sight, and brought it with him to Marseille on the train, broken down and hidden in the bag. A week ago he'd rented a dented Renault from Agence Centrale on the Prado, ostensibly to play a few rounds at the golf course in Cannes-Mandelieu, but actually to align the Zeiss rifle sight in the secluded forests of Haute Provence.

The man carried the valise and the rifle back to his chair by the window. Placing the rifle across his knees, he laid the valise on the broad windowsill, undid the straps and opened it. He first removed a pair of black wool stockings, which he had loosely filled with beach sand he'd collected several days previous while strolling on the Promenade de la Plage.

He placed the weighted pads on the windowsill, then took out a brown leather cylinder, eight inches long, stitched at one end and capped at the other. Opening the cylinder he slid out a one-inch-diameter Maxim Model 15 silencer, which he then fitted over the muzzle of the rifle, using the broad nut at the bottom end of the device to firmly attach it to the threaded end of the barrel.

The Maxim silencer had been introduced for sniper use during Pershing's Punitive Expedition into Mexico in 1916, but even after almost twenty years it was still the best noise suppressor available. The twenty interior baffles within the metal tube would reduce the sound of his shot to something no louder than a ruptured paper bag or the muffled slamming of a door. Almost as useful to him was the fact that the silencer would considerably reduce muzzle flash—a bonus on the off chance that someone was looking in his direction when he fired.

Reaching into the valise again the man took out a single six-shot magazine and carefully snapped it into place. He slipped the index finger of his left hand into the large ring at the end of the bolt action, pulled smoothly, then turned it counterclockwise and let it slide forward again, releasing the safety. That done, the man stood again, placing the rifle carefully across the chair.

He went to the window and looked out once more. The crowd was noisier now, many of the onlookers waving small French and Yugoslavian flags. There were policemen every twenty or thirty feet along the way, most of them wearing the navy-blue uniforms of the rural gendarmerie rather than the darker blue of the better-trained, and much better armed, Gardiens de la Paix.

Two blocks away, on the other side of the wide cobbled avenue, the man could see the large sign above the blue-and-white-striped canvas portico of the Hotel Bristol. On the roadway directly in front of the awning there was a connecting Y in the streetcar tracks that ran up both sides of the street. The Y in the tracks was exactly 175 yards from his position at the window—the distance paced off several times on the street, then triangulated using the distance up to the fifth floor and taking into account the difference in the slope of the hill that lay between the two hotels.

The man took one of the sand-filled stockings and placed it carefully on a scratch he'd made on the windowsill during an earlier sighting session in the room. He then balanced the second pad on the back of the chair. Finally he picked up the rifle and set it down on the pads, the forward stocking cradling the front end of the stock at the barrel's midpoint, while the second pad held the butt of the rifle. The silencer on the end of the barrel poked less than three inches out through the narrow window opening. From below or across the street, it would be invisible, lost in the dark shadows of the room behind him.

Placing his right knee on the chair seat, the man lowered his cheek to the butt plate and curled his index finger into the trigger guard. Squinting slightly, he looked through the sight and used his free hand to adjust the focus. The cobbled street and the Y intersection of the tracks leapt into view as though he was standing no more than a dozen feet away. The crosshairs of the sight marked a spot in the air a little more than six feet above the street.

The overcast October sky was flat and gray, and no breeze turned the leaves of the ornamental trees planted on either side of the thoroughfare. It was perfect shooting weather. Breathing in a slow, easy rhythm now, the patient man took up the first pressure point of the trigger and waited for the target to appear.

The man in the dark hotel room waiting to kill a king had the black, Huguenot-French look common to the southern counties of the Irish Republic—Cork, Waterford or Kerry. His birthplace was the last of these, a small, wretched Kerry village called Drumdean, cold in the bleak, forbidding shadows of the McGillicuddy Reeks.

His name was John Bone, with no middle name or initial—an odd state of affairs for a child born at the century's turn in Catholic Kerry. His father had been a farmer and his mother worked boiling sheets for the local hotel as well as doing piecework sewing when it was offered. John Bone had five sisters and a brother, none of whom had lived to their majority. He had been the last born and the only one to survive. His mother was dead of influenza before John Bone was ten, and his father died not much later, leaving him hostage to the predatory local priest who used him as a scullery boy.

Past the tempting blush of preadolescence, John Bone was sent to a Jesuit orphanage at twelve, and after four years of a classical education, he ran away to join the Republican cause just in time for the Easter uprising in 1916. After that ill-fated event reached its predictable and tragically Irish end in the rubble of Dublin's blasted main post office on O'Connell Street, a bounty of five hundred pounds was put on John Bone's head.

Two years later, still at large and barely nineteen, John Bone was a crack shot with the long-barreled Krag rifle he'd come to favor, and the price on his head had tripled. Seeing little future for himself and having little use for either the Cause or self-imposed martyrdom, John Bone fled Ireland after taking part in Michael Collins's so-called Bloody Sunday, when fourteen British army officers in Dublin were taken from their various beds and executed in front of their families.

An Irish accent and a knowledge of the works of Catullus being more of a hindrance to employment than an asset, John Bone continued in his occupation as a soldier of fortune, honing his deadly skills. There was no lack of employment opportunities. His trade took him far and wide, from the African Rif Wars to the Afghan uprising and then across the seas to Mexico for their civil war.

By 1928 he had moved on to Brazil, and from there, he crisscrossed South and Central America, going wherever his services were needed, taking the side of whatever faction was willing to pay him best. Cuba in 1931, the Chaco Wars a year later, then on to Nicaragua, Uruguay, and back to Cuba in 1933. In addition to his killing abilities he learned how to fly light aircraft, handle most kinds of explosives and track his quarry, human or otherwise, over any terrain, including dense jungle.

His Irish accent faded with both time and distance, and on those rare occasions when he thought about Drumdean and his past at all, it was only in unremembered dreams. He spoke Spanish fluently, French well and Italian when necessary.

Now, at the age of thirty-four, John Bone understood that he was nearing his prime and that with the passing years his reflexes and his eyes would start to falter and, he knew, eventually betray him. He lived simply and cheaply in Havana, saving most of his money. Another five years and he would have enough safely invested to retire to a life of relative ease. Bone lifted his eye from the rifle sight and listened to the growing roar of the crowd gathered along the Canabière. Five years? He could just as easily be dead within the next five minutes.

At 4:15 P.M. the first outriders in the procession appeared—a group of eight mounted soldiers in full dress uniform, complete with hanging swords. Behind the eight men on horseback, the open touring car containing the king moved slowly up the hill. The automobile was a narrow-bodied black Mercedes-Benz Kurz with wide running boards and elegantly scalloped doors. Riding in front with the uniformed driver was General Alphonse Georges, the renowned French war hero. In the rear, directly behind the general, was the king, in the full dress uniform of a Yugoslavian naval commodore, and beside the king, wearing a formal morning suit, was the diminutive, white-bearded figure of Louis Berthou, the French foreign minister.

The Mercedes drew level with the portico of the Hotel Bristol and right on cue John Bone's partner, a florid-faced Croatian fanatic named Velitchko, jumped up on the running board, a large broom-handle Mauser automatic pistol in his fist. He began firing wildly, aiming at the king, unaware that at the request of his bodyguards Alexander was wearing his usual bulletproof vest beneath his uniform. Almost by accident, two shots struck the king in the neck and face.

Ignoring the king entirely, Bone moved the rifle slightly, the crosshairs finding Berthou, the anti-Nazi foreign minister. Bone took up the slack on the trigger. The butt of the rifle jerked back into his shoulder as he fired. Keeping his eye to the sight Bone saw the heavy bullet tear through the base of Berthou's throat, dark arterial blood spraying up onto the snow-white beard. The little man's hands reflexively came up to his neck and Bone fired a second time, striking the foreign minister high in the chest. Both were killing shots and Bone knew that he had accomplished his primary task.

Easing the rifle fractionally to the left Bone was amazed to see that Velitchko was still on the running board, his pistol now empty. One of the mounted guards was hacking at the Croatian's head with a sword while Velitchko tried to fend him off with an upraised arm. People were running in all directions, uniformed policemen were trying to hold back the crowd, and for a moment Bone saw the figure of a newsreel cameraman recording the whole thing on cine film.

The king, bleeding from the throat and head, had sagged against the back of his seat. Bone fired a third time and watched the impact of the bullet in Velitchko's chest. There had been several others involved in the plot to kill Alexander, but Velitchko was the only one Bone had dealt with directly.

The task complete and the only witness to his involvement now silenced, John Bone stood away from the window, taking the rifle with him. He began counting off the seconds in his head as the crowd on the Canabière now began to scream in panic. Working methodically, Bone unscrewed the Maxim silencer from the end of the rifle, then shoved it and the sand-filled stockings back into the leather valise. After moving to the center of the room, he threw back the oval rug at the end of the bed, took a nail from his pocket and, bending down, inserted it into a small hole in one of the floorboards he had loosened the previous day.

The board came up easily. Working quickly, Bone slid the rifle down into the narrow cavity, seating it snugly between two crossbeams. He pushed the satchel down into the space as well, then put the floorboard back in place and fitted the nail into its hole. Using the heel of his boot he stamped hard on the nail, pushing it down flush; then he replaced the rug. It was by no means a perfect hiding place, but for the short term there was now nothing to connect the occupant of room 506 at the Hotel Louvre et Paix to the terrible events that had taken place in front of the Hotel Bristol, two hundred yards down the Canabière.

Bone went back to the armoire, opened it and removed a dark brown, finely made leather jacket. He shrugged it on, then left the hotel room, locking the door behind him. Turning to the left, away from the elevator, he walked down the corridor, went through the stairway exit door, then down to the main floor. The stairway let him out close to the rue d'Aubagne entrance to the hotel rather than the main entrance on the Canabière, which he knew would now be hopelessly blocked.

John Bone stepped out into the chilly October air and found himself instantly caught up in a pressing surge of spectators from the Canabière being pushed back into the side streets by the local gendarmerie. He let himself be shoved back along the street for a dozen yards or so; then he slipped down the narrow alley behind the hotel and retrieved his motorcycle, which he had chained to the wrought-iron grating of a basement window. He'd purchased the muscular French-made 500cc Dresch for cash from a local dealer, using a false *carte d'identité* to obtain a license from the prefecture a few blocks away on the rue de Rome. If, by some unlikely chance, the motorcycle was ever connected to the assassination of Berthou and the king, an investigation into its ownership would lead nowhere.

Bone switched on the ignition, kick-started the engine and turned away from the crowds now being pushed back along rue d'Aubagne. Instead he wove through a series of back alleys, keeping his speed down as he picked his way around piles of refuse, empty carts and abandoned furniture. A few minutes later and he was deep in the Vieux Carré, the oldest section of the city, directly under the looming presence of the basilica high above on the summit of the hill. Half the streets here had no names and most of them were too narrow to allow two cars to pass each other. Pursuit, except with another motorcycle, would be impossible.

When he was well away from the Canabière, John Bone turned the motorcycle south toward the sea. Five minutes after leaving the hotel he had found his way down to the narrow coast road that serviced the port facilities. Increasing his speed considerably, he headed west. By now he knew that the first alert would have gone out to the ferry terminal at the Quai de Belges, the Gare Maritime and the Gare St. Charles. The first police cordons and checkpoints would be going up and within another ten minutes there would be roadblocks on the N8 east to Toulon, the coast road to La Ciotat and Bandol, and the same roadway heading northwest to Aix-en-Provence. In less than half an hour every way out of the city of Marseille would be sealed up tight.

Except one.

With the throttle fully open John Bone flew along the

narrow road, empty now since the entire port had been closed in honor of King Alexander's arrival. He squinted against the dust that drove up into his eyes and mouth, and tried to ignore the stench of the abattoir and cattle pens that stood between him and the sea.

Bone reached the shunting yards, backed by the gasworks with its giant tanks, and the huge engineering works of the Société Provençale de Construction Navales beyond. He turned to the left, following the road down toward the freight sheds along yet another quay, then turned west once more, pounding past the tall, soot-belching smokestacks of the power station. Above the road to the right the ground rose up in shelves and cliffs of bald broken rock, where no highway could ever go.

The port road turned again. Rounding the corner, Bone could see the mass of the Kuhlmann smelting works. Beyond that, at the end of the road, was the dark cavern that marked his objective, the entrance to the Rove Tunnel. Above it, cut into the spiked limestone crags like a lace collar made of stone, was the Arles Railway bridge. The four-and-a-half-mile run had taken him slightly less than five minutes. In all, eleven minutes had now elapsed since the first shot had been fired.

The Rove Barge Tunnel had been designed as an extension of the Rhone-Marseille canal system, with preliminary engineering studies done in the late 1890s, when most industrial barge traffic was still using teams of dray horses instead of engines. Based on these studies the original designs included a twelve-foot-wide metaled towpath on either side of the seventy-foot-wide canal. Work on the project had begun in 1911 but construction was halted for the four-year duration of the Great War. The 29.7-kilometer tunnel wasn't opened until 1927.

A small workman's village had grown up around the entrance during the seven years since the tunnel had gone into operation, but like the rest of the port its sheds, café and ship chandlers were closed and empty on this day. Barely slowing, Bone roared along the top of the stone breakwater at the water's edge, skidded deftly around a pile of nets and rope, then reached forward and switched on his headlamp as he entered the tunnel. Leaving a thundering echo in his wake, Bone rocketed down the towpath, balanced precipitously over the dark, flat water of the canal barely six feet below him. Bone knew from an earlier reconnaissance that the towpath was regularly used by pedestrians and bicyclists even though such use wasn't strictly legal, and he also knew that the entire length and both entrances were unguarded.

After thirteen noisy but uneventful minutes in the tunnel, John Bone exited at the artificially enclosed Etang de Bolmon, which was actually no more than a small bay in the much larger saltwater tidal ponds of the Etang de Vaine and the Etang de Berre. By using the shortcut through the tunnel he had bypassed almost thirty kilometers of travel and had completely avoided any roadblocks.

Bone angled the motorcycle up the steep dike of the channel exit, found a rutted farm track and finally reached a single-lane back road that took him into and through the sleepy little town of Marignane. It was a surprising landscape beyond the town after the bleak, broken hills of Marseille only a few miles behind him. The farmers' fields were almost perfectly flat, sloping gently down toward the sea, the black, rutted soil turned under for the coming winter. A mile beyond the town he turned west, following the roadway past the small railway station to the Marseille-Marignane Aerodrome.

The airport was made up of two runways laid out in a lopsided V, a row of hangar sheds and a rectangular white terminal building topped with a five-story observation tower. The grass strips between the concrete runways and the hardstands were little more than stubble, stunted and burned by the past summer's sun. A service road connected the terminal building to the ramps of the Base de Hydroavions at the water's edge.

The seaplane base was a key stop for the huge flying boats of Imperial Airways on the Far Eastern routes, as well as the somewhat smaller aircraft of Air France and Lufthansa. As usual, the airport—the second largest in

France—was busy. There was an Imperial Airways C-class flying boat moored to the passenger loading dock beside one of the ramps, a Netherlands Airline Dornier moored nearby and more than a dozen assorted aircraft pulled up around the main terminal.

Bone eased back on the throttle as he approached the terminal, then turned aside and parked behind one of the hangars. Switching off the machine, he dismounted and stretched, smelling the salt water of the etang and listening to the rattle and roar of an airplane taking off. He looked at his watch. It was 4:45, thirty minutes since the shooting. Even at high speed there would be only just enough time for the police to reach Marignane and no reason for them to do so unless something had gone terribly wrong.

Standing beside the motorcycle Bone pulled a packet of Gauloises from the pocket of his jacket and lit one, glancing toward the main entrance to the terminal. As usual there were two gendarmes on guard outside the doors. The two men were smoking, their heads bent in serious conversation, but there was no sign of any untoward activity around them. Bone took a few more puffs on his cigarette, then tossed it away and walked casually around the hangar to the side entrance of the terminal. The doorway led to the baggage area and the consigne counter. Bone gave the uniformed attendant his ticket, reclaimed a medium-size suitcase and took it to the WC a few meters down the corridor.

He emerged less than five minutes later, transformed. The leather jacket was gone, replaced now by a slightly rumpled but obviously expensive cream-colored linen suit, a white shirt and a blue-and-red-striped silk tie. His hair was combed back off his face and he now wore a pair of gold-rimmed, plain glass spectacles, the lenses lightly tinted in a smoky brown as though he suffered from a sensitivity to light. He looked like a well-dressed businessman, which was exactly what the freshly minted Brazilian passport he carried said he was.

Carrying the suitcase, Bone went out onto the main concourse and paused for a moment before crossing to the Lufthansa desk on the far side of the room. A cluster of airport workers including a trio of blue-jacketed *douaniers* was gathered around the swinging doors leading out onto the tarmac. Once again there seemed to be no official alert in place.

Bone went to the Lufthansa desk, handed over his passport, ticket and the suitcase, then waited as the clerk took his bag, stamped his ticket and checked his name off on the manifest.

The clerk smiled. "Your flight leaves in ten minutes, Monsieur Ramirez. You may board anytime you wish."

"Merci," Bone answered. He walked across to the customs-and-immigration kiosk, showed his ticket and his passport, then went out through the double doors. Fifty feet to his right a two-engined Fokker DC-2 waited, the red, white and black Nazi insignia gleaming boldly on the aircraft's tail, its propellers already whirling as the engines warmed up.

Bone walked across the cracked concrete of the hardstand, smiled at the male steward standing by the short stairway at the rear of the aircraft and climbed aboard. The Fokker, an American-manufactured Dutch-assembled Douglas DC-2 had a standard single-aisle seating arrangement, single seats along both the right and left sides.

There were already a dozen or so passengers on board, but Bone found a seat over the wing and dropped into it gratefully. He watched out the window but saw nothing out of the ordinary happening at the terminal. A few minutes later the plane swung around, taxied to the far end of one of the runways and took off, turning northeast above the rolling hills of Provence and leaving the Mediterranean behind. John Bone let his head fall back against the seat, closed his eyes and slept. An hour and fifty-five minutes later the Lufthansa flight arrived at Geneve-Cointrin Airport.

Alexander Karageorgevic died of his wounds almost immediately after being shot, while the seventy-two-year-old French foreign minister, Louis Berthou, officially expired while being taken to the Hospital St. Pierre. Velitchko, the assassin who jumped on the running board of the Mercedes, died instantly, although the official report lodged with the Sureté Nationale in Paris stated that he had died several hours after the attack, the cause of death being the sword cuts delivered by Colonel Poillet, the man on horseback beside the car. No mention was made of the bullet wound in Velitchko's chest and no explanation was given for the disparity of calibers between the bullets found in the king's body and the ones that killed Louis Berthou.

The only survivors of the murderous attack were General Alphonse Georges, struck by four bullets from Velitchko's weapon, and the driver, who escaped unscathed. Between the king, Berthou and General Georges, ten bullets were recovered, nine from the bodies of the gentlemen concerned and the tenth from the upholstery of the Mercedes where Berthou had been seated. Although the C12 Mauser used by Velitchko did in fact hold ten bullets, only seven had been fired when the weapon was recovered. No explanation was ever given for the three extra bullets.

Immediately following the death of the king and Berthou, a full-scale search was done for other members of the assassination plot. Within forty-eight hours three men had been arrested trying to cross the Swiss-French border at Col de l'Iseran. The men, all Croatians like Velitchko, had been seen in his company in both Avignon and Marseille. Upon interrogation all three men insisted that the mastermind of the plot had been a dark-haired man known only to Velitchko. They claimed he called himself Petar. After a brief trial the three Croatians were found guilty and sentenced to life imprisonment. No trace of the man known as Petar was ever found.

Chapter 1

Monday, March 13, 1939
New York City

Jane Todd stared at her cards and tried not to yawn. Pelay, the little Brazilian bellhop, had managed to get them a room overlooking the park this time. Dawn sunlight was already leaking in around the drawn curtains. All four people at the table were smokers and the cigarette haze was thick as fog. The green felt tossed over the table to protect it was covered in ashes, beer bottles, poker chips and cards. The radiator under the window was hissing and the big bed on the other side of the room was starting to look very tempting. Jane and the others had been at it since midnight, and even the sandwich trays Pelay had cadged from his pal down in the Oak Room couldn't soak up the sour taste of too much beer and coffee and far too many cigarettes.

Since it was Jane's deal they were playing Slop, a ladies' game—a two-draw version of poker she'd learned on a Moore-McCormack cruise to Hawaii. Jane let out a small unladylike belch and looked down at the cards again. She'd dealt herself a pair of fives and not much else. Everybody had anted up for the hand and four bucks' worth of chips lay in the pot. Pelay, sitting on Jane's left, drew three cards, then wriggled back in his seat with an irritated expression on his face. Rusty Birdwell, her scrawny pal from the *Daily News,* was seated directly across from Jane. Like the bellhop, he drew three cards, then used a wetted index finger to smooth down his Clark Gable.

"Well shit," he muttered and took a slug from the bottle of Pabst in front of him. Dick Walsh, the handsome, dark-haired headwaiter from the Stork Club, tapped the table and held up three fingers as well. Jane dealt them out, then took three for herself. Still nothing but the pair of fives.

Pelay shook his head. "You a rotten goddamn dealer. You know that, Jane?"

"Yeah," said Walsh. "But at least she's democratic. She doesn't deal anyone a good hand."

"Bet," said Jane. She shook a Lucky out of the pack in front of Pelay and lit it with his slim, solid-gold lighter. "Where does an evil little dwarf like you get the money for a Dunhill?"

"A gift," said the bellhop. He tossed a dollar chip into the pot.

"From a guest?" asked Birdwell, who threw in a dollar as well.

"A grateful guest, my friend." Pelay arched an eyebrow. Walsh folded, tossing in his cards, then stood up and wandered off toward the john.

"Grateful for what?" asked Birdwell, playing into it.

The bellhop leered, then reached down with his free hand and squeezed the crotch of his uniform trousers. "I gave her what no woman can give herself."

"What would that be?" Jane asked. "One of those little cocktail wieners they serve down in the bar?" She added her dollar to the pot. "Anybody worth shooting in the hotel?" she asked.

Pelay shrugged. "Miss Bankhead is here. The Duke and Dukette of Windsor arrive tomorrow, but they do not allow pictures. You know that, Jane."

"I think that's duchess, my little South American friend," said a grinning Birdwell.

"I don't care for a shits what you want to call her," Pelay snorted. "All I know is she has too much luggage and never tips."

"Nobody else?" Jane asked. Because she was a free-lance news photographer, information from people like Pelay at the Plaza and Walsh from the Stork Club was worth its weight in gold. Which was half the reason for the regular once-a-week poker game, of course.

Pelay sighed. "Mr. Dewey is having a party here on Friday. Mr. Astaire arrives on Thursday. Mr. Powell is here on Saturday and Sunday before heading to Cape Cod." He gave a little laugh. "Then there are the regulars, of course: wives playing *fec-a-fec* on their husbands, husbands playing *fec-a-fec* on their wives, assorted kings and queens without countries."

"Think the King and Queen of England will stay at the Plaza when they come to the States?" Birdwell asked.

"If they stay in New York they would stay nowhere else," said the little man, lifting his head proudly. "I would see to it personally, me, Juan Auguste Pelay!" He poked a thumb into his chest.

"Not if the duke and duchess are here," said Jane. Everybody knew England's new queen and the duchess hated each other. Now that would be something worth seeing, Jane thought—a down-and-dirty catfight complete with hissing and scratching and hair pulling, tiaras and crown jewels flying in all directions. What a picture that would be. You could make enough with a shot like that to retire. "Anybody want cards?"

They went around the table again and Jane gave herself a pair of eights to go along with the fives. She bet two dollars. Pelay and Rusty called and they put down their cards. Birdwell took it with queens and treys.

"Royalty has always looked kindly upon me," Birdwell said, screwing up one eye as though he was wearing a monocle. Then he leaned forward and raked in the pot. He lit a Spud and leaned back in his chair. "They'll go over big, those two," Birdwell predicted. "Just you wait."

"From what I hear, he's kind of dull," said Jane. "Not like his big brother."

"Not what the Brits need right now," Birdwell said, shaking his head. "He went shooting tigers in India, flying around in airplanes, kicking up his heels with Mrs. Simpson. Old George and Elizabeth are just what the doctor ordered—Fairbanks and Pickford all over again, mark my words. He's shy, she's charming and both of them are salt-of-the-earth types. Just what you want in a war."

Walsh came back from the john with splashes of water on his wrinkled white shirt and Jane handed him the cards, begging out of the game for a hand or two. She stubbed out her cigarette, then stood up and went to the window. She pulled back the drapes and hauled up the lower pane six inches, letting in a waft of fresh, cold air. She eased herself down onto the radiator, tucking her dark skirt under her thighs, leaned back against the window frame and looked out over the park. Nothing was moving except a cop on horseback going around the pond to Inscope Arch. Jane took a deep breath and closed her eyes for a moment.

Jane Mary Todd was almost thirty-nine years old, born with the century in Brooklyn, New York, on March 31, the same day McKinley officially put America onto the gold standard, making her her mother's personal Golden Girl, as she was called when she was a little girl, much to her shame and horror.

Jane's mother had been a seamstress and her father had worked for the New York Central Railroad. Her father had died in a trench in France in late 1917 and her mother died a year later during the influenza epidemic, leaving eighteen-year-old Jane to take care of Annie, her blind, dull-witted older sister. Helped by friends of her father, Jane managed to find work as a telegraphist's assistant with the railroad, but the money she made wasn't nearly enough to support both herself and Annie. In the end she was forced to have her sister committed to the Metropolitan Hospital Lunatic Asylum on Welfare Island.

Jane lasted two years on the railroad, then found a job as a copy girl on the *New York Herald Tribune,* where she eventually earned enough money to buy a ten-year-old Speed Graphic and set herself up as a freelance reporter and photographer. That was in 1923 and she'd been doing the same thing ever since, bouncing around from one city to the other all over the United States, including a couple of years as a publicity photographer in Hollywood, which was where she'd first met Rusty Birdwell.

For the last three years she'd been back in New York, living and working out of a two-room office in a run-down block on Twenty-third Street that was occupied by jobbers, bail bondsmen, second-rate lawyers and even a couple of private detectives. She'd come close to marriage a few times but had never taken the final plunge. Thankfully she'd never sunk as low as sleeping with any of her poker partners, no matter how desperate she'd found herself. Even though she was pushing forty, most men agreed she was a looker, like a slightly out-of-focus Glenda Farrell in the Torchy Blane films, blond bob and perm, big eyes and a mouth that made you think about all sorts of things, but so far no one was willing to live with her longshoreman's vocabulary, the constant smell of photographic chemicals and a parrot named Ponce de Leon, who only said rude things in Italian. Jane had been given the orphan bird by Dan Hennessy, a cop friend, after covering the murder of its previous owner for the *Daily News*. The dead man, a low-level gunsel for the Gambino family, had been named Vinnie the Mook.

"You gonna play or you gonna jump out the window?" asked Birdwell. Jane opened her eyes and yawned, putting her hand in front of her mouth. She glanced out the window. The horse cop was gone and the park was empty. Somewhere far away she heard the howling of a police siren.

"Play," Jane said finally. She closed the window and went back to her seat. Birdwell was dealing now. Jane anted up and then checked her cards. Junk. She thought about folding before she wasted any more money but decided to stay in for the draw.

"So why you think they coming to America?" Pelay asked.

"Who?" asked Jane, lighting another cigarette.

"This king and this queen," said Pelay.

Birdwell drew a pair. "Depends on if you're a Democrat or a Republican," he said, arranging his cards in a fan.

"I do not understand," said Pelay.

"If you're a Democrat you think it's a nice gesture, hands across the sea and all that, the result of a friendly invitation with no political significance at all," Birdwell replied.

"And if you're a Republican," Jane explained with a smile, "you think it's a secret plot by FDR to get America into the war."

"This is twice you have spoken it. What war?" Pelay asked nervously. "I have not heard of this."

"The war with Hitler," said Birdwell. "Which you can bet your socks is coming, slick as shit."

"I don't want your socks. I want your money," said Walsh. "Three cards." He took them and then it was Jane's turn. She drew three as well and came up with a pair of jacks. She bet two dollars.

"You think the king is coming to make some kind of deal with Roosevelt?" Jane asked, looking across at Birdwell.

The skinny reporter lifted his narrow shoulders. "Hard to say. There's never been a British king on American soil before, so it must mean something."

"I can tell you what it means," said Walsh. "It means that we're already up to our armpits in crap from the World's Fair out in the Meadows and now we're going to be buried in more crap pasted with pictures of the Limey royals—that's what it means." He shook his head. "Billingsly's probably going to come up with a whole new goddamn menu for us to memorize. Quail à la queenie and king crab cakes." He drew two cards, frowned at his hand and folded again.

"I guess we'll just have to wait and see," said Jane. A few minutes later Pelay took the hand with three queens and Jane went home to her office and Ponce de Leon the parrot.

Alan "Tommy" Lascelles stepped out of his office on the ground floor of Buckingham Palace, his outstretched arms loaded down with a half dozen red leather dispatch boxes for His Majesty's attention, and no doubt, the meddlesome attentions of Her Majesty as well. The thin, tall and slightly stooped man turned right and headed down the long gloomy corridor. It was ten minutes to ten, and like everything else in the ill-lit pile that was the royal residence in London, the enormous size of the building had to be factored into any estimation of personal punctuality.

From his office at one end of the Privy Purse Corridor, Lascelles had to walk the entire length of the northeast wing, passing all the Household Offices, then wait for the ancient and interminably slow King's Lift, which would then, if it didn't stop halfway up, deposit him in the King's Corridor, directly in front of His Majesty's study.

Hardinge, the king's private secretary, had made a study of the journey over a period of two years and had discovered that the regular 10:00 A.M. delivery of the dispatch boxes required a lead time of a full ten minutes if the lift was on the upper floor and had to be summoned, and seven minutes if the lift was already on the main floor. According to Pendrell, the deputy master of the household, it was even worse for the kitchens; the average distance traveled by a Buck House meal was the better part of half a mile, and the elapsed time for a bowl of soup to go from royal ladle to royal lips was roughly eighteen minutes.

Delivering the boxes was usually Hardinge's job, but Sir Alexander Hardinge, KCB, GCVO, Military Cross and Bar was, damn his bloody eyes, indisposed after what his note that morning had cryptically referred to as a "trying" weekend in the country. If Lascelles knew anything about it, he was fairly sure that the trying part of the weekend had involved far too much Scotch and God only knew what with one or more of his young friends from the grenadiers.

Lascelles reached the tiny elevator just in time to be bowled over as Elizabeth and her younger sister came charging out into the corridor, shrieking with laughter.

Both the young princesses were dressed in plaid wool skirts and light blue wool sweaters against the ever-present chill of the palace. Neither the skirts nor the sweaters were particularly becoming, not surprising given the somewhat rural background of their mother.

"Dreadfully sorry, Tommy!" said Elizabeth. She helped Lascelles retrieve the scattered boxes while Margaret watched solemnly, a thumb tucked wetly into the corner of her mouth like one of Churchill's cigars. With the boxes back in Lascelles's arms Princess Elizabeth gave him a quick little curtsy, pushed the button to open the narrow elevator door, then grabbed her sister's hand and skipped away down the corridor.

The tall man smiled, watching the future Queen of England race away, thinking fondly of his own two children, John and Lavinia, and wondering briefly what the future held for them. Lascelles stepped into the elevator, vowing that if either one of them showed the slightest sign of marrying into the royal family he'd have them committed to the Cane Hill Asylum just outside Croydon. Grinning broadly, he nudged the UP button with his elbow and the coffin-size lift began to move.

Not for the first time Tommy Lascelles found himself wondering just what he was doing as an assistant private secretary to yet another royal. He'd spent nine years as assistant private secretary to the Prince of Wales, and then, fool that he was, he'd taken on the job again when the prince became, however briefly, Edward VIII. By that point, already in his late forties, he really had very few employment choices. Both unwilling and unable to support a family on his military pension, he reluctantly accepted the post as assistant private secretary to George VI. At the time he'd assumed, optimistically, that nothing could be as bad as being APS to George's older brother, Edward. He was wrong.

Having had reasonably close relations with the royal family for the last twenty years, Lascelles had come to the reluctant conclusion there was something inherently "wrong" about virtually all of them. Edward, now the Duke of Windsor, had appalling taste in women and certain personal practices Lascelles found both revolting and embarrassing. Henry, the Duke of Gloucester, was almost cretinously stupid, and the duke's sister, Mary, married to Lascelles's uncle the Duke of Harewood, was interested in virtually nothing but horses and had the intellect to match her passion.

Prince John, never mentioned in the press and rarely within the family, had been born a "backward" child, and epileptic. Dead of the terrible disease at fourteen, almost twenty years ago, he was buried secretly on the family estate at Sandringham and all but forgotten.

The only one of the lot with any spirit or real backbone was the other George, the Duke of Kent, and even he was something of a spendthrift, especially when it came to exotic, expensive bijous and bric-a-brac. There were also tales concerning the young man's late-night catting about in the London clubs that belied his supposedly happy marriage.

George, the present king, was sovereign purely by the disastrous default of Edward's abdication. He had a childhood stutter that had left him horribly lacking in confidence. A kind man certainly, and a doting father to his daughters, but terribly unhappy with the role unhappily thrust on him by fate. Like Edward, the king's taste in women was magnificently naïve at best, although there were plenty of people at the palace who would tell you that it wasn't the king's taste at all—it was the Scots belle of Glamis Castle who'd set her porridgy sights on the poor stammering man right from the start. Lascelles, privy to most of the secrets in the royal closet, knew that both the little princesses had been conceived through a new and somewhat offensive procedure called artificial insemination due to a "recurring medical condition" afflicting His Royal Highness. Lascelles wasn't sure if it was a medical condition at all and not just simple fear of the woman he'd found himself married to. It certainly wasn't something he held against the king. Quite the contrary, in fact—it showed a certain inborn sense of self-preservation in the face of danger.

The elevator reached the upper floor and thumped to

a stop. The door opened and Lascelles stepped out into the King's Corridor. Directly behind the lift was the Throne Room, and directly in front of him, across the long, slightly tatty carpet, was the King's Study. Balancing the boxes on one arm Lascelles first checked the bow tie at the tall collar of his morning suit, then gently tapped at the door.

"Enter," a woman's voice called out.

Oh God, thought Lascelles, the witch is in there with him. He opened the door and stepped into the room. The study was large, high-ceilinged and memorable only for the tall bow window that looked out across the wall and over to Green Park. The window was set with French doors leading out onto a small balustraded balcony. The French doors, like all the windows at Buckingham Palace, were fitted with long, heavy drapes in deep red. A door on the left side of the study led into the king's private dining room, while an identical door opposite led into the king's bedroom.

There were three comfortable-looking green-and-gold armchairs arranged around the marble fireplace, a matching settee, and several small tables. The dark oak floor was covered with a balding but obviously valuable Persian carpet and a number of paintings were hung on the walls. Lascelles had attended to the needs of the room's previous tenant and knew that every single picture had been changed at the queen's direction and according to her baldly sentimental tastes.

One in particular, a Frank Holl titled *No Tidings from the Sea,* was fit only for a biscuit tin and depicted a sobbing woman who has been out all night looking for her sailor husband in a storm. Given the torrent of tears on the woman's face and the grizzling of a small girl clinging to her grandmother's skirts it could be assumed that the sailor husband has been found dead.

Another painting, Sir Joseph Noel Paton's *The Return from the Crimea,* was equally mawkish, depicting a one-armed corporal back from the war, bloody bandage around his head, his mother weeping on his shoulder and his wife kneeling at his feet, embracing him. Paton had been appointed official painter for Scotland by Victoria and the hanging of the picture in the King's Study was as much a trophy for the Bitch of Glamis as was the Russian helmet at the foot of Paton's amputee soldier.

As Lascelles came into the room the queen, dressed in yet another of her ghastly kilts, was arranging a vase of her favorite pink Betty Prior Polyantha roses on the mantelpiece. The king, dressed in a plain gray suit, was seated behind the cluttered desk that stood in front of the bow window. The desk was large, gilt-edged with a matching lyre-back chair and laden with stacks of paper. There were a pair of wicker IN and OUT baskets, a small ormolu clock, two telephones, a silver inkstand, a framed photograph of the queen and the children, an adjustable brass lamp, and, on the leather-bound blotting pad, a large, overflowing cut glass ashtray that held one of the king's fuming, ever-present Players cigarettes.

As it had been since Victoria's time, the blotter on the desk was jet black to ensure absolute privacy. Glancing past the king's shoulder Lascelles could see over the wall to the upper deck of an omnibus moving along Constitution Hill and found himself wishing almost desperately that he was on it. The king gestured to a small table adjoining the desk and Lascelles gratefully put down the red leather boxes.

"Well, Tommy?" Once again it was the queen who spoke, forcing Lascelles to turn his head uncomfortably, unwilling as he was to look away from the king but forced by protocol to recognize the queen.

"Yes, ma'am?"

"Anything of interest in this morning's boxes?"

As though they contained copies of the *Times,* thought Lascelles, or in her case, the *Picture Post.* "A number of bills requiring His Majesty's signature and seal," he answered quietly.

"What about the trip?" asked the queen, proffering a small half smile in his direction. Presumably she was asking about the upcoming royal tour of North America and not a jaunt out to the greenhouses at Windsor Castle for more Betty Priors.

"Yes. Wha-wha-t about the trip?" the king repeated. He picked up his Players and drew on it, holding it in the European style, just the way his brother Edward did. "And do sit dow-down, Tommy, you make me awfully ner-nervous looming over me like that." Once again the queen was putting him in an awkward position. The king had given him leave to sit, but the fact that the queen remained standing prevented it. Lascelles stood his ground.

"Presumably the problem with that funny little man in Canada has been solved," said the queen.

The funny little man in question was Mackenzie King, the prime minister, who was also that country's foreign minister and who had insisted on accompanying Their Royal Highnesses on the entire tour, including the few days they would be spending in the United States. Normally on such a tour they would have been accompanied by the governor general, but Tweedsmuir had graciously stepped aside, making himself unavailable by arranging to be on a fishing holiday.

"Yes, madam, the problem has been solved." Lascelles nodded. "Lord Tweedsmuir shall not attend."

The queen nodded and turned back to her vase of roses.

"That's ra-ra-rather a shame," said the king. "I've enjoyed his st-st-stories. Particularly the one about the sub-submarine."

"*The Thirty-nine Steps,* sir."

"Common stuff, if you ask me," muttered the queen, fiddling with her flowers.

"An-anything else of con-consequence, Tommy?" asked the king.

"The itinerary has been set," Lascelles answered. "Eight cities in Canada with a one-day rest at Banff in the Rocky Mountains, then the United States. Two days in Washington, a day in New York City to attend their World's Fair, and then a rest day with the president at his country estate on the Hudson River." Lascelles paused. "Following that, the royal train proceeds to Halifax and Their Royal Highnesses board ship for England."

"Sounds a bit gru-grueling," said the king with a sigh. "I'm not terribly good at this sort of thing, as you well know, Tommy."

"You'll do fine, sir. The Canadians are a friendly lot. I spent quite a bit of time there some years ago."

"I *do* hope there's very little of the tour spent in automobiles," said the queen. "Bertie suffers dreadfully from car sickness, as you are aware."

"Yes, ma'am," said Lascelles, knowing perfectly well that it was the queen who hated car travel, not the king. "Virtually all travel will be aboard the royal train." Lascelles also knew perfectly well that this wasn't entirely true, but any last-minute changes by the queen would be like ripples in a pond, inconveniencing literally thousands of people on two continents. "We have also been informed that the interior refitting of the *Repulse* has now been completed and she'll be ready on schedule."

The queen gave the spray of flowers a final adjustment, then walked across the room to stand behind her husband, one hand on his shoulder. "Bertie and I have been discussing that."

"Yes, ma'am?" said Lascelles, his heart sinking.

"Yes. The king feels that it would be improper for him to use a warship like the *Repulse* considering the situation with Mr. Hitler."

Give her credit for political shrewdness, even if it was almost certainly self-serving, thought Lascelles. *Repulse* was a battle cruiser, and even refitted as she now was, hardly the sort of ship one wanted to cross the North Atlantic in. *Repulse* was also one of the few ships in the Royal Navy capable of catching the German navy's new fleet of pocket battleships, which had been recently spotted lurking around the Spanish coast.

"Actually it was Bu-Bu-Buffy's idea really, although I quite agree with her."

"Perhaps I should begin looking for alternate transportation," Lascelles said finally. Tens of thousands of pounds wasted, not to mention several months of work. At this stage of the game the only other option would be to charter a transatlantic liner, and God only knew what *that* would cost. Since the tour had been suggested more than a year ago, the king had offered up one excuse after another and Lascelles had come to the conclusion that His Highness didn't want to go at all.

"I know it's a bo-bother," said the king. He raised a hand and placed it over the queen's. "Bu-but Buffy *is* right, you know." The look on the king's narrow face was almost pleading. Lascelles flinched and felt color rise in his cheeks. He hated it when the king and queen used their pet names for each other in his presence. Not only was it embarrassing, it was also distinctly un-royal.

The queen smiled brightly. "Perhaps you could talk to those nice people at Cunard," she said. "I'm sure they'd be most happy to help."

"Yes, ma'am," said Lascelles, suppressing a sigh. "I'll attend to it immediately." He bowed to the king, bowed again in a slightly lesser movement to the queen and withdrew.

"I really don't know why you keep that man around," said the queen, pushing at her flowers again.

"To-Tommy is a tradition. He worked for Fa-Fa-Father, he worked for my bro-brother and now he works for me. For me."

"All the more reason to be quit of him," answered the queen. "Doesn't do to have a man know too many family secrets."

The king stabbed out his cigarette angrily. "I'm too bloody stupid to have any secrets, don't you see?" Temper flaring, his stutter vanished instantly.

"Now, Bertie," cautioned the queen.

"There's no 'Now, Bertie' about it. David was the handsome one, the smart one, the one who was good at sums and reading, and Mary was the pretty one. We visited Great-granmama at Balmoral once and she didn't even mention me in her diary." He lit another cigarette. "I was a funk at school, worse in the navy and I'm no bloody good as the King of bloody England either!" He swept the dispatch cases off the writing table and onto the floor.

"Now, Bertie," the queen repeated. She bent and began retrieving the red leather boxes. "You may well have been a funk at school, and your stomach troubles kept you out of the war, but at least you had the good sense to marry me, unlike your dear brother who gave up the throne for an American . . . tart!" She stacked the cases back on the desk and patted her husband on the shoulder.

"It's this damnable trip that has me worried," he muttered. "I shall make a fu-fu-funk of it as well."

"Don't be silly, Bertie. You'll do admirably, and besides, I'll be with you every step of the way, so there's really nothing to worry about, is there?"

"I just wish things could be the way they were before!"

"Well, dear, they can't, and that's that, I'm afraid. You're the king, I'm the queen, and we have our duty to do." She patted his shoulder again. "Why don't you go to the nursery and see what Lilibet and Margaret Rose are getting up to?" She placed one plump and dimpled hand on the pile of dispatch cases. "I'll look through these and see if anything really merits your attention."

Puffing on his Players the king stared at the cases for a moment, then stood and left the room without another word. The queen smiled, closed and locked the door behind him and then sat down at the writing table. She opened the first case and began to read.

Chapter 2

Thursday, March 16, 1939
Palm Beach, Florida

The short, fat-faced little man wearing wire-framed spectacles and the black suit and collar of a Catholic priest stood on the seawall of the large and very private estate at 1095 North Ocean Drive. Small hands clasped behind his back, he stared out at the quiet sea and contemplated his future, the ways of men and destiny.

His name was Francis Joseph Spellman, fourth-generation Irish, son of a grocery store owner from Whitman, Massachusetts, presently auxiliary bishop of Boston and soon, if all went according to plan, archbishop of New York, the single most powerful position in Catholic America. During his climb up the ecclesiastical ladder, the fifty-year-old Spellman had made a great many enemies, but he had also made a number of strategically important friends, not the least of them being the newly elected Pope, his old friend and colleague at the Vatican State Secretariat, Eugenio Pacelli, now Pius XII.

Spellman glanced over his shoulder. The huge white-stucco and red-tile mission revival mansion behind him belonged to another friend, Joseph Kennedy, the United States ambassador to the Court of St. James and the first American Catholic diplomat to formally attend the crowning of a new Pope. Even though Spellman and Pacelli were old friends, both the new Pope and Kennedy had agreed that Spellman, not well liked by many of his peers in both Boston and Rome, should not attend either the convocation or the crowning, and as a small sop to the bishop's ego, Ambassador Kennedy had offered Spellman the seclusion of his winter residence in Palm Beach. He'd eagerly accepted the invitation. Everyone in the Mother Church knew of Spellman's close relationship with Pacelli, and if he was to have any chance at all of being given the position in New York, it was key that he stay out of the limelight for the time being.

Spellman took out his cigar case and lit one of the Juan Lopez Coronas he favored, then turned back to the sea again. He sucked in a mouthful of the rich, aromatic smoke and smiled. Six weeks ago the world had been a different place. He'd been very much the dark horse for the New York archbishopric, well behind Donahue, the man groomed for the position by his late predecessor Cardinal Hayes, as well as John T. McNicholas, archbishop of Cincinnati. On top of that, his archenemy Cardinal O'Connell of Boston wasn't above sabotaging Spellman's career both in the United States and Rome. With the death of Pius XI on February tenth all that had changed and the tables were turned. With Pacelli's ascendancy it looked as though all he had to do now was wait patiently and the New York job would be his.

He glanced at the expensive gold watch on his wrist, a gift from his onetime friend, the Long Island socialite Genevieve Brady. Waiting was something that Francis Spellman was very good at, patience a virtue he shared with a rattlesnake poised to strike. And strike he would when the time came, at enemies who'd mocked and spurned him over the years since he'd first attended Rome's North American College Seminary, enemies who'd lied maliciously about him, spreading rumors of his deceit and hidden lusts, would all be silenced, once and for all. The round-faced grocer's boy would be the closest thing there was to a pope in America.

The bishop turned at the dull sound of a car door slamming. A few moments later a hawk-nosed, balding man in a white shirt and tie appeared, framed in the French doors at the rear of the house, his suit jacket over his arm. He walked halfway around the swimming pool, then seated himself at the umbrella-shaded table at the right, a few feet from the diving board. Spellman walked back up the sun-browned lawn and joined him. The man stood again as the bishop approached, making a gesture that was half a nod and not quite a bow.

"Your Excellency," he said and seated himself again. His name was James A. Farley. He was presently postmaster general of the United States, a position he abhorred, as well as national chairman of the Democratic Party. He had been Franklin Roosevelt's campaign manager for the last two elections and a high-ranking figure before that in the New York Democratic machine. Now in his mid-fifties, he felt he deserved something better than being the nation's mailman, but under Roosevelt's administration it seemed unlikely that he was going to get it.

A white-jacketed house servant brought out a tray holding a pitcher of iced lemonade and a pair of tall glasses, put the tray on the table and then withdrew.

"No word yet?" said Farley, pouring. He handed a glass to the bishop, then took one for himself.

"Nothing yet," said Spellman, shaking his head. "A telegram from His Holiness shortly after the election. A call from Joe every few days."

"And how is Joe doing?" Farley asked.

"Having the time of his life, I think," said Spellman. "An Irishman running about in Rome."

"And two more Irishmen in Palm Beach." Farley smiled, his expression sour. "Why is it that an Irishman can get nowhere in his own country, yet thrives everywhere else?"

"This is our country," said Spellman. "The Irish is only in our blood." It was true; the era of emigration was long over, and few if any of Spellman's or Farley's peers had ever set foot on Irish soil. The bishop paused, took a small sip of his lemonade, then a puff on his cigar. He stared across the table at Farley, the sun flashing off the lenses of his spectacles, hiding his eyes. "You've had your meeting, I assume?"

Farley nodded.

"And the result?"

Farley stared back at Spellman. "I'm assuming our conversation here is that of a parishioner to his confessor?"

"As always," Spellman said. "I'm still really just a parish priest, after all."

Farley smiled. Calling Francis Joseph Spellman a simple parish priest was like calling Abraham Lincoln a country lawyer. "Everyone is agreed," Farley said. "If Roosevelt is elected for a third term he's almost certain to bring us into war."

"A war that hasn't started yet," Spellman cautioned.

"It's only a matter of time," Farley answered, shaking his head. "Hitler will play the hand out and Roosevelt will go against him."

"You're sure the president will try for a third term?"

"He says not, at least to me." Farley grimaced. "I don't believe it, though. He's already done his housekeeping. Anyone who's not with him completely is against him—that's his philosophy."

"Yourself included?"

"He knows my feelings well enough. He'll keep me on until after the election and then I'll be gone."

The bishop heard the undertone of bitterness in Farley's voice. Like Spellman, the man across the table from him had reached a point in life where the opportunity to leave a passing mark upon the world was beginning to fade. Historians rarely included postmasters in their texts.

"What about Garner?" Spellman asked. As far as he knew, Roosevelt and the vice president rarely talked, and it was well known that the only reason the aging congressman from Texas had agreed to play second fiddle to FDR was because William Randolph Hearst had ordered him to do so.

"He'd do anything to see Roosevelt out of the White House." Farley paused and let out a long breath. "The plan is that, once Roosevelt is gone, Garner will appoint Lindbergh as his vice president and finish out the term.

Lindbergh will easily get the party nomination for president next year and that will be the end of it. John Nance Garner goes down in the history books as the thirty-third president of the United States, and when you get right down to it, that's all Cactus Jack really wants."

"Lindbergh has agreed to all of this?" asked Spellman. "He knows about your . . . course of action?"

"He agrees in theory," Farley said. "He knows we're meeting here to discuss the situation."

"You'll need a great deal of support."

"We have it. Hearst is backing us, of course. The Morgan Bank. Several members of the DuPont family. Ford. Pew from Sun Oil."

All natural enemies of the president, thought Spellman. "What about political support?"

"Ten senators, including Byrd, Wheeler and Nye. A half dozen congressmen. Fish, Stratton, Jennings Randolph. We even have people with us at the War Department."

"Impressive."

Farley cleared his throat. "We were hoping for the support of the Church as well, Your Excellency."

Spellman let out a small laugh. "A blessing on the greatest betrayal since Cassius and Brutus conspired to kill Caesar?" He shook his head. "I think not."

"We were thinking along more practical lines than a blessing."

"Such as?"

"In a few more days you'll become Archbishop of New York—that's almost certain."

"You flatter me," said Spellman, lifting a hand in a deprecating wave.

Farley ignored the false modesty. He knew perfectly well that Spellman was fully aware of his present power within the Church and the greater power that would come to him as Archbishop of New York. "There are twenty thousand policemen in New York City, most of them Irish, most of them Catholic and most of them belonging to their own Holy Name societies. You would only have to reach out and every one of them would follow you."

Spellman laughed again. "I hardly see myself at the head of a column of New York's finest."

"We only need their passive cooperation, not their active help."

"I see." Spellman thought hard and quickly. Farley was offering a simple, direct and violent solution to a problem that would have a direct influence on the Church, not only in America but everywhere else in the world. The priest who heard the confessions of the men involved in such a plot the way he was hearing Farley's would wield an incredible amount of power, even if the plot failed.

He smiled. There was even ecclesiastic precedent for what Farley and his people were suggesting. Tisserant, the dean of the College of Cardinals, was privately convinced that Pacelli's predecessor had been murdered in his bed with an injection of poison, most probably for his dangerously violent views about Hitler's Nazis and Mussolini's *Fascisti.* It wasn't so far-fetched when you considered that the daughter of the senior Vatican doctor was Claretta Petucci, Mussolini's mistress, and that Pacelli's last post outside the Vatican had been papal nuncio in Berlin. If the Vatican was capable of such a thing, then why not here?

"Oh, what a tangled web we weave, when first we practice to deceive."

"I beg your pardon?" Farley said, confused.

"An admonition on your labors from Sir Walter Scott." The bishop examined the tip of his cigar. A gust of wind rushed up from the sea and blew ash across the table and into the pool a few feet away. "Ten senators, a half dozen congressmen, assorted financiers and industrialists. A vice president. A national hero." He shook his head. "A great many disparate desires and philosophies." Spellman looked across the table at Farley. "Can you accommodate them all, satisfy them?"

"It's what I've done all my working life, Your Excellency. Bringing people together at the right time and in the right place. The same means to different ends makes common purpose."

"An interesting turn of phrase."

"Machiavelli," Farley answered.

"Ah," murmured the bishop. He puffed on his cigar, recharging the smoldering end with each sucking breath until it was red-hot. "The means you refer to . . . are they still in the planning stages or have you proceeded to something more concrete?"

"A man has been chosen. He'll be approached within the next day or so. An offer will be made."

"Do you know who this man is?" asked Spellman, a small note of worry in his voice. If Farley had used any of his God-given brains he would have distanced himself from any such close information, and by extension, distanced Spellman.

"The actual execution of our decision has been left to . . . others. The fewer of us who know the details of it the better for all concerned."

"Quite so," Spellman agreed.

There was a long silence. Farley finished his glass of lemonade, the ice cubes already melted in the Florida heat. He stood. "Well . . ." he said, uneasily. "I should be on my way."

"Yes," Spellman said and stood. Farley stretched out his hand and the bishop took it.

"We have your support then?"

"Theoretically," the bishop said. "We'll have to see how things unfold. Keep me posted."

Farley couldn't tell if the pun was intentional or not. He kept his expression neutral. "I will," he said, then turned and walked away.

Spellman stayed where he was, rolling the cigar around in his small mouth, watching the little freshets of wind from the shore riffle the surface of the pool, sending quick snaking shadows along the pale blue concrete of the bottom. Ten senators, a half dozen congressmen, the Lone Eagle—Charles Lindbergh—Henry Ford, Morgan and Hearst. Roosevelt had been given the Democratic

Party's nomination by Hearst's decree, and then, at least in Hearst's mind, the president had betrayed him. Lindbergh loathed Roosevelt on principle and both Ford and Morgan had enormous European interests that they could easily lose in the face of a Continental war with Germany under a dozen or more provisions of the Trading with the Enemy Act.

The vaguely stated collusion and condonement of the plan by the senators and congressmen were just as easily understood. The New Deal in all its octopuslike incarnations had eroded the long-held powers of patronage in their constituencies, and allowing an unchecked Roosevelt to push them into an unpopular war would be even more damaging. You didn't vote for the man who'd been party to having your child killed in some place with a name you couldn't pronounce, blown to pieces in some foreign trench, buried in a distant grave. The last war was only twenty years ago, half a generation gone, more than a hundred thousand American mothers weeping for their lost sons. Memories still painfully raw.

The fat little man in his plain black suit stubbed out his expensive Havana and pursed his lips thoughtfully, staring out from under the striped canvas umbrella, watching the sea. Farley was right, even if his plans had more to do with his own political ambitions than the ultimate fate of the nation. If something drastic wasn't done in the very near future, Franklin Delano Roosevelt would drag the United States into a war that could easily change the world forever. If Farley's plan was the only way to stop him, then so be it, *miserere Deus*.

The postmaster general drove the big Buick convertible through the open gateway of the Kennedy estate, turned left onto North Ocean Boulevard and headed south, back to the Breakers. High overhead the endless rows of palms on both sides of the broad street filtered the late-morning sunlight, turning the boulevard into a cool green tunnel.

He glanced into the rearview mirror and picked up the green Ford Tudor a hundred feet back, making no attempt to conceal the fact that it was following him. Farley lifted his hand and waved at the two FBI men behind him in the government car. Two years before, he'd launched a campaign to have Hoover replaced, mostly because the FBI director refused to take part in any of the patronage games that were bread and butter to a man like the postmaster general. The top G-man had never forgiven him, even though the attempt to have him unseated had ultimately failed. He knew for a fact that both his home and office telephones were tapped, and the two men in the Tudor, in various incarnations, had dogged his steps ever since. Virtually everywhere Farley went he was accompanied by his government shadows, presumably hoping to catch him engaging in some questionable activity.

"If only the pie-faced bastard knew," Farley muttered to himself. He put his foot down on the gas, giving his watchers a run for their money. Mostly he found his constant companions a mild irritation, but today they had served a useful purpose. Farley had little anxiety about the federal agents discovering the real reason for his visit to Palm Beach since they had no idea who he had met with at the Breakers. On the other hand he was absolutely sure the two men in the car behind him knew who was presently occupying 1095 North Ocean Drive, not to mention J. Edgar Hoover himself.

Soon a file would cross Hoover's desk, testifying to today's events with neatly noted times and places, his meeting with the bishop written out in black and white, a bureaucratic fact. Eventually the file would be taken to some basement corner of that great gray, gloomy building on Pennsylvania Avenue, where it would remain, one small hidden jewel of proof. If by some terrible twist of fate the plan failed and he went to the mat, files like that one would break his fall.

Farley found himself humming one of the Bobby Breen numbers from *Way Down South,* a movie musical he'd seen only the night before. He tapped his fingers on the steering wheel as he drove, lifting his foot from the gas pedal, letting the Tudor catch up. There was an Eastern Airlines flight out of Anderson Field in an hour and he was already packed. If the weather held, he could be back in Washington before supper was served at the Mayflower, where he kept rooms close to the White House and the Capitol. He felt some of the tension of the last few weeks begin to dissipate. His part in these terrible affairs was over, at least for the moment. The rest of it was now in other hands.

Chapter 3

Friday, April 14, 1939
Havana, Cuba

The thin, red-haired lawyer sat in the forward compartment of the Pan American Airways flying boat and looked down at the glittering, ruffled expanse of the Florida Straits ten thousand feet below. He was thirty-eight years old and his name was Howard Raines, a junior partner at the law firm of Fallon and McGee in New York City. On the seat beside him the topcoat he'd worn against the harsh winds and rain leaving the city the previous night was draped over a bulging briefcase, his only luggage. In the seats across the aisle the newlyweds billed and cooed, the woman snuggling into the man's collar, the man pulling her closer and nuzzling her ear, whispering promises he wouldn't keep. The woman used her thumb to constantly twist the ring on the third finger of her left hand, and Raines noticed that her red nail polish matched the color of her lipstick perfectly. It was all too sweet and he turned away, looking out the window again.

The lawyer grimaced, feeling the oily grumbling of his stomach. He'd had a fruit cup breakfast an hour ago at the Biscayne Bay terminal in Miami and it wasn't sitting well with the three cups of coffee he'd been served since. He looked up at the clock on the compartment bulkhead above the newlyweds. It was 9:30. Another quarter hour before they reached Havana. The engines on the high-slung wing droned on monotonously and the air in the cabin smelled of stale cigarette smoke combined with the faintly disturbing scent of hot oil and gasoline.

The aircraft was almost full, not unusual at this time of the year. Of the thirty-five people on the passenger manifest for the early-morning flight most were New Yorkers like Raines. All of them were rich enough to buy their escape from the wet, blustery city, able to afford a week or so on the sunny beaches of the Playa del Este or to lose a few dollars at the racetrack or in the casinos. Among them were a few the nervous young lawyer recognized, either from the newspapers or his own business dealings.

Martha Gellhorn, the writer and Ernest Hemingway's current mistress, was on board, as were Red Levine and Bo Weinberg, two of Meyer Lansky's aides, probably on their way to meet the boss at the Hotel Nacional. In the rear compartment, traveling with a few of his junior legmen and his own picnic basket, was Ernest "Fatso" Cuneo, the crumb-covered three-hundred-pound slob who was La Guardia's famous "assistant" and supposedly some kind of behind-the-scenes heavyweight for the New York Democratic machine. The only thing missing was Walter Winchell, making up stories about the passengers.

Raines looked up at the clock again and shifted in his seat, feeling the aches and pains of all-night travel beginning to catch up with him. He yawned and stretched. It would be over soon enough now. He was booked out on the 3:00 P.M. flight that afternoon, which would get him back to Miami in plenty of time to catch the New York–Florida Limited at 9:00 that evening. A couple of stiff belts to bring on a good night's sleep in the bedroom he'd already booked and he'd be back in Manhattan just after breakfast the following morning, his odious task concluded.

He looked across at the honeymoon couple, still obliviously entwined, feeling the power of his secret. They had no idea who he was, or what business he was about, not the faintest thought that the man across from them was going to change the future of the world, stop the progress of a war yet undeclared, save millions of lives. Like flotsam on the water of a rushing river they were unknowingly being swept along on the swift current of the history he was making right at this moment.

The lawyer smiled to himself, leaned back in his seat and closed his eyes. Heady stuff and true enough, even though he was no more than a pawn in the game that was unfolding. He let out a long breath and flattened his hands on the armrests of his seat, trying to relax. Better to be a pawn than no piece on the board at all. If the game played out, perhaps there was a chance to play the knight in this new world they were inventing.

The flying boat reached the city right on schedule, sloping quickly down through the hot, cloudless sky, following the broad bisecting line of the Canal del Puerto through to the harbor itself, the sharp blade of the hull slicing into the water and sending up a feathering crown of spray, showering the windows on both sides. As the flying boat settled into the water the engines were throttled back and they made a sweeping turn to starboard, bringing them majestically to the landing wharf.

Because he was seated in the forward cabin, Howard Raines was one of the first off the aircraft. With nothing but his briefcase to carry he quickly passed through the minimal customs formalities, made his way through the noisy, crowded, echoing hall and stepped out onto the Alemeda de Paula, where he hailed a taxi, his already wrinkled business suit wilting even more in the oppressive humidity and heat.

With a chattering driver at the wheel they hurtled through heavy morning traffic, horn blaring as they raced up the quays until they reached the foot of Calle Obispo, careening through a tight left turn and threading their way into the confines of the narrow street that ran behind the Palacio de Los Capitanes Generales—the massive gray stone building that housed Havana's City Hall. Less than a minute later they reached the intersection of Calle Mercaderes and the taxi came to a jolting stop in front of the five-story redbrick pile that was the Hotel Ambos Mundos.

The driver called out a fare in pesos that Raines couldn't

calculate, so he gave the man a handful of American pocket change, which seemed to please him well enough. The lawyer stepped out of the car, and even before he'd fully closed the rear door the car was already driving away, probably racing back to the Pan American docks to catch another fare.

Hefting the briefcase, Raines stepped into the small, dark lobby and approached the front desk. To his left he could see through an archway into what appeared to be a dimly lit bar, and on his right there was a split stairway leading upward with the wrought-iron open shaft and cage of an elevator between the two sets of steps. The green-blue carpet under his feet was old and worn, and the arrays of potted palms and rubber plants in the corners of the lobby were coated with dust. Above the lawyer's head a pair of desultory wood-vaned fans stirred the languid air, wobbling slightly with each wickering turn.

Following the instructions he'd been given before leaving New York, Raines approached the man behind the reception counter and asked for Señor Delmonico's room. As expected the man behind the counter asked Raines to identify himself, which he did with one of the firm's engraved business cards. The hotel clerk then unlocked a drawer below the counter and handed the lawyer an envelope. Tearing it open Raines found a room key with an oval metal tag stamped with the number 503 and a brief printed note, unsigned:

Give him twenty dollars.

It was an absurd amount for such a small service—more than the price of his flight from Miami—but once again Raines followed his instructions to the letter and gave the clerk a well-worn bill from the sheaf of money he'd been given for expenses.

"Piso cinco," said the clerk, indicating it was on the fifth floor as he peered over the counter at the key tag.

"Muchos gracias," Raines answered, stretching his knowledge of Spanish to its limits.

"De nada." The clerk smiled.

Raines dropped the key into the pocket of his jacket, crossed the lobby to the elevator and rode the squeaking, rattling cage up to the fifth floor. He found 503 at the end of a narrow corridor that smelled faintly of cats, used the key and entered the room. It was small, barely twelve feet on a side, filled with a sagging iron bed, a freestanding wardrobe and a washstand fitted with a chipped enamel basin. There was a matching chamber pot under the bed and no sign of an adjoining bathroom.

An inset balcony looked out onto Obispo Street and the soot- and pigeon-stained rear facade of City Hall. The sound of the traffic crowding the narrow street was deafening, but with the balcony doors shut the room was like an airless, claustrophobic steam bath. Enduring the noise, Raines sat down on the edge of the bed and waited resolutely, briefcase on his lap and the room key clutched firmly in his right hand like some sort of talisman.

Ten minutes later there was a short knock.

Raines cleared his throat. "Enter!"

The door opened and a short, fat man in a poorly cut blue suit stepped into the room. He peered nervously at the lawyer. "Señor Delmonico?"

Raines bobbed his head up and down. "Yes?"

The fat little man gestured toward the open door behind him. *"Viene con me, por favor."*

Raines nodded—the man's meaning was clear. Still gripping the briefcase and the room key, he got to his feet and followed the man out of the room. They rode the elevator silently, then crossed the lobby and stepped out onto the street. There was another taxi parked in front of the main door. The fat man got behind the wheel and Raines climbed into the back. The whole process was becoming tedious but Raines saw its ultimate value. Each step was isolated from the next, thus providing near perfect anonymity. The clerk in the hotel had no connection with the man who'd given the envelope to him, and this taxi driver had no connection with the room clerk. There would probably be at least one more of these handoffs before he met the man he'd come to see.

The taxi ride was a brief one, taking the lawyer back to the harbor and depositing him at the steps leading down to the San Francisco docks, directly across the Avenida San Pedro from the ancient bulk of the St. Francis of Assisi Monastery. The docks were a labyrinth of narrow wharves and jetties, home to most of the Havana fishing fleet, scores of charter boats and dozens of private cruisers.

"Where do I go now?" asked Raines, climbing out of the car and reaching for his wallet.

The driver waved away the offer of money. *"Quédaté,"* the man said, pointing to the ground at Raines's feet. Stay here. The lawyer nodded and the taxi drove off in a cloud of blue exhaust fumes. Raines stared down at the sea of boats bobbing up and down at their berths. Gulls were wheeling over the fishing trawlers, their skirling calls rising wildly into the air. The whole place reeked of fish. Raines sighed; he was definitely beginning to regret taking on the job at hand, no matter how much grace and favor it earned him with the senior partners at Fallon and McGee. His suit was ruined, probably for good, and standing hatless in the hot sun was making him feel even more nauseous than on the flight from Miami.

A few moments later a dark-haired man wearing grease-stained white ducks and a striped jersey came jogging up the steps and motioned to Raines. "Señor Delmonico?"

Sighing again the lawyer nodded at the name and followed the man down the steep flight of steps and through the maze of floating docks until they reached a well-used, broad-beamed Elco cruiser with an upturned nutshell dingy lashed down to her after cabin. The name board on the bow said she was the *Spindrift*. The paint on the name board looked a lot fresher than the boat itself, the black lettering crisp and shining almost as though it was still wet. Raines was willing to bet that a week ago or less the *Spindrift* had been called something else.

The man in the stained ducks stepped aside and gestured, inviting Raines on board. The lawyer stepped off the dock while the other man cast off the bow and stern lines, then hopped aboard himself. The wheelhouse and the rear cabin took up most of the deck all the way back to the transom. As the cruiser's engines fired and they warped away from the dock, Raines had little choice except to duck his head and enter the wheelhouse.

It was surprisingly spacious. The whcel itself was on the port side with a well-worn pilot's chair behind. To starboard, close by Raines's left hand, was a broad chart table, and behind that was a set of lockers and a narrow berth. A bulkhead door aft led to the rear cabin and another door forward led down to the forward cabin.

For the most part *Spindrift* looked innocuous enough, a lot like the pleasure boats Raines had been on during occasional weekends with clients in the Hamptons. The sound of the engines vibrating beneath his feet was different, though, deeper and more powerful. *Spindrift,* if that really was her name, was something more than a rich man's toy.

The dark-haired man behind the wheel shunted slowly out into the main channel beyond the docks, then turned toward the mouth of the long channel, which was bracketed by the Castle of San Salvador de le Punta on the left and the remains of the even older Morro Castle on the right. The pilot pulled back evenly on the twin throttle levers and *Spindrift* lifted slightly as her speed increased. A few minutes later they reached the castles and headed between their great white stone hulks, then straight out into the darker waters of the open sea.

The man at the wheel continued on his course for another quarter of an hour, the skyline of Havana receding quickly behind them. Then without comment, the pilot dropped a small wooden ring over the upper spoke of the wheel to lock it in place, turned and disappeared into the rear cabin of the boat, closing the bulkhead door behind him and leaving Raines alone in the wheelhouse.

Raines swallowed dryly, wondering just what the hell was going on. For the first time since leaving the hotel room he took his hand away from the briefcase. He stepped away from the chart table and took a step toward the lashed-down wheel. Outside, a brilliant sun was shining down onto a sparkling, inoffensive sea, but suddenly the young man felt fear. He was reaching out for the wheel when a careful, vaguely accented voice stopped him.

"Don't touch that."

A man in a dark blue sweater and brown whipcord trousers stood in the open doorway of the forward cabin. He was neither tall nor short, his coal-black hair thinned into a widow's peak, edged with gray at the temples, his skin pale, almost translucent. He wore blue-tinted steel-rimmed spectacles, but the eyeglasses did nothing to soften the cold aspect of his slightly hooded eyes.

His hands were small, the fingers long and delicate, but strong, like those of a pianist, thick tendons knotted across his wrists like twisted metal cable. There was a slightly paler patch of skin on the man's right cheek in just the place where the buttstock of a rifle would rest. Although Raines had seen no photograph he knew instantly that this was the man who was the subject of the slim file he'd been given to read in New York. This was John Bone.

Raines moved silently back to his position beside the chart table and without another word Bone closed the cabin door and walked to the swivel chair behind the wheel. Leaving *Spindrift* on her lashed-down course, the man sat down in the pilot's chair, folded his hands in his lap and waited. His breathing was calm and even and he sat with absolutely no motion, the expression on his face blank.

The lawyer swallowed hard again. Bone's eyes were like those of a hook-billed shrike as it chose the appropriate thorn to impale its victim on. All of Raines's senses suddenly took on a terrible intensity and he found himself preternaturally aware of the slapping sound of the waves against *Spindrift*'s hull and the mottled scatterings of reflected sunlight on the whiteness of the cabin roof above his head. A wooden beam creaked with a sound like small bones snapping and his nose and mouth were full of the smell and taste of salt and iodine from the sea.

Bone spoke at last and the spell was broken. "I've been informed by a mutual acquaintance that you might have something for me."

Raines nodded his head. This much he knew about—the mutual friend was Frank Hague, the longtime mayor of Jersey City, a hard-nose Mick sprung out of the pest-hole of the Jersey City Horseshoe, close to the Hudson River docks. Publicly Hague was an iron-spined Calvinist who neither smoked nor took strong drink, but he took payoffs from both sides of the river, dined regularly with Charlie Yanowski and Eddie Florio, gangster bosses of the longshoreman's union, and sent Christmas gifts to Longy Zwillman, another big-time hoodlum. According to the rumors Frank Hague had a long arm—long enough to install Mary Teresa Norton as his personal stooge in Congress.

The lawyer snapped open his briefcase and pulled out a thin manila envelope, the gummed flap closed and stamped with a red wax seal. Raines looked back at the closed door to the aft cabin.

"Don't worry," said Bone. "Carlos is very discreet and he speaks almost no English."

Raines nodded again and handed the envelope across to Bone, who took it from him and stood. "I'll be a minute or two."

The lawyer smiled nervously. "It's okay to leave the wheel like that?"

Bone glanced out through the front windscreen of the wheelhouse. "There's only the Gulf Stream out there," he said, turning back to Raines. "We're not likely to run into anything except one or two of those sharks Mr. Hemingway and his friends like to shoot so much." With that, he went to the forward cabin, entered it and closed the door behind him, leaving Raines entirely alone with his thoughts of the deep blue sea and sharks.

According to his watch, John Bone was gone for slightly more than seven minutes, not two. When he came back up to the wheelhouse there was no sign of the manila envelope. He sat down in the swivel chair, unlashed the wheel and turned it hard to starboard, taking *Spindrift* in a broad, lazy turn that eventually pointed them back in the direction they had come.

"We're going back," said Raines, stating the obvious, not knowing what else to say.

"Yes," Bone answered.

"You've read the contents of the file."

"Yes."

Raines cleared his throat. "Are there any questions?"

Bone turned to him. "If I did have any questions would you be able to answer them?"

Raines felt his face flush and he made no response, his bluff called. He had no idea what the envelope contained and now this man knew it.

"They didn't tell you anything?" Bone asked.

"Only to follow the instructions I was given. To contact you in Havana."

"Which you did."

"Yes. Which I did," said Raines, some small bitterness in his voice.

"Did they give you any other instructions?"

"They said you might have a reply."

"I do, I do. You can tell them that I'm interested, but that I'll need more money. A great deal more. If they wish to discuss the matter they can contact me by placing an advertisement in the classified section of the *Havana Post*. The advertisement should begin with the words 'Dear Uncle Charles' and should include a New York telephone number where they can be contacted, the numbers reversed." Bone paused. "Do you have that?"

"Dear Uncle Charles. Reverse the telephone number."

"Good," said Bone. "That's that then." Using his left hand John Bone pushed the throttle levers forward and *Spindrift* responded, the tone of the engines deepening as her twin propellers dug into the foaming water. Her bow rose, taking them back toward the distant shore. Half an hour later they reached Havana Harbor once again and Bone dropped Howard Raines at Washington Docks. Even before the New York lawyer had reached the top of the stairs and the Avenida San Pedro, *Spindrift* was putting out to sea again.

Raines took another taxi, this time telling the driver to take him to the Hotel Nacional, the only other address he knew in the city. Using more of his expense money he treated himself to lunch from the lavish terrace buffet, purchased an enormous Romeo y Julietta cigar from the hotel shop and, smoking it, went into the Grand Salon. He ordered a Courvoisier from a sad-eyed young waiter with the name Fidel stitched on the breast of his white jacket, then nursed the brandy and cigar for a leisurely hour watching the ebb and flow of people as they lost small fortunes at the tables, their rich smiles undiminished no matter how much of their money found its way into the croupier's slot.

But then it was time to go. He finished the last drops of the brandy, then let the uniformed doorman under the hotel portico whistle up a taxi. He rode back to the Pan American terminal on the docks and boarded his flight with time to spare. Slipping away from the harbor's embrace and climbing high above the dark blue water of the Florida Straits, Raines found himself looking down toward the sea, searching for *Spindrift*'s wake, knowing he wasn't going to find it, and thinking about the last sight he'd had of John Bone and the odd expression on his face.

Pity.

Chapter 4

Sunday, April 16, 1939
New York City

Jane woke up to the nightmare sounds of Ponce de Leon, her screaming parrot, and the earsplitting clatter of the telephone a few feet away on her desk. She groaned, threw off the thin blanket covering her and sat up on the couch. Her head was pounding from the effects of one too many bourbons the night before at the China Doll and her tongue felt like the bottom of Ponce de Leon's cage. She realized she'd gone to bed with her clothes on and made a small noise of self-disgust. Torchy Blane would definitely not sleep in her clothes, except under very trying and worthwhile circumstances. Jane pushed the palms of her hands into her eye sockets and tried to swallow away the taste in her mouth but it didn't do any good. The telephone continued to ring and the bird screeched out a stream of foul-mouthed Italian, shuffling back and forth on its hanging roost in the open-doored cage at the far end of the couch.

The bird made a grating, ratchet noise somewhere at the back of its throat then swore again. *"Eh, paisan! Fungulo mi!"*

"Shut up," Jane croaked weakly. Neither the bird nor the telephone paid any attention. Jane stood up, staggered over to the desk and dropped down into her ancient wooden swivel chair. She picked up the phone, and when the ringing fell silent, so did Ponce de Leon.

"What?" said Jane.

"It's Hennessy." Dan Hennessy was a detective sergeant on police commissioner Lewis J. Valentine's so-called Confidential Squad and the best contact Jane had at police headquarters on Centre Street. His hobby was making passes at her and being told exactly what he could do with himself. Still, he persevered.

"I don't care who it is, you Mick snatcher. It's Sunday." Jane blinked at the old Lady Bulova on her wrist. "Jesus, Dan, it's eight-thirty in the morning."

"And I don't care what day it is, or what time." Hennessy laughed. "Get your sweet ass off that flea-bitten couch of yours. I've got one you might be interested in."

"One what?" Jane asked. She reached out, tapped a Camel out of the pack on her desk and lit it. It made her mouth taste even worse, but each drag of the stale cigarette woke her up a little more.

"A corpse."

"What's so interesting about a corpse?" She reached out again, this time pulling her notebook closer and picking up a pencil. On any given day there were all sorts of corpses in New York to choose from, but a corpse from Dan Hennessy was probably going to be a special one.

"This one's in Englewood."

"As in Englewood, New Jersey?" Jane asked, surprised. What was a headquarters cop doing on the other side of the Hudson?

"Closer to Tenafly, actually," Hennessy answered. "The Palisades on 9W. A little roadhouse called the Rustic Cabin."

"Sounds charming. A Jersey Copacabana?"

"More like a black and tan," said the detective. A black and tan was a nightclub that catered to white people as well as colored. In Tenafly the whites would probably be Italians since Wops weren't allowed in most of the right nightspots.

"Who is it?" Jane asked.

"A lawyer. His name is Howard Raines. According to his business card he works for Fallon and McGee." There was a grim little pause. Jane felt her heart give a little flip. "He also happens to have your business card in his wallet. You mind giving me the skinny on that, Jane, before I have to answer some awkward questions from upstairs?"

Fallon and McGee was a company with well-known connections to both Tammany and the Mob. Jane swiveled around in the chair and looked out the grimy window and down to the street. Six stories down Fifth Avenue, Broadway and Twenty-third Street came together in a deserted, Belgian brick plaza. As usual there were a couple of two-tone Checker cabs parked in front of the Walgreens Drugstore at the foot of the Flatiron Building's pointy end.

Jane sighed, remembering. "He used to be a friend of mine."

"Used to be?"

"We grew up together. Went to school together. He was the only friend I had who didn't make fun of my sister."

"So what happened?"

There was a long pause as Jane debated with herself how much to reveal to Hennessy. Finally, she said, "I went my way. He went his."

"And the business card?"

"Just that, business. We talked once in a while."

"What did you give him?"

My cherry, when I was eighteen years old in the back of his old man's Durant, was the thought that ran through her head. But all she said was, "Nothing that wasn't legal. Nothing at all really. We had a drink once or twice at the Plaza. I haven't seen him in a year, maybe more. I don't think he had too many friends and I don't think he was a very good lawyer. Not the way he talked, anyway."

"Well, he's a dead lawyer now. You want to come down here and take pictures or not? Kill two birds and all since you can officially identify the body while you're down here."

"Give me the exact address of this place and I'll go get a cab." Jane turned around in her chair again and stubbed her cigarette in a Stork Club ashtray she'd filched on her one and only visit to the place. "And you can also tell me why you sound like you've got the jitters about it."

"I got the jitters because we're getting a lot of heat to bury it already. Someone doesn't want this one getting even *close* to page one."

"The address," said Jane.

"East Clinton Avenue and 9W," Hennessy said. "Looks like a big log cabin. You can't miss it."

"Half an hour."

"I'll be here. Got a couple of witnesses to talk to—the owner and some crooner he hired to sing with the band."

"On my way." Jane hung up the phone. Across the room Ponce de Leon ducked out of his cage and flew noisily to the hat rack by the front door of the office. "Shit on my raincoat and I'll eat you for dinner," warned Jane. She picked up another cigarette, lit it and headed for the adjoining bathroom.

Five minutes later she came out of the bathroom with her hair wet and her teeth brushed. Jane pulled slacks, blouse and a pair of old deck shoes out of the standing cupboard she kept by the door, found some fresh underwear and got dressed. She took an already loaded Contax out of the second drawer of her filing cabinet, grabbed her shoulder bag and left the office, blowing Ponce de Leon a kiss on her way out and locking the door behind her. Two minutes later she was climbing into one of the hacks in front of Walgreens and heading up Broadway toward the George Washington Bridge.

It being Sunday there was virtually no traffic to slow them down all the way up Broadway and even less on the bridge, so Jane wasn't far off on her predicted half hour. Pulling into the gravel lot of the roadhouse, Jane handed the driver a five and two ones, more than an hour with a Carey Limousine would have cost, but fair enough since the driver had to deadhead back to Manhattan from the Jersey side. Jane blinked in the harsh, hot sunlight, dug her Ray-Bans and her cigarettes out of her bag and lit up as the taxi backed and turned, then headed down 9W toward the bridge.

The Rustic Cabin was pretty much the way Dan Hennessy had described it—a large log building with a wraparound veranda and a wire frame and lightbulb sign that ran along the roofline. It was set in the middle of a half-acre triangular-shaped parking lot with an entrance on both 9W and the narrower strip of Clinton Avenue that intersected with the highway. The back of the triangle was a scruffy strip of trees, tall grass and weeds running beside something that looked like a ditch or a small stream. Beyond that, Jane could see a farmer's field. Not the center of the universe by any means, but Tenafly was only a few miles up Clinton Avenue and Hoboken wasn't that much farther. Not a bad spot to get away from the wife and kiddies and maybe even bet on a horse or play some poker in a windowless back room.

There were three vehicles in the parking lot—two Hoboken Police Indian motorcycles and Dan Hennessy's familiar dark green La Salle. No meat wagon and no sign of any other press. Hennessy, minus his regulation brown suit jacket and wearing a short-sleeved white shirt, was standing with the Hoboken cops by the line of trees at the far end of the property. They were all smoking and staring down into the ditch. A skinny-looking kid with a face as sharp as a hatchet was standing on the veranda by the front door, smoking a cigarette in short, jerky puffs as though he was nervous.

The kid had a pompadour, his shoes looked like Johnston & Murphy's and the suit was definitely expensive. Too young to be the owner of the place, which meant he was probably the crooner Hennessy had mentioned. The detective turned, saw Jane and waved her over. Jane crossed the parking lot with the kid on the veranda watching her every step of the way, taking in everything from the way her tits moved around inside the silk of her blouse to the swing of her can as she passed by. She wrinkled her nose like she'd smelled something bad but she knew he was smiling at her with one of those know-it-all grins and there wasn't anything she could do about it. She sighed and wondered if there'd come a time when men weren't wolves and women weren't sheep.

She reached the far edge of the property and Hennessy introduced her to the Hoboken cops, who'd been the first ones called to the scene. Jane looked down into the ditch and saw the body for the first time. Her heart did a little flip again but she bit the inside of her cheek, forcing herself not to get the slightest bit teary-eyed, because if she did, Hennessy would never let her forget it. The corpse was lying on its back, feet pointing up the slope, ankles crossed, the back of the head sitting in the slow-moving water trickling down the streambed.

The body was dressed in a dark brown suit and a white shirt with a large red stain in the middle of the chest. There was another wound in the left temple, a small dark hole and a patch of blood-matted ginger hair marking the spot. It was as hot in Jersey as it was in Manhattan and the dark, sweet scent of rot was already oozing up out of the ditch and into the air.

"That him?" Hennessy asked.

"Yeah." The first dead friend she'd ever had. Probably not the last. "Not a lot of blood," Jane commented. "A dump job?"

Hennessy nodded. "That's what we're figuring." The detective cleared his throat and gave the state cops a long look. They bobbed their heads and moved back toward their vehicles. "You going to take some pictures?" Hennessy asked.

Jane nodded briefly, still looking down at the body, the strap of the camera case still looped over her shoulder. She turned and looked back at the cop, suddenly realizing how she'd been conned. "You really are a son of a bitch."

The big, flat-faced Irishman tried to look innocent, eyes widening. "What's that supposed to mean?"

"It means it's Sunday and you couldn't get the regular police photographer to drag his sorry ass out here."

"He was taking his family to church and then out to

his poor old mother's grave," said Hennessy. "Besides, you knew the guy."

"Bullshit." Jane shook her head and sighed. "How much?"

"Dollar a glossy. Eight-by-tens."

"The hack cost me seven."

"We'll pay it."

"How many?"

"At least a dozen."

"Sixteen."

"Done," said Hennessy, and Jane began popping the Contax out of its case.

Jane eased herself down into the ditch and squatted low. She took a close shot of the head wound, trying to think of anything else but whose head it was. "Looks like the Mob," she said, clicking the shutter. "Two to the heart and one to the head, just to make sure."

"That's what I thought," Hennessy said, standing above her. The big detective reached into his pocket and took out a wooden direction marker. "Here, use this," he said and tossed it down to Jane. The marker had two arms, riveted together in the center. At the end of each arm was a letter, E, W, N, S. Jane opened it up and placed it on the soggy ground beside the head with the N lying roughly parallel to 9W.

"That good?" asked Jane, glancing up at Hennessy.

"Good enough," he said and nodded.

Jane noticed that Howie was wearing his nice Omega Chronograph, the one his father had given him for passing the bar exam about a week before the old man died. She took a shot of it in case one of the morgue boys got a little light-fingered. Jane continued to shoot. "You said there was heat."

"The owner of the place called the cops. They found Raines's wallet and radioed the identification in to their headquarters. Since Raines comes from Manhattan they called Centre Street too."

"You caught it?"

"Yeah," said Hennessy. The Irishman was regularly

on the outs with his wife, Maureen, and he often slept on a cot in one of the police headquarters dormitory rooms. "I wasn't even out the door when I got a call from the PC's office. They already had Raines's name and they told me to go slow on the investigation. Play it by the book."

Jane finished shooting, picked up the direction marker and climbed up out of the ditch. "What does that mean?" she asked, ignoring the hand Hennessy was holding out to help her up out of the ditch. She grabbed a root instead and boosted herself back up onto the gravel of the parking lot.

"Send the body off to the morgue and forget about it until I'm told otherwise." He shrugged. "Gonzales and his people have bodies stacked up like cordwood down there. This one just goes to the bottom of the pile, that's all." Thomas A. Gonzales was the chief medical examiner for New York, with his shop at Bellevue Hospital.

"You going to sit still for that?" Jane asked.

"I like my job," Hennessy responded. "I intend to keep it." He turned and glanced in the direction of the two Hoboken officers. Both of the motorcycles were pulling noisily out of the parking lot. "They want to keep their jobs too."

"They had the same word come down on them?"

"The order of the day seems to be get amnesia." He nodded toward the ditch. "Our Mr. Raines would seem to swing a lot of weight."

Jane slipped the camera back into its case. "Anything in his pockets?"

Hennessy nodded. "Claim check from the Ariston and a bar receipt from Gloria's."

Jane nodded. The Ariston was an apartment hotel on the corner of Broadway and West Fifty-fifth Street that had a luxurious steam-bath arrangement in the basement. Gloria's was a bar on Third Avenue at Fortieth Street. Jane knew about both of them and the kind of men who went there. "Somebody want to make it look like he was a pansy?" she said.

"Sure looks like it. You knew him. Was he?"

Jane brushed it off. "Not that I know of. What about your witnesses? They see anything?"

"The owner says no."

"What about the kid on the veranda over there. The one in the swank suit with the gash eyes."

"Name's Frankie Sinatra. Also answers to Frankie Satin. The owner says he's a waiter who sings sometimes. The kid leaves out the waiter part. He's the one who found the body in the first place."

"How'd he do that?" Jane asked.

"Said it was about four in the morning. Place just cleared out. The toilets in the club were plugged up so he came out here to take a leak. That's when he saw Mr. Raines there." Hennessy nodded toward the ditch again.

"He see anything else?"

"No."

"Maybe he killed him."

"Kid's too skinny to hurt a fly."

"Sinatra," said Jane. "Italian?"

Hennessy laughed. "Don't go getting big ideas, toots. I did a little checking. Frankie's a nobody. His mother's a rabbit killer and his father is a fireman." Rabbit killer was a cop term for abortionist. "If they have any connection with the rackets, it's the wrong kind," the detective added.

A black Willys panel truck came off 9W and crunched its way onto the parking lot. The only marking on the meat wagon was the word MORGUE in white letters across the back doors. Two men in black uniforms climbed down out of the truck and approached Hennessy.

"Where is it?" said the older of the two men.

"The ditch," Hennessy said and walked back toward his own car, Jane beside him.

"So that's it?" Jane shook her head. "A junior lawyer for a Mob firm gets bumped and the PCO tells you to bury it. It stinks."

"Sure it stinks," said Hennessy, pausing to light a cigarette. Jane joined him and they both watched as the two men from the morgue brought up Raines's body on a stretcher and loaded it into the back of the meat wagon.

"You telling me I'm supposed to forget about this? Howie wasn't much of a friend but he deserves better than this."

Hennessy sucked on his Lucky Strike, squinting into the sun as the meat wagon doors were slammed shut. "Make two sets of pictures. Send one set to me so I can show something in the file, and keep a second set somewhere safe just in case the ones in the file disappear."

"And then what?" Jane asked. The two morgue attendants climbed back into the Willys and drove away.

"This thing smells so bad no cop is ever going to find out anything."

"So it's a dead end?"

"I said no *cop* is ever going to find out anything. I didn't say anything about reporters."

"What am I supposed to do? We were friends from a long time ago. I wasn't married to the guy," said Jane. "There's divorce dicks in my building who know more about investigating murders than I do."

"They don't have keys to the murder victim's house," said Hennessy. He reached into the pocket of his trousers and pulled out a small set of keys. He dropped them into Jane's hand. "It's a basement on Washington Square North, 26B." He shrugged. "Who knows what you might find out." He reached his car and pulled open the driver's side door. "Come on. I'll drive you back into town."

Chapter 5

Sunday, April 16, 1939
London, England

Following the instructions he had been given to be discreet, Detective Inspector Thomas Barry decided to approach his destination on foot, going out through the main gate of Scotland Yard and turning left up the Victoria Embankment. Across the bustling strip of road was Victoria Pier, while ahead of him were the Embankment Gardens and beyond that the sooty, utilitarian hulk of the Hungerford Railway Bridge.

It was overcast, not surprising for April in London, and there was a nip in the air, but Barry was happy for any air at all after spending most of the day in the stuffy confines of the red and gray brick pile behind him, surrounded by a thousand men in cramped offices wearing wool suits or uniforms who sat smoking endless cigarettes and reeking pipes.

The policeman allowed himself a quick smile. If the glimmers and dips out there waited long enough, Jacks like him would wind up dying of asphyxiation. His throat was dry as dust, there was a distant but distinct little rattle in his chest and his eyes were burning. Notwithstanding all of that he reached into the pocket of his overcoat, pulled out an almost empty tin of Players and lit his twentieth cigarette of the day, letting the first inhalation clutch at his lungs for a rich moment before releasing the smoke into the chilly atmosphere.

It was dusk and most of the automobiles moving along the roadway had their headlamps on. Across the Thames he could see the twinkling lights of Southwark. As a cab rattled by with a window down Barry briefly heard the sound of a woman's high-pitched laughter. Hardly the sights and sounds of a great city on the verge of going to war, but then again, even the prime minister was still denying it would come to that.

That afternoon he'd lunched at Overton's with two friends, Bob Fabian and Morris Black, both colleagues at C.I.D. Over the fish course he'd tried to bring up the possibility that Herr Hitler had designs on more than Czechoslovakia and the port of Memel in Lithuania, his most recent acquisition, but neither man had seemed very interested in the subject.

In Morris's case it was at least understandable. The poor bugger had lost his wife, Fay, to cancer only a few months before and was still in mourning, but he'd expected more from Bob. Detective Inspector Fabian, however, seemed far more concerned with the fact that his cousin, a footman at Cliveden, Lady Astor's country house, was making more in gratuities from her famous and infamous guests than Bob was making in salary. Nobody, it seemed, was concerned with impending doom unless it was at their doorstep.

Keeping to his roundabout course Barry turned away from the Embankment at Horse Guards Avenue and made his way toward Whitehall. His summons to the meeting at hand had only come on his return from lunch and had been delivered in a sealed envelope by none other than P. C. Childers, secretary to Ronald Martin Howe, assistant commissioner of the Criminal Investigation Department, or C Division, of Scotland Yard and the man who, ultimately, was Barry's boss.

The note, written in Howe's own tight, neat hand, was, like Howe himself, brief and to the point. Using utmost discretion Detective Inspector Barry was to present himself at the Horse Guards entrance to Treasury at precisely 6:00 P.M. that evening, where he would be met by

Mr. Charles Calthrop, a clerk of that office, who would escort him to his final destination.

Mr. Calthrop would be wearing a dark suit, a red tie and spectacles and would be standing at the reception desk to the right of the doors. Detective Inspector Barry would identify himself to Mr. Calthrop by showing his warrant card. All very cloak and dagger, which led Barry to believe that the summons probably had something to do with the Irish situation. God only knew what *that* had to do with Treasury, unless the boyos had planted one of their ill-made bombs there, which in the light of recent events seemed unlikely. The Republicans had taken credit for almost a dozen incidents in Birmingham and London the past week, all the explosions taking place in public toilets.

The IRA had been active in London and elsewhere in England since January, and even though there'd been a number of arrests there was no sign that the activity was slacking off. Normally the *Sinn Feiners* were handled by Special Branch, but Barry, Morris Black, Fabian and a dozen detective inspectors had been pressed into service as well since the attacks had become so widespread. Barry had been particularly useful since he still had enough of the Shandon in his voice to ask questions where others couldn't.

Thomas Patrick Barry had been born January 19, 1899, in the gloomy gray confines of Mercy Hospital, Cork City, Ireland, at three minutes past midnight. The following day he had been moved to the foundlings ward and his mother, Mary Margaret Barry, was escorted by a priest and two nuns across the old wrought-iron footbridge spanning the River Lee to the Magdalene Laundry in Sunday's Well. Mary Margaret had been eighteen at the time of his birth, a chambermaid at the old Victoria Hotel on St. Patrick Street. She never disclosed the name of the man who had impregnated her, even after being severely beaten by her own father, a malter for the nearby Murphy's Brewery.

Raised by monks at the Capuchin Orphanage in Cork,

young Thomas Barry received a good enough education, but ran away at fifteen and joined the British army by lying about his age. He fought in the infantry and managed to survive four years of war unscathed from the First Battle of the Marne to the Second Battle of the Somme, and finally, Amiens. He'd gone into the war as a private and demobbed out in London in January 1919 as a sergeant. With nothing to look forward to in Cork or anywhere else in Ireland except strife and poverty, the twenty-year-old successfully wrote the British Civil Service entrance examinations, applied at Peel House, and was accepted as a candidate for the London Metropolitan Police Force.

After eight weeks at Eagle Hut, the training school in the Strand, named for the YMCA soldier's center that had previously occupied the building, Thomas Patrick Barry, late of Cork and the Great War, was made a probationary constable. Slightly less than two years after that, he was promoted to detective sergeant. Then he followed the regular line of promotion for the next twelve years and eventually the assignment to the elite Flying Squad at about the same time as Morris Black and Bob Fabian. In 1929, on forced leave after rupturing a ligament in his hip during a chase, Barry went back to Ireland for the first time in almost fifteen years, taking the packet steamer from Fishguard to Rosslare, and from there down to Cork City by train.

Enlisting the aid of the local Garda office he was told that the commercial laundries operated by the Magdalene Order all over the Republic were little more than prisons for young women deemed to have sinned, and since they had never been arrested or charged within the court system, the inmates had no recourse in law. The women had been given into the hands of the Church by their priest or parent, and only the Church had the power to release them. Since the women worked fifteen hours a day for the most meager room and board and were paid no wages, releasing them was hardly cost-effective and rarely occurred.

Barry was advised that a direct confrontation with the

mother superior or the local bishop would be inflammatory and unproductive, but discreet inquiries were made on his behalf and he eventually learned that his mother had died of pleurisy and pneumonia after being held prisoner in the laundry above Sunday's Well for almost seventeen years. Barry was directed to the graveyard where the women who died at the Magdalene Laundry were buried and found that the graves were all nameless, marked only by whitewashed wooden crosses. He left Ireland that same day and never returned. Nor had he set foot in a Catholic church again.

Barry passed under the looming shadow of the black-spired pile of Whitehall Court and continued on past the bulk of the War Office to Whitehall itself, pausing to let a pair of No. 18 omnibuses growl by in opposite directions before he crossed the wide thoroughfare and turned west again. Finally, after having made a meandering three-quarters circle that he hoped was discreet enough to meet with Assistant Commissioner Howe's approval, Barry went up a short flight of steps and entered the Treasury Building. According to his wristwatch and the booming chimes of Big Ben only a few blocks away it was spot-on six.

As promised, Calthrop, a tall, slim man with thinning hair, spectacles and a red tie was standing beside the reception desk. After Barry introduced himself and showed his warrant card, he was given a brief, tight smile in return. Calthrop then led the detective inspector down a maze of interconnecting stairs and narrow corridors, most of which seemed to lead in a roughly southwesterly direction. The tall windows were all shuttered, and after two or three minutes Barry was thoroughly disoriented.

Eventually they reached a narrow, unmarked oak door guarded by a young uniformed police constable. The PC had the bored, slightly pained expression of a man enduring a punishment detail. Calthrop stood away. "Someone will see to you on the other side," he said. Calthrop nodded to the constable, who reached over and opened the door for Barry.

The detective went through, almost tripping as he

stumbled down a short flight of steps, then stepped through an open doorway into a long, narrow room beyond. He suddenly realized where he was. He'd seen this exact spot in a photo in the *Picture Post* the week before. Just as it had been in the pictures, at the far end of the room in a niche above a small coal fireplace there was a pale marble bust of Wellington, and to the right of the fireplace was a row of pegs in the wall hung with hats and coats. It was madness. This was the antechamber to the Cabinet Room in 10 Downing Street, the official residence of the Prime Minister of England.

Immediately to Barry's left there was a broad stairway and on his right were a number of darkly varnished oak doors. He looked over his shoulder, positive that Calthrop had somehow led him astray, and he had already begun to turn back toward the steps he'd come down when the door on his right opened and a man a little younger than himself stepped out into the hallway.

The man was dressed formally in a black suit, white shirt and celluloid collar that made him look very much like a shorter, clean-shaven version of Prime Minister Chamberlain himself. He wore a signet ring with a carved armorial crest and a regimental tie. The handkerchief in his breast pocket showed three points and appeared to have been starched and ironed.

"Alec Douglas-Home," he said, pronouncing the last as Hume in the Scottish fashion. "I expect you're the policeman." The voice was pleasant, layered with Eton and Oxford and just imperious enough to raise Barry's hackles. He added a little too much lilt to his response, watching for the man's reaction.

"Right enough, sir. Detective Inspector Thomas Patrick Barry, at your service."

"Ah," Douglas-Home responded, a little coolness creeping into his voice, "like the tea."

Barry smiled. "No, sir. Like the architect who designed the Parliament Buildings. A great-uncle, I believe." It wasn't true, of course, but that didn't matter.

"Um," said Douglas-Home. "I'm PPS to Mr. Chamberlain. He couldn't attend the meeting so he asked me to be his proxy."

Barry had no intention of asking what a PPS was, assuming that it meant either Principal Private or Principal Parliamentary Secretary. Instead of saying anything he just nodded.

"The others are waiting," Douglas-Home went on. He turned, walked down the corridor a little way, then opened another door, standing aside to let the Scotland Yard man precede him. Barry found himself in a small vestibule with a surprisingly tatty little piece of blue and green Axminster on the floor. Through a tall window directly in front of him he could see across the garden and a low stone wall as dusk settled on Horse Guards Parade. On his right there was another plain, dark door, on his left a set of double doors, painted white.

Chamberlain's man walked past him, knocked lightly on the left of the double doors, then opened it and stood aside again. Barry took a single deep breath and let it out, wishing there'd been time for another cigarette. He walked past Douglas-Home and entered the Cabinet Room, once again recognizable from the story in the *Picture Post.*

It was at least thirty or forty feet long, high-ceilinged, the immense green-felt-covered table that ran the room's length lit by three electric candelabra. The walls were cream colored and bare except for a single small portrait hanging above the fireplace. There was a plain wooden case clock ticking away on the white marble mantelpiece below the painting. The carpet on the floor was the same pattern and color as the Axminster in the vestibule. Two tall windows faced north, another two west, and all four were hidden behind heavy green drapes that matched the color of the table covering. All in all it was surprisingly drab.

There were four men seated at the far end of the table. To Barry's left he could see prim, thin-lipped Ronald Howe, deputy assistant commissioner for C.I.D., and beside him was Sir Norman Kendal, the gaunt, austere head of Special Branch and one notch in rank above Howe. Across from the two Scotland Yard men was a tall, balding figure wearing round, steel-rimmed spectacles and the uniform of a lieutenant colonel in the Royal Engineers. At the end of the table, seated in the only chair with arms, was the home secretary, Sir Samuel Hoare. In front of each place at the table was a green blotting pad, a leather folder, an inkstand and a cut glass ashtray. Both Hoare and the man in the army uniform were smoking cigarettes and Kendal was smoking a pipe.

Douglas-Home closed the door to the Cabinet Room, walked the length of the table and sat down to the right of the uniformed man. Barry remained standing at the far end of the table, waiting. Finally Howe spoke, his voice mildly irritated.

"Sit down, Inspector."

"Yes, sir," said Barry. He pulled out the chair at the end of the table and seated himself. He could feel the tin of cigarettes against the top of his thigh but he wasn't about to light one up here unless he was invited. He folded his hands over the leather-covered folder on the table in front of him and waited while Douglas-Home made the introductions, discovering that the man in uniform was an intelligence officer named Joseph Holland.

"Do you have any idea at all why you've been asked to come here?" Hoare asked from the opposite end of the table.

"None whatsoever, sir."

"Theories?"

"No, sir."

"We have a situation," said the home secretary. He took a long pull on his cigarette, then let the smoke dribble slowly from his nostrils.

"Yes, sir?"

"Indeed," Hoare murmured. "A grave situation." He turned his head slightly and nodded toward Holland.

The balding man pulled his spectacles up onto his nose and flipped open the leather folder in front of him.

"We have received information about a plot to assassinate Their Majesties on their upcoming tour of Canada and the United States. We have reason to believe that the Irish Republican Army is involved." Holland paused and looked across the table to Kendal and Howe. Barry saw Kendal's head move fractionally as he nodded. Holland turned and looked down the table. "Presumably you know who Sean Russell is."

"The IRA chief of staff," Barry answered quietly. "And not well liked."

"Quite so," said Holland. "Odd sort of fellow. Early forties. Big, red-haired, drinks too loudly and talks too much. Two years ago he was thrown out of the movement for embezzling money for an automobile. Red sport coupé, actually. Last year he was elected chief of staff." Barry saw the bald man's lips twitch in a fractional smile. "They really are a strange lot."

"What evidence is there that Russell is involved?" Barry asked.

"Lieutenant Colonel Holland is not at liberty to divulge that information," said Hoare. "Suffice it to say that such evidence does exist." The home secretary paused. "Regardless of that, Inspector Barry, what are your feelings about such a plot and this Russell man's involvement?"

"I don't think I know enough to express an opinion on the subject," Barry answered, carefully trying to be diplomatic. Express the wrong opinion and he could easily be back patrolling the East End as a constable. He still had no idea why he had been summoned to a meeting at this level—certainly not because his opinions were of any particular value to the home secretary or the mysterious Lieutenant Colonel Holland.

"Don't be coy, man!" Howe snapped. "Hazard a guess."

Barry tried to arrange his thoughts. He finally sat forward in the chair. "I don't believe it. Not Russell's involvement anyway."

"Why?" Hoare asked.

"Because it doesn't make any sense, sir. Russell is fighting for full Irish independence, North and South together. If the IRA was involved in such an assassination Russell would get his unification by way of an English invasion and martial law being declared." Barry looked directly at the home secretary. "I don't think Prime Minister Chamberlain would have any other choice." The policeman shook his head. "As I said, there's no logic to it."

"But the plot exists," reiterated Holland. "There's no doubt about it." He lifted his shoulders. "And no doubt that Sean Russell is somehow involved. He sailed for New York from Le Havre this afternoon on a German ship, the *Stavangerfjord*. It has been suggested he's gone to raise funds, and we have some information regarding his connection with a well-known American film star." He blinked. "Another Irishman, as a matter of fact. A Mr. Flynn."

"From what you've been saying, there is presumably some reason to think that the assassination is to take place either in Canada or the United States."

Holland nodded. "The United States."

"Curious," said Barry. "Much easier to kill them here I should think. His Majesty likes to shoot and the queen spends a great deal of time in the country."

"We're assuming a political reason for the location," said Holland. Barry nodded. He glanced quickly in Hoare's direction. The home secretary was well known for his strong position supporting appeasement. The death of the king and queen on American soil would cause a rift between England and the United States that would take decades to heal. "This is an extremely important diplomatic mission, among other things. We all know how difficult His Majesty finds being in the public eye, let alone speaking in public, yet he is doing it, and doing it at a very difficult time."

"I assume appropriate security measures have been taken," said Barry.

Kendal, the head of Special Branch, made a small snorting sound, presumably annoyed by what he considered to be the detective's effrontery. "You assume correctly, Inspector. We've already dispatched a team of men to go over every foot of rail the royal train will cover in both Canada and the United States. The Royal Canadian Mounted Police are rounding up any potential troublemakers and we're getting the same level of cooperation from the FBI. Their Majesties will be accompanied by Cameron and Perkins, the royal bodyguards, and there will be at least a dozen of my men aboard the train who will accompany the king and queen everywhere. Local police and highway patrol officers will further protect Their Majesties in the United States, and they will also be provided special agents from the State Department's Office of Security."

"More than enough protection, I should think," commented the home secretary. "And of the best sort by the sounds of it."

Barry said nothing, but he could almost hear Brother Emmett as the tonsured bastard stripped the First Place rugby ribbons from the low walls of his little cubicle in the orphanage: "Pride goeth before a fall, boyo. You'd be wise to remember that, wise indeed." This done a day after the sinking of the *Titanic* in April 1912. Barry had been thirteen years old.

"Cui bono," he said, dredging up some hard-earned Capuchin Latin. "Who does it benefit?"

Hoare's small mouth pinched even more. "I beg your pardon?"

"In a crime, look to see who profits. Find the motive, find your man. The best way to protect against a threat is to discover its source and remove it."

"Rather what I've been saying about all of this," said Holland gratefully. "If such an assassination attempt were successful, who *would* profit?" He tapped his cigarette nervously on the edge of the glass ashtray in front of him, looking around the table. No one spoke. "The Nazis," he said finally. "Germany."

"One nation assassinating the sovereign of another?" said Hoare. "It's preposterous! Not done!"

Holland wasn't fazed by the outburst. "It's the most logical answer to the inspector's question, I'm afraid. The murder of the king and queen in America would have a devastating effect. It would drive a wedge between our two countries that would last an age, let alone the duration of a European war." He paused, glancing down at the open folder in front of him. "The German government couldn't directly orchestrate such a thing, but they could use someone like Russell to do it for them, and we already know the Nazis have actively supported the IRA for years." He paused and cleared his throat. "Kills several birds with one stone, actually—dividing and conquering in the first instance and leaving the throne vacant in the second."

"I'm not quite certain what you're suggesting," said Douglas-Home.

Holland answered, a note of unease appearing in his voice. "There is some evidence of a recent meeting between Mr. Flynn and the king's brother at the Hotel Meurice in Paris. There were also two high-ranking members of the Nazi Party present."

"By the king's brother I assume you mean the Duke of Windsor?" Douglas-Home asked.

"I'm afraid so," Holland said. "The duke may no longer be in formal line of succession, but then neither is the Princess Elizabeth old enough to assume the throne. A regent would have to be appointed until the princess reached her majority." Holland paused again, then reached out and took a sip of water from the glass in front of him. "I doubt there could be a more popular choice among the people than the Duke of Windsor for the appointment." He put the water glass down on the table. "In effect, he would be king again and the duchess would be his morgantic queen."

"Ridiculous!" said Hoare. "Utter madness!"

"Perhaps so, sir," said Douglas-Home smoothly. "But I'm quite sure the prime minister would just as soon we erred on the side of caution in this matter."

"Um," said Hoare, "perhaps."

"I've reviewed the material myself," Douglas-Home continued. He glanced at Holland. "It is clearly substantive."

"What do you suggest then?" Hoare asked.

Douglas-Home smiled across the table at Kendal. "I think we can assume that Special Branch has done as much as possible to ensure the safety of Their Majesties, but there would be no harm in having a discreet, independent inquiry into the matter."

"What would this inquiry of yours entail?" Hoare asked.

"It has already been discussed," said Kendal. "All we need is your final approval." He tilted his head toward Howe. "Deputy Assistant Commissioner Howe has offered to second Inspector Barry to Special Branch and our mutual friends at St. Anne's Gate have agreed to let us use Lieutenant Colonel Holland for the time being. The inspector reports to Holland. Holland reports to me."

At the far end of the table Thomas Barry was beginning to realize that he had absolutely no say in his own fate. He remembered the Capuchins at the monastery-orphanage in Cork doing exactly the same thing, talking about him as though he wasn't in the room, discussing various options for his future, most of them religious, none of them even vaguely considering the idea of personal fulfillment or pleasure of any sort at all. It wasn't much later that he'd run off to join the army. There'd be no running away from this, however.

Douglas-Home leaned forward and looked down the table, bringing Barry out of his brief fugue. "What's the matter, Barry? You don't seem terribly interested in these proceedings. I thought it was every Irishman's dream to go to America."

Barry looked down the table at the pompous little ass of a man. He smiled. "Now that's an engaging theory, Mr. Douglas," he said, letting his voice fall into a music-hall lilt, purposely cropping the priggish man's name. "The only trouble with it, though, is the fact that I'm not every Irishman." Chamberlain's parliamentary secretary reddened visibly, and even Hoare was amused. Douglas-Home snapped his leather folder shut.

"I think our business here is at an end," he said crisply, and that was that.

Following the meeting, at the lieutenant colonel's invitation, Barry dined with Holland at his club, the Army and Navy on Pall Mall. It being Sunday, the small dining room at the rear of the club was almost deserted. Barry had the fish while Holland worked his way quickly through a trio of lamb chops, all of it served by a stooped and grizzled waiter with a limp and the disdainful look of a man who had almost certainly once been a sergeant. Neither man spoke very much during the meal except to exchange biographies, although while reciting his, Barry realized his companion probably knew it chapter and verse already.

Holland's own story had the flat, bland ring of truth, although given his association with the Secret Intelligence Service it could just as easily have been totally false. According to the balding lieutenant colonel he had been educated at the Royal Military Academy, commissioned in the Royal Engineers and attached to the Royal Flying Corps as an observer in 1916. He served in the Balkans. He was mentioned in Dispatches, given the Distinguished Flying Cross, and demobbed as a brevet major.

According to Holland he'd spent most of his time since then wandering from one boring Whitehall appointment to the next, although he did make a vague reference to having been in Dublin for a brief period during the Troubles. He also mentioned that a chest wound during an operation in Sofia had left him with chronic lung problems, which he assumed would keep him out of any front-line posting should war come. All in all his little set-piece biography made him sound like a benign military bureaucrat with a mildly interesting past. A future club bore in the making.

Dinner over, Holland led the detective down a narrow corridor to the large, oak-paneled Coffee Room overlooking Pall Mall, directing him to a small table and a vacant pair of comfortable-looking red leather armchairs beside one of the tall, arched windows. Like the Dining Room, the Coffee Room was almost empty and the only sounds were the occasional snapping of a newspaper being folded back and the hiss of a coal fire burning in the grate at the far end of the room. They ordered coffee and brandy, and when it came, Holland offered Barry one of his Craven A's and lit it with a plain gold Dunhill lighter.

"I'm still not sure what the purpose of that meeting was," said Barry. "Howe or Kendal could have briefed me privately at the Yard."

"Fog," said Holland, smiling broadly.

"I beg your pardon?"

"Fog," repeated Holland. "My own terminology. Stands for Fear of God. You were meant to be suitably impressed by being allowed into the Cabinet Room. Impressed and cowed. It's a game they play, the Eton-Oxford set, people like Douglas-Home." Holland paused and puffed on his cigarette. "Know anything about his background?"

"Nothing," said Barry.

"Hereditary Scottish lord. Home of the something or other. Eton, third-rate degree in history from Oxford. Never worked a day in his life. Played cricket and shot grouse until he decided he wanted to go into politics. Hasn't looked back. They'll give him a knighthood eventually, just for sticking it out, and if he sticks it out even longer he'll probably be prime minister himself one day. A political dilettante who likes to play at power. Exactly what we don't need in this next war."

Barry smiled. "I gather you don't like him."

"Not him so much," Holland answered, warming to the subject. "His type. We gave Kendal the information on Russell and Kendal passed it on to Chamberlain's Scotty dog. Home doesn't believe there's any plot and neither does Hoare. They think it's going to be a gentleman's war and gentlemen don't go about shooting kings and queens." Holland shook his head. "Well Herr Hitler's no bloody gentleman, believe me."

"If they don't believe there's any real assassination plot, what am I supposed to be investigating?"

"We're a sop, you and I," Holland explained. "They have to make some sort of response to the information simply because we sent the information their way. Our so-called independent investigation is what they've decided on. If, by some terrible chance, something *does* go wrong, then you and I will be the scapegoats." He smiled bleakly. "It's the kind of contrivance our cricket-playing friend thrives on. Damned if we do and damned if we don't, just so long as none of the damning damns him."

"What do you think about the plot?" Barry asked. He stubbed out his cigarette and took a sip of coffee. "Do you take it seriously?"

"Historically most assassinations are senseless, the acts of lunatics or zealots."

"Like Russell."

"I think you know better than that, Inspector. Russell's neither zealot nor madman. He swaggers about O'Connell Street in a bright red MG to match his hair, looking for young ladies to impress. He's six feet two inches tall and as far as the records show he's never shot at anyone in his life. He's a drinker, a talker, a fund-raiser. Hardly my first choice for an assassin."

"Sometimes the Irish can fool you." Barry smiled.

Holland smiled back. "Oh, I'm aware of that, Inspector. Have no doubt on that score. Which is precisely why I think you're just the right man for this job."

Barry laughed. "As a sop?"

"As a detective, and a good one too if your record is any indication." He paused and shook another cigarette from the packet on the table between them. "I could be wrong, of course, but I trust my intuitions about things like this. Whatever Sean Russell's involvement, there's rarely smoke without fire, and these days most fires have names like Fritz and Ernst and Heinrich, the de Valeras and McGarritys aside."

"We've got a dozen IRA men under lock and key in the Scrubs but they'll not likely have much to tell you about Russell, or tell me, for that matter."

Holland laughed and lit his cigarette. He leaned back in his chair, smiling. "No, we won't find answers at Wormwood Scrubs."

"Where then?" Barry asked.

"Dublin, for a start," Holland answered.

Chapter 6

Sunday, April 16, 1939
New York City

Dan Hennessy dropped Jane off at the Flatiron Building, then headed back to Centre Street to put his report together. Jane went into Walgreens, picked up a Dixie of coffee and a doughnut at the soda fountain, then went up to her office, riding the slow, moaning elevator and thinking about the dead man she'd just immortalized on film.

Howie Raines, a kid she used to play nurse and doctor with, no queer then certainly, who worked for a shady law firm like Fallon and McGee and wound up bopped in a New Jersey ditch on a Sunday. So what got him killed? The shyster part of the equation, or the queer part? And much more interesting, why was Dan Hennessy being told to zip lips? Howie was no big-time Mob mouthpiece. So far it wasn't making much sense at all. The elevator jerked to a halt two inches below floor level. Jane stepped out, went down the quiet corridor and let herself into her office.

Ponce de Leon shrieked an obscene hello and she gave the bird a piece of doughnut just to shut him up. She took her Contax into the bathroom/darkroom, threaded the roll of film into her Reelo Tank and developed the negatives. When she was finished she clothespinned them up in strips over the sink to dry, then went back out front and finished her cooling coffee. She glanced at her watch. It was one-thirty—lots of time to get over to the dead man's apartment and have a look-see before she went to visit her sister.

On her way out the door she pulled another camera out of the filing cabinet, this time choosing her smallest: a fully loaded Model E Leica that fit easily into the pocket of her jacket. She rode the elevator to the ground floor and stepped out into the early-afternoon sunshine.

Instead of taking a hack, this time she went to the bus stop on Fifth Avenue and waited for a Sunday schedule No. 1, smoking two Camels in the process. When the bus finally pulled up she was pleased to see that it was one of the older-style double-deckers. Jane got on, paid her dime and took the little spiral staircase up to the top level. She sat down, lit another cigarette and rode to the end of the line at Washington Square, feeling a bit like a tourist as she watched the sights go by from her elevated perch.

The bus drove through the arch and pulled to a stop just past it. Jane climbed down and stepped out into the sunlight again. The big rectangular park was full of life. Italian boys and girls in their Sunday best played running games among the scattered pin oaks and locust trees while their parents sat on blankets, some of the men stripped down to their undershirts to catch the sun. There were students here as well, reading on the benches or stretched out on the grass, escaping the drab buildings of New York University on the eastern side of the park.

Jane dug into her shoulder bag and touched the ring of keys Dan Hennessy had given her. Taking a path that would lead her out to Washington Square North she wondered how many of the people enjoying their afternoon outing knew that once upon a time the park had originally been New York's potter's field and that there were more than ten thousand nameless graves beneath their feet, or that some of the big elms giving them shade had once been used for gallows.

Washington Square North ran for a block on either side of Fifth Avenue and was made up of an almost intact line of early-nineteenth-century Greek Revival town houses of red brick and white limestone trim sitting on land that had once been part of the old Warren estate. Once upon a time the houses had been part of one of New York's most elegant residential areas, but times had changed. At least half of the buildings had been transformed into rooming houses, several were closed up, windows blinded by heavy shutters, and two or three were for sale, although the signs advertising their availability were so old the paint on them had partially faded away.

The street numbers ran from east to west, which put number 26 west of Fifth Avenue at the MacDougal Street end of the park. Except for the fact that the low hedge in front of the building was neatly trimmed the building wasn't much different from its neighbors on either side—three and a half stories tall, three windows across, the front door accessible up six stone steps leading to a false portico, the inset oak door flanked by a pair of outsized Ionic columns. The windows and the door were shaded with green-and-white-striped awnings, but the fabric was washed out and stained and tears were developing here and there. Twenty-six Washington Square North was on the way down.

Behind a low wrought-iron fence a steep flight of steps led down to the basement apartment. Two small windows were filled with glass blocks cemented together. Jane went down the steps, took out the ring of keys and let herself into the apartment.

She found herself in a narrow foyer with a hat rack on the right and an oval mirror on the left. There were a homburg and a topcoat hanging from the hat rack and a pair of toe rubbers on a sisal mat at its base. Jane closed the door and locked it behind her, tasting the air. Stale with a back-scent of cigarette smoke. No blood tang, no smell of death. Howard Raines had been dumped in that ditch, but he hadn't been killed here.

An archway on the left led into a small, low-ceilinged sitting room, the walls cheaply decorated with movie posters, an oval rag rug on the floor, brown sofa on the right, dark green upholstered easy chair opposite under the glass block windows and a gas fireplace in between. There was an ashtray and a small pile of magazines on a low table beside the easy chair. Jane leafed through the magazines. *Saturday Evening Post, Liberty, Newsweek, Baseball* and *Flying Aces*. Two of his favorite things. Ball games and a kid's dream about being a fighter pilot. Did queers read *Flying Aces* or *Baseball* magazine?

She glanced at the movie posters. Another one of Howie's little passions, what he talked about most often when they talked at all. Most of the posters were from a few years back, nothing really recent. *Dawn Patrol* with Basil Rathbone and Errol Flynn, *The Invisible Ray* with Boris Karloff, *Last of the Mohicans* and *Trade Winds*. Jane had seen them all except *Trade Winds,* which appeared to be a romance-on-an-ocean-liner story with Fredric March and Joan Bennett. Not her kind of movie, but that didn't make it something a fairy would like. Or did it?

The kitchen was next, narrow and old. Yellow linoleum on the counter, a chipped GE monitor-top refrigerator with a clattering compressor and a tall, rust-rimmed hot-water heater standing beside the small gas stove. Against the side wall there was a small breakfast table with a blue oilcloth cover and three white kitchen chairs. Jane checked the refrigerator: two bottles of Coca-Cola, three cans of Pabst, eggs, butter, a piece of cheese and two or three small parcels wrapped in butcher's paper. A half-empty tin of Dole Pineapple Gems—no telling clues there. Canned soup, Tender Leaf Tea and Ovaltine in the cupboards. A bottle of Teachers and another of Fleischmann's Gin under the sink. Howard Raines was beginning to shape up as a fairly normal bachelor.

The bathroom was a little more informative, but not by much. Howie Raines the grown-up used Vaseline Hair Tonic for dandruff, Ipana to brush his teeth and Odo-Ro-No for his armpits. He also had packets of Sal Hepatica and Saraka, both of them partially used, which meant he was constipated a lot. He lathered up with Colgate and shaved with Gem blades. Jane smiled. Every inch the lawyer on his way up—tight-assed, sweet-smelling and smooth-cheeked. Except he wasn't on his way up anymore. He was on his way to the morgue.

The small bedroom was at the rear of the apartment and sported another pair of glass block windows that probably looked out onto a back alley. A bed, bedside table, a desk and a bureau were crammed into the room. The bed was covered with a dark green spread, the bedside table was wicker and the bureau was older than Jane, its shellac gone piss yellow with time. The desk was from the same era and held a green blotter, a Stork Club ashtray just like Jane's, a gooseneck lamp and a telephone. The number on the dial was CIrcle 6-7350.

Jane checked the desk drawer first. Old bills, a few new ones, some Fallon and McGee letterhead and envelopes, paper clips, a few stamps, three or four Mongol Number 2s and a sharpener, a bottle of Waterman's blue ink, an old, dried-out tortoiseshell Shaeffer fountain pen that looked as though it might have belonged to Howard's father and a crumpled pack of Skeets with two very stale cigarettes inside. No address book, which was a little odd.

The narrow closet revealed three pairs of brown shoes, one blue suit and a dark brown one that was the twin of what Howie had been wearing when someone blew his brains out. A striped Arrow tie was looped over each of the suit hangers. There were a half dozen paper-wrapped parcels with laundry tags on the low shelf—most likely white shirts like the one he'd been wearing. Jane didn't bother opening one to look. She did check the pockets of the two suits and came up empty. Not even lint. There was a small Hartmann overnight case on the floor of the closet but there was dust all over it—the luggage hadn't been used for quite a while.

There was nothing in the drawer of the bedside table and nothing on top except a lamp and an alarm clock that had run down. She finally struck pay dirt, such as it was, in the second drawer of the bureau under a pile of underpants: a full deck of nudie playing cards and a yellow quarter-dozen tin of Caravan prophylactics with one missing. To Jane's knowledge pansies didn't like looking at naked women and she didn't think they used cocksafes either. The queer-boy story was starting to come unstuck and it was beginning to look as though the Ariston baths claim check and the bar receipt from Gloria's had been planted on Howie Raines like a bad smell.

By whom and for what reason? Jane put the cards and the tin back in the drawer, closed it and sat herself down on the end of the bed. She was reasonably sure she knew why the damning evidence had been planted—to make it look as though the poor schmuck had been involved in some romantic falling out between perverts. The papers didn't take much interest in running that kind of story and the cops wouldn't put much effort into solving the murder. Without some other kind of angle it would all just fade away, and by appearances someone had gone to a great deal of trouble to make that very thing happen.

Which meant that for some reason Howard Raines was important, and that led inexorably back to Fallon and McGee. Both Jimmy Fallon and Eugene McGee had been dead for years, but the firm carried on in the same tradition, representing anyone who was anyone in the underworld and in the realm of unsavory city politics. There was even a rumor going around that the firm had been the ones who hired Lloyd Paul Stryker to represent Jimmy Hines, the Tammany leader, earlier in the year.

She closed her eyes and tried to imagine Howie the way he'd been, in his stupid glee-club jacket, trying to get out of it and getting caught in the sleeves, with Jane all the while on her back with her prom dress up around her waist and her panties already off, feeling like a dozen kinds of fool in the backseat of his father's car, waiting for the magic moment and finding out in the end it was more moment than magic. Innocent as sheep, both of them—no wolf, Howie—but it had been something special. If nothing else he'd been so grateful and so sweet, even if he was faster than lightning and not too well endowed.

Jane sat on the bed with her eyes closed and allowed herself what she wouldn't allow in front of Hennessy. She wept, for Howie and that long-ago moment in the car, for the past they shared and for the future Howie'd never have. Dying in a ditch. The poor bastard didn't deserve that.

She gave herself a few minutes, then found a single white glove from her darkroom in the bottom of her bag, wiped her eyes with it, and pulled herself together. She lit a cigarette and thought about things—the hard, cold reality of it. Howie was dead. Whatever he'd been to her once wasn't important now. Finding out who'd killed him was the thing. The story. At least she could tell herself that, make the image of the boy she'd known go back into tones of gray where it belonged, just like the pictures she'd taken.

Dan Hennessy was a good cop and he smelled a rat. When Danny boy smelled a rat, Jane smelled a story, and a story meant money. But the scent was fading fast. The connection between poor old Howard and the law firm he worked for was a dead end. No one at Fallon and McGee was going to tell her anything about Howard Raines, what he had been up to, or who his clients were. Jane chewed on her lip and looked around the small room. She hated like hell to give it up so early in the game but she didn't see any other way to go. Sometimes when she went to visit her sister she thought she could see fleeting instants of recognition, like lightning flashes in the dark that said *I'm in here. You just can't see me.* That was what she was feeling now, except from Howie. *I'm dead and gone but I was here. I existed. I deserve a better epitaph than I'm going to get, so tell my story for me.*

Jane leaned back on her splayed hands and closed her eyes, trying to imagine what Hennessy would do. She visualized the apartment again, going through it room by room, wondering if she'd missed something important, but there was nothing—nothing out of place, nothing strange except the lack of an address book, nothing pointing to a motive for murder.

She got up from the bed and went back down the hall to the front door. She put her hand on the doorknob and then paused. Just for the hell of it she turned to the hat rack and went through the pockets of the topcoat. It hadn't rained since Thursday, which was probably the last time Howie had worn it.

She felt something in one of the pockets and pulled it out. It was a pack of smokes with a book of matches tucked in under the cellophane. The matches were from Pan American Airways, and when Jane pulled the book out she saw that the cigarettes were a brand she'd never heard of—*ALAS*. She flipped over the pack and looked at the bottom. *Hecho in Habana.* It figured. If she remembered right, *alas* was Spanish for wings, and that was the stylized motif on the red, white and blue wrapper.

She tapped a cigarette out of the pack, held it up to her ear, then rolled it between her thumb and forefinger. It didn't crackle too much and no tobacco fell out. She lit it and dragged in a lungful of smoke. A bit on the strong side for her tastes, but not harsh and burning. The smokes were fresh. It looked like Howard had been on vacation.

"Well now, Howie, maybe we've got ourselves a story after all."

Jane tucked the pack into her shoulder bag and went back into the bedroom. She sat down at the desk, picked up the telephone and dialed the operator. A few seconds later she was connected to the Pan American Airways office on East Forty-second. The main office was closed, but after a few questions the Sunday duty operator transferred her to the Marine Terminal office in Port Washington, Long Island.

"Pan American Airways Marine Terminal. My name is Doris. How may I be of assistance?" She said the words as though she'd learned them from a script, which was probably the case.

Jane closed her eyes and went into her own act. "Hi there, Doris. My name's Sara Wackerman. I'm the bookkeeper for Fallon and McGee. The lawyers?"

"Yes, Miss . . . Wackerman?"

"Well, you see, the thing of it is, Doris, I'm sitting here with Howie's expense vouchers and there's no dates or times or anything, and I was wondering if you could clear a few things up for me." She paused and put her best smile into her voice. "Think you could help me out here, Doris?"

"I'll do my best, Miss Wackerman. You said Howie?"

"Howard Raines. I've got him down here for a flight from New York to Havana."

"When was this?"

Jane thought about the topcoat and took a stab at it. "Thursday, I think. The big rainstorm."

"Just a moment." Doris went away and Jane tapped her ash into the Stork Club ashtray. A few moments later Doris came back on the line. "Miss Wackerman?"

"Still here."

"We show Mr. Raines on the passenger manifest for our Miami overnight on Thursday the thirteenth, connecting with our Havana flight at 8:30 A.M. on Friday."

"And the return?"

"His ticket included a voucher for the 3:00 P.M. return flight from Havana to Miami."

"And back to New York?"

"He had a ticket but he turned it in." Doris sounded a little disappointed.

"Any reason?"

"Um, under Refund it says 'decided to take train.' "

"Well, that pretty much explains things, Doris." Jane thought for a second. "One more thing, Doris, if you don't mind."

"Not at all, Miss Wackerman." Doris was starting to sound a little put upon.

"How did Mr. Raines pay for his tickets?" Jane screwed the butt of her cigarette out.

There was another short pause and then Doris spoke. "They were on account."

"Who authorized them?"

Doris sounded hesitant. "I'm not sure I should say, Miss Wackerman."

"It's the Fallon and McGee account, Doris, and I'm the Fallon and McGee bookkeeper."

"But the tickets weren't put on that account. That's the problem."

Now *that* was interesting. Jane pushed a little. "Come on now, Doris. You've got to know I'm on the up and up here. I'd like to be outside enjoying this nice Sunday afternoon along with the rest of New York, but I'm stuck here trying to make sense of Howie's travel vouchers." She breathed a long-suffering sigh into the mouthpiece. "Obviously what's happened is that Mr. Raines was doing business for a client and had the travel authorized by the client instead of the firm, and now that's got me all confused."

Doris sighed back at her. "Me too."

"So if I know who the client is, I can clear the whole thing up."

"Shalleck," said Doris after a moment. "The account is with Mr. Joseph Shalleck."

Who the hell was that? "You're a peach, Doris. Thanks a million." Jane hung up the telephone. She waited for the line to clear, then picked up again and dialed, this time to Billy Tinker, one of Winchell's researchers down at the *Mirror*. The skinny, pock-faced kid wasn't much on looks or personality but he had a photographic memory and a noggin like an encyclopedia. As usual, when he wasn't at the *Mirror* building next door to the abattoirs on East Forty-fifth, he was at home with his three sisters in Brooklyn. One of the sisters answered the phone, and when Jane asked for Billy, she yelled for him. A long minute later he came on the line. The voice had the rusty, self-conscious tones of someone who spent more time reading than talking.

"Tinker."

"Jane Todd, Billy. Two bucks says you can't tell me who Joseph Shalleck is."

"You lose."

"Impress me," said Jane. She opened the drawer of the desk and took out a sheet of Fallon and McGee stationery and a sharpened pencil.

"How do I collect?"

"Name your pleasure."

"Lunch. That little Greek place on West Twenty-fifth."

"The Spartacus Club," said Jane, remembering. A greasy little dive between Seventh and Eighth.

"That's the one," said Tinker. "Where they pour booze on the goat cheese and set fire to it."

"You're on," Jane agreed. "Now what about this Shalleck guy?"

"You want the short story or the novel?"

"Both."

"Short of it is, he's a Mob shyster from a long way back. Pol connections too."

"Tammany?"

"Once upon a time maybe, but for the last twenty years he's been a back-room boy with the local Democrats."

"Okay, now give me the details."

"For two simoleons you want details?"

"I'll buy you a beer with your shish kebab."

"Shalleck started off apprenticing for Jimmy Fallon just after the war. Wound up representing everyone from Arnold Rothstein to Frank Costello and Eddie Moretti. Owney Madden in the old days, Lepke Buchalter, Dutch Schultz—you name it. He also represents Dandy Phil."

"Kastel?"

"The same," said Billy. Dandy Phil Kastel was the brains behind half a dozen bucket-shop fraud operations flogging nonexistent penny stocks on Wall Street. Everybody was predicting big things for him in the Mob.

"What's the connection to the Democrats like these days?"

"He was Jimmy Hines's lawyer of record and you can't get any more connected than that. Until Dewey came along and broke up the party, Hines had the D.A.'s office in his pocket, not to mention the fact that he was a bagman for Farley. Some people say Shalleck even has FDR's ear, knows where some bodies are buried." Billy fell silent.

"That's it?" Jane asked.

"You want more it's coffee and dessert."

"Pass," Jane said, grinning into the phone, "for the moment."

"I really do want the lunch," Billy warned.

"Don't worry. You'll get it," Jane promised.

"I'd better," said Billy. There was a click as he hung up.

Jane looked down at the notes she'd made on the Fallon and McGee stationery. A junior shyster who works for a Mob law firm winds up going to Cuba on business for another, even bigger Mob lawyer and then winds up getting bumped off and thrown in a ditch in New Jersey for his efforts. She drum-tapped the Mongol on the blotter, trying to see Howie's last day as a series of photographs, black-and-white strips of time hanging on a clothespin over the sink, starting with him arriving back in New York after the breakneck visit to Havana.

The lawyer doesn't take a suitcase, but he goes on business, so that means he's carrying a briefcase when he climbs up out of Penn Station. Probably he gets a taxi out front since Shalleck is paying the tab, then rides home. Comes in, hangs up his topcoat, puts down the briefcase. Not much time goes by because he doesn't even take the fancy smokes out of his coat before someone comes calling, that quick because they're probably watching the place, waiting. Not Shalleck himself because he wouldn't involve himself directly. One of his Mob pals and someone Howard knows, because there's no sign of a struggle, no mess. Raines takes the briefcase with him because it's business, but he leaves the topcoat behind because it's sunny now.

Jane lit another one of the Cuban cigarettes and sat back in the chair. Raines would have taken a sleeper, probably on the Seaboard Silver Meteor, which meant there'd be a record of it somewhere, and she might even find the hack who took Raines from Penn Station home, but what was the point? None of it would tell her much more than she already knew, and when you got right down to it, she didn't know much except that it was likely Shalleck had ordered the young lawyer murdered immediately upon his return from Cuba. To go any farther with the story Jane was going to have to find out why Shalleck sent Howard Raines to Havana in the first place.

She looked at her watch. She'd spent the better part of an hour in the apartment and it was getting late. She tidied up the desk, put her notes into her pocket, and took out the Leica. It was loaded with DuPont Superior and she had the lens wide open. She spent the next ten minutes going through the place, room by room, taking pictures, not so much because she wanted a record, but mostly because she knew Hennessy would want to see them. When she was finished she put the Leica back in her pocket and let herself out, locking the door behind her.

It took her two buses and a streetcar to go uptown and crosstown into Yorkville and Germantown. By the time she reached Cherokee Place and the ferry slip at the foot of Seventy-eighth Street, it was four-thirty. Dusk was already settling over the litter of old gray buildings, brooding in exile on the flat, low island in the middle of the East River's dark, uncoiling ribbon. Jane showed the ferryman her permanent visitor's pass for the hospital, then paid her nickel and was handed her punched ticket.

She sat down on the front thwart of the flat-bottomed scow and a few seconds later the boat's engine coughed into life and they chattered out into the river. As she did every time she took the bleak ride, Jane thought about Edmond Dantes in chains as he rode across to the ghastly prison of the Chateau d'If in *The Count of Monte Cristo,* wondering if he would ever return to the mainland and to freedom.

Three minutes later they reached the island and Jane stepped out onto the narrow, vacant dock.

"Last ride at six," said the ferryman. "No exceptions."

"I'll be here."

"If not, you stay the night," the ferryman warned.

"I'll be here," she said again.

The ferryman nodded and backed the boat away from the dock. Jane watched him go, watched the sun beginning to go down behind the city for a moment, then turned and followed the gravel path up to the main building with its octagonal, fortresslike tower and two massive wings, stretched out at an angle on either side with smaller towers of their own, like curled fists at the end of monstrous, enfolding arms.

The narrow, barred windows were blank plates of brass reflecting the dying sun. Jane tried to swallow the small terror that always accompanied her here, the suffocating fear that she would enter the building and become lost and never find her way out again. Feeling her heart begin to pound, Jane reached the main entrance and dragged open one of the heavy wooden doors. She stepped into the octagon tower and paused, letting her eyes adjust to the gloom.

Things had changed little since Charles Dickens visited the asylum during the final stages of its construction almost a hundred years before—dark-stained wainscoting with cold brick and stone above, dim yellow light leaking out from sconces bolted to the walls and booming granite floors that echoed with every step. Hateful then by Dickens's description, and hateful still.

The core of the tower was taken up by an elegant spiraling staircase that wound upward to serve the multiple floors and open galleries above, while at its base stood a broad, high counter like that of a hotel. There were two people behind the counter. One, a woman, was dressed as a nurse, while the other, a huge man with ham hands and the flattened face of a prizefighter, was wearing an orderly's white cap and uniform.

Jane showed her pass to the nurse and she nodded, but the orderly's eyes followed her suspiciously. Or was he leering? Ignoring the look, Jane continued on and turned up the stairs. With each step she climbed the noises from above grew louder; moans and cries and wailing screams that echoed and reechoed, the gibbering of idiots, the cataclysmic dreams and aspirations of tortured souls. Stepping out onto the third floor she was suddenly among them.

They were everywhere in the corridors, like traffic on a busy street, moving in all directions. Men and women, all of them gaunt, some in pajamas or long, old-fashioned nightshirts. Some shuffling in slippers making mad whispers as they moved, others barefoot on the cold stone, hair wild, eyes listless, hands twitching or gesticulating, fingers pointing in accusation or picking at ears and arms and chests. Teeth munching on lips.

A marching soldier back from a war, chest out, proud of his medals, except there were no medals on his naked sunken chest, only the flapping breasts of an old man. A woman sitting on the floor, filthy with her own evacuations, laughing frightfully at an endlessly funny joke only she could hear. A mad conductor with an invisible baton and an orchestra of the insane.

None of them with names.

Once, early on, before she'd gone to California and deserted her sister for all those years, she'd come down the wrong stairs and found herself in the basement of the asylum and seen the most frightful sight of all—thousands upon thousands of dusty boxes, suitcases, carpetbags and valises in piled aisles and rows, a hundred years' worth, ten thousand patients' worth, the last evidence of lives lived outside the walls of this place, the last remnant of who each man and woman had been before they'd been consigned to their awful, anonymous exile here. Sometimes she still dreamed of it.

Jane shook off the thought and moved with the ebb and flow of the lunatic tide, threading her way along the corridor until she came to the large ward of beds where her sister was. She showed her pass to another nurse on duty at the ward desk, and like the first nurse, she passed Jane through with no more than a nod.

Here in the dark ward, windows shuttered, there were only the sounds of sleep and dreams, soft muttering and whisperings and small moans. Creaking bedsprings and small coughs, the steady rattle and tick of a ventilating fan. The smell of carbolic soap and urine and the yeasty pall of hard-laundered sheets. Rows of iron beds, the bodies within them already shrouded, like a muttering, whispering waiting room for death.

Jane found her as she always found her, motionless,

on her side, curved like a bent old woman, her lank hair against the striped pillow ticking, her face turned so that only one blind, roving eye was showing, shifting endlessly, moving back and forth and rolling side to side, seeing nothing in all these years, knowing nothing. If the eyes were windows to the soul, then her sister's spirit had vanished long ago.

"Hello, Annie," she said softly and sat down on the edge of the bed. "How you doing, sis?" There was no response. There never was, but she sometimes told herself that she knew the sound of her voice, knew she was visiting, knew she hadn't forgotten her. She reached out and touched the soft skin of her hand, surprised as always at its warmth, its life. She took the hand in her own and held it and talked to her, leaning forward a little so she wouldn't have to raise her voice.

She spent an hour with her, telling her about Howard Raines, and Cuba and Doris at Pan American and her lost bet with Billy Tinker. Told her about Joseph Shalleck the Mob lawyer, Dan Hennessy's clear worries about burying the case and about her own sense that this was only the beginning of something much bigger than a small-time shyster's murder.

Ominous was the word for it. Ominous as the trembling of leaves before a storm, the flat dead calm of a hurricane's approach. Ominous as the seemingly steady sweep to war again—that is, if you believed what you read and saw in the pages of *Life* magazine.

The time passed and then it was fully dark outside. Jane looked at her watch and saw that it was almost six. The ferryman would be making his last trip soon. Jane squeezed her sister's hand. "Better for you to be here, better you don't know what's going on in the world." She released her hand and stood, preparing to leave. The wide, polished planks of the old floor creaked beneath her feet. In the gloom someone angrily recited the Twenty-third Psalm like a curse.

Jane stood and looked down at the blind, lost shell of her sister and shook her head in the gathering night. She shivered and looked up toward the ceiling high above her, almost expecting to see the huge black wings of some creature that would give substance to the dark sense of foreboding that had suddenly come upon her, a nightmare of her own, harvested from the dreadful anguish of the sleeping souls around her. "Terrible things are coming, Annie," she whispered, shivering again. "Terrible things."

Chapter 7

Monday, April 17, 1939
Dublin, Republic of Ireland

As arranged over coffee the previous evening, Barry met Lieutenant Colonel Joseph Holland at the Irish Sea Airlines offices on Lower Belgrave Street at 9:00 A.M. the morning after his so-called Fear-of-God meeting at 10 Downing Street. Holland was wearing a light worsted suit and Barry had dressed in his inevitable tweeds. From Belgrave Street the two men took the airport coach out to Croydon in time to catch the flight to Bristol.

Their aircraft was an elegant, eight-passenger DeHavilland Rapide, a twin-engined biplane, freshly painted in the Aer Lingus green-and-white livery. It was a lovely spring day with clear skies, and they took off exactly on time, flying due west toward the sea. The sound of the engines made conversation virtually impossible, but Barry was more than content to stare out the window at the unfolding landscape a few thousand feet below.

It was the policeman's first flight and he enjoyed it immensely, ignoring the occasional shudder and swoop as well as the moanings of a female passenger in the seat directly behind him. Beside him, Holland slept for the entire hour, waking only as they started to land at Whitechurch Aerodrome, a few miles south of Bristol.

The aircraft refueled, Barry and Holland each had a fried-egg sandwich and coffee in the aerodrome café, and then the flight resumed. For the first hour of the ongoing journey Barry kept watch at the window as they flew northwest across the Severn, then on above the Welsh hills of Monmouth, Brecknock and Cardigan, leaving the land entirely at Aberystwyth, heading out over Cardigan Bay, and finally the Irish Sea.

The engines droned on monotonously, sending a light, continuous vibration through the airplane. The sun glinted brightly on the ruffled sea far below and eventually Barry turned away from the window, put his head back and closed his eyes. When he opened them again it was to discover that the weather had deteriorated to a dullish overcast and they were preparing to land at Dublin's brand-new Collinstown Airport. As they touched down on the runway Barry glanced at his wristwatch. Not quite one in the afternoon. An arduous, exhausting journey that would have taken at least twenty hours via train and ferry had just been accomplished by air in less than four. Barry commented on it as they climbed down out of the aircraft and walked across the tarmac to the broad curve of the snow-white, multistoried terminal building.

"Yes, wonderful." Holland nodded as they went through the swinging doors and into the Arrivals hall. "And all things being well we'll be back in London by midnight."

Since they carried no luggage Customs was merely a formality. They showed their passports to a uniformed official and Barry was given a second look when the man saw first his place of birth and then his occupation.

"Come home to join the Garda then?" asked the official. "Or is it to take a job with Special Branch?"

"Neither," Barry answered, ignoring the man's tone. "Just over for a pint of Guinness and a stroll across St. Stephen's Green."

"Mile failte"—a thousand welcomes—said the official without meaning a word of it, handing Barry back his passport.

"Go raibh mile maith agat"—And may as much good fortune be yours—Barry answered without hesitation. At first the official looked surprised, then confused. He fi-

nally scowled, waving him onward. There were no thousand welcomes for Holland, ill-meant or otherwise.

Once out of the Customs hall they crossed the echoing concourse and stepped outside onto the pavement. The sky had darkened even more since they had landed, making the white concrete arc of the terminal building even brighter and the grass of the roundabout in front of them a startling green.

There was a small, blunt-nosed Leyland coach in Aer Lingus colors parked beside the curb as well as half a dozen taxicabs of varying vintages and states of repair. "Which shall it be?" Holland asked. "Coach or cab?"

Barry shrugged. The officer inside the terminal had almost certainly begun to spread the news of their arrival, either by telephone or into the ear of a mate, and the coach driver and cabbies were either IRA themselves or had friends who were. One way or another their presence in Dublin would be common knowledge before the day was done. It was an odd feeling, but there was no doubt in Barry's mind that in most ways, this deceptively familiar place was actually enemy territory and potentially dangerous.

"I don't suppose it really matters," Barry said finally.

"I don't really fancy the coach," said Holland, watching as it began to fill up. "Let's splurge and take a cab." They went to the end of the queue, waited their turn, then climbed into a fragile-looking Swift at least a decade old with a bit of rag stuffed into the radiator plug and skinny tires completely barren of tread. The driver was old and fat with thin white hair over a scalp that was frighteningly red. He was reading *The Irish Press* and puffing on the fuming stub of a wet-ended cigarette.

"Where to?" he asked, barely shifting to turn in his seat as Barry and Holland climbed into the back.

"Two Foster Place," said Holland. "You know where it is?"

" 'Course," said the cabby. "Three punt."

"Two," Holland answered.

"Done," said the driver. "Since you're not having luggage wit' ya." He flipped the cigarette end out the window, turned the key and pressed the starter. The engine caught and the automobile chattered away from the curb. They made their way around the traffic circle, then followed the newly paved access drive to Swords Road, where they turned right and headed south toward Santry and the city beyond.

The driver plucked another short end of a cigarette from a rusty Players tin on the seat beside him and lit it with a Vesta, blowing clouds of smoke at the windscreen. "A fine soft day it is," he said, turning his head slightly toward his passengers, smiling around the cigarette fixed to his lower lip.

"It is that," Barry answered, accenting the words.

The driver looked back in his mirror. "In from London, are you?"

"We are," Barry said.

"But not from there," said the driver. "Not you, at least."

Barry smiled. "No, that's true, that's true. Born in Cork I was. You've got me there," he answered, laying the accent on with a trowel, turning the *o* in Cork into a broad, flat *a*.

"Ah," said the driver. "A *culchie*." The word was untranslatable, combining backbiting, gossiping, cheating and conniving with a general sense of uncultured rural stupidity. It was a word that Dubliners had applied to Corkmen for as long as anyone could remember.

"Being *culchie* is a state of mind," Barry answered. "I've seen it as often on the banks of the Liffey as I have on the banks of the Lee. And at least the Lee has swans, *culchie* though they may be."

"Well, that's true enough." The driver grinned. He paused and puffed on his cigarette. "On the other hand, I've heard that Corkmen have been known to hunt the poor bloody birds down and eat them on occasion. A very *culchie* thing to do, that."

"It's true," muttered Holland. "Put two Irishmen in a room and you'll have an argument." He shook his head. "You're all mad."

"Driven to it without a doubt by a thousand years of

British oppression and occupation," the driver responded pleasantly. "We fight among ourselves to keep in training to deal with the likes of you."

As they continued on in silence, open land gave way to built-up estates and small factories, and by the time they crossed the narrow trench of the Santry River there was little greenery to see at all. They kept on Swords Road through Whitehall and Drumcorda, a brownish haze gathering around them the farther south they drove. By the time they crossed the Royal Canal in sight of the brooding stone pile of Mountjoy Prison, the air was thick with the yeast and sawdust smell of hops and barley spreading up and out in a dense pall from the massive Guinness Brewery at St. James Gate, still more than two miles away on the other side of the Liffey.

"My God," said Holland, wrinkling his forehead and pushing his spectacles up onto the bridge of his nose. "I'd forgotten the stench."

"If beer could shit, that's what it would smell like," Barry answered.

"Meat and drink to me," the cabby said, without being asked for his opinion. "Even a beggar won't starve in Dublin if he has a nose. Food of the gods is Guinness."

"Sounds like an advert," Holland said with a laugh.

The driver finally found his way down to the broad reach of O'Connell Street and they drove its length, going past the elegant facade of the Gresham Hotel, the black finger of Nelson's Column, the General Post Office—still bullet pocked from the 1916 Rising—and finally the statue of O'Connell himself, peering balefully at the clattering dark green trolleys crossing the wide bridge over the Liffey that was named for him.

A No. 17 omnibus turned in front of them with a large Gold Flake tobacco advertisement on its side, and out of the corner of his eye Barry caught a glimpse of the huge *Players Please* illuminated sign attached to the roofline of the Hopkins Store on the corner. On the opposite side of the wide street there was another sign, this one vertical, advertising Craven A. The might of the British Empire had failed to conquer Ireland's heart and soul, but British commerce had certainly conquered her lungs.

The taxi veered slightly to the right up Westmorland Street and soon reached College Green, the sooty Georgian expanse of the Bank of Ireland on their right, the walled white confines of Trinity College on their left. They sputtered around the columned arc of the bank, once Ireland's Parliament and House of Lords, then took the first right turn down a narrow, tree-lined cul-de-sac.

"Foster Place," said the driver, pulling to a stop. In front of them at the end of the street was a looming blank wall of cut stone and to their right was a side entrance to the Bank of Ireland. To the left was a short row of tall, mid-Victorian buildings, the last with a strong neoclassical porch supported on cast-iron columns. "It'll be the Royal Bank you're going to then?" asked the driver.

"Quite right," said Holland. He climbed out of the Swift with Barry close behind, and paid the driver. He stood on the curb for a moment, waiting for the cabby to make his turn in the narrow street, but instead the white-haired man simply lit another cigarette end and picked up his newspaper. He glanced up at Holland and Barry. "Changed your mind, have you?" he asked.

"No." Holland smiled.

The driver shook his newspaper, folding back a page. "Thought I might be of assistance when your business is concluded."

"Very thoughtful of you," Holland answered. "We shan't be long." He turned away from the taxi and went up the low steps to the porch of the bank.

"Keeping an eye on us," said Barry.

"Of course," Holland said. "Only to be expected, really." He pulled open one of the doors and stood aside to let Barry enter before him.

The central banking hall was enormous, a beautiful barrel-vaulted-and-coffered ceiling in cream and brown supported by cast-iron Corinthian columns, the roof artfully lit by hidden clerestories that flooded the upper part of the room with light. The floor was marble, a long foyer bound on the left by a waist-high, dark oak counter and on the right by several arched niches set with comfortable-looking leather chairs for waiting patrons. At the far end of the entranceway the counter was fitted with an opening, allowing access to the rows of desks in the main portion of the hall.

"They have their little spies everywhere," Holland said as he grinned. "I should think this all started when we arrived at the Irish Sea Airlines office this morning."

Barry agreed. The uniformed ticket clerk had taken his information for the passenger manifest from their passports and could easily have placed a call to Dublin. The strawberry-faced driver of the Swift would stick to them like glue for the duration of their visit.

"What do we do about him?"

"Follow me," said Holland. He marched down to the far end of the counter, walked through the opening and smiled politely at the frowning young man who rose up from behind his desk. He was wearing a dark suit with the trousers too short and a white shirt with a very frayed collar. He had sandy hair and freckles across his nose. He looked no more than twenty.

"Help you, sir?"

"Certainly," Holland said, his voice clipped and imperious. "Meeting with Mr. Louth about my accounts."

"Yes, sir," said the young man. "I'll fetch him, shall I?"

"No need, no need," said Holland, brushing past him. "Know the way. Use your facilities first, if you don't mind."

"No, sir. Of course not, sir," the young man said, calling after them. "It's—"

"Know the way there too, lad," Holland said with a wave.

They threaded their way between the desks until they reached the rear of the hall, then went through a pair of glass-windowed doors onto a rear landing. A narrow flight of stairs led up, another, shorter flight led down. Holland went down. Reaching the foot of the stairs he turned to the right and they walked past doors marked

WC-GENTS and WC-LADIES. Continuing on down the passage they reached another short flight of steps, went up, turned right and then went down yet another, even narrower hallway. Barry was thoroughly lost but Holland seemed to know exactly where he was going.

At the end of the hall Holland pushed through a swinging door with a tarnished brass palm plate and Barry suddenly found himself in what was obviously the bank's luncheon room. There were a half dozen plain wood tables and chairs, a coffee urn and a doorway leading into the small kitchen beyond. Barry could smell sausages and chip grease. There were several people at the tables, all dressed in dark suits like the young clerk upstairs. Two of them were drinking tea and reading their newspapers while the third, an older man, was fast asleep, his head tilted back in the chair, his mouth open.

There was a heavy-looking wooden door at the far end of the room, and someone had jammed an old shoe into the crack to keep it open, letting in fresh air. The two men reading their papers never even looked up as Holland and Barry crossed the room and went through the door. As he passed by, Barry noticed that the door was fitted with a large brass lock and several bolts and that there was no handle on the outside at all. He smiled to himself as he stepped out onto a narrow cobbled lane at the rear of the bank. The door had been designed to keep unsavory characters from getting in, not out.

"This way," Holland instructed, turning to the left, heading out toward Dame Street.

"You've done that before," said Barry, smiling.

"Once or twice."

"Chancy."

"Not really. I do have an account at the bank, as a matter of fact, and I've dealt with Mr. Louth before. If he remembers me at all it's as the English fellow who goes off to pee and never comes back."

They reached the head of the cobbled lane and stepped out onto the pavement of Dame Street, four lanes divided by a narrow stone median. The traffic was as heavy as a broad street in London, filled with bicycles, taxis, buses, trucks and trolley cars ebbing and flowing in both directions.

"Where to?" Barry asked.

"Not far now," Holland answered. "But let's put some distance between us and our friend the curious cabby."

Holland turned right and together he and Barry made their way briskly down Dame Street, past Crow Street and Temple Lane, finally crossing Dame Street at the point where Great George Street curved down to meet it, moving south. By now they were well away from the taxi driver waiting beside the curb in Foster Place but Holland was taking no chances. They continued up Great George Street until they reached the entrance to the old covered market, then turned in, moving quickly between the rich-smelling stalls of meats and cheeses, fish and produce, finally exiting onto Drury Street.

They paused there long enough to smoke a cigarette, waiting to see if anyone was following them. Satisfied that they were on their own, Holland nodded to Barry and they turned left this time, moving north again, walking in single file down the narrow crumbling pavement through what passed for Dublin's garment district—an assortment of ground-floor wardrobe shops and milliners topped by narrow-windowed factories on the floors above. Eventually they reached Exchequer Street, turned right, then left again onto St. Andrew's Street, finally ending up in front of St. Andrew's Church itself, a squat and unattractive seventeenth-century pile of soot-stained granite.

"We're going to mass?" Barry asked as they stopped in front of the entrance to the church. A woman as squat as the church scuttled in through the doors, pulling a black shawl over her head as she disappeared into the gloom within.

"We're going for a pint, just like you told the man in the Customs hall," said Holland, pointing to an elegant Victorian structure of polychrome brick and timbered windows directly across the street. The ground floor was a public house, with O'Neill's inscribed in gold on the green wooden name board above the long, curtained windows. They crossed the street and went inside.

The interior was noisy, dark and hazed with smoke. It was also crowded with the remnants of the lunchtime trade, mostly barristers and bankers from the well-dressed looks of them. The pub was made up of a long bar on the left and a series of stall-like niches on the right running the length of the room, with benches and several tables in each stall.

They found a table halfway down the room and sat down. "You fetch the drinks," said Holland. "I'd only attract attention."

"What'll you have?" asked Barry, standing.

"Guinness."

Barry edged his way between the patrons chatting at the rail and ordered Holland's Guinness and a black and tan for himself. He carried the tall glasses back to the table and sat down again.

Holland took a small sip and licked the foam from his lips. "They say if you drink enough of this you don't mind the smell of the city so much."

"Drink enough of that and you don't mind the smell of anything," Barry answered. He took a pull at his own ale-and-stout mixture and tried to recall the last time he'd taken drink in a Dublin pub. Too long ago to remember. He lit a cigarette and glanced at Holland. "You said we were coming here to get answers," the policeman said, pitching his voice low enough not to carry far.

"In time," said Holland.

Barry sighed; he'd had enough of secret meetings and cryptic phrases. "Are we waiting for someone?"

"Yes," said Holland. He took another sip of the Guinness, looking over Barry's shoulder toward the door.

"Who?"

"A young lad. His name is Brendan. A cutout."

"Cutout?"

"A go-between," Holland explained. "Nothing more than an errand boy, really."

"You know him?"

"I've used him before." Holland paused, looking over Barry's shoulder again. "There he is." He lifted his hand and waved. "Behan!" A few moments later a young man appeared and slid onto the bench beside Holland. He was no more than sixteen, short, square-shouldered and fat-cheeked with hard-brushed mouse-brown hair that seemed to stand straight up on his large head. He had the soulful eyes of a basset, a large nose and a small, almost girlish mouth. He glanced down at the glass of Guinness.

"Finished with that, are you?" he asked.

Holland smiled and pushed the pint in front of the boy. He picked it up and drank deeply, almost emptying the glass. He set down what was left and gave a little sigh of contentment.

"Thirsty?" Holland asked.

"Always." The boy glanced across the table at Barry, then turned to Holland. "Who's this then?"

"A friend, Brendan."

The eyes narrowed. "Not of mine."

"A countryman," Holland soothed.

The boy stared, then lifted the Guinness and drained it away, his eyes never leaving Barry's face. He put the glass down, belched lightly and then began to sing to the tune of "The Rising of the Moon."

They told me, Francis Hinsley,
they told me you were hung . . .

He left it hanging in querying invitation.

Barry grinned, took a pull on his black and tan and finished the verse.

With red protruding eyeballs
and black protruding tongue.

Behan laughed and continued the test. "Up a long ladder . . ."

"And down a short rope . . ."

"To hell with King Billy . . ."

"And God bless the Pope."

"And if he don't like it . . ."

"We'll tear him in two . . ."

"And send him to hell with his red, white and blue." Behan nudged Holland in the ribs. "No offense to the flag meant, yer honor."

"None taken," said Holland.

Behan pointed to Barry's black and tan. "Done with that?"

"I suppose I am," said the policeman, repeating the ritual of pushing the glass in the young man's direction.

"It's laid on then?" Holland asked as Behan finished the drink.

The round-faced boy nodded and put down the glass. "I'll go out first and then you follow. I'll be ahead on my bike, a hundred feet or so. If there's trouble I'll get off and give you a signal."

"What kind of signal?" Holland asked.

"How about if I scratch me arse?" said Behan. "Will that be clear enough to ya?"

"Abundantly."

"You see me doing that, clear out of it, quick. Either it's the Boys or it's the Garda, which means tomorrow they find me *bolg anairde* in the Liffey, or having my horrible cobble in the Joy, neither of which would please me or my sainted mother very much, thanks but no thanks." He stood up and slipped out from behind the table. "Give me a minute to get clear." And then he was gone.

"A bogman in the making," said Barry. "Or trying to be." At sixteen the boy was already familiar with the broken bodies of informants floating belly-up in the river and the quality of the food in Mountjoy Prison.

"Fancies himself a writer," Holland commented. "Joined the *Fianna Eireann* when he was twelve and started publishing articles in their magazine." Barry nodded. *Fianna Eireann* was the Republican version of the Boy Scouts and bore a disturbing similarity to Germany's Hitler

Youth. Like that organization, *Fianna Eireann* was also a way of breeding recruits for the more serious activities of its adult counterpart.

"Do you know where he's taking us?" Barry asked.

"Haven't the faintest," Holland said.

As it turned out, the young boy on his bike led the two men, on foot, back across the river to O'Connell Street, then down Talbot Street past the bookstalls and haberdashers to Amiens Station. At no time did young Behan climb down from his bicycle and scratch his arse, so they assumed they were safe, at least for the moment. The two men followed him into the plain brick railway terminal, sat down on a bench and watched as the boy leaned his bike against a wall. He went to one of the ticket windows, spoke to the agent briefly then turned away, purchasing an orange from a vending cart. He brought the fruit over to where they were sitting and peeled the orange in one long strip of rind, standing in front of the rubbish bin beside the bench.

"There's a train to Wicklow Town in five minutes, track five. You'll be met." The pie-faced young man finished peeling the orange, split it and popped a section into his mouth. "For the scurvy." He grinned and popped another section into his mouth, then walked away. Holland and Barry did as they were told, purchasing their tickets and climbing aboard just as the train began to move.

Chapter 8

Monday, April 17, 1939
County Wicklow, Republic of Ireland

The train went from Dublin to Rosslare along the coast, stopping at almost every small town along the way. The passengers were mostly country folk, women and children returning home after shopping or a visit to relations in the city. They sat in the straight-backed wooden seats and laughed and drank and ate and smoked and talked, sometimes buying tea from the trolley as it rattled past.

Barry sat closest to the window and stared out toward the iron-tinted sea. They went through the ferry port of Dun Laoghaire, past the beaches at Dalkey, then came to Bray, where they followed a narrow stone-hewn path along the flinty cliffs and through half a dozen short tunnels.

The weather had cleared slightly, giving the air a little brightness, and under other circumstances Barry might have enjoyed the trip. As it was he was finding himself feeling more and more impotent in the face of events, no more than a student or companion of Holland's, that truth made all the more irritating by the fact that this was *his* birthplace and should have been hostile territory for the man sitting beside him. The man who was presently looking calm as oiled water, spectacles perched on his bald forehead as he leafed through an abandoned copy of the morning *Independent*.

The train reached Wicklow Town an hour after leaving

Dublin. They stepped out onto the platform with a score of others as half a dozen new passengers clambered on. A moment later, after a warning toot of its whistle, the train puffed laboriously past the small whitewashed station and disappeared around a corner, hidden in the deep cut it followed around the turn.

By then the platform and the station itself were empty, the other passengers having quickly streamed out through an opening in the high stone wall that stood a few feet away. They were alone except for the trainman in his raised signal box high above the track. The Irish name for Wicklow, Cill Mantain, was picked out in whitewashed stones on the sloping bank on the other side of the track and flanked by two red pots of dark earth that might hold pansies later in the season.

"I thought we were being met," said Barry, looking around.

"Someone will show up," Holland answered. He'd kept the newspaper and now had it tucked under his arm. He looks British enough to make your teeth ache, Barry thought. A perfect target.

"What if this is all some sort of elaborate trap?" the policeman asked.

"Doubtful," said Holland. "If they'd wanted to do us harm they'd have done it in Dublin, not in the countryside."

"Tell that to Michael Collins," Barry said with a snort. Collins, onetime head of the Irish Republican Brotherhood and eventually commander in chief of the Irish National Army, had been assassinated in the narrow valley of Beal Na Blath in County Cork, not far from his birthplace in Clonakilty. Barry was fully aware and so was Holland that the IRA was capable of killing them anywhere.

"You're no Michael Collins and neither am I," scoffed Holland, lighting a cigarette. "They'd have nothing to gain by killing us."

"They have nothing to gain from blowing up lavatories in London and Manchester either," said Barry. "But that doesn't stop them from doing it." He shook his head.

"You're not talking about logic, Colonel. You're talking about fanaticism and zealotry."

"Well said. But I still don't think we have anything to worry about." Holland puffed on his cigarette and smiled. "Young Brendan would have scratched his arse, remember?"

Barry sighed. "Brendan's scratched arse aside, and just so I won't be taken entirely by surprise, I *would* like to know who we're meeting, if that's not divulging vital state secrets."

"You haven't actually signed the Official Secrets Act yet, have you?"

"No."

"Then it probably *is* divulging vital state secrets if I tell you, but I don't see what harm it can do at this point, since you'll know soon enough anyway." He paused. On the other side of the wall they could hear the sound of tires crunching on gravel as a car pulled up into the small lot beside the station. Holland dropped his cigarette end onto the platform and crushed it out with his shoe. "We're meeting with Stephen Hayes."

Barry stared. "Sweet shitting Jesus! Stephen Hayes is Russell's second in command!"

"Quite right," Holland said. "He also happens to be a Special Branch informant."

Both men turned at the sound of a voice behind them. "Colonel Holland?" The man speaking was gray-haired and in his sixties, wearing the plain black suit and white collar of a Catholic priest. The older man stepped forward and extended his hand. The thick fingers were yellowed with nicotine and the voice was whiskey-burred and tired. "I'm Father O'Hara. There's a car waiting."

The automobile in question turned out to be a flatulent black Austin 10-4 almost as old as the taxi they'd used in Dublin. Barry and Holland sat crammed together in the rear seat while Father O'Hara sat alone in the front, bolt upright behind the wheel, clutching it stiffly in both hands except when he ground the gearshift as he drove along the rising unpaved track that led away from the station.

A half mile away at the main road a steep hill rose, covered in gorse and gnarled trees. There were lower hills and hedgerow-broken fields both left and right, planted in clover for the grazing sheep. It was the breeding season and the rams had broad patches of beetroot dye on their bellies, which would rub off on the backs of the ewes to show that they'd been mounted.

Barry was still stunned by the announcement that they were about to meet with Stephen Hayes, and more than that, bewildered by Holland's blandly couched revelation that Hayes, the second-highest-ranking officer in the Irish Republican Army, was an informer for Special Branch. Barry was no specialist in IRA affairs, but he knew that Hayes was a lifelong Republican and well known to be wedded to the cause.

Over the past two years or so there had been dozens of arrests both here and in the north, thinning the already depleted ranks of the paramilitary organization. Almost as bad were the divisive squabblings of half a dozen factions of the Irregulars from Belfast all the way down to the Cork Brigade. Because of this, formerly low-grade officers within the IRA ranks were suddenly being thrust into prominence.

In 1937, Russell, a Dublin cabinetmaker, had been the IRA's quartermaster, but the interim chief of staff at the time, a barrister named Sean McBride, accused Russell of tampering with IRA funds and squandering the organization's money. McBride, a member of the Army Council, had Russell drummed out of the IRA altogether, an odd event in itself, since usually the only way to retire from the IRA was by way of a bullet through the back of the head.

Russell, undaunted and now with a taste for power, managed to ally himself with another Dublin faction of the group and twelve months later, with few others left to choose from, Russell was made chief of staff and brought Hayes with him into the spotlight. Up until then Hayes had been an on-again off-again supporter of the organization as a town councilman in Wexford, a man known to be a soccer lover and someone who enthusiastically enjoyed his drink. Now, with Russell apparently already gone to America, Hayes would be the de facto leader of the entire Irish Republican Army, and, if what Holland said was true, a traitor to it.

Father O'Hara managed to guide the backfiring Austin up to the main road, then turned left, following the line of the gorse-and-bracken-covered hill to the right. In the distance Barry could see the dark slate roofs of the town's outlying buildings and what appeared to be a narrow high street between them, but O'Hara abruptly turned sharply to the right, geared down with a grinding clatter and pointed the car up a steep and very narrow roadway that suddenly appeared, flanked by a pair of high stone walls. Barry caught a quick glimpse of a whitewashed boulder at the side of the road, a name painted on it in tar black: FRIAR'S HILL.

As the Austin struggled upward along the narrow snaking roadway there was very little to see—both sides of the rough thoroughfare were screened by dense and ancient ramparts of blackthorn and holly. Then, just as suddenly, they were out of it, climbing to the crest of the bare-topped hill.

On the left there were a few stony fields set with more sheep and the barely visible ruins of some old stone buildings, perhaps the long-vanished monastery that had given the hill its name. On the right the precipitous slope of the hill dropped away, offering a windswept vista ranging down to the railway station in the distance with the single line of track that ran northward up the coast, and then to the beach and the flat gray sea beyond. Inland from the railway track Barry could see stands of forest, farms and other hills, but here there was nothing except the road and a single small cottage on the right surrounded by a low stone wall. Yeats had written about places like this, called it a "terrible beauty." Terrible indeed, and like a dark stone within his own heart, unutterably sad.

The cottage was like ten thousand others in the country, low to the ground, almost as though its shoulders were hunched against the cold winds that came off the sea and roared over the stony fields around it. The spackled gray walls were thick, mildew stained and uneven, the windows small, their panes cheaply made, whorled and rippled, spotted with bubbles and oily occlusions. The roof was local slate, the cracks between each piece deep green with moss. Better than a crofter's hut perhaps, but not really what anyone would want to call a home with any pride. The simple door was made of iron-strapped planks, once blue, now scoured to smooth silver by the winds.

The priest ground the Austin to a halt in front of a gateless opening in the wall around the cottage and all three men clambered out, instantly feeling the wind as it plucked at their clothes and hair, stinging their eyes. Holding his jacket tightly closed with one gnarled hand, O'Hara led the way up to the cottage door. He thumbed down the latch without knocking, ducked his head under the lintel and disappeared inside. Holland began to follow him but Barry put a hand on his arm, stopping him.

"A priest? And Hayes an informer?" He shook his head. "I can't believe it."

"The R.C.s have been against the IRA from the start—you know that. The Church has never shared power lightly. Being a member in good standing is grounds for excommunication."

"Then there are IRA priests hereabouts celebrating mass without authority," Barry scoffed. "And that still doesn't explain Hayes." He shook his head. "It's got to be some sort of trick."

"No trick," Holland answered, gently removing Barry's hand from his arm. "Hayes is a traitor to his own because he has no choice."

"Why?"

"Because he's a poofter," Holland answered flatly. "A fart-catcher, that's why. We caught him at it one night in the public loo on St. Stephen's Green. If his friends in the movement knew about his fancy they'd do things to him you don't even want to think about before they finally topped him. There are no queers among the heroic brethren of the IR bloody A, nor will there ever be."

"Does the priest know?" Barry asked.

"The priest is the one who told us where to look," said Holland. "Now come along. We've work to do." He followed O'Hara into the cottage, Barry close behind him.

The Scotland Yard detective stepped through the doorway and paused, letting his eyes adjust to the dim light. The inside of the cottage was as rough and simple as the exterior. The door opened into a low-ceilinged front room that ran from one side of the house to the other. A narrow archway to the left led into a tiny kitchen and a doorway on the right opened into a small, dark bedroom. The whole place was filled with the dark, oily scent of burnt peat and the musk of rising damp. As Barry took a step within the room the pegged floors squeaked under his feet.

Close to an iron fireplace against the far wall, Stephen Hayes sat at a roughly made table, O'Hara standing at his back, a protective hand on his shoulder. Hayes was a large man, forty or so, broad-shouldered, relatively tall for an Irishman, with red bushy hair, a strong jaw and the florid cheeks of a drinker. There were two empty bottles of Beamish Stout on the table in front of him, and a half-filled one in his clasped hands. He looked up for a moment as Holland and Barry entered the house, then looked down at his hands and the bottle in them once again.

"I'll leave you then," the priest said quietly. "When you've a mind I'll see you safe back to the city." He patted Hayes on the shoulder, then turned away and went into the bedroom, closing the door behind him.

"There's tea in the kitchen if you're wanting it," Hayes said. "I think. 'Tisn't my house so I really don't know." He nodded toward the closed bedroom door. "Belongs to one of Father Bunloaf's flock." Barry barely suppressed a smile. He hadn't heard the term since he was a boy.

"We're not here for tea, Mr. Hayes," said Holland. He pulled another chair out from the table and sat down across from the man. Barry seated himself to the left.

"This is Detective Inspector Barry," Holland continued. "He'd like to know some things concerning the whereabouts of your superior."

"Sean, you mean?" said Hayes. He lifted the bottle of stout and took a swallow.

"Sean Russell, yes."

"Gone to America," Hayes answered. His voice was blurred with drink.

"We know that."

"Sunday week," Hayes went on. "A Norwegian liner out of Le Havre, the *Stavangerfjord.*"

Barry did the calculation in his head. Eight days out of Le Havre. Even for a small liner, more than enough time to reach New York.

"Rumor has it he's gone to raise funds from his friends of *Clan na Gael,*" said Holland. Clan na Gael was the wealthiest and most powerful of the expatriate Irish ogranizations in America and had been a source of arms and finance for the Republican cause from the start.

"Rumor's wrong," Hayes grunted. "We've plenty of funds; it's brains we're lacking." He reached into the pocket of his coat and Barry stiffened, but Hayes only produced a little packet of papers and a pocket tin of Players tobacco. He began rolling himself a cigarette, his broad fingers surprisingly deft.

"Then why did he go?" Holland pressed. "It must have been important for the IRA chief of staff to leave his post in the middle of a major campaign."

"The bombings?" Hayes made a snorting sound. "That's nothing. That's just—" Hayes stopped talking. He licked the cigarette paper, twisted one end and lit his creation with one of the wooden matches he kept in the tobacco tin.

"That's just . . . what?" Holland asked.

"Nothing," Hayes grumbled stubbornly. "I've nothing more to say."

"Suit yourself," said Holland. "But you know the consequences." He pushed back his chair, scraping it across the plank floor and stood up.

"Wait." Barry could visibly see the man's bravado

fade, his shoulders sagging as though under some great weight.

Holland stopped, hands holding the back of the chair. "Well?"

"Sean's not gone for money. There's more to it than that."

"Tell me."

"There's some of us who think there's going to be another war soon now. There's some of us who think that, if it comes, we'll be dragged into it like we were before. De Valera says we'll be neutral but there's some that don't believe him or anyone else in the Dial."

"Like Sean."

Hayes nodded. "Like Sean. He who hates my enemy is my friend—that's his creed."

"The Germans?" asked Holland.

Hayes nodded again. "One in particular. A man named Goertz. They've come up with a plan, God bloody help them."

"To kill the king and queen in America," Holland offered.

Hayes stared at him, eyes widening. "You know?"

"About the plan, but not the details. That's why we've come."

"All I know is that it's made Sean enemies within the organization. Gilmore's bunch, along with Ryan and O'Donnell. Then there's McCaughey in the north, with Liam Rice and Charlie McGlade. They all think it's madness. If Frankie Ryan hadn't gone off to fight with the Spaniards he would have topped Sean himself for his foolishness."

"They're not backing him?"

"They don't have to," said Hayes. "Sean has enough friends to carry him along in the United States, not to mention Goertz and all the Germans can bring to bear. Kill the Royals and the Yanks will stay out of the war, that's his idea. With the Yanks out, Hitler's mob invades England and Ireland is free at last."

"Russell actually believes that?" Barry asked, dumbfounded. The simple logic was good enough to a point, but what made Russell think that Hitler would stop after invading England? With Heinkels and Dorniers flying out of Liverpool or Manchester, Dublin could be bombed in a day and Belfast the following morning. The Irish Sea hadn't stopped Cromwell and it wouldn't stop Goering's *Luftwaffe,* that was a certainty.

"Sean believes it with all his heart," Hayes answered, nodding. "He has to believe in it, because nothing else is working in this godforsaken country and we're being made fools of." He tapped the ash of his handmade cigarette into one of the empty beer bottles. "Bombs that don't go off. Exploding toilets. Bombs that blow up the people setting them." Hayes paused, shaking his head wearily again. "The organization is a joke. Sean knows it and so do I." He gave a hollow little laugh. "Bunch of yobbos skulking about playing soldiers and silly buggers, drilling with broomsticks and waiting for action that never comes." He paused and took another swallow of his beer, slamming the bottle back down onto the table. "Sean wanted to strike a blow for once! To do something that mattered, something that would be remembered!"

"You know nothing of the details?"

Hayes lifted his shoulders slightly. *"Faic,"* he answered. "Nothing."

"Russell didn't confide in you?"

"Sean confides in no one, least of all me."

"He said nothing at all?"

"The only thing he told me was that the plan was a case of foils, whatever that means. He thought it was a great joke, that."

Hayes lifted the bottle again, but this time Barry reached out and gripped the man's wrist, stopping him. "We have to find him, Stephen," he said quietly. "If he does the job he's set upon, and with the Germans' help, he'll put back the cause a thousand years. Winston Churchill will come across that little bit of water out there and make Oliver Cromwell look an amateur before he's through. Ireland won't see freedom again for an eternity. Do you understand?" He dropped his hand away from Hayes's wrist.

The red-haired man put down the bottle of his own accord. He looked at Barry and nodded, ignoring Holland now. "There's a woman," he said slowly. "A courier bringing him documents that he needs and news of those against him here."

"Her name," Barry insisted.

"Sheila," Hayes answered. "Sheila Connelly. Traveling false and using the name Mary Coogan."

"Where do we find her?"

"She sails in five days from Southampton. The *Empress of Britain*."

Chapter 9

Thursday, April 20, 1939
New Orleans, Louisiana

After the appearance of the appropriate classified advertisement in the *Havana Post,* there was an exchange of telephone calls between John Bone and his prospective employers that resulted in an agreement to meet face-to-face in New Orleans on Friday, April 21, a date and venue agreeable to both parties. In aid of that meeting Bone had been sent a Chicago and Southern Airlines ticket for a flight that would have brought him in to Shushan Airport on Lake Pontchartrain on the morning of the meeting, but he elected to ignore the ticket and instead booked passage on the United Fruit Company steamer S.S. *Tivives*. The comfortable two-day voyage on the well-equipped cargo-passenger vessel left Bone rested, relaxed and in New Orleans a full twenty-four hours before he was expected to arrive.

The *Tivives* docked at the Thalia Street pier shortly after eight in the morning after the last slow leg of the journey up from the Gulf of Mexico. It was hot, without a hint of cloud in a weak blue sky, but the air seemed almost palpably damp—normal weather for New Orleans. Bone left the ship and went through a cursory customs and immigration check, traveling on a well-worn Canadian passport identifying him as a petroleum engineer named Edwin Dow. The passport was quite legitimate, although Dow had been dead for the last six years—a victim of yellow fever in the jungles of Uruguay while looking for likely drilling sites on behalf of British Petroleum.

When the passport came into Bone's hands it was almost out-of-date, so he simply removed Dow's photograph, replaced it with one of himself, and then had it renewed at the Canadian Consulate in Montevideo. A year ago he'd renewed it again, this time at the embassy in Havana, further muddying the trail of his adopted identity.

Leaving the immense, swelteringly hot passenger shed he carried his single small bag onto the street and out of the sickly sweet reek emanating from the banana warehouse next door. He found a taxi at the stand in front of the shed's main doors. Following Bone's instructions the driver headed up to Tchoupitoulas Street, then turned right until they reached Canal Street. They swung onto the broad avenue with its paved center boulevard of so-called neutral ground and then drove northwest into the hotel and thcater district, the broad hazy breadth of the Mississippi retreating behind them.

The driver turned left onto Baronne Street and deposited Bone in front of the huge, red-brick pile of the seven-hundred-room Hotel Roosevelt. He went to the front desk, announced himself as Edwin Dow, with a confirmed reservation made by telegram from Havana. The clerk gave him his key. Bone waved off the bellhop and took the elevator up to his room. Depositing his case on the bed, he removed a lightweight, pale green cotton shirt, equally lightweight cotton trousers, fresh socks and a pair of cool, open-weave rattan loafers. He also took out a small, cased pair of Zeiss binoculars and the most recent edition of the AAA guide for the eastern United States. That done, he went to the adjoining bathroom and showered.

Refreshed, he returned to the bedroom, changed into the clothes he'd laid out and then used the AAA guide to find a nearby garage where he could hire an automobile for the next three or four days. He found one on

Gravier Street only a few blocks over from the hotel, which promised to deliver a vehicle to him within the hour.

Pleased with his progress so far, Bone picked up the binoculars, went down to the coffeeshop, bought a newspaper and ate a light breakfast of poached eggs and dry toast, then went to the cigar store in the lobby. He purchased a road map of New Orleans and its environs, a small pocket diary with its own pencil, two bottles of Pepsi-Cola from the cooler and an odd-looking souvenir bottle opener in the shape of what appeared to be a flattened crawfish. He also purchased a pair of green-lensed Cool Ray sunglasses from a display beside the cash register and wore them out of the shop.

With the strap of the binocular case over his shoulder, his purchases in a brown paper bag and the folded newspaper under his arm, Bone went back to the lobby, where he found the young delivery driver from the garage already waiting for him. Bone filled out and signed the rental form and paid a twenty-dollar cash deposit. Using the road map and the stub of a pencil, the driver showed Bone the best and shortest route to his destination before they went out to the car.

The vehicle waiting at the curb was a dark blue Ford, six or seven years old by its boxy, squared-off look, but well kept and in good running condition according to the young man from the garage. It had been freshly oiled and watered and the gas tank was full. Bone got behind the wheel, took a moment to familiarize himself with the controls, then drove the young man back to the Gravier Street garage, promising to return the car sometime before the following Monday. Bone checked his watch. It was now ten o'clock.

Leaving the garage he continued on down Gravier Street until he found himself back in the riverfront district. He jogged slightly, putting himself onto a much-narrowed Canal Street, then thumped across the jumble of interweaving railway lines and drove down to the ferry slip squeezed in between a pair of giant, rusty-roofed warehouses. It was well past the morning rush and he had no trouble getting a spot on the broad-beamed flatboat. Ten minutes later, with the half-mile breadth of the sluggish mud-colored river behind it, the ferry pulled in to the Boumy Street pier at Algiers Point.

On the east bank of the Mississippi, New Orleans had grown into a modern, industrialized city, but Algiers on the west bank, without a connecting bridge and isolated except for the ferry, had retained its original river-town flavor. There were no skyscrapers or grand cathedrals here. The tallest buildings in Algiers were grain elevators, and the churches were small and usually made of wood.

The streets were paved with asphalt now, and there was electricity here as well, but the casual visitor was more likely to see Algiers as a rough-and-ready bayou town than as the Fifteenth Ward and Fifth District of the great city of New Orleans. The best food in Algiers was the pickled egg and pretzel lunches in the bars on Opelousas Avenue, the best entertainment in the semipublic gambling houses run by Sylvestro "Sam" Carolla and his friends, and the best women in the single cribs and brothels that hugged the low, mean streets around the Southern Pacific yards.

Following the penciled instructions on his map, John Bone turned left toward the point itself. Reaching the old Johnson Iron Works and Shipyard he turned right onto Patterson Avenue, following it along the downstream course of the river until he reached the tall chain-link fence surrounding the abandoned Algiers Naval Air Station. The barbed wire on top of the fence was brown with rust and the hangars and buildings were paint-faded, their windows grimy and smashed. Even from the road Bone could see that the runways were cracked and weedy, and it didn't look as though the strawlike stands of grass between the buildings had been cut for years.

Boxing the compass on three sides, Bone skirted the desolate acreage, eventually returning to the unpaved public road that stretched out along the levee above the muddy currents of the broad, snaking river. On the far side, just visible through the heat haze, were the Poland

Street docks and the narrow entrance to the ship canal that led up to Lake Pontchartrain.

At the old Quarantine Station Bone followed his directions and turned right down a narrow oiled road bearing a single sign indicating that he was now on the way to the village of Behrman and State Highway 31. Algiers was all but gone now, the townscape replaced by small truck farms and undeveloped grazing land posted with signs advertising a variety of futures for people willing to put down ten percent on their dream house of tomorrow. By the weathering of the placards and the empty land it didn't look as though there were too many takers.

At State Highway 31 he turned left again and drove for a mile or so, passing the entrance road leading to the Alvin Callender Airport, New Orleans's first, its single runway and out-of-date facilities now relegated to use by cargo operators and small charter companies. According to the signs he was now nine miles from New Orleans proper. Bone finally reached the Mississippi once again at Belle Chasse, a down-at-the-heels plantation house and property that stood like a languorous, time-wilted monument to the past. Directly across were the clattering ramps, cranes and railyards of the Seatrain terminal, a huge, noisy operation that lifted entire freight cars of produce onto waiting ships that would take them downriver to the gulf and eventually to Havana, or Edgewater, New Jersey.

At Belle Chasse, Louisiana State 31 hooked hard right following the levee, but Bone turned instead onto the one-lane country road that ran north. On the landward side of the road there were smallholding cotton fields and acreage planted in slash pine. On the river side were the long rolling fields of an indigo plantation long since gone to seed and scrub, the perimeters of the fields barely defined by rickety rail fences half turned to rot and lines of low trees planted for windbreaks every hundred yards or so.

The entranceway to the plantation was marked by a pair of rusty iron gates and a stone fence choked with vines. On the far side of the gates two lines of twisted, arthritic oak trees flanked a rutted carriageway leading up to a low hill close to the levee. Perched on the hill, overlooking the river and the fields, was an old plantation house, smaller than Belle Chasse, and not as old but in much worse shape. The name of the plantation was still visible, worked into the scrolled wrought-iron design of the gates: LA FLORA.

Bone drove on for another half mile, making sure that the car couldn't be seen by anyone driving in toward the plantation. He pulled the car up into the shade of half a dozen cypress trees that stood in a cluster by the side of the road, their limbs hung with long gray rags of Spanish moss. He switched off the engine, climbed out of the car and raised the hood, propping it open, then went back for his binoculars and the bag containing the two bottles of soda pop, the bottle opener and the pocket diary he'd purchased from the cigar store in the lobby of the Hotel Roosevelt. Anyone happening along the road would assume that the owner of the car had gone looking for a garage.

Carrying his supplies, Bone headed out across a wedge-shaped field that led to a low, boomerang-shaped ridge, its crest topped with willow and alder. The indigo fields hadn't been worked for a good thirty or forty years, but the snake patterning of the plant rows meant to prevent erosion was still vaguely discernible even though the low-growing legumes had gone to seed decades before. At one end of the ridge there was a small, ramshackle building, and just beyond it, weaving down through the trees, Bone could see the twinkling line of a small stream as it jumped and twisted down the rocks. A spring, obviously, and the building had probably once been a pump house, built to carry cool, fresh water to the house.

Reaching the foot of the ridge, Bone made his way up to the treed crest, keeping well below it as he worked his way across to the source of the stream, a small pool almost directly above the old pump house. The pool was no bigger than a round dining table, fringed with moss and giving the air a fresh, earthy tang. Bone found a narrow stone ledge no more than a foot below the surface and immersed the two bottles of Pepsi in the chilly water. He turned away, crouched down and made his way to the edge of the trees, taking care to keep himself fully in the dappling shadows cast by their leaves and branches.

Below him the ridge dropped down steeply to a sweeping field of tall grass, tips brown and wilted with the heat. Only the hundred feet or so directly around the house had been roughly trimmed down, probably with a handheld scythe, just the way Bone had seen barley mown when he was a small child in Drumdean so long ago.

The two-storied house was of good size, at least forty or fifty feet on a side, columns rising all around in the Greek Revival style of the early 1800s. The straight mansard roof was copper gone dull, streaked verdigris and topped with a square cupola set with a pair of windows on each side. Most of the glass in the cupola windows was gone and half the windows of the house itself were smashed as well.

Except for the freshly cut grass, La Flora appeared to be derelict. There were only small clues that spoke of recent attention. Two of the tall windows to the left of the heavy-looking double doors were still intact, and gleamed as though they had been freshly washed. On the front and side verandas, leaves and other refuse had been swept into several neat piles, ready to be collected and disposed of. Bone took the binoculars out of their case and took a closer look at La Flora, keeping the lenses out of the sun to prevent reflections.

Using the binoculars he quickly picked up the shadowy marks of tire tracks in the newly cut grass and followed them to a large outbuilding behind the house. One of the outbuilding doors was slightly open and Bone could see the glint of sunlight on an automobile's brightwork. He turned his attention back to the house, scanning the windows carefully. A moment later he caught a hint of movement in the cupola. Keeping the binoculars steady he waited, and the movement came again, the silhouette of a seated man, regularly bringing his hand up to his mouth—someone smoking a cigarette, posted as a lookout.

Bone put down the binoculars and closed his eyes, listening. A cicada was sounding in the distance, like a high-pitched trill in his ear. There was the faint sound of the little stream behind him. He focused harder, pushing the natural sounds away, trying to pick out anything else, anything out of place. Eventually it came, very faintly, a cough from inside the house, repeated twice, and then the sound of hard shoes on wooden floors.

He opened his eyes again, used his index finger to wipe away a few beads of stinging sweat and looked down at the bed of brown and green pine needles in front of him. Lit brilliantly in a patch of hot sun a few feet away was the carcass of a bird, a jay from the color of its feathers, its breast a cage of gristle and bones that fluttered with the nervous movement of dozens of iridescent bluebottle flies, their maggot castings piled like tiny tubes of parchment beneath the fragile ribs. The flesh of the head was desiccated down to skull and yellow beak, the eyes withered, sucked dry of life by the sun. A line of ants marched up from the splayed, curled feet and disappeared into the cave of the dead bird's corpse.

Bone smiled, enjoying the simple elegance of the small, unmarked tragedy and transformation, then edged back deeper into the shadows before climbing to his feet. He went back to the pool, took out one of the Pepsi-Colas and opened it with the crawfish device. He drank the Pepsi slowly, enjoying the cold sweet bite of the soda, thinking about what he had seen. He put the bottle down, took out the little diary and used the pencil it came with to quickly sketch the layout of La Flora. The upper rooms could be discounted with the exception of the cupola, since tomorrow's meeting would almost certainly take place on the ground floor.

If it was like other homes of its kind Bone had seen before, the interior would be divided into three main rooms, a dining room to the right, a larger living room to the left and a kitchen in the back. Between dining room and living room there would be a wide front hall and a staircase leading upward. Entrance at the front, exit through the kitchen and the only clear approach to the house being the lane through the aisle of oak trees stretching back from the main gate. Behind the house were the outbuildings and some upwardly sloping marshland leading to the levee and the river beyond. La Flora was like a funneling crayfish trap—once in, escape would be virtually impossible.

Bone finished the first of the two sodas then went back to his shadowed vantage point. Over the course of the next three-quarters of an hour he spotted five men. One was black and carried a broom and pail. The other four wore dark suits and heavy shoes. Three of them were of average height with dark curly hair and Mediterranean features that were alike enough to suggest they were brothers or possibly close cousins. Sicilian, perhaps, Italian certainly, which meant that they were probably members of Sam Carolla's New Orleans–based criminal organization.

The fourth man had appeared carrying a hunting rifle and Bone assumed he had been the lookout in the cupola. He was taller than the other three, broad-chested and blond with pale, sunburned skin. He handed over the weapon to one of the Italians and lit a cigarette. Changing shifts, perhaps, arguing over whose turn it was to climb up onto the roof. It was just past noon now and the interior of the boxlike cupola would be swelteringly hot.

Bone stayed in position and waited. Another hour passed with nothing of note occurring beyond the occasional sound of an airplane landing at the nearby airfield and once, the distant shriek of a train whistle. Then, just after one o'clock, two cars, both Packards, both black and dusty, came down the lane between the oaks and parked in front of the house. Four more dark-suited men appeared out of the first car, their clothing and looks apparently cut from the same cloth as the other three Bone had already seen.

Three men climbed out of the second car and went up onto the front veranda of the house. These three, older, better dressed in lighter-colored suits, ignored the younger men around them. One of them, in his late fifties or maybe even older, with the blowsy open face of a heavy drinker and thinning dark hair, was recognizable to Bone almost at once. He'd seen him from time to time in the casino of the Hotel Nacional in Havana, and occasionally in the newspapers. This was Sam Carolla, boss of the New Orleans Mob, and by the looks of it he was taking the other two men on a tour of La Flora.

The heavier and shorter of the two men Carolla was guiding was clearly uncomfortable in the heat and mopped his forehead every few seconds with a large white handkerchief. The other man didn't seem to be bothered at all. He was much taller than his companion, very tall, with large ears, a long nose and exceptionally fair skin that he protected with a white Stetson. After a few moments on the veranda Carolla and his guests disappeared inside the house.

Bone had seen enough. He eased back for a second time, then went to the pool and retrieved the full bottle of soda pop from its hiding place and put it and the already empty bottle and the crimped metal cap back into the paper bag. He slid the binoculars back into their case and walked back to the car, careful to keep the ridge at his back, blocking any potential view from the lookout in the cupola.

Returning to the automobile Bone lowered the hood, climbed in behind the wheel and opened the second bottle of Pepsi, holding it between his knees as he drove back down the country road, sipping the cold beverage as he put his thoughts in order. The reason for using La Flora was logical and clear. The property was away from prying eyes, relatively easy to secure and close to the old airport so that anyone flying in for the meeting could do so with anonymity, but the very need for that anonymity was distressing since it meant that the men attending the meeting were well enough known to require such a high level of discretion.

Carolla's presence was equally worrisome. Contrary to the lurid stories the yellow press reported, there was no code of silence within the Mob, in New Orleans or anywhere else. Given the right circumstances and incentives any one of them could be made to tell all that they knew. Conspiracies were dangerous, political ones even more so, and by all appearances this one was spreading out of control. As Bone drove back toward Algiers and the city he noticed a heavy line of deep gray clouds massing like a huge, dark curtain in the south. Before long it was going to rain, and rain hard.

Bone was back in New Orleans just after three o'clock. He parked the car in the lot next to the hotel, returned to his room briefly to drop off the binoculars and the brown paper bag, then walked the few short blocks down to the main branch of the public library on Lee Circle. The large building, designed in what Bone liked to call the Roman Temple tradition, had a more than adequate supply of newspapers and periodicals in the main reading room as well as a superior clipping file. Within an hour, diary and pencil in hand, Bone had names for most of the people he had seen that afternoon.

He had been right in his immediate identification of Sam Carolla, and the three similar-looking young men of Italian origin were Carlos, Peter and Michael Marcello, all of them associated with various enterprises of Carolla's. The tall blond man with the rifle was one James Moran, also an employee of Carolla, and previously a bodyguard of the assassinated former governor of Louisiana, the infamous Huey Long, the "Kingfish."

Far more important were the two men Sam Carolla had been taking on a tour of the old plantation house. The heavyset man continuously mopping his face was Huey Long's deputy, a onetime Bible-thumping minister from Wisconsin named Gerald L. Smith. A look at his recent clippings file was revealing—it was almost empty. Since Long's murder, Gerald Smith's standing had fallen to an all-time low. Within days of the murder of his onetime boss in September 1935, the various factions within the Kingfish machine had begun squabbling over who would succeed their fallen leader in the Senate, who would be the next governor and, most important, who would control Long's immense financial warchest.

Smith had been pushed out of the running almost immediately by Louisiana insiders, including Huey Long's brother. The best the preacher had been able to do since then was insert himself into the madcap but popular Old Age Revolving Pension movement being vigorously promoted in California by a white-haired doctor from the Black Hills of South Dakota named Francis Everett Townsend. Apparently Smith had now also inserted himself into the meeting at La Flora scheduled for the following day.

The second man with Carolla was also interesting, but for different reasons. A thirty-one-year-old, recently elected Texas Democratic congressman from the oil-powerful Tenth District who had strong ties to the man who had helped put him there—John Nance Garner, thirty years a Texas congressman and senator and now the vice president of the United States. The young Texan's name was Lyndon Baines Johnson, and according to his file of clippings, he knew how to pull all the right patronage levers in Washington. What a collection—the local Mob, a washed-up back-room boy and a give-a-favor get-a-favor congressman with less than a single term under his belt. Bone returned the clipping envelopes to the periodicals desk and left the library.

He walked back to the hotel, noting that the clouds he'd seen coming up from the south on his return from La Flora were now massing overhead. As he reached the Roosevelt and ducked under the awning over the main entrance on Baronne Street it began to pour. Bone went up to his room and lay down on the bed, watching the heavy rain smear the glass of the window, tapping on the panes with small, skeletal clicking sounds, ghostly, ancient come-hithers he tried to ignore.

On the wall at the end of the bed was a cheaply framed and poorly rendered watercolor of a yacht race on Lake Pontchartrain, the sky an unbelievable blue, two boats running with the wind but in opposite directions on dead-calm water unruffled by any breeze at all. The work of an amateur.

Amateur, of course, was the operative word. In his experience it was the very amateurishness of the people who wanted his services that made the purchase of those particular services necessary. By nature, those of his profession were a breed apart. Virtually all men who killed for a cause wound up dying for it as well. He'd seen enough of that from his brethren in Ireland and more again on his travels.

Listening to the rain, Bone lifted his hands up in front of his face and examined them. They were relatively small, but the fingers were long and very strong. Over time, though, his knuckles had thickened and ropes of vein and tendon had begun to appear. The skin itself seemed to have lost much of its elasticity and had turned to a faintly shiny parchment texture. He thought about the dead bird on the ridge above La Flora and wondered what had brought about its death. An incautious movement? A split second of careless inattention? A trick of the sun that had blinded the creature for a fatal instant?

John Bone clenched his fists and felt small twinges of painful tension that he wouldn't have felt ten years ago. Not arthritis, just age. He was closer to forty than he thought he'd ever be, and if his hands didn't betray him soon it would be his eyes. Buying the Cool Rays in the lobby shop had been a necessity; his eyes were far more sensitive to light than they'd been only a few years ago and any kind of glare was painful. At night, his depth perception was half of what it used to be. Any work requiring the cover of darkness was now out of the question. This job and perhaps one or two more after it and then he would be forced into retirement by his own physical inadequacies.

On returning from the library John Bone's initial reaction had been to pack his bag and leave, taking the first available transportation back to Havana. Instead he turned to the night table and picked up the telephone. He first placed a call to the Shushan Airport Terminal on Lake Pontchartrain and then, with the help of the hotel operator, he was connected to a number in New York City. The call to New York was answered on the second ring.

"Yes?" The voice had the slightly muffled electrical echo of most long-distance calls.

"I'd like to speak to Uncle Charles," Bone said quietly.

"This is Uncle Charles."

"Do you know who this is?"

"Yes," answered the voice from New York. "Is there a problem?"

"Yes. The venue for the meeting is now unacceptable."

"It was acceptable to you before."

"Not any longer."

"May I ask why?"

"Certainly," said Bone. "It would appear that your people are now employing the services of the Carolla family in New Orleans. It would also appear that a number of other people will be at the meeting, including a congressman from Texas and the ex-assistant of a United States senator, now deceased." Bone paused. "The presence of either one of these men at any possible meeting is also unacceptable."

"Why is that?" The voice wasn't particularly defensive, just curious.

"Too many people are involved in this already. These men are politicians. Politicians are by their very nature unable to keep secrets for very long."

"Two people can keep a secret as long as one of them is dead," said the voice from New York.

"I beg your pardon?"

"A quote from Benjamin Franklin," the voice explained. There was a long pause. "There must be a meeting to conclude our business." He paused again. "There are terms to be discussed."

"Not with those men. And not in that place."

"Then who?"

"You," said Bone. "And one other. No more than that."

"Tomorrow?"

"Yes," said Bone. "I won't risk being here more than another day."

"I suppose I could get a flight out this evening."

"You can," said Bone. "I checked to make sure. There's an Eastern Airlines flight leaving Newark Airport at ten-thirty tonight traveling by way of Washington and Atlanta. It arrives in New Orleans at seven-thirty in the morning."

The pause was shorter this time. "All right."

"Will you be alone?" Bone asked.

"No. I'll have one other person with me if he can arrange to get on the flight in Washington."

"All right."

"How do I contact you?"

"Check into the Roosevelt Hotel under the name Thorn. I'll leave a message for you saying where and when the meeting will take place." Bone hung up the telephone. He looked out the window; the rain had ended as quickly as it had begun.

John Bone spent the remainder of the day making arrangements for the following day's meeting, which included renting a room above a restaurant in the French Quarter. With his business done, Bone walked over to Canal Street, then a few short blocks down to Royal Street. He bought an old suitcase at a pawnshop on the corner, then walked another block over to the Hotel Monteleone, almost as large as the Roosevelt and equally anonymous.

He checked in, paid for three nights' lodging in advance, and after dropping his empty suitcase off in his room he went down to the hotel's Carousel Lounge with its slightly idiotic revolving bar, had a drink and then enjoyed a crab cake dinner in the hotel dining room. Appetite satisfied, he went back to his room, switched on the complimentary radio to the Monteleone's own radio station, WDSU. At that time of the evening the local station combined with the NBC Blue Network, and for the better part of an hour Bone lay in the dark listening to Guy Lombardo and the Royal Canadians doing a medley of songs from *Show Boat*. Eventually he fell asleep.

At 10:00 A.M. the following morning John Bone stood in the shadows of a doorway across the street from the restaurant he'd chosen and watched as a bright yellow Nola cab pulled up in front. The restaurant, Antoine's on St. Louis Street, occupied the main and second floors of a well-kept four-story building. As Bone had discovered the previous afternoon, the shuttered rooms on the third and fourth floors were accessible by walking up a staircase leading from the ornate ironwork of the second-floor veranda.

Two men climbed out of the cab. As the taxi drove off Bone saw that both men were dressed in dark three-piece suits far too heavy for New Orleans weather. The shorter of the two men had gray hair, wore metal-rimmed spectacles and had a mustache. He appeared to be in his mid-forties. The second man, broad-chested, big-bellied and at least ten years older than his companion, had dark thinning hair brushed back from a broad forehead and large, slightly protruding eyes. He was clean-shaven, wore no eyeglasses and smoked a large black cigar.

Bone kept watch as the two men consulted with a white-aproned Negro sweeping the sidewalk in front of the restaurant's dark-paneled entrance. The man with the spectacles and mustache reached into his pocket, took out a folded bill, then pressed it into the sweeper's hand. The Negro nodded, leaned his broom up against the open doorway and led the two men into the restaurant. A few moments later, the two men, alone now, reappeared on the fire escape and climbed slowly up to the fourth floor of the building. The bigger man seemed to have some difficulty and paused several times before they reached a small, metal-grated platform at the top of the fire escape. Finally, the two men stepped through the open French doors set into the dormer and disappeared into the room Bone had rented for the meeting.

Bone, who had been at his post across the street for almost an hour before the arrival of the two men, waited five minutes more, making sure that they had come alone. When he was satisfied he crossed the street, entered the restaurant, and followed the two men up into the fourth-floor room.

At John Bone's request the room had been emptied of all furniture except a small plain desk and three chairs. Two of the chairs had their backs to the French doors, while the third had its back to the door that led to an interior staircase. At Bone's request the door had been locked from the inside, ensuring that the only way in or out was via the exterior fire escape. The two men had taken the chairs obviously meant for them. As Bone stepped down into the room they both turned to look at him. Looking over the shoulder of the gray-haired man with the spectacles and the mustache, Bone saw that he already had a stenographer's notebook and a pen ready on the table.

"I'd advise against putting anything down on paper," said Bone. "For everyone's sake." Bone went around the table, checked to make sure that the door was still locked, then sat down across from the two men. "Which one of you is Uncle Charles?"

"I'm Uncle Charles," said the gray-haired man. The flat, slightly nasal accent was clearly New York. "I always take notes," he said firmly.

"No," said Bone.

"Do as he says, Allen," the other man suggested. The voice was quiet and rang with a rich Texas twang, which, to Bone's ear, was almost a contradiction.

"Who are you?" Bone asked.

The big man smiled and took a tug on his cigar. "Just a country boy," he said softly, "doing my part." Keeping his eyes on Bone he put out his right hand and pushed the offending notebook and pen toward his companion. Uncle Charles took the broad hint and put the notebook away. "I understand y'all didn't like the meeting place we arranged. That so?"

"It is," Bone said. The man across from him was going to some lengths to make himself out to be some kind of country bumpkin, but his eyes were hard, cold and calculating.

"Didn't care much for the people we were bringing either, now, did you?"

"As I said before, they're politicians."

"Young Lyndon's more than a politician, sir, believe me. Bound for glory, that boy is. No telling how far he'll go." The Texan smiled even more broadly. "Depending on the circumstances."

"How much does he know?" Bone asked, glancing at the man from New York.

"Nothing," Uncle Charles responded. He gestured toward the Texan. "Only that my friend here requested he be at a meeting of some importance."

"And the others?"

"The same," said the Texan. "Lyndon knows some people here in Louisiana. Next-door neighbors, so to speak. He talked to Gerry Smith. It was Smith who laid on the security measures you objected to. Mr. Carolla and his people, that is." The Texan lifted his big shoulders and dropped them, smiling. "Sorry if we gave you offense, but I have to say, sir, that we don't do this every day." He paused. "We have our professional talents, but when it comes to . . . this sort of thing, we're amateurs."

"I understand," Bone said.

"Perhaps we should get down to business," said the man from New York. "We don't have a great deal of time."

"Suits me," said the Texan. Bone said nothing. There was a long, almost physically unpleasant pause. Outside on the street Bone could hear a barker for the Pelican Lottery hawking tickets:

"Four, 'leven and forty-four,
Four 'leven and forty-four,
Bring that number 'fore I lose my head
'Cause my woman's in that yeller-man's bed"

Finally the man from New York spoke up. "My friend here and I represent interests who find the thought of America involving itself in another world war abhorrent. Clearly, however, Mr. Roosevelt intends to take us into just such a conflict." He paused and cleared his throat. "He must be stopped. At all costs, he must be stopped."

Bone remained silent. The big man smoked his cigar and waited for his friend to continue. Eventually he did so.

"A number of us feel that through political scheming, blandishments of one kind and another and outright lies, the president has positioned himself in the American public eye as some sort of savior. He has the entire nation hoodwinked."

"And you intend to save the nation from Mr. Roosevelt?" said Bone, unable to resist. He'd been at a dozen meetings like this one, had heard variations on this same theme as many times. Cain had probably used the same justifications to himself before slaying Abel.

The Texan took the cigar out of his mouth and leaned forward across the desk, his large, slightly goggled eyes staring at Bone. "No, sir," he said, his voice still soft. "We intend to save ourselves and the people we represent from Mr. Roosevelt. Powerful people, sir, people who don't much care for what the president has done to business in this country, and who care even less for what he intends to do if, God help us, he is elected to another term."

"And these are the people who wish to hire my services?"

"Indeed," said the Texan. He clamped his teeth down on his cigar and leaned back in his chair.

"We were going to discuss terms," said the man from New York.

"Two hundred fifty thousand dollars," said Bone, his voice flat and unemotional. "Half deposited into an account I keep in Bermuda within the next seven days. The rest on the satisfactory completion of the task."

"Good Lord!" said the man from New York. "That is a great deal of money, sir."

"I agree," said Bone. "But you and your friends are getting a great deal in exchange."

"He's quite right," the Texan said. "The visit of Their Royal Majesties is most definitely part of Roosevelt's third-term campaign strategy. It is meant to be a triumph.

This will turn it into tragedy." He paused. "There will be no third term."

"Do you think you can actually accomplish the task?" asked the man from New York.

"Certainly." Bone nodded. "I wouldn't be having this meeting if I believed otherwise."

"How will you do it?" the Texan asked.

"I'm not sure," said Bone. "It's not important that you know."

"When?"

"I'm not sure of that either."

"It must take place on American soil," insisted the man from New York. "That is of primary importance. It cannot take place during the Canadian portion of their visit."

"I understand," Bone said.

"Can we be of assistance in any way?" asked the Texan. "The people we represent have resources you might find useful."

"I prefer to work entirely alone," said Bone. "In my experience most plots such as this die stillborn due to lack of security." He paused. "The fewer people who know of my existence the better." Bone stared across the table at the two men. "I'm quite certain that by now too many people already know too much, but that can't be helped."

"Then we're agreed?" said the Texan. "We can proceed?"

The man from New York hesitated, his lips parting as though he was about to speak, but the Texan brought up a large hand and placed it on his companion's shoulder. The man from New York nodded. "We're agreed."

"How will we contact you?" the Texan asked.

"You won't," Bone answered. "I'll contact you, if necessary." He stood up. "Now if you'll excuse me."

"A name?" the Texan asked. "We'll need one." The man sounded almost eager, as though he didn't want the meeting to end, as though he relished it. "I don't suppose you'll be using the one you gave us any longer."

"Green," Bone said. "Green is as good as any other."

He glanced at the man from New York. "I'll call you with the necessary bank information." Bone bowed his head slightly. "If you will, gentlemen, wait five minutes or so before you leave." He glanced at his wristwatch. "You could even have some lunch downstairs. The oysters are delicious." With that he went around the desk and went through the French doors and out onto the fire escape. Then he was gone.

The two men sat for a moment and then the Texan stood and climbed up onto the dormer. He glanced out through the opening. "He's gone."

"He may be good at what he does," said the man from New York, "but he's not much of a businessman."

"Why do you say that?"

The gray-haired man got up from his seat and joined his friend at the window. "What if he succeeds and we decide not to pay him the rest of the money?"

"We won't do that, Allen," the Texan answered, shaking his head. His cigar had gone out and he relit it carefully with a small gold lighter that seemed oddly dainty for a man of his bulk. He blew a plume of heavy smoke back into the room.

"Why won't we?"

"Because," said the Texan, puffing hard on the cigar, "if we were that foolish, the pale-faced son of a bitch would find out who we were and track us down and kill us, one by one by one."

The man from New York reached into his pocket and took out a pipe. He lit it with the Texan's lighter, then sent up his own blue cloud of smoke. "Well at least he doesn't know about the other thing." The pipe made a small gurgling noise and the man took it out of his mouth and peered into the bowl.

"Yes," said the Texan. "Our ace in the hole." He glanced out the window again, a faint shadow of worry flashing across his features. "Let's just pray that your friend Mr. Green never finds out about *that*."

Chapter 10

Saturday, April 22, 1939
Southampton, England

Thomas Barry took the early-morning train from Euston Station and arrived at the cavernous Southampton Terminal just past noon, carrying his single suitcase. The inside of the huge, gloomy departure terminal was filled with milling crowds of passengers, porters and well-wishers and the scores of vehicles that had brought them to the docks. In addition to the train there were lorries bringing last-minute supplies to the ship warped against the dock just outside, dozens of taxis, buses and limousines from London and a fair number of private cars. Luggage trolleys moved to and fro, tourist-grade and third-class passengers checked in at the trestle tables set up close to the pier-side doors that opened up to a view of the huge ship's high, gleaming white-liveried flank, while first-class passengers and their farewell parties took one of several large cage elevators to the upper level of the terminal building and then crossed onto the ship over the canvas-topped D deck gangway.

As arranged, Barry met Holland at the magazine kiosk across from the ticket agent's table, half pushed along by the other passengers rushing off the train. It seemed as though everyone in the cavernous building was calling loudly to someone else, but even through the welter of sound Barry could hear the steady rumble of the idling ship's engines. He felt a sudden stirring within himself that he found surprising and almost embarrassing. This was Drake and Cook and Voyageurs in grand canoes, James Fenimore Cooper, Red Indians and all the myriad other fantasies every young boy had, rich or poor. Spotting the bald-headed figure of Holland standing at the kiosk, blithely smoking a cigarette and leafing through the *Times,* Barry put on his sternest face, careful to hide anything that even whispered the word *adventure*. Suddenly a massive, basso-profundo blast from the ship's horn rang out, shaking the entire building, energizing the crowds around Barry to a new frenzy. Holland looked bland as a lamppost. He flipped his newspaper closed and pushed out his cigarette in a wooden sandbox bolted to the side of the kiosk.

"I suppose we should be getting on board." He glanced down at the cream-colored canvas-covered suitcase in Barry's hand. "Your only luggage?"

"Yes."

"No evening clothes in there, I presume."

"I didn't think they'd be necessary," Barry answered, evading the point, since the only evening clothes he'd ever worn had been rented to attend a friend's wedding.

"Never mind," Holland said. "We'll make do." He took Barry by the arm. "Come along."

Holland led the way, pushing gently but firmly through the throngs of people, eventually reaching the cage elevators leading to the upper level. He stepped aboard one of the cages and gestured for Barry to join him. Together with half a dozen other passengers they slowly jerked their way upward. A few moments later they stepped out onto the airy second-level concourse, a broad, shaded breezeway that ran the length of the terminal building. Halfway along the concourse Barry could see the covered gangway spanning the chasm between the building and the ship, the huge vessel painted a brilliant white except for a thin line of royal blue around her hull at the Main Deck level and her buff-colored funnels. The promenades on the upper two decks were already lined with passengers throwing streamers and calling out to friends.

"Stunning," said Holland as they headed for the gangway. "We'll be at war within a year and they're all acting like it's a bloody church fete."

"You sound very sure," said Barry.

"Those aren't toy soldiers Herr Hitler is playing with, nor are those wind-up airplanes being flown about by Mr. Goering. One doesn't make weapons unless one intends to use them, Barry." They reached the gangway and Holland dug into the pocket of his overcoat and pulled out a packet of ticket vouchers done up with a rubber band. "Believe me, there'll be a war. He's already been practicing in Spain for the last three years or so."

Barry followed his taller companion across the canvas-covered bridge that led into the ship, trying not to look down. A few days ago he'd flown in his first aircraft, now he was setting sail on his first ocean liner. They reached the far side of the gangway and stepped off into the first-class entrance hall, a dazzling confection of multihued wood veneers, cast aluminum and sandblasted glass. A broad set of carpeted stairs led upward from D to C deck.

"Where are we?" Barry asked.

"B deck," Holland answered, pointing up the stairs. "The same as Miss Connelly."

"She's traveling first class?" said Barry, surprised.

Holland nodded as they climbed the stairs, first to C deck, then upward to B. "All those shillings and pence gathered arduously from supporters of the 'Cause' and one of their couriers spends it on having her linen changed once a day and her bed turned down each night." They reached B deck and Holland paused for a moment to catch his breath as other passengers ebbed and flowed around them. "Actually it makes sense. In tourist and third class you're traveling with at least two other people, sometimes three, none of whom you're likely to know. Miss Connelly has what they refer to as a Special Stateroom, designed for one person. Posh, but not as posh as a suite. She'll have her privacy."

"I'm not sure why she'd need it," said Barry. "All she's doing is carrying information to Russell, probably committed to memory."

"According to Hayes that's all she's doing. But who's to say that he knows everything that's going on?" Holland pointed to a large club chair. "Wait here for a moment, would you?" Barry dropped down into the chair while Holland crossed to a long counter facing the stairway. An illuminated sign above the counter read BUREAU. He spoke briefly to a uniformed officer, who then handed Holland a telephone handset. Holland dialed a number, listened for a moment, then hung up and returned to Barry. "She's been on board for the better part of an hour and a half and she hasn't set foot outside her stateroom. She came down from London on one of the omnibuses provided by Canadian Pacific."

"You have people on board?"

"Of course. Her cabin steward for one, a man in the purser's office for another."

"What about her luggage?"

"No special check at customs. Didn't want to upset the woman this early in the game. You and I will attend to that later." Holland paused, smiling. "In the meantime why don't we take your case down to our cabin and then go somewhere for a drink?"

Somewhere turned out to be the Knickerbocker Bar on the Lounge Deck, a relatively small room with a horseshoe-shaped bar, the teal-blue walls covered with an original and characteristically bizarre Arthur Rackham mural depicting the discovery, pursuit and inevitable capture of a creature known as the Cocktail Bird. Even before sailing the bar was crowded, so after being served the two men took their drinks around to the Writing Room on the other side of the funnel casing. The lonely other occupant of the library-style room was a middle-aged woman in tweeds who was working her way steadily through a pile of identical Canadian Pacific postcards, writing, addressing and stamping in a methodical series of movements that were almost hypnotic.

"A schoolteacher," said Holland, taking a sip of his whiskey and soda. "Writing to her students. She'll have them all done before we cast off and down at the purser's before we reach the Solent." A crackling whistle came over the public address system and a nasal voice gave out the "all-ashore-that's-going-ashore" announcement. The woman writing postcards continued without pause. "Have you ever heard of a newspaper called the *New Yorker Staats Zeitung und Herold*?"

"Of course," said Barry, taking a swallow of his cold Canadian beer, feeling the icy bite of it against his teeth. What did they say about Canada? The land God gave to Cain. "Read it all the time. A favorite."

"It's published by a man named Victor F. Ridder."

"A German?"

"There you have the question," said Holland. "Technically he's an American citizen, naturalized. Among other things he's on the National Boy Scouts Committee, a member of the New York State Board of Charities and he was appointed a New York WPA administrator by Roosevelt himself."

"Salt of the earth then," said Barry, waiting for the other shoe to drop.

"In addition to being a Boy Scout, Herr Ridder has also met privately with the führer on a number of occasions over the past ten years, goes from New York to Berlin like other people go from London to Greenwich, and according to reliable sources employs half a dozen people at his newspaper who don't exist."

"Pardon?"

"Dummy employees. He's having monies funneled to him to support what is euphemistically called German-American cooperation."

"I don't quite see how this ties in with our Miss Connelly."

"Ridder has traveled to the Continent eleven times in the past five years. On two of those occasions he took the *Hindenberg*; on the other nine he took a variety of North German Lloyd ships out of Bremen or Hamburg. On none of those eleven trips did he ever set foot on British soil."

"He's on board?" said Barry.

"Such an agile mind," said Holland with a pinched smile, taking another sip of his drink. Across the room the schoolteacher completed her task, tapped the stack of postcards into a neat pile and left the room. "Both Miss Connelly's room and the one occupied by Ridder were booked through the same ticketing agent within twenty-four hours of each other. The ticket agent is the same one who has all of the German Embassy's business in London."

"So we assume they know each other."

"At this point I think we assume nothing. Ridder is in stateroom B217. Miss Connelly is in B241. Mr. Ridder has an unfortunate bone condition that requires the use of canes and sometimes a wheelchair. They may have been placed close together for ease of access."

"It strikes me as being a little naive of them," said Barry. "With a few simple checks you've connected them like dots on a child's puzzle. If there is a relationship between them they've done nothing at all to hide it."

Holland finished his drink and stared into the bottom of the glass. Then he shrugged again and put the glass down on the writing table in front of him. Beneath their feet the plates of the decking began to shiver and the sound of the engines deepened. "You give them all too much credit, Barry. These aren't master criminals. They're not even very good spies. They're amateurs. Worse than that, they're true believers." The bald man shook his head. "The thing of it is, you see, a true believer will believe in anything given half a chance. Ridder thinks he and his Nazi friends in the United States are the advance guard of a new order in the world and Miss Connelly believes so deeply in the cause of a United Ireland that she and Russell and all the others like them will get into bed with the Germans and think they'll be able to get out again with their virtue intact." He laughed and took off his glasses, polishing them on the sleeve of his overcoat, then pinched them back across his nose. "Hayes said it himself—a bunch of yobbos skulking about playing soldiers and silly buggers, drilling with broomsticks and waiting for action that never comes."

"You really do have a dark philosophy of life, don't you?"

"Developed in a number of dark and ghastly places," Holland responded. "Belfast and Belgrade not the least among them." He rubbed the top of his head lightly and smiled. "Let's go out on deck, shall we? Bid the Old World good-bye and turn our faces toward the New." He smacked his lips happily. "Then another drink."

Jane met Hat Rack Levine under the elevated station at Chatham Square. The ten-cent Venice Theater was showing a Randolph Scott double feature, but no one seemed very interested at eleven o'clock in the morning and the only thing keeping the fat woman awake in her glass ticket booth was the roar and rattle of the trains overhead.

Hat Rack was a *schlepper* for the unbroken line of women's apparel stores that went south on Division Street from Eldridge to the Bowery, drawing and cajoling, often lying outright to get prospective customers into the stores. He also had some very good ear-to-the-ground sources of information about the Mob and its activities. The name Hat Rack came from his habit of constantly changing hats. Today it was a homburg set squarely on the tall man's large, round head. When Jane came down the steps from the platform above, Hat Rack was leaning up against one of the el support girders, reading a newspaper and smoking a cigarette. Jane could smell his breath from a yard away—nicotine, spearmint toothpaste and gin.

"Hat Rack."

"Jane." The tall man levered himself away from the girder, folding the paper under his arm with a quick little snap. He looked around nervously as though he was worried that someone might be watching, which was nothing new. Hat Rack Levine always thought someone was watching him, as though he might have the secrets of the pyramids under his hat rather than a few dribs and drabs of information that trickled down to him through the *schmata* trade and the occasional overheard back-room conversation at the Old Sicily Club on Mulberry Street.

"Let's take a walk," said Hat Rack. He led the way out

from under the shadows of the el tracks, criss-crossing over the square, down a block on New Bowery to a little triangular cemetery between James and Oliver Streets. As he pushed open the rusty gate he pulled off the homburg, revealing his large bald head, edged with a clown-fringe of curly black hair above his ears. Jane followed him into the cemetery, noting that each stone had a Star of David on it.

"I didn't know there was a Jewish cemetery here," she said.

Hat Rack found a stone bench that stood in front of a tall, dark, red-granite monument and sat down. Jane joined him. "It's the oldest Jewish cemetery in Manhattan," said Levine. "All Portuguese and Spanish, like this guy here." He pointed to the name on the monument in front of them across the little pea-gravel path. "Gersholm Mendez Seixis. I mean, what kind of a Jew name is that?" He shrugged. "I think he was some kind of big-time rebbe or something back in 1776 or something." Hat Rack shook his head. "You never think of Spics and Wops being Jews, but there must be some, I guess. Mostly you think of Krauts and Russians and Polacks like me." He laughed. "Maybe there's even a Jig Jew or two out there, who knows."

"I never really thought about it," said Jane.

There was a short silence between the two. Jane stared at the marker for Rabbi Gersholm Mendez Seixis. Finally Hat Rack spoke. "So you come down here to ask me the time of day or what?"

"Howard Raines."

"Never heard of him."

"Junior lawyer at Fallon and McGee, but a guy named Shalleck was paying his way."

"Shalleck's big-time. What's this Raines character got to do with it?"

"Raines wound up in a ditch in Jersey with three bullets in him."

"This the stiff they found out by the Rustic Cabin?"

"That's the one."

"I couldn't put a name to it there for a second."

"He was an old friend of mine."

"Sorry to hear it. Friends are supposed to die peacefully in bed, maybe a year or so before you do, so you don't have to mourn their passing too long." He shook his head. "Shouldn't have friends who get whacked."

"So what can you tell me?"

"About your friend? Nothing. But I can tell you why he was dumped there."

"Go on."

"The Rustic Cabin's all on its own, not part of Willy's organization." Willy being Willy Moretti, the onetime enforcer for Abe Zwillman who now owned all the gambling concessions in New Jersey and half the ones in Manhattan in conjunction with Frank Costello.

"What's Moretti got to do with my friend Howie?"

"Probably nothing, except to make the owner of the Rustic Cabin look bad. There's a singer there Will likes. He wants to make him big time, but the kid's got a contract."

"This Frankie Sinatra guy?"

"I heard it was Frankie Silk."

"Same difference. Skinny kid in expensive clothes."

"Never met him. Anyway, Moretti thinks he can go places. Maybe figures a corpse next door to the Rustic Cabin will make the owner think twice about trying to hold on to the Frankie Silk contract."

"You think the singer knows anything?"

"Maybe. I mean, he must know Moretti. No one dumps a stiff in Jersey without Moretti knowing about it, so go figure."

"Can I approach this singer kid without losing some part of my anatomy?" Moretti had a reputation for being savagely protective of his "assets" and Jane didn't want to wind up in a ditch like poor old Howard.

"You got such nice anatomy too." Hat Rack grinned.

"Just answer the question."

"I'll set it up for you."

"Thanks, Hat Rack. You're a pal. Can you get me some background on the kid, maybe something I can work with?"

"Cost you twenty and a big, wet kiss, sweetheart. I'll be in touch." Hat Rack gave Jane a wave, then headed out of the cemetery, leaving her still sitting on the bench. A Second Avenue express came scratching and screeching along above the street, spitting sparks and groaning like an old ghost. Jane stared at the tombstone of Gersholm Mendez Seixis and wondered how at peace the old rebbe was resting, being shaken around in his coffin every few minutes by the gigantic city that had grown up around his grave. Howard Raines was probably faring a little better in the meat locker in the Bellevue Morgue, except for the fact that he'd be blue with cold. Jane got up and followed the path between the stones toward the exit. When you got right down to it the best kind of death was to be like her sister, Annie, alive but not knowing it.

She used a nickel to make a call in the booth at the foot of the el steps, then hopped an uptown Third Avenue local to the Plaza. Her friend Noel Busch was already waiting for her in the Oak Room when she arrived, sitting at one of the prestigious niche tables in the gloomy old paneled room, a smoke-stained mural of what was supposed to be a romantic castle on the Rhine looming above him. As usual, the magazine writer was dressed to the nines. Today it was a double-breasted blazer with silver buttons, and white flannels—probably from Arnold-Constable and certainly not from off-the-rack at Gimbels—the richly polished shoes from Rogers-Peet, a custom-made white silk shirt from some poor benighted genius of a Chinese tailor on Mott Street, all of it topped off by a demure University Club tie.

The tall, elegant Princeton graduate had once worked for the *Daily News* and the *New Yorker,* followed by a stint as the movie and theater critic for *Time,* and was now a feature writer for *Life* magazine. Jane had supplied pictures for Busch at *Newsweek* and less often at *Life,* where you had to go through half a dozen pipe-smoking picture editors before your shot ever saw ink.

Busch was drinking a gimlet and smoking a cigarette as Jane sat down opposite him.

"Ah," said the man, "Margaret Bourke White in a skirt. How's the lady photographer today?"

"Don't give me a hard time, Bushy. I'm not in the mood. That time of the month, you know." It wasn't, but she liked to see him blush. "Not to mention the fact that my first love is cooling off on a slab at the Bellevue Morgue."

"Sorry to hear it," said Busch. "Have a martini and tell me your troubles."

A waiter shimmied up, took Jane's order for coffee and shimmied away again. Jane looked at her watch. It was just past noon and they were the only people in the room, which wasn't surprising. The place didn't really do much business until the sun went down.

"Missed you at the poker game last week," said Jane.

"Blame it on Hitler," Busch answered. "Every time he invades someplace I have to stay up half the night writing something new and interesting about the son of a bitch."

"Think there's going to be a war?"

"Of course. Germany's whole economy is based on it now. It's too late for him to turn all those tanks into plowshares."

"We going to get involved?"

"When it becomes economically useful."

"You really believe that?"

"Sure I do," said Busch. "Wars are good for business. When this one is good for American business we'll get right into it."

"You really are a cynical bastard, aren't you?"

"Cynical enough to know you don't want to sit around chatting about foreign affairs." He grinned. "You can read *Time* for that."

"Or *Newsweek,*" Jane parried. Her coffee arrived and she lit a cigarette.

"So," said Busch, "tell me how your first love arrived at the morgue."

Jane told him, right through to her conversation with Hat Rack Levine. "I can see all the pieces," she complained, "I just can't see the connections." Jane lit a second cigarette and sat back in her chair. Above her the turrets of the magic castle floated like the fairy-tale remnants of some forgotten kingdom, in a mythical time of chivalrous knights when corpses didn't turn up in Jersey ditches. "You're the hot-shot analyst. What do *you* see?"

"Okay," said Busch, letting the fingers of his right hand smooth the linen tablecloth in front of him. "Let's put it in order. Joe Shalleck, who's right up there on the top of Dewey's shit list, tells a young lawyer working for Fallon and McGee named Howard Raines to go down to Havana. He stays there long enough to do whatever it is Shalleck told him to do, then he turns around and comes back. Raines gets professionally whacked then dumped in a ditch behind a New Jersey roadhouse. Am I missing anything?"

"Not so far."

"Okay. The body gets discovered, the New Jersey cops call in the New York cops because the lawyer is from Manhattan and they really don't want any part of it. Your friend Hennessy is assigned to the case and somewhere along the line he's told to go easy, maybe even put a lid on the whole thing. He thinks the whole thing stinks like the Fulton Fish Market, so he tweaks your ear and gives you the keys to the young lawyer's apartment." Busch paused and stared across the table at Jane. "Hennessy the kind of guy who'd set you up?"

"Set me up for what?"

"To take a fall."

"No. We've been friends for a long time. He wouldn't do something like that."

"Not even to cover his own ass?"

"No." Jane frowned. "What are you getting at?"

"A straight Mob hit they wouldn't bother with the phony queer stuff, trying to make out that Raines was the victim of some kind of pervert love spat. It's the cop angle that bothers me."

"How?"

"When was the last time you heard of any police force

handing a case over to another one? The Jersey cops should have been fighting for Raines. Instead they hand him over without a whimper and the New York bulls proceed to sweep it under the rug. Raines sits in the icebox at Bellevue for a month and then he gets shipped off to Hart Island with a number instead of a headstone. Case closed and forgotten. Sound about right to you?"

Jane nodded. "That's the way it seems to be going."

"Maybe not. Maybe you just have to ask the right questions."

"Such as?"

"Such as, why?"

"Why what?"

"Why did he go to Havana? What did he do there that got him killed?"

"From what I can tell, Raines was pretty much a nobody at Fallon and McGee."

"Perfect for a messenger. Disposable after doing his job, like toilet paper."

"And delivering the message gets him murdered?"

"Makes sense if you want to protect the person the message was delivered to, or cover up the fact that it was delivered at all. Makes sense if a guy like Shalleck wants to distance himself from whatever's going on. Makes sense if it's a big enough deal that someone big in the cops is stepping on the whole thing."

"It still doesn't add up."

"Ask another question."

"Such as?"

"Such as, why did the manager of the Rustic Cabin call the Hoboken police? The proper jurisdiction would have been Tenafly or Fort Lee—they're a hell of a lot closer."

"The fix was in?"

"Right from the start. It's like beads on a string. Forget the Mob. This is political."

"Explain," said Jane. "I'm a photographer, not a pundit."

"Shalleck is a Mob lawyer, but he's also a Democratic Party lawyer. Who runs New Jersey like it was his own personal country? A Democrat named Frank Hague. Where does Hague live? Hoboken, which is run for him by the McFeeley family from the mayor all the way down through the police department and the city commission. Do a bit of careful digging and dollars to doughnuts you'll find out it was a McFeeley who got called by the manager of the Rustic Cabin."

"You're trying to tell me that the Democratic Party is going around murdering people?"

"No," Busch answered. "But it would appear that they have something they very much want to hide."

Chapter 11

Tuesday, April 25, 1939
Washington, D.C.

John Bone sat at one of the long tables in the eighth-floor South Reading Room of the Library of Congress Annex on South Second Street and continued to make his neatly penciled findings in a three-ring student's notebook. He had been working in the annex for the past two days and had collected a great deal of the background information that he felt was necessary to complete his task. In Europe or in Latin America such information was a tightly guarded secret. Here it was available by consulting the thirteen thousand trays in the Card Index Room across the hall, or the Newspaper Reference Room on the ground floor.

According to various newspaper accounts and several volumes Bone had checked describing royal tours by previous English monarchs, security around the royal figures was surprisingly light. When traveling within England the king and queen had only their personal constables for protection, both from A Division of the London Metropolitan Police. In the case of the king, the policeman was a man named Hugh Cameron, while the queen's policeman was named Giles. Both the royal bodyguards had offices in Buckingham Palace, and unlike the rest of their colleagues in Scotland Yard, Giles and Cameron were invariably armed with Belgian Browning 9mm automatic pistols worn in underarm shoulder rigs. Cameron had been a royal bodyguard since 1932, Giles since 1934. Prior to that both had been uniformed policemen. Both were much taller than either the king or queen and both came from strongly athletic backgrounds.

On trips abroad the king and queen traveled with an added contingent of Special Branch officers as well as the bodyguards, but for the most part the only real function of the Special Branch men was to coordinate security efforts with the police of the city or country where the royals were traveling. According to what Bone had read so far, this meant that the bulk of the security duties during the Canadian portion of the royal visit would fall to the Royal Canadian Mounted Police, while in the United States, the onus, at least from a federal point of view, would be on the State Department and a little-known force of agents known collectively as the Bureau of Secret Intelligence.

The Bureau had originally been created to investigate passport and visa applications, but over time their operations had expanded to include security for U.S. diplomats abroad and the well-being of foreign dignitaries, diplomats and heads of state visiting the United States. Bone smiled at the thought. The broadening of the Bureau's mandate was presumably to avoid such embarrassing incidents as the assassination of the Yugoslavian king, Alexander Karageorgevic, on French soil.

Reading between the lines, however, Bone saw that even if every one of its forty agents was assigned to the royal party the Bureau could not hope to provide any real security for the king and queen. While they were with Roosevelt they would fall under the protective umbrella of the White House Secret Service Detail, but since the majority of their time in the United States would be spent in Washington and New York, responsibility for the royals' safety would fall chiefly to the Washington Metropolitan Police, the New York State Troopers, and the New York City Police Department. In other words, it was a logistical, tactical and jurisdictional nightmare. This was complicated even more by an itinerary that included side trips to Mount Vernon in Virginia, a possible cruise on the Potomac aboard the presidential yacht, as well as travel by train, automobile and even the *Warrington*, a U.S. navy destroyer. Initially, Bone had been surprised to discover that the Federal Bureau of Investigation and its publicity-hungry director were playing no active role in the royal tour. Now he knew why—the security plan for the visit was a ship without a captain, and unless Hoover was at the helm he wasn't interested in simply being part of the crew.

The protection of the United States president was also a matter of public record, and as far as Bone could see the general security around Roosevelt would be very little altered by the presence of King George and the Queen Consort. At all times, whether at the White House, the Warm Springs, Georgia, polio spa or the Roosevelt estate in Hyde Park, New York, the president would be guarded by the White House Secret Service Detail headed by Colonel Edmund Starling, an ex–railway detective who had been with the White House detail since 1914 and directing its activities since the Coolidge administration. In addition to the official detail Roosevelt also had two private bodyguards from his days as governor of New York—Gus Gennerich, an ex–New York City policeman, and Earl Miller, a veteran of the New York State Troopers.

Day or night the White House detail consisted of a minimum of eight agents and sometimes as many as thirty. The presidential automobiles, mostly Lincolns, Packards and Cadillacs, were all bulletproof with extra-wide running boards and exterior handles for up to six agents, and the vehicle used by the president was always guarded front and rear by Secret Service cars, each one carrying four agents, all armed with automatic pistols, sawed-off shotguns and Thompson submachine guns. Roosevelt considered the safeguards excessive, but there had already been one attempt on the president's life in February 1933 in Miami, shortly before his inauguration. Colonel Starling was on record as stating that there would be no president assassinated while he was head of the detail. Bone glanced at the tall window on his left, then checked his wristwatch. It was past six and daylight was beginning to fade. He reached out and switched off the little parchment-shaded lamp at the front of the table. He closed his notebook and stood up, a faint smile on his face. Colonel Starling's statement would soon be put to the test.

Taking the elevator down to ground level, Bone exited the annex building, stepping out into a light spring rain. Slipping the notebook under his jacket, he turned up his collar, crossed Independence Avenue, then followed First Street as it ran behind Capitol Hill. The dull skies and the rain had driven almost everyone from the sidewalks, and the city was quiet except for the hissing of tires from passing taxicabs on the wet streets. Continuing down toward D Street, enjoying the misty rain, Bone thought about the trail he was leaving behind and wondered if it was cause for significant worry. He'd traveled from Louisiana to Washington by train, paying for a drawing room under the name of Nash. Arriving here he'd booked into his hotel under the same name, and so far he hadn't been asked to formally identify himself to anyone and doubted that he would be.

At the Library of Congress he'd continued to use the name Nash, explaining to the librarian he'd dealt with that he was a reporter for the *Oakland Tribune,* using the facilities of the library to research the upcoming arrival of the king and queen, scheduled to arrive in six weeks or so—hence his interest in the couple and his request for detailed information about them, and also about President Roosevelt. It was unlikely that the librarian would even remember him after six weeks, but his requests for both books and periodicals would be on file somewhere. Given the monumental importance of his targets he could presume that any investigation following the completion of his work would be incredibly thorough, and there was no doubt at all in Bone's mind that Hoover's FBI would be the agency in charge. While his visits to the Library of Congress as Charles Nash of the *Oakland Tribune* might not be noticed, they would however be noted and a fragile hidden link would be established. It was a link he could not abide.

Bone crossed Louisiana Avenue to North Capitol Street, turning into the anonymous eight-story bulk of the Hotel Continental. Retrieving his key he rode up to his room, packed his single small case and rode back down to the lobby. He checked out of the hotel, shook off the doorman who offered to get him a taxi, and walked across Capitol Plaza to the gigantic white granite arches of Union Station. Stepping out of the rain and into the grand concourse that stretched the length of the station, he purchased a sleeping car ticket to New York as Bill Joyner, a name he'd seen on the jacket of the assistant manager at the front desk of the Hotel Continental. An hour later, with darkness falling and the rain coming down much harder, the New York train left Washington. By the next morning Charles Nash and Bill Joyner would be no more, and finally after years of faithful service, Edwin Dow, petroleum geologist, would vanish as well.

Jane Todd sat in the Schrafft's at Forty-seventh and Fifth, waiting for the Sinatra kid to show up. The waiter from the Rustic Cabin was supposedly doing a fifteen-minute singing spot at WNEW, a few doors down on Fifth, but he was already an hour late. The restaurant was its usual genteel self, lots of padded leather, artificial flowers and a menu to suit the needs of matrons out shopping, blue-haired old ladies and their equally ancient dogs searching for something sweet and soft enough to slip past their dentures and through their digestive tracts. Jane was already on her third pot of tea and her second plate of chocolate-covered biscuits, which was going to give her a complexion just like Ricky the soda jerk in Walgreens if she didn't watch out. She ate the last one on the plate, silently cursed herself for agreeing to meet in a place where they didn't sell beer and lit a cigarette.

According to the information she'd received from Hat Rack, Sinatra wasn't really a kid at all, he was just a young-looking twenty-four. He was determined to be the next

Crosby, but so far the best he'd done was a brief stint as one of the Hoboken Four, now the Hoboken Trio, and his present job as singing waiter and emcee at the Rustic Cabin. He was married to a girl named Nancy and his mother's nickname for him was Slacksy because he bought so many clothes. The mother really was an abortionist, presently on parole for almost butchering a teenager. She was also a longtime ward heeler, doing favors for the local pols and the people in her Madison Street neighborhood. She thought Frankie was a fool for trying to be a singer, but on the other hand he hadn't had any other kind of job since he was seventeen, so she'd called in a couple of favors and made sure he got a membership in the Musician's Union local so he could keep on singing at the Cabin and even do some side work like the WNEW spots.

Sinatra slid into the booth across from Jane, a big, tight grin on his thin face. He was wearing a dark green suit, a white shirt, a blue-and-white polka-dot bow tie and a porkpie hat. He took off the too-small hat and dropped it onto the seat beside him. His hair was slicked down and shiny with hair cream, showing off his round, protruding ears. With his big forehead and his knife-sharp high cheekbones he looked like some sort of bright-eyed rodent. He shot his cuffs a couple of times, making sure Jane saw the big gold and onyx links he was wearing and he gave her a practiced look that probably worked pretty well on seventeen-year-old girls. It was even working a little bit on her. She crossed her legs under the table and tried not to think about it. When Sinatra spoke Jane could tell that he'd spent a fair amount of time putting a polish on his voice and shaving off the corkscrew New Jersey vowel sounds.

"You're the chick I saw at the Cabin." He gave it just enough sneer to irritate, but not quite enough to anger.

"You're the singing waiter."

"I ain't no waiter. They don't hire waiters to sing on the radio, do they?"

"And they don't get chicks to snap pictures of corpses." Jane smiled.

Sinatra ignored the comeback. "Dolly said I should talk to you." Dolly, Jane knew, was the mother. A twenty-four-year-old who did what his mother told him meant either she was a tough old lady or he was a mama's boy. Maybe both.

"Why would she want you to do that?" asked Jane. It was a serious question, not a taunt.

"Because that guy getting whacked and thrown in the ditch ain't what you think, and Dolly and some other ginks don't want you to get the wrong idea."

"What would the wrong idea be?"

"The wrong idea would be that Mr. Moretti or his people had anything to do with the dead guy and him getting that way."

"Everything about it says it was a Mob hit, Frankie."

"It's Frank, not Frankie, and the guys that dumped the body weren't from any Mob I ever heard of."

"You saw it happen?"

"I saw the body being dumped."

"You told the cops you were taking a piss in the ditch and that's when you saw the body."

"Nice dirty mouth on you."

"I like it. Why didn't you tell the cops what really happened?"

"What I tell the cops is what I tell the cops."

"So you did see it happen?"

"Not him getting whacked. I told you that. I saw him get dumped. Maroon Lincoln, couple of years old. New York plates."

"Bet you don't remember the numbers."

"You'd be a loser." The easy smile came on again, then switched off just as fast. He reached two fingers into the breast pocket of his jacket and took out a folded piece of paper. He flipped it onto the table. Jane opened it up.

"It's 5N 30-94."

"You got it, sweetheart." He started to slide out from the table. "And that's all you're going to get."

"One more thing," said Jane.

"What?" Sinatra paused, half standing, his small hands on the table.

"You said the guys you saw weren't from any Mob you knew about. Why?"

"Mob guys don't dress that way." He lifted one hand and ran his thumb and forefinger down one lapel of his jacket. "Most Mob guys got style. Sharp dressers, maybe a bit flashy."

"And these guys weren't like that?"

"No. I mean, it's like the Lincoln. What Mob guys drive around in a maroon Lincoln Zephyr? If they did, at least it would be this year's model." He stood up fully and shot his cuffs again. "No cars like that, and no brown suits. All three of them, brown suits, brown shoes, brown hats." Sinatra let out a short, barking laugh. "You ask me, babe, they looked like FBI agents or something." He reached down, tipped the porkpie onto his head and snapped his index finger against the brim. "So long, toots. See you in the funny papers." Sinatra turned and left the restaurant, his walk a rubber-kneed strut that would have looked great in a Fred and Ginger movie. Jane watched him go, then looked down at the little slip of paper in her hand.

"A clue," she said. "I'll be damned."

Holland and Barry sat in the Mayfair Lounge taking afternoon tea, watching their quarry doing the same on the other side of the cavernous, glass-ceilinged eighty-by-seventy-foot space, the largest public room on the *Empress*. It was decorated like an Edwardian men's club, with deep, comfortable upholstered chairs and walnut paneling, and as a backdrop to a raised stage at the far end of the room there was a huge tapestry depicting the hunting exploits of Emperor Maximilian I.

A frieze running around the edge of the amber-colored glass ceiling included snowshoes, maple leaves and canoe paddles in a discreet homage to the ship's Canadian ownership. A six-piece chamber orchestra was playing on the stage and a dozen or so stewards made the rounds with trays of tea and biscuits and small sandwiches of various kinds. After four days on the ship Barry had decided that he liked the salmon pâté sandwiches the best, and the cucumber least, since they gave him gas. By observation he had noted that Miss Sheila Connelly, also known as Mary Coogan, purportedly from Enniscorthy, seemed to favor cheese and ham and drank coffee rather than tea. He'd also noted that she was extremely attractive, a classic Irish type with long, ink-black hair done up in a twist and dark Spanish eyes a man could drown in if he wasn't careful. He tried not to think too hard about her, about the eyes and the way her legs moved under her skirt. The truth of it was that the strength of his feelings, his feelings as a man, sometimes frightened him with their power, and he knew perfectly well that those feelings could never be reciprocated by the likes of Miss Sheila Connelly, if for no other reason than he was a policeman, and worse, a policeman whose ineptness with the opposite sex almost certainly shone like the beacon of a lighthouse. Maybe the monks were right, better to abandon such feelings entirely.

"By God, she is a peach, isn't she?"

"I beg your pardon?" Barry felt completely the fool and knew his face was beginning to flush with embarrassment like a schoolboy.

"Don't be a prig, old fellow. She's a spectacular bit of fluff and don't tell me you hadn't noticed."

"We're supposed to be keeping a watch on her."

"Precisely, and a very enjoyable watch it is."

"Please. I'd rather you didn't speak that way."

"Make you feel a little uncomfortable?"

"I suppose you could say that." He could feel the flush darken and he felt ridiculously light-headed, his secret revealed. He'd noticed everything about her, of course—her skin, the line of her jaw, her breasts against the fabric of her blouse, the eyes, the hair. He gritted his teeth and forced down the images rising in his mind's eye.

"I wonder if Ridder will ever show up at all," Holland murmured, blessedly changing the subject.

There was no sign of Herr Ridder in the lounge, or anywhere else for that matter. Since leaving Southampton the man had only left his cabin for dinner, making his painful two-caned way to his table in the Salle

Jacques Cartier Dining Room. He invariably took the first seating, while the Connelly woman appeared at her table for the second. There was also no sign that the two had ever met.

"Maybe there is no connection between them," Barry said, swallowing one of the tiny triangular sandwiches whole.

"I don't believe in coincidences, Barry, and neither do you. Ridder could have traveled on a ship that took him directly to New York instead of roundabout via Montreal. It makes no sense." Holland sipped his tea, his eyes on the woman across the room. "Did you notice the book?"

Barry nodded. *"The Mask of Dimitrios."*

"Written by that Ambler fellow. Quite good, I hear, if you like that sort of thing." Barry did like that sort of thing, but he wasn't about to tell that to Holland. "Notice anything odd?" Holland continued.

"She never reads it," Barry said. "Not while she's in here anyway."

"I don't think she reads it at all," said Holland. "No bookmark, the dust jacket isn't poked into the pages. She just carries it about with her."

"You think the book is significant?"

"Not really. Just odd. Like a crippled man taking a ship that doesn't go where he wants to go."

"We dock in Montreal the day after tomorrow. Once they're off the ship we're sure to lose one or the other of them."

"You're suggesting action of some kind?"

"Yes."

"I agree. It may be our last chance," said Holland. "Just so long as we don't flush our birds prematurely. If either one of them discovers that they're under surveillance they'll get a message to Russell and ensure that he goes to ground. We can't have that."

"So?"

"So I suggest a visit to Herr Ridder's cabin at the earliest opportunity."

Barry glanced at his watch. "Five-thirty. First sitting for dinner is in half an hour."

"Our sitting," said Holland a little wistfully. "They're having Gateaux St. Honoré for the sweet tonight."

"Ah, well," said Barry, "we all have to make sacrifices."

Ridder's B-deck cabin was on the port side, midship, almost directly opposite the barber shop and the telephone exchange. While Holland fetched a pass key from his friend in the purser's office, Barry stayed in the exchange, pretending to place a ship-to-shore call. At five past six Ridder appeared in the corridor, dressed formally and leaning on his canes. He locked the door of his cabin, then made his way painfully down the passage toward the elevator, his progress slowed even more by the slight corkscrewing motion of the ship. Barry peeked out the door of the exchange and watched as the crippled man tapped the elevator call button and waited. The elevator arrived quickly and Ridder climbed into the cab and disappeared. A few seconds later Holland returned, coming from the direction of the forward first-class stairway. He ignored Barry, using his newly acquired key to let himself into cabin 217. Barry left the telephone exchange, crossed the corridor and followed suit, closing the door firmly behind him.

Like all of the cabins on the *Empress,* 217 had a porthole and an ocean view. The room was long and narrow, the walls paneled in a light fruitwood, the curtains, light fixtures and bedclothes done in varying shades of pale yellow. There was a wood-veneered chest of drawers between the beds, a desk under the porthole and several chairs. On the bulkhead wall across from the beds there was a brass-cased octagonal clock. The small table on the bed closest to the door had an empty cup on it and the coverlet was rumpled, so presumably that was the bed Ridder actually slept in.

Holland slid back the mirrored doors on the cabin's single closet and began going through the two suitcases he found there. Barry, meanwhile, began going through the chest of drawers, the desk, and finally the bedside table. The policeman made a small noise of surprise and lifted an object from the drawer. "Another copy of the Ambler book," he said.

"Perhaps it's just a coincidence," Holland offered, sliding the cupboard door closed. He crossed to the bed and sat down beside Barry. The two men looked at the book. There didn't seem to be anything special about it. The book was a standard edition with a white theatrical mask as illustration on a bright blue background, the title and author's name in white as well, the type and colors clearly designed to evoke a Greek flavor. Barry flipped through the pages. No turned-down corners, no obvious markings or underlining.

"Nothing that I can see."

"Hold the pages up to the light. Maybe he's pricked words with a pin," Holland said. Barry held the book up to the overhead fixture, flipping the pages slowly. It was all very silly, really, like something out of Baden Powell's Boy Scout Manual or a novel by John Buchan.

"Nothing."

Holland poked his glasses back up onto his nose. "There's got to be *some* meaning to it."

"A recognition signal?" Barry offered.

"A little cumbersome, don't you think?" Holland answered. "Why not a red carnation in a buttonhole or a couplet from a sonnet? 'Fair stood the wind for France.' " He held out his hand and Barry gave him the book. The policeman glanced up at the clock over the bed. They'd been in the room for a little more than ten minutes. Ridder had probably barely begun to eat.

Holland opened the book until it was almost flat, letting the pages hang down from the spine. He shook the covers but there was nothing hidden between the pages. He peered down the space between the spine and the binding but there was nothing there either. "Bloody hell," he muttered.

Barry felt the corners of his mouth twitch upward and he quickly lifted one fisted hand and cleared his throat, dismissing the rising smile with the gesture. Holland, the hardened professional, self-professed grizzled veteran of the Balkans and the Ulster Counties, was being confounded by a pair of amateurs, one of them a woman.

"So," said Barry, "what do we do now?" He looked up at the clock again. Ridder would barely be past the soup. They still had lots of time but very little to do with it.

Holland stood up and looked around the narrow room, hands on hips. "I suppose we could search her cabin."

"To what end?" Barry asked. According to Holland's information Ridder was in the employ of a colonel in Nazi Military Intelligence named Erwin Von Lahousen, whose forte was sabotage and sedition and who was also in charge of the Irish Section. Since Ridder was an American it was assumed that it was he who would be passing information to the Connelly woman and not the other way around.

"All right then, what's your suggestion?"

"Wait. Their Majesties aren't due to arrive in Canada for the better part of a month, and it will be another two weeks after that before they cross into the United States. Anyway, the object has always been to let Miss Connelly lead us to Russell, not to arrest her."

"And lead us she will," said Holland. "But a little real evidence of this so-called plot would go a long way to proving a case to our American friends. One way or another we are going to need their help. The Republican cause has a lot of supporters in the States—when we do get Russell we're going to have trouble keeping him for very long unless we can prove he was going to kill Roosevelt and the royals."

"Well, it doesn't look like we're going to find any evidence here." Barry shrugged. "I doubt we'd find anything in Connelly's cabin either." He leaned over, slipped the book back into the open drawer of the night table and then closed it. He stood up.

"I suppose you're right." Holland adjusted his glasses again. "But it's damnably frustrating."

"Now isn't that just like the Irish for you," Barry said and smiled. "Come along. If we hurry we can get up to the dining room for some of that Gateaux St. Honoré."

Sir Stewart Menzies, Deputy Director of MI6, England's secret intelligence service, sat having a late dinner in one of the private rooms at the Army and Navy Club in Pall Mall, methodically trimming the fat from a large slice of prime rib while waiting for Chamberlain's young toadie to get to the point. Like a true politician Douglas-Home had managed to be utterly evasive all the way through the soup and the fish, but so far Menzies had managed to keep his temper. The fact that Douglas-Home was PPS to the prime minister was irrelevant—PMs came and PMs went with regularity, but Douglas-Home, like Menzies himself, *knew* people, which, if you wanted to get ahead, really was the most important thing. Obsequious little twit or not, the man had to be cultivated.

Menzies speared a small square of fatless meat, added a cube of Yorkshire pudding and popped the end of the fork into his mouth. He put down his knife and fork, chewed, swallowed, patted lips and neatly trimmed mustache, then picked up the knife and fork again while smiling pleasantly in Douglas-Home's general direction. The younger man cleared his throat and Menzies deferred his next mouthful, waiting for him to speak.

"We have a delicate situation before us."

"Ah," said Menzies. "We being . . . ?"

"The prime minister's office."

"I see."

"As you are no doubt aware, the prime minister is not well."

Something of an understatement, thought Menzies, considering Chamberlain had cancer of the throat. "Yes, I was aware of that."

"Given the state of his health it has been decided that certain . . . events and circumstances shouldn't be brought to his attention unless absolutely necessary."

"Events and circumstances?" Menzies ate another bite of food.

"Ones which the Prime Minister might find particularly . . . vexing."

"Such as?"

"Security questions relating to the royal tour of North America."

"Ah," said Menzies.

"Indeed," said Douglas-Home.

Menzies put down his knife and fork again, deciding to put the man out of his misery. "Presumably you mean the question of the Irish assassination plot."

"Sean Russell."

"We are aware of a rumor concerning an assassination attempt but I was under the impression it was just that, a rumor."

"Yes. So far we have very little to go on."

"I would have thought Special Branch and the local authorities in Canada and the United States would have security well in hand."

"They do, certainly." said Douglas-Home. "It's just that . . ."

The man had an irritating habit of letting sentences dangle. Menzies allowed himself a small sigh, then smiled once again. "It's just that you'd like to be kept advised if we come up with anything at MI6."

"Precisely." Douglas-Home sat back in his chair, clearly relieved that it was out in the open. The politician paused, smoothing a nonexistent crease in the tablecloth with his index finger. "About this Holland fellow of yours . . ."

"What about him?"

"He seems a little . . . independent . . . if you know what I mean."

"No, actually, I don't," said Menzies. He tipped a little horseradish onto his next bite of beef and waited for Douglas-Home to go on.

"Some of our people are having second thoughts about the investigation of Russell."

Here it comes, thought Menzies. He's finally getting down to it. "What sort of second thoughts?"

"There is some concern that any adverse publicity arising out of the investigation could exacerbate the situation here."

"More bombing of water closets, you mean."

"Quite so."

Menzies put down his knife and fork for good, the erosion of his appetite complete. It was clear now that Douglas-Home had never really believed there was an assassination plot and that the prospect of continued Republican bombings in England was obviously a more relevant concern. Menzies wiped his mouth and tossed the napkin down on the table. "In other words you want the investigation to end."

"Curtailed would be a better term, I think."

"By withdrawing Holland?"

"It had occurred to us."

"On what authority?"

"I thought perhaps you'd know of some discreet method."

Menzies smiled. The little shit seated across from him would go far and Menzies had every intention of going along with him. Chamberlain was sick, but Admiral Sinclair, head of MI6, was even sicker and not expected to last out the year.

"He was wounded in the Balkans," said Menzies.

"Oh dear," said Douglas-Home. "Health problems?"

"Chronic," Menzies offered. "Lungs." A good enough excuse to have him brought back to England and put behind a desk in the research division again.

"What about the other one, the policeman?"

"That would be up to the Yard." Both men knew that without Holland the investigation would effectively come to an end. Detective Inspector Barry could be seconded to the Special Branch contingent traveling with the royal party, or simply recalled.

"You'll keep me informed?"

"I don't have any problem with that." Menzies made a calculated assumption. "I'm assuming that rather than formally advising the prime minister's office you'd prefer that any information be passed on to you personally."

"Quite so," agreed Douglas-Home.

"So as not to vex Mr. Chamberlain unnecessarily."

"Indeed."

Knowledge is power, thought Menzies, and secret knowledge is the most powerful of all. Douglas-Home would go very far indeed. Menzies reached out and picked the dusty chateau bottle out of its basket in the center of the table. "More wine?"

Chapter 12

Wednesday, April 26, 1939
New York City

John Bone arrived in New York on the morning of April 26 and immediately took a taxi from Grand Central Station to the Gramercy Park Hotel at Twenty-first and Lexington, the hotel being a random choice taken from a guide book he'd purchased in Washington. He registered and took a moderate-size double room on the fourth floor overlooking the small, fenced square of greenery that gave the hotel its name. He returned to the lobby, then had a bacon-and-eggs breakfast in the old-fashioned European-style dining room. His meal over, he consulted briefly with the desk clerk. Following the young man's directions, he made his way to the Walgreens Drugstore at Broadway and Twenty-third Street on the ground floor of the Flatiron Building, putting him within a hundred yards of Jane Todd's office in the Tamblyn Building.

At the drugstore he purchased a pair of black-framed magnifying eyeglasses for reading, a package of twenty Grand single-edge razor blades, a small jar of Dart Household Glue and a bottle of Instant Clairol in black, as well as a four-ounce bottle of Marchand's Golden Hair Wash, which was essentially a five-percent hydrogen peroxide solution. He went to two more drugstores, buying another bottle of Clairol in each, one blond and one red.

Carrying his purchases in a brown paper bag, Bone returned to the hotel by way of Broadway, stopping at the Woolworth on the corner of Twenty-first Street to purchase a broad cold chisel from the hardware department, a cheap straw Panama hat, six lengths of colored ribbon from the sewing department, a $1.88 Excello shirt with a celluloid collar stiffener and a box of small envelopes. This done, he returned to the hotel, stopping at the newsstand to purchase copies of the *New York Times,* the *Herald-Tribune,* the *Daily News,* the *Journal-American,* the *Post,* the *Brooklyn Daily Eagle,* the *Bronx Home News* and the *Mirror.*

Back in his rooms, Bone spread out the newspapers on the table under the window, concentrating on the obituary pages from all the dailies as well as the shipping news from the *Times,* the *Herald Tribune* and the *Daily News*. For the next hour and a half he went carefully through these pages, using the razor blades, mucilage and his notebook from Washington to assemble a collection of eleven possible obituaries, as well as a list of passenger liners due to arrive in New York on that day, Thursday and Friday. Cross-referencing his clippings with the telephone directory in his room he then matched addresses and telephone numbers with the names of the deceased given in the obituaries, as well as gathering listings for the offices of the relevant shipping lines, jotting the information down in his notebook.

Bone's plan for creating several new identities for himself was simple, straightforward and involved very little risk. It was also a method he had used to good effect on several occasions in the past, including the Karageorgevic contract, several jobs in Romania and Bulgaria and, more recently, the Sandino affair in Nicaragua. In Bone's experience the best prospects were usually Catholic. A Catholic funeral service took much longer than a Protestant or Jewish one, and if there was going to be a special, and longer, requiem mass, the obituary invariably mentioned it. Such a funeral could easily take as long as four hours from beginning to end, which often meant that the dead person's home was empty and vulnerable for that period of time.

The first funeral on his list was set for the following

morning with a requiem mass at the Church of St. Andrew on Duane Street, just off Foley Square near City Hall. Interment would take place at Holy Cross Cemetery in Queens. The dead man's name was Harold E. Moss, a forty-two-year-old lawyer survived by a wife, but apparently with no children. The only Harold E. Moss listed in the telephone directory lived at 410 Central Park West, which according to the map in Bone's guide book put it roughly at 101st Street.

The next morning Bone ate breakfast in the hotel restaurant, then returned to his room. He pressed the magnifying lenses out of the reading glasses, then put the frames in the side pocket of his suit jacket along with the collar stiffener from the shirt and one of the envelopes from the stationery box, which he'd already addressed to Mrs. Harold E. Moss. He put the straw hat back into the Woolworth bag, then returned to the lobby and went out through the revolving door onto Lexington. He walked up a block to avoid using the doorman, then hailed a cab and took it to Central Park, traveling up the east side on Fifth Avenue. He got out of the taxi at East 100th Street, then crossed Fifth Avenue and used the public telephone there, calling the directory number for Harold Moss. He let it ring eleven times, then hung up, assuming that the apartment was empty. Bone continued on, entering the park by the children's area at the Transverse Road, putting on the empty eyeglass frames and the straw hat as he strolled casually across the North Meadow Playground, exiting just below the pool at West 101st Street.

The address he wanted was a sixteen-story building on the southwest corner of 101st and had the name Edith painted on the green-and-white-striped awning over the main door. A uniformed doorman was standing behind a narrow counter just inside the main entrance, an array of darkly varnished pigeonhole letterboxes behind him.

"Help you?" said the doorman.

"I'm here to see Mrs. Moss."

"She's at the funeral."

"Then perhaps I can leave this card for her."

"Sure thing."

Bone took the envelope out of his pocket and handed it to the doorman. He glanced at the address, turned and popped it into the box marked 601. There were already half a dozen other envelopes stuffed into the pigeonhole.

Bone reached into his pocket and took out a dollar bill. He handed it to the doorman. "You'll see that she gets it?"

"You bet," said the doorman, folding the dollar and putting it into the breast pocket of his uniform jacket. "Soon as she gets back."

"Thank you," said Bone. He turned away and left the building. The rear entrance to the Edith was down a service alley that ran behind the apartment block, connecting West 101st Street to West 102nd. In the central air shaft he found a row of battered garbage cans, and a heavy, dark green metal door with the address of the building splashed across it in rough strokes of white.

The door was equipped with an impressively large pin tumbler lock, but there was no shielding metal flange across the door and the jamb. Bone took out the celluloid collar stiffener, eased it between the frame and the door, then slowly sawed the strip back and forth, easing it down on the lock catch, pushing it out of the strike box in the frame until it popped open. Had the door been fitted with a flange he would have used the cold chisel in his other pocket to bend it back out of the way, and if the door had been fitted with a more efficient lock he would have simply gone to the next address on his list, hoping for better luck there.

As it was, he put the collar stiffener back in his pocket and opened the door. He found himself in the rear stairwell, which smelled faintly of garbage. He paused, listening for a moment, hearing nothing but the buzzing of a large bluebottle fly and a distant echo of rattling pipes coming from below. Reasonably confident that his entry had gone unnoted, he eased the door closed behind him, leaving it barely ajar. The garbage cans were empty and the smell in the rear vestibule was faint, which meant the refuse had already been picked up. It was unlikely that the rear door would be used in the next hour or so, and even if it was, whoever used it would conclude that it had been left open by accident.

There was almost certainly access to a service elevator in the basement, but Bone ignored the possibility on the off chance that there was some sort of in-use indicator behind the doorman's position by the front door. Instead he climbed the stairs, walking up six flights to ease the stairwell door open an inch or so. He found himself looking out into a small public hall tiled with black and white squares of marble. On the opposite side of the hall were a pair of elevators, a short corridor leading away to the left, and to the right three doors numbered 602, 603 and 604. Four apartments to each floor, with 601 at the end of the short corridor to his left.

The locks on the three doors that he could see were the same pin tumbler types as the rear door of the building and just as easy to slip. There was no reason to think that 601 was any different. Bone took the collar stiffener out of his pocket, pulled open the stairwell door and stepped across the open space and into the corridor. A few seconds later he was inside apartment 601, the door closed safely behind him.

Once again he paused, listening, his nose tilted to taste the air. Silence except for the steady thump of a large clock somewhere and the muffled sound of traffic moving down Central Park West. No smell of cooking in the air, nothing but furniture oil, floor wax and stale air. Bone glanced at his wristwatch, marking the time and giving himself a thirty-minute maximum limit within the apartment. He did a quick survey of the rooms, walking softly, keeping to the sides of hallways on the off chance that someone in the apartment below could hear his footsteps.

Directly in front of Bone was the living room, connected to the dining room by a pair of glass-paned pocket doors. Across a narrow hall from the dining room was a small kitchen with three rooms beyond—a pair of bedrooms, each with its own bath and toilet, and a small study sandwiched in between. The living room, dining room and one of the bedrooms looked out onto Central Park while the study, the second bedroom and the kitchen were windowless. The foyer and the hall were floored with diamond-patterned parquet, the kitchen with dark blue battleship linoleum and the rest of the rooms in highly polished blond oak.

The living room and dining room were both overdone in Louis XVI gold and tapestry. A large, ornately framed portrait of a plain, middle-aged woman wearing a gauzy pale blue evening dress hung over a marble mantelpiece in the living room. The mantel itself was cluttered with lacquer objects and a japanned bowl filled with carnations that were beginning to rot.

The hall leading down to the bedrooms and the study was hung with botanical prints in colors chosen to match the pastel stripes of the wallpaper behind them, while the bedroom overlooking Central Park was done up like the boudoir of a nineteenth-century English duchess in reds and greens and corals, a massive gilt pier mirror on one wall reflecting a delicate lady's bed piled high with pillows, its head lovingly swagged with ornate draperies. Definitely a woman's room, presumably occupied by the person depicted in the oil painting over the fireplace.

The second, smaller bedroom had clearly been decorated for a man's taste. Instead of oriental carpeting the wood floor was covered with a large rag rug. The furniture was brown, varnished and Victorian. A dark suit jacket had been hung carelessly over the back of a narrow-seated chair and there was an expensive-looking pair of black shoes beneath it. The bed had been stripped down to the ticking but a wallet, a ring of keys and a pair of eyeglasses had been left on the bedside table. All accessories unnecessary for the dead. Bone picked up the key ring. Three Yales, an automobile ignition key, a thin brass safe-deposit key and a second brass key with SEARS-ROEBUCK stamped on it that probably belonged to the inner cash box of a safe. A small skeleton key that probably fit a desk. Bone slipped the key ring into his pocket, then checked the wallet.

A driver's license in the name of the deceased, fifteen

dollars in assorted small-denomination bills, several business cards—all from lawyers and tucked away behind a slit in the satin lining of the billfold—and a small, deckle-edged snapshot of a young woman in a bathing suit, sitting on a beach with a line of sand dunes behind her. The young woman was definitely not the person in the living room portrait. He slipped the wallet into his pocket with the keys. Bone did a quick check of the closet and the adjoining bathroom but found nothing of particular interest. There was a prescription pill bottle of nitroglycerine tablets for Harold Moss's heart in the medicine chest above the sink, and a matchbook from the Stork Club in the pocket of one of the suit coats in Moss's closet. Bone checked his watch then went to the study.

Another man's room, the walls a rich Napoleonic green, had a modern-looking oriental carpet on the floor and two brass-tacked green-leather club chairs facing a small gas fireplace. The mantel was set with a pair of decorative marble urns with a portrait above, smaller and more plainly framed than the one in the living room, but showing the same woman, this time dressed in riding clothes, one arm raised and resting on another mantelpiece, the mirror above it reflecting the interior of what appeared to be the drawing room of a large house in the country. There was a small couch, a drooping palm tree in a pot, leaves gray-green with dust, a large rolltop desk in darkly varnished oak, a wooden office swivel chair, and in the corner, half hidden behind the palm, a steel safe on brass casters.

Bone sat down in front of the desk and rolled back the top. Five minutes later he had a picture of the life led by Harold Moss and his wife. She was a Whitney of one branch or another and controlled most of the money. Presumably Moss had been brought in to breed a new line of Whitney heirs but had failed. Moss, an attorney, had no real practice of his own beyond a sinecure at one of the Whitney charities, spent most of his time in New York while his wife, Deirdre, lived at a more substantial residence in Connecticut. Bone opened all the drawers in the desk, finally discovering the combination for the safe penciled on one of the file drawers' side panels.

He fished the key ring out of his pocket, knelt in front of the safe and entered the numbers on the rotating lock. There was a solid clicking noise as he turned to the last number, and he gripped the nickel-plated handle, turning it sharply. The safe opened. Deeds, insurance policies, Moss's will but not his wife's, an envelope of cash and two morocco-bound ledger books for the household accounts.

Using one of the small keys on the ring, Bone opened the box welded to the upper-left-hand side of the safe's interior and found what he was looking for—Moss's passport, up-to-date, the most recent stamp showing that he had gone to England the previous spring.

Under the passport there was a bundle of letters done up with a frayed black shoelace, four more deckle-edged photographs, several multicolored tin boxes of Ramses prophylactics and a small black leather case containing a glass-and-steel hypodermic syringe and a green vial containing a sweet-smelling white powder. The label on the vial was from the same doctor as the nitroglycerin tablets in the medicine chest. There was nothing on the vial to identify its contents, but Bone presumed that the powder was either heroin or morphine. Prescribed or not, Harold Moss was a drug addict.

Bone flipped through the small collection of photographs. All were of the same woman as the picture in Moss's wallet. Pretty, young, in one of the pictures wearing a tennis outfit, in the other three light cotton dresses. Bone checked a few of the letters. "My Dearest Darling," "My Own Darling," "Cherished Darling." Letters from the woman, Allison, to Moss, all of them pledging love eternal and describing the length and breadth of their passion and desires in rich, almost embarrassing detail.

The daughter of one of Deirdre's friends, a secretary from Moss's workplace, a chance shipboard meeting on the way back from England? The letters were all postmarked Long Island and the dates ranged from the previous May up until three weeks ago. For a moment Bone found himself wondering if she was going to be at the funeral, holding back her tears in deference to the widow, and he also thought briefly that the kindest thing might be to remove the bundle of letters, the syringe and the prophylactics from the safe. Why cause Moss's wife unnecessary pain at her husband's weakness and infidelity? He slipped the passport into the pocket of his jacket along with the wallet, then put everything else back into the metal-skinned lockbox. He was no more than a fleeting, ghostly presence in the life of Deirdre Moss and the death of her husband, and he was here for a single purpose, with no place or right to interfere in the unraveling of their separate destinies.

Bone closed the safe and spun the combination dial. He allowed himself a brief, sour smile as he stood up. The sympathetic thought for Deirdre Moss's feelings was as telling and as alien to him as his failing night vision and the slight arthritic ache he sometimes felt in his hands. Ten years ago such an emotional twitch in the middle of an assignment would never have occurred to him. He checked his watch again. Twenty-three minutes. It was time to go. He returned to Moss's bedroom, put the key ring back on the night table and then left the apartment. Half an hour later he was back at the Gramercy Park Hotel, consulting his notebook and planning his next move.

Chapter 13

Saturday, April 29, 1939
New York City

Despite pack ice in the Gulf of St. Lawrence, the *Empress of Britain* arrived in Montreal as scheduled, shortly after midnight on the twenty-seventh. After breakfast the passengers began leaving the ship, but not before Holland and Thomas Barry had settled themselves in a small room behind the Customs table in the dockside embarkation shed. Carefully observed, both Ridder and Sheila Connelly went through Customs without incident, collected their baggage and then took separate taxicabs to Windsor Station. They both purchased through-tickets to New York via Albany and the Twentieth Century Limited, Ridder taking a drawing room to himself while Connelly, still traveling as Mary Coogan, chose a less expensive section sleeper in the same car. Holland and Barry watched as first Ridder and then Connelly changed pounds for American dollars at the Bureau de Change in the station. Following the exchange, Ridder, moving awkwardly on his two canes, went to the Restaurant de la Gare for lunch while the Irish courier sat herself down on one of the wooden benches in the large, echoing waiting room.

"Now what?" asked Barry.

"We follow them," Holland answered.

Shortly after one in the afternoon their train left Montreal, traveled to the border crossing at Rouses Point, where everyone's passports were looked at again, and then continued on to Albany, where they arrived late in the evening. They dined in the station restaurant, and an hour later transferred to the Twentieth Century. At no time during the entire process did Ridder or Connelly exchange so much as a glance.

"There's always the chance that Hayes was sending us up," Barry offered, dropping his one small bag onto the floor of the small bedroom he and Holland would be sharing. The train's steam whistle let out a shriek, bells rang and they began to move out of the brightly lit station and into the darkness.

"He'd have to be some kind of terrible fool," said Holland, slumping down into one of the plush chairs by the window. He stared at his own worried reflection in the dark glass. "He knows we'd throw him to the dogs if we thought he was lying. And it's just too bloody Byzantine. Connelly was on the ship, so was Ridder, and they're both carrying that idiotic book. All of that a ruse to send us off playing hare and hounds? I really don't think so, Barry. It just won't wash."

"She may be an innocent in all of this. There's a chance she has no idea she's acting as a courier at all."

"You've either gone mad or been taken by the turn of the woman's ankle."

"Don't be silly." Not just her ankle but every other part of the woman. He felt like a fool, but some part of him was positive that she was innocent of any involvement in the whole scheme, and that if she was involved it was under duress.

"She's a member of the organization," Holland said flatly. "That's a matter of record."

"And a hundred reasons to be one, not all of them to do with politics. Fear makes as many members of the Cause as the cause itself. They're a ruthless bunch, as you well know."

"Good Lord, I believe you really are in love." Holland laughed. "Defending the woman as a victim of her own people."

"I thought that it was a basic tenet of English law that the accused are innocent until proven guilty."

"A law that doesn't apply to the Irish, because they don't apply it to anyone else. Theirs is the law of the gun and the bomb, Detective, and that woman is one of them, believe you me."

"And what if there's no exchange before we arrive in New York?"

"It certainly won't prove her innocent. We have Ridder's office under watch as well as his home. According to the purser, the Connelly woman asked to have a room booked for her at the Hotel Taft on Seventh Avenue for three nights."

"I thought you said we barely had anyone in place in New York."

"We don't," Holland answered. He took off his spectacles for a moment, pinching the bridge of his nose and closing his eyes for a moment. "Two people in the passport control office."

"MI6."

"Umm." Holland replaced the glasses and lit a cigarette, coughing heavily as he inhaled. "Fellow named Paget and two or three assistants."

"Then who's watching Ridder?"

"The FBI," said Holland, leaning back against the banquette and yawning. "Apparently Mr. Hoover has a particular thing against Nazis, so he was glad to help. Ridder is an American citizen, so the Bureau is within its jurisdiction." Holland closed his eyes as the train clattered onto a bridge. Through the window Barry could see the lights of the city reflecting off the broad, dark reach of a river. He suddenly felt very far from home.

"So presumably we concentrate on Miss Connelly."

"You presume correctly," Holland murmured.

"Why don't I get the porter to make up the upper berth?" Barry said. "If we keep the door ajar we can see anyone coming or going from the banquette and the other person can sleep." Ridder's sleeping car was in front of them, Connelly's behind.

"Excellent idea," Holland said sleepily. "You'll take the first shift, umm? Keep an eye out for that shapely ankle."

"Delighted," Barry answered with a sour smile. He rang for the porter.

Just after seven in the morning Barry and Holland enjoyed a surprisingly good breakfast of bacon, eggs and sausage in their compartment. By prearrangement with the conductor Holland was escorted to the forward baggage car while Barry remained where he was. The train arrived at Grand Central Station at precisely 9:30 A.M. Saturday morning. As the Twentieth Century came to a full stop at the end of track thirty-four the platform instantly turned into a sea of people heading for the front of the station. Barry, clutching his one small bag, stood close to the steps leading down from his car, scanning the dense ebb and flow of the passengers, trying to pick out his quarry. Surprisingly it was the crippled Ridder who showed up first, seated in a wheelchair, his copy of *The Mask of Dimitrios* in his blanket-covered lap. The wheelchair was being pushed by a young man wearing a dark suit who kept his head bent, engaging Ridder in conversation. The wheelchair effectively parted the crowd in front of it. To keep them in sight Barry had to follow close behind in the vehicle's wake. He was less than ten feet away from Ridder and his companion. Through the hollow rush of blasting steam and the echoing roar of the crowds on the platform he could just hear them in conversation—animated German that he didn't understand at all.

Almost on cue Sheila Connelly stepped down from her car, turning against the oncoming rush of people just as Ridder grew close to her. She took a single step forward, scanning the crowd as though looking for someone, and Barry suddenly knew exactly what was going to happen.

The left front of the wheelchair clipped her just above the knee and she went down, letting out a small screech of fear, her handbag and her copy of the Ambler novel flying out of her hands. The young man raced forward to retrieve the book and the fallen handbag while Ridder himself leaned forward, solicitously trying to help Connelly to her feet. In the process he managed to give her his copy of the book from his lap while his companion handed her the handbag, but retained her book, dropping it into Ridder's lap as he adjusted the wheelchair. The entire exchange took only a few seconds, and amateurs or not, it was extremely well done. Barry felt his heart sink at the clear evidence of her culpability. His conversation with Holland the night before came back to him like sour bile.

Barry continued to follow the wheelchair, keeping well back. As they reached the gate at the end of the platform he saw Holland talking angrily to a middle-aged man wearing a severely cut dark blue suit and carrying a bowler hat in one gloved hand. English certainly and possibly a diplomat. Connelly went through the gate first, followed a few seconds later by Ridder. The wheelchair went through the gate and continued on, squeezing in behind Holland and his companion, then headed up the ramp to the main concourse of the station.

Barry slowed, uncertain what to do. Looking over the shoulder of the man carrying the bowler, Holland gave the Scotland Yard man a quick warning look. It must have alerted the man with the bowler because he half turned and looked down the platform, but by then Barry had continued on. Clearly Holland had encountered some kind of bureaucratic difficulty, since the man with the bowler was almost certainly from the consul's office. Just as clearly, Holland wanted Barry to keep on with their surveillance. Since the FBI was keeping a watch on Ridder, Barry decided to concentrate on Connelly, especially now that the book had been switched.

The Scotland Yard detective strode up the slightly rising tunnel to the main concourse, passing Ridder, his eyes on Connelly, who was now wearing a three-quarter-length Burberry travel coat with a matching suit and a bright green scarf around her neck. She wore no hat. Reaching the top of the tunnel they came out into the immense main concourse, and for a brief moment Barry found himself lost in the architectural drama of the cathedral-size space, great streams of light flooding down from the immense curved windows high above. He blinked hard, bringing himself back to earth, and spotted Connelly going down a set of stairs to the station's lower level. He followed her down to the lower concourse shops and into a Rudley's restaurant, where she spent the next hour at a table eating a leisurely breakfast and reading a copy of the *Daily News* while Barry drank coffee after coffee at the counter. At 10:30 the IRA courier paid her bill, returned to the main level and went across to the baggage room.

Barry followed, then paused at the octagonal information booth in the center of the concourse and pretended to examine a brochure about the Super Chief, trying to remember enough of his geography to visualize just where Los Angeles and Chicago would be on a map of the United States. When the Irish woman simply stayed waiting at the baggage counter Barry went to one of the long wooden benches and sat down, his eyes half on the brochure and half on the baggage claim area.

Finally Barry saw a shirtsleeved baggage attendant return from the rear of the large, cluttered room and place Connelly's two suitcases on the low, zinc-covered counter. A brief conversation between Connelly and the luggage man ensued, ending with a pair of orange tags being tied to the suitcases and a piece of paper money changing hands. The only thing Connelly kept was the copy of *The Mask of Dimitrios* and her pocketbook. It looked less and less likely that the woman intended on a stay at the Taft.

She put the other half of her orange baggage tags into the pocketbook, shook the baggage man's hand, then turned away, heading to a long line of ticket windows that lined one entire south wall of the station. She went to the closest one, consulted briefly with a clerk and purchased a ticket, slipping it into her pocketbook. She then turned and made her way up the stairs to the main level of the terminal, leaving the building at the Vanderbilt Avenue exit.

Barry's heart sank when he spotted the long row of

cream-and-green taxicabs parked along Vanderbilt. He quickly looked both ways and saw she had walked only a few feet farther on to the corner and crossed Forty-second Street. Barry followed her, still carrying his own small suitcase, and watched as she paused under the broad marquee of the Embassy movie theater to examine the posters. According to the marquee the Embassy was playing *Union Pacific,* starring Joel McCrea and Barbara Stanwyck. Barry wasn't much for pictures, but he had seen Stanwyck in *Stella Dallas* a couple of years back and quite enjoyed it. As Barry reached the corner and stepped up onto the sidewalk he saw Connelly purchase a ticket for the first showing at 11:30. She disappeared into the theater and a few moments later Barry followed suit, fumbling a little with the unfamiliar coinage. By the time he reached the concession stand his quarry had already gone into the auditorium. Barry gave the popcorn girl a quarter to mind his suitcase with the promise of another when he returned to fetch it, then went into the theater himself, standing just inside the doors to let his eyes adjust to the gloom. There was a cartoon showing before the feature that concerned the misadventures of a criminally minded flop-eared rabbit named Bugs and his bumbling archenemy, a hunter named Fudd.

Barry's vision cleared. It wasn't too difficult to spot Connelly since there appeared to be fewer than a score of people in the theater. There were also two fire exits, one on each side of the screen. Barry stood and watched until the cartoon finished and several trailers for coming attractions appeared. He didn't like leaving Connelly alone, but eventually he decided the risk was necessary. He went back into the lobby, found the public telephone booth in an alcove beside the men's toilet and spent several minutes trying to figure out the mechanism, eventually realizing that the money had to be inserted before a connection could be established, the reverse of the British system. Eventually he managed to connect with an operator, who in turn connected him to the British consul's office. Remembering Holland's conversation from the night before he asked for Mr. Paget in passport control, was informed that it was actually "Sir" as well as "Captain" James Paget, R.N., and he was duly connected. After almost ten minutes spent establishing his bona fides to someone named Bell in Paget's office, Barry heard Holland come on the line.

"Where the bloody hell are you?"

"A movie theater called the Embassy. Right next to the train terminal."

"The Connelly woman?"

"Watching the film."

"Was there an exchange?"

Barry paused, his breath a long sigh. "Yes. On the platform. She has Ridder's book now."

"What did I tell you?"

"She may have reasons for what she's done."

"You're beating a dead horse, Barry, even if it's a very pretty one. What I want to know is why she hasn't gone to the Taft."

"Would you like me to go into the theater and ask her that?" Barry wedged the telephone between his shoulder and jaw and lit a cigarette. "I don't think she has any intention of going to a hotel. She's kept her luggage at the station and she's bought another train ticket."

"Where to?"

"I have no idea."

"Why didn't you ask the man who sold it to her?"

"I would have lost her." There was a pause as Holland digested the information, and Barry intruded on the silence with a question of his own. "What happened at the train station?"

"The man you saw me with was one of Paget's associates. According to Paget orders have come down from on high that I am to return to England forthwith."

"Any explanation?"

"Apparently my health is none too good," Holland answered dryly. "Under the circumstances I really can't say much more than that."

In other words, Paget or the man in the bowler hat was in the room with him. "You're not alone?"

"That is correct."

"Is the entire case being dropped?"

"I wouldn't go that far."

"This has something to do with Sean Russell."

"Indeed."

Barry blew smoke out through his nostrils and stitched it together for himself. Russell had high-ranking friends in America, including a couple of congressmen and at least one senator. Tread too hard on his toes and there were likely to be repercussions back in England—an escalation from bombing toilets to exploding mailboxes perhaps. "Was this Douglas-Home's idea?"

"I'd say that's a reasonable guess."

"He's trying to stop us, isn't he?"

"Possibly."

"At least slow down the investigation of Russell."

"Probably. Almost certainly that much."

"And you're out of it completely?"

"So it would seem."

"What about me?"

"You're Scotland Yard. That's Home Office, not my bailiwick."

"Fucking hell!" Barry seethed. He leaned down and pushed the stub of his cigarette into the sand-filled canister beside the telephone.

"Yes, I'd say that sums it all up quite neatly."

"What am I supposed to do with the Connelly woman?"

"We bring her in for interrogation, forthwith. I want to ask her a few questions of my own before I head back to Merry Old England."

"And if she doesn't want to come?"

"What Miss Connelly wants, wishes or expects is irrelevant at this point. She'll be taken by force if necessary. All you have to do for now is play Bill the Minder. Sir James has enlisted the aid of one Percy Foxworth of the FBI and several of his minions. Give them twenty minutes or so and we should have the joint surrounded, as the saying goes."

"She's in the eighth row, five seats in from the center aisle."

"Good man. Now go and enjoy the movie. We'll sort the rest of this out later."

Chapter 14

Saturday, April 29, 1939
New York City

After a visit with her sister at the hospital on Welfare Island, Jane made her way back to Manhattan for a prearranged meeting with Dan Hennessy. It was late afternoon by the time she reached Reuben's on Madison Avenue. She found the police detective seated in a relatively quiet booth in the back, working his way through a stacked pastrami on sour rye, washing it down with a bottle of Knickerbocker. There were three other bottles on the table other than the one the cop was drinking. Jane slipped into the booth, snagged a cigarette out of the crumpled pack of Skeets on the table in front of her friend and lit up.

Hennessy chewed, swallowed, then took a sip of beer. "Visiting your sister?"

"Yeah."

"Nice that you do that. Lot of people wouldn't."

"She's the only family I have."

"Still." Hennessy waved a hand in front of his plate. "You should eat something." He lifted his bottle and took a belt. "Drink something too."

Jane shrugged. "Maybe later." She took a drag on the cigarette and leaned back against the worn leather of the booth. "You find out anything about the car?"

"Sure," Hennessy said. "I found out the plate was taken off a '34 Dodge owned by an old bird named Hector Weakes who runs a hardware store in some little burg up the Hudson. A maroon Lincoln turned up on a hot sheet in one of the Brooklyn precincts."

"Gabbie Vigorito," said Jane.

"You got it."

Gabriel Vigorito, otherwise known as Bla-Bla for his talkativeness or the Black Man for his dark Mediterranean coloring, had controlled an interstate auto-theft empire from his Greenpoint headquarters until a conviction in 1934 earned him a ten-year spot up the river in Ossining. He'd done five years at Sing-Sing and had been released for good behavior two months previously. The word was he'd gone right back to his old ways, now operating as something called Boro Hall Auto Exchange. Rumor also had it that he'd bought himself a hundred copies of J. Edgar Hoover's *Persons in Hiding,* which had a whole chapter in it devoted to his exploits.

"I guess it's a dead end then."

"Maybe not." Hennessy finished his sandwich, then pushed the plate away and lit a cigarette of his own. It was early evening and Reuben's was filling up. The air was filled with aromatic steam, the clatter of dishes and orders being called out for Clark Gables, Carol Lombards and FDRs with ketchup. More than once Hennessy had said he'd die a happy man if they named a sandwich after him at Reuben's.

"Spill," said Jane.

Hennessy leaned back, relaxing. "We picked up the car on a tip from Henry Franzo." Once upon a time Franzo had been the Black Man's brother-in-law and also a master at changing the registration numbers on stolen cars. "Henry said some Harvard guy approached him, said he needed a car."

"Harvard guy?"

"Boston accent," Hennessy supplied. "Educated. Anyway, Franzo tells him no problem, tells him how much it's going to cost and the guy says fine, he'll pay half down in cash, the rest on delivery. Then he gives Franzo a card with a telephone number on it, says call when he's got the car, which he does."

"Who has the telephone number?"

"New York division of a company called Somerset Importers."

"What is it?" Jane asked. "One of Costello's operations?"

"No. Your friend the singing waiter was right, they weren't Mob guys. Somerset Importers is a booze distribution operation owned by Joe Kennedy."

"You've got to be kidding," Jane whispered. "Joe Kennedy as in the Joe Kennedy who's the U.S. ambassador to England?"

"The very one," said Hennessy. "Pal of FDR's and onetime head of the Securities and Exchange Commission." He tipped up his bottle, draining the last inch of beer in it. "Which brings me to my other piece of news."

"You can do better than tell me that Joe Kennedy is ordering hits on Mobbed-up lawyers?"

"I've been promoted."

"What the hell are you talking about, promoted?"

"Just what I said." Hennessy tapped an inch of ash into his empty beer bottle. "Yesterday I get called into Valentine's office and he tells me I'm now a lieutenant and second in command of the Safe, Loft and Truck Squad under Captain Ray McGuire."

"You don't sound too pleased."

"After he tells me I'm promoted the commissioner says I'm lucky it's Safe and Loft, since it could have been Traffic or BCI, but at least this way I'll live to see my pension."

"A threat?"

"No. I think it's just a warning. He told me to hand over all my active cases to Joe McNally, but he makes a special point of telling me he wants McNally to have everything I've got on Howie Raines, our boy in the ditch at the Rustic Cabin, and then he asks me if anyone else has anything on Raines, such as the freelance broad who took the crime scene snaps."

"How'd he know it wasn't one of your guys?"

"Because he had the pix right there on his desk, the ones you gave me, each one of them rubber-stamped on the back with your name, address and telephone number, just like always."

"Another warning?"

"Or maybe he's fishing. Wants to know about anything else you might have going."

"I thought you told me Valentine was one of the good ones."

"He is, but he's also been a New York cop for thirty years. In this town that doesn't necessarily mean you're dirty, but it doesn't mean you're clean either. One way or the other he owes a few favors and now someone is calling a marker."

"Why?"

"Because something isn't square with the Raines thing. It was sour right from the start. That's why I brought you in on it. But now it's gone too far. This Kennedy thing is the last straw, my girl. I'm out of my depth and so are you. It's time to bow out gracefully. Drop it. This is politics, and I don't mean the old-fashioned Tammany kind. This is Big Politics."

"You're making me nervous."

"Good."

"Also curious."

"Not good."

"Howie works for a firm of Mob lawyers. Howie goes to Cuba, which also means the Mob, and when he comes back he gets snuffed. So far nothing really too strange—you work for the Brunos, you expect a little grief from time to time. Maybe he screwed up, maybe he screwed the wrong frail, maybe he's just a screwball. So what? Who cares?" Jane paused and stubbed out her cigarette in the little tin ashtray at the far end of the table. Then she lit another one. Hennessy just watched her, waiting, his features slack and a little sleepy from the beer, but his eyes awake enough.

"So why all the interest?" Jane continued. "Howie's nobody special. Then all of a sudden there's all this pressure on. From the sound of things the mayor of Jersey City has his finger in it, so does the commissioner of the New York Police Department, and now you tell me Joe

Kennedy's got a string attached as well, and if you really wanted to go out on a limb you could say there's a string attached all the way to the White House."

"Drop it, Jane."

"It sounds like something awful big is going on."

"Maybe you're right, but it's the kind of awful big something that could get you seriously hurt." He tapped the side of his plate with a fingernail. "One less lady photographer in the world is like one less lawyer—no one's going to miss you too much."

"Gee, Dan, I didn't know you cared."

"Try and be serious for a minute, would you?" Hennessy shook his head. "You're right, girlie. This is something big and the likes of you and me don't belong, so let's keep our noses out of it, understand?"

"Then why did you tell me about Somerset Importers and all that?" Jane asked.

Hennessy let out a long-suffering sigh. "Because I thought you should know how high up this goes, and because I figured that no matter what I said you'd probably keep on digging into this." He paused. "I'm telling you not to. I'm telling you to stop right now. Forget it ever happened. If you took another set of prints from the Rustic Cabin, get rid of them right now, along with the negatives."

"Like a blackboard slate," said Jane. "Howard Raines gets wiped off and doesn't leave so much as a smudge."

"That's it exactly," said Hennessy. He slid out of the booth and rose a little unsteadily to his feet. He reached into his pocket, drew out several crumpled bills and tossed them down onto the table. "Have a beer and a sandwich on me and Commissioner Lewis J. Valentine of the NYPD. Think about what I said."

Hennessy leaned down, both of his big hands spread across the table to support himself, his beer-and-mustard breath in Jane's face. "Better still, sweetheart, don't think about it. Just do it, okay? You've got a reputation in this town as a tough-talking broad, one of the guys—try and make sure you don't get a reputation for being a dead tough-talking broad, okay?"

He pushed himself upright, gave his friend a little salute with one hand, then turned on his heel and tottered out of the restaurant. Jane watched him go and decided to do what Dan had suggested, at least as far as the beer and sandwich was concerned.

The interrogation of Sheila Connelly, traveling as Mary Coogan and using a forged passport in that name, took place on the fourth floor of the U.S. Court House in Foley Square. The entire floor and the one above it were occupied by the New York office of the Federal Bureau of Investigation. The interrogation room itself was usually used for meetings and conferences relating to specific cases, and one of the short walls in the room was fitted with a half dozen spring-loaded roller maps of New York State and New York City. The other short wall held a large blackboard, and the space in between was taken up by a plain rectangular conference table set with eight equally plain chairs.

On the table in front of each chair was an ashtray. To the right of the ashtray at one position partway down the table there was also a telephone and a message pad. A small table by the door held a large Bakelite water carafe and a stack of paper cups.

In the interrogation room were Percival "Sam" Foxworth, assistant director and head of the New York FBI office, an unnamed male clerk-stenographer, FBI Special Agent William G. Friedemann, FBI Special Agent James C. Ellesworth, Sir James Paget from MI6, and seated closest to the door, Holland and Barry. Sheila Connelly was being held in a small cell-like room next door.

Paget went through an attention-getting bout of throat clearing before speaking up from the far end of the table. "I think there are some questions of protocol that should be made clear before we proceed."

"What questions would those be?" asked Foxworth quietly, his speech tinged with a well-educated Mississippi accent.

"Which of us is in charge of the interrogation, for instance."

"Well, I don't really see how that makes much of a difference, all things considered. According to you this woman is a courier for the Irish Republican Army who is also connected to our man Ridder, who we're pretty sure is a Nazi. You say she's traveling on a forged British passport, which she used to gain illegal entry into the United States. It would appear, Sir James, that both of us can pick the meat off her bones equally, unless you just want us to deport her, which means she'd have to be out of the country within the next twenty-four hours."

"She's bringing information to Sean Russell."

"About this so-called assassination attempt you told me about."

"Yes."

"Which you now say isn't much of a threat at all, at least according to your people in London."

"According to our information it would appear to be unlikely, yes."

"But you still want to interrogate this woman about it."

"Not so much the assassination plot as Russell's whereabouts." Paget cleared his throat again. "As we discussed earlier, Mr. Russell is also traveling with a false passport."

"So you say." Foxworth smiled. The thin, pale man had a faintly aristocratic air about him and Barry could easily imagine him well seated on a horse and wearing a Confederate army uniform. "According to you the passport is genuine enough but refers to him as John Russell, not Sean."

"Quite so. False information."

"I always thought John and Sean were one and the same," said Foxworth. "But it's hardly the same as going around with a totally forged document like this Sheila Connelly of yours."

"Nevertheless . . ."

Foxworth smiled. "Nevertheless you'd like to talk to her."

"Yes." Paget cleared his throat again. "We'd also appreciate it if your people could have a look at that book she was carrying."

"Already in the works," said Foxworth. "Which brings me to a protocol question of my own."

"By all means," said Paget.

"Director Hoover has made it abundantly clear that under no circumstances will he countenance any espionage activities by a foreign nation to take place within the United States. There are no exceptions to this. Is that understood?"

Paget did not look pleased but he finally nodded his assent. "Yes."

"Good." Foxworth took a breath. "Therefore any actions taken as a result of the interrogation of the Connelly woman will fall under the aegis of the Federal Bureau of Investigation and no other agency, including yours. Is that also understood?"

Again Paget's agreement was grudging. "Yes. Although presumably there will be some kind of liaison between my office and yours."

"As I understand it Colonel Holland here is on his way back to England."

"That would appear to be the case, yes."

"Which leaves us with Detective Inspector Barry here." Foxworth flashed his small, bright smile at Paget again. "Correct me if I'm wrong, but he is the only real policeman in your group. Isn't that so?"

"Yes."

"Mr. Hoover has a great deal of respect for Scotland Yard. I don't think he'll mind Inspector Barry sticking around for a while to see how things shape up." Foxworth smiled down the table at Paget. "That okay with you, Sir James?"

"I suppose it will have to do."

"Good," Foxworth said. He turned to Special Agent Ellesworth, seated on his left. "Bring in the woman."

She'd been picked up at the Embassy Theater shortly after noon and it was now almost dinnertime, but even after six and a half hours in custody Sheila Connelly still looked calm and self-possessed. Ellesworth seated her at the head of the table and then went and stood by the door, almost as though he expected her to make some desperate attempt at escape. Barry looked for any signs of distress or fear and saw none. She gave the appearance of a beautiful woman irritated with a delay in her plans.

"You've been treated well?" Foxworth asked kindly.

She shrugged. "Well enough."

"Anything we can get you?"

She didn't hesitate. "I'd like a cigarette and some coffee."

"How do you take your coffee?"

"Milk and sugar. Plenty of both, if you don't mind."

Foxworth nodded at Ellesworth and the agent left the room, presumably to fetch the coffee. The assistant director reached into the pocket of his own suit coat and pulled out a green and red package of Lucky Strikes and a slim, almost ladylike Ronson lighter with its electroplating worn at the corners. He slid the cigarettes and lighter across the table and Barry passed them along, the tips of his fingers touching hers as she took them from him. She lit a cigarette and then put the lighter down on the package of Luckies, lining up the corners neatly.

Paget began the questioning, opening up a thin file that lay in front of him.

"Your full name is Sheila Grace Connelly?"

"My name is Mary Coogan, just as it says on my passport."

"From Craigavon in County Armagh."

"That's right."

"No, that's wrong," said Barry quietly. "You're from County Cork without a doubt. No farther north than Mallow, no more than a stone's throw from Cork City itself."

"And how would you be knowing something like that?"

Barry noticed that the cigarette was shaking a little between her fingers. "I recognize the voice," he answered, trying to keep some caring in his voice, not wanting to come on all hard policeman, not wanting to frighten her.

Or lose her. He watched as she put the cigarette between her lips and drew on it. "You've spent a little time in Belfast perhaps, but more in Dublin."

"You're an expert in such things, I suppose?"

"I grew up in the Capuchin orphanage by Parliament Bridge. The brothers would take us to sing the mass at Saint Anne's every Sunday." He smiled at the woman, staring into her eyes. "You grew up within hearing of Shandon Bells, Miss Connelly. I'm afraid there's no getting past it."

"I don't know what you're talking about." She smiled brightly, looking him right in the eye. "And the name is Coogan. Mary Coogan."

A message had passed between them, a recognition signal of some kind, but he wasn't quite sure what it meant. "Sheila is a much nicer name."

"Unfortunately not my own. And I still don't know what you're talking about."

"We're talking about Stephen Hayes," said Holland. "He told us all about your little errand on behalf of Sean Russell and the Cause."

"I don't know any Sean Russell." Still no fear in her tone, and Barry was probably the only one to catch it, but her accent thickened slightly, taking her home in her heart if not in reality.

"Sean Russell. Tall, red-haired chap," said Holland. "Drives a sports car at high speed all around Dublin. Drinks too much and spends too much time with the whores in Irishtown."

"I told you, I don't know any Sean Russell."

"We know he's already in America. He arrived in New York two weeks ago on a Norwegian ship named the *Stavangerfjord.* Sir James and Assistant Director Foxworth were advised that he was coming but Russell managed to give them the slip. We think you know how to find him. We think you're supposed to give him some information supplied to you by Herr Ridder, your friend on the *Empress of Britain.*"

"I don't know anyone named Stephen Hayes, I don't know anyone named Sean Russell, and I certainly don't have a friend named Ridder." She stubbed out her cigarette.

"That's a lot of people not to know," said Holland. He took off his glasses, wiping them with a handkerchief, and leaned his head back, eyes closed. "You're stubborn, Miss Connelly, but you aren't stupid. You know when the jig is up."

"This is all some kind of mistake."

Holland tapped an earpiece of his spectacles against his nose. "No mistake. Sheila Connelly, daughter of Michael and Mary Connelly, both killed by the Blueshirts in '33, lover of Sean Glynn, who hanged himself in his cell at Arbour Hill three years later. Sheila Connelly, who doesn't really give a damn about the Cause and only knows it seems to kill the people she loves. You do as you're told by these people because that's what you've always done. You don't know any other way to live."

Barry watched as the woman's features hardened. The dark eyes burned. "You're one of the Specials, aren't you? One of the Specials who killed my Sean!"

"Your Sean killed himself with a twist of blanket after getting himself drunk with his mates on some kind of spirits they made in the prison kitchen. The last anyone heard he was crying to himself and declaiming Jimmy Steele's poetry from the *Wolfe Tone Weekly* in a loud voice up and down the cell row. There's even some who say those same mates strung him up because he knew too much and was about to break down and tell it all like a blubbering baby."

"That's a bloody lie! Sean was no grass! He was a patriot! A hero!"

"He was neither," said Holland, sitting forward again, hooking his spectacles over his ears. "He was a young boy. Someone who got in too deep and saw no way out. Like you."

The telephone in front of Foxworth rang loudly, shocking everyone into immobility. It rang a second time. The FBI man leaned out and picked up the receiver. "Foxworth." He listened for several moments, making small notations on the file folder in front of him, then replaced the receiver back on its hooks. "That was our Identification Division. They found the message Miss Connelly received from Herr Ridder."

"In the book?" said Holland.

Foxworth nodded. "On the inside of the dust jacket. They used protoxide of mercury. Turns black under ammonia vapor."

"What was the message?" asked Holland.

"I'm not at all sure that it would be a good idea for Miss Connelly to hear it," said Paget.

"Oh, I don't know about that, Sir James," Foxworth said and smiled, loosening the reins on his Mississippi accent a little. "Maybe it's time Miss Connelly here knew the kind of folks she's running with."

"What would you know about it?" the woman answered hotly, her own accent broadening. "I live in a country that's been torn in two and lies bleeding for no good reason except for the fact that men like your Sir James want it to be that way."

Foxworth smiled. "We fought our own civil war a while back, Miss Connelly, and by and large we've come to terms with the results of it." He paused. "You have the slightest idea what your friend Russell is up to in this country?"

"Fund-raising, the same as it was when he came before."

"Not this time, I'm afraid."

"Mr. Foxworth . . ." Paget cautioned.

Foxworth ignored him. "The information passed along by Ridder is a complete schedule of the movements of the King and Queen of England while they're in the United States from the time they cross at Niagara Falls until they leave again, as well as several contact telephone numbers for people who can help him get hold of what he needs in the way of making bombs." He nodded across the table to Holland and Barry. "These people also have information that leads us to believe that Russell intends to assassinate the king and queen, and if our president happens to be standing next to them, well so much the better." Foxworth paused. "As you well know, Mr. Roosevelt is no friend to your precious Cause."

The woman sat there, a stunned expression on her face, already ashen. "You're lying," she whispered after a long moment.

"Why would I do that?" Foxworth asked gently. "What would I have to gain?"

"And what do we gain by giving her this information?" Paget snapped.

"Perhaps her cooperation," Foxworth suggested.

"Not from the likes of her."

She picked up the Ronson and lit another cigarette. Holland leaned toward her. "He's going to kill them, Sheila, and probably some others as well. Russell and his lot are working with Hitler's people to keep the Yanks out of the war. They think somewhere along the line there's going to be a quid pro quo. You've got to believe me."

"That's what you all say. Even them," Connelly answered, drawing hard on the cigarette. " *'You've got to believe us, Sheila, for the Cause.' 'Sean died for the Cause.'* My poor bloody parents died for the Cause." She stabbed the cigarette out in the ashtray. "Well may the good Lord Himself curse the fecking Cause. I've had enough. I'm done. Put me in one of your jails and let me rot because it'd be better than a life fighting for the Cause." She looked around the table. "I'm just so bloody tired of it all." Tears were streaming down her cheeks and the fire in her eyes had fallen to dull embers.

Watching her closely Barry realized that this was no sudden, miraculous conversion. It wasn't the first time she'd questioned her life in the IRA and her reasons for living it, nor the hundredth. It was something that had haunted her half her life, a wound that never had a chance to heal. At that moment his only thought was that he was that chance for her and would be willing to do almost anything for it. Madness!

Foxworth gave Agent Ellesworth the nod. The FBI agent stood up, gently eased Connelly out of her seat and led her out of the room. Foxworth tapped a pencil on the table in front of him.

"I'm not sure I see the purpose of the little drama we just witnessed," said Paget.

"Intelligence gathering," Foxworth answered.

"And just what is it that you think we've all learned?"

"That she's human," Barry said tightly, ignoring Paget's sour look. "That she's vulnerable."

"And what possible difference does *that* make to the situation at hand?"

Foxworth smiled. "It means that she can be used."

It was getting dark by the time Jane climbed up out of the subway. Most of the shops were closed and the streetlights were already flickering on. It was the weekend, so the Flatiron Building was dark, but the Walgreens was still open and lit up. She crossed Fifth, ducked under the striped canopy and went into the drugstore.

She ignored the leers from a couple of cab hacks having dinner at the lunch counter, picked up a tin of Golden Bear cookies in case she got hungry later on and then asked Ricky the soda jerk to make her up a Dixie of coffee. Ricky had a heartrending crush on her and she always tipped him double and gave him her best smile, even though he had a farmer's field of pimples on his forehead and God knew where else. Let the kid have a few furious dreams—if she could boost his confidence a little, why not? She carried her purchases back across Fifth and let herself into her own, dark building, juggling her keys, the coffee container and the bag with her fattening can of bridge assortment inside.

Riding up in the cranky, clanking elevator she tried to put the puzzle pieces together once again, trying to keep the sadness down and concentrate on the facts. Howie the low-end Mob lawyer led to Shalleck the high-end Mob lawyer, who in turn led to one of Joe Kennedy's companies, and that in turn fit in with Bushy's proposition that the Democrats were involved in whatever was going on, which also fit in with a Democrat police commissioner warning off one of his homicide detectives from anything to do with Howie. Full circle, but what a far-reaching circle it was, and even with the pieces all put together, what the hell was the picture she was looking at?

The elevator came to a thumping halt and Jane made her way down the gloomy corridor as much by habit as by sight. Reaching her office door she put the paper bag and the coffee cup down on the floor, took her keys out of her shoulder bag and unlocked the door. She bent down, retrieved the paper bag and the Dixie full of coffee, turning sideways to push open the door with her shoulder.

As the door opened the string wrapped around the inside knob took up the slack, tightening through the small eyebolt that had been screwed into the jamb, the taut string in turn jerking the pull ring out of the homemade spring-loaded striker that had been pushed into a half-pound charge of safecracker's explosive left on Jane's desk. The striker, jury-rigged from a piece of copper tubing and the firing pin of an old Remington automatic pistol, smacked down onto a .38-caliber percussion cap, which in turn set off the main charge.

Jane's brain barely had time to register what was going on before she was mercifully knocked unconscious. The massive concussion from the explosion blew the door back into her face, throwing her forcibly across the corridor and slamming her into the far wall, the Dixie of coffee and the contents of the ruptured can of Golden Bear cookies spattering Jane, the ceiling and the corridor wall with a sugary yellow-brown paste that acted like glue on the cloud of bloody, iridescent blue and green feathers that filled the air like a whirling blizzard of multicolored snow. Her skirt was torn to shreds, her Real-Silks actually vaporized off her legs and her eyebrows were singed off along with half an inch of her hair.

A few seconds later the remains of Ponce de Leon the parrot began to settle to the floor and the earsplitting thunder of the exploding bomb was replaced by the rising crackle of small flames. Beyond the demolished office there was the distant, tinkling echo of shattered window glass striking the Belgian-block pavement on the street half a dozen floors below.

Chapter 15

Thursday, June 1, 1939
Jasper, Alberta, Canada

As far as the king's assistant secretary, Tommy Lascelles, was concerned, the royal tour across Canada had been an unqualified success from almost every perspective, at least so far. In the end, rather than using a Cunard vessel, it had been decided that a Canadian liner, the *Empress of Australia,* would be used as the royal yacht on the outward journey while its sister ship, the *Empress of Britain,* would be used for the return trip. The day after the *Empress of Britain* arrived in Montreal carrying Barry, Holland, Herr Ridder and Sheila Connelly, it went back down the St. Lawrence to Halifax for a monthlong refit to royal standards.

The tour began in Portsmouth on May 6 as the king, queen and the royal retinue boarded the white-painted ship to begin their journey, their leave-taking witnessed from the royal family enclosure on shore by Queen Mary, the king's mother, the dukes of Kent and Gloucester and their duchesses, the Princess Royal and her husband and members of the royal household and local dignitaries and officers. Neither Princess Elizabeth nor Princess Margaret was accompanying their parents on the tour, although both children were there to see their parents off.

Although the original reason for using a commercial liner had supposedly been to save any fighting ships of the line from leaving England's defense, the cruisers H.M.S. *Repulse,* H.M.S. *Glasgow* and H.M.S. *Southampton* accompanied the *Empress* out into the Atlantic. After the third day at sea the *Repulse* turned back for England but the other two cruisers remained as a royal escort.

Shortly after reaching the mid-Atlantic the weather began to worsen, first with dense fog, then with roving ice fields and bergs, all of which the king recorded on the new Kodak movie camera he'd purchased for the tour. Eventually though, after eleven days rather than the scheduled six, the *Empress of Australia* reached Wolfe's Cove and Quebec City.

After a grueling day of sightseeing, presentations and processions, the royal entourage enjoyed a lavish banquet at the Chateau Frontenac Hotel and then made an early night of it, even though thousands of well-wishers kept a cheering vigil around the hotel until the early hours of the morning. After a simple private breakfast the king and queen then traveled by car to the royal train, which was waiting for them at Quebec Station.

The train consisted of twelve cars, five of which were coaches, all painted royal blue and silver. The two rear coaches each bore the royal crest and were designated Car 1 and Car 2. Both coaches were usually used by the Canadian governor general, Lord Tweedsmuir, better known to the reading public as the thriller writer John Buchan, whose novel *The Thirty-nine Steps* had been made into an exciting and popular film by Alfred Hitchcock several years before.

Car 1, at the very rear of the train, contained the two main bedrooms, the king's decorated in blue and white chintz, the queen's in blue-gray with dusty pink damask chair covers and curtains to match. There was also an oak-paneled office for the king, dressing rooms, a private bath for both royals, a sitting room with a radio and a small library. In Car 2 there were two bedrooms for senior staff, as well as offices, dressing rooms and bathrooms.

Farther forward there were living and working quarters for McKenzie King, the Canadian prime minister.

The remaining cars were given over to accommodation for roughly fifty people, including members of the royal entourage, the prime minister's staff, stenographers, railway workers, maids and valets, as well as the king and queen's personal bodyguards, a contingent of Royal Canadian Mounted Police and the commissioner of the entire RCMP, Stuart Wood. Two baggage cars were filled to overflowing with literally hundreds of wardrobe changes for Their Royal Highnesses.

Pulling the train was the enormous Canadian Pacific Locomotive 2850 equipped with a massive stainless-steel Hudson engine refitted for the occasion. The locomotive had been dressed in royal blue, silver and gold with imperial crowns attached to the running boards and the royal coat of arms emblazoned over the headlight. Although rated and tested at over eighty-five miles per hour on the tracks it would utilize, the train would rarely exceed thirty-five miles per hour on the outward leg of the trip from Quebec City to Vancouver, except during the night.

Running half an hour ahead of the royal train at all times was the very ordinary-looking pilot train that housed the radiomen, extra RCMP officers, post office, telegraph and telephone officials, a special darkroom for photographers and film crews and accommodations for more than sixty-five correspondents. Most of the newspapermen were also aware that the pilot train itself was a safety and security precaution for the royal party, which was pointed out in a story filed from the train to the *New York Times*:

> *If a bridge fails, if a freight train gets shunted onto the main line or somebody leaves a bomb on the track it will be 30 minutes before the train bearing King George VI and Queen Elizabeth across Canada this week comes upon the wreckage of its pilot train and the mangled bodies of the correspondents and photographers who are covering Their Majesties' trip.*

For the next two weeks, with the royal train as home and refuge, the royal couple rumbled across the country, avoiding controversy with the fascist-loving mayor of Montreal, exhausting their bodyguards and the RCMP protective contingent by breaking every security rule in Ottawa when the queen suddenly decided to mix with the crowd around the new war memorial they were dedicating, meeting the Dionne quintuplets and dedicating a new horse race, the King's Plate at Woodbine racetrack in Toronto.

In Winnipeg they endured a downpour, soaked to the skin in their open Packard limousines, and a daunting radio speech of eight hundred agonizingly enunciated words on the occasion of the king's grandmother, Queen Victoria's birthday. In Manitoba the king and queen received two elk heads and two black beaver pelts in lieu of the ancient rent demanded by King Charles II of the Hudson's Bay Company, and it was estimated by one of the newspapermen that the king had shaken three thousand hands and would shake ten thousand more before the tour was ended.

Somewhere along the way the king was made Great Chief Albino of the Blackfoot Duck Clan, and then they were into the mountains, eventually reaching the small resort town of Banff with its huge, chateau-style hotel, the Banff Springs, where they listened to a fifteen-hundred-voice children's choir sing "Springtime in the Rockies," walked alone briefly by the banks of the Bow River and then had buffalo steak for dinner. Several quiet comments were made that the king seemed to be exhausted.

After a day's rest in Banff they continued west to the Pacific, and by first light on Monday the 29 they were out of the mountains and into the Fraser Valley. By ten in the morning the royal train reached the Canadian Pacific Railway station by the docks in downtown Vancouver. There was a brief welcoming ceremony at the new and faintly totalitarian Art Deco City Hall, a visit to a veterans hospital and the University of British Columbia, and then a luncheon at another one of the CPR's chateau-style hotels, the Hotel Vancouver. Then they crossed the newly built Lions Gate Bridge, where they joined the CPR vessel *Princess Marguerite* docked at the foot of the bridge on the opposite shore. By the time the small ship, briefly transformed into the royal yacht, reached Victoria, the king had rested sufficiently to attend to his duties, enduring another round of receptions and gatherings, including yet another lavish luncheon in yet another lavish CPR hotel, this time the ivy-covered Empress.

Given the king's speech problem, even the briefest addresses given at these receptions tended to be nerve-racking, especially for Tommy Lascelles, who did most of the speech writing. When a newsreel crew suddenly appeared in the Empress dining room, bathing the head table with their hot lights, Lascelles was furious, terrified that the king would be seized by one of his attacks of nerves, especially since this particular speech was being broadcast by radio. In fact the king carried the speech off without a single moment's stuttering and was quite proud of his performance, demanding a recording of it for a souvenir, which was promptly made for him.

The following day they left Victoria, traveled back to Vancouver and drove by automobile to New Westminster, where they boarded the royal train again, this time traveling on Canadian National Railway tracks and drawn by a Canadian National locomotive. Traveling through the remainder of the day and all the next night they arrived for a day of rest in Jasper, Alberta, early on the morning of Thursday, June 1.

A general order for privacy was published, restricting the newsfilm operators and photographers from following the royals, who, by noon, were firmly ensconced in Outlook Cabin, an adjunct to the much larger Jasper Park Lodge. While the king ran off a few hundred more feet of home movie film, the queen picked flowers and the rest of the party from both the pilot train and the royal train generally took a day off, occupying themselves with fishing or swimming or tennis or golf.

Sitting in his drawing room compartment on the royal

train, Tommy Lascelles was far from relaxed, even with a majestic mountain view to be seen in every direction. In his mind the Canadian portion of the tour was almost without interest; the country was a loyal dominion, bound to England by hundreds of ties and treaties, not to mention, with the exception of Quebec, popular favor and patriotism.

Lascelles was well aware that England was on the verge of war, but throughout the tour so far it had been the ill-educated wee Scots girl from Glamis Castle who'd dominated everything, deciding which speeches "Dear Bertie" should give and where, stepping forward into the limelight, supposedly in an attempt to combat her husband's shyness and regularly making naïve and sometimes idiotic statements about the present political situation around the world.

There had already been a few reflections of this in the American press, including a pair of inflammatory articles in *Time* and *Newsweek* saying that the whole purpose of the visit was to draw first Roosevelt and then the people of the United States into what was clearly going to be an unpopular war with Germany. The king and queen would only be in the United States for five days, but that could easily be enough time for opinions to polarize, especially if there were mistakes made by one royal or the other.

For the past hour he'd been trying to put his thoughts down in his journal, but the entry was bleak, with the possible exception of the rumor going up and down the train that he was on the King's List and up for a knighthood. After all the years he'd put in to the Windsor family it seemed like a fair enough exchange.

There was a short, rapping knock on the door to his compartment.

"Enter."

Stuart Wood, the tall, powerful-looking commissioner of the RCMP ducked into the room. It was one of the few times Lascelles had seen the man out of his scarlet, heavily medaled uniform. The commissioner had what appeared to be a sheaf of yellow telegraph tear sheets in his hand. Lascelles gestured to the banquette on the other side of his portable table and Wood sat down, letting out a long breath. Lascelles offered his tin of Senior Service and both men lit up.

"A problem?" Lascelles asked, pointing to the pile of telegraph forms.

"Possibly. As you know, the FBI and a Scotland Yard representative have been keeping tabs on Sean Russell."

"The IRA chief?"

"Yes."

"Supposedly he's in the United States to raise money."

"There's more to it than that. There's information that would lead us to believe there is an assassination plot against Their Royal Highnesses, with Russell as the plot's chief conspirator."

Lascelles shrugged. "If there's evidence then surely he can be arrested."

"It's not that easy by the looks of it."

"How so?"

"The FBI has orders to keep Russell under surveillance only."

"Whose idea was that?"

"Believe it or not, the orders would appear to come from Mr. Roosevelt."

"I'm not surprised." Lascelles shrugged. "Next year is an election year for him. Russell may be a thug in England, but in Ireland and America he's a bit of a hero. Roosevelt doesn't want to alienate the Irish vote. He'd lose New York, Boston and Detroit, and they're key to his winning the presidency for another term."

"You seem to know a great deal about American politics."

"When I was secretary to the Canadian governor general I had to learn Canadian politics too." Lascelles offered up a baleful grin. "Once upon a time all you had to do was count the number of gunports on a navy's ships. Now it's all done with voting booths and expensive campaigns. The point is, it's unlikely Roosevelt will allow any action to be taken against Russell unless it's absolutely necessary." Lascelles made a small face. "Anyway, he does seem rather an unlikely assassin. He's far too much in the public eye."

"Even more so now," said Wood. "Someone named Dr. Dinsley gave a press conference in Los Angeles telling a gathering of reporters that he was a British Secret Service agent with an F10 designation who was there to announce that Sean Russell was in the United States for the express purpose of assassinating the king and queen."

Lascelles frowned. "There's no such Secret Service ranking as F10."

"No, there isn't, as the next day's editions of the newspapers were quick to point out. This Dinsley person was utterly ridiculed in the press and so was his idea of Russell as an assassin."

"What happened to Dinsley?"

"Disappeared without a trace, the damage done."

"Who organized the press conference?"

"A man named Lechner from the American Legion Los Angeles Public Relations Committee."

"And the FBI?"

"Russell no longer has any priority. I cabled Hoover asking for photographs and descriptions of Russell in the event that he tries to cross the border, but I've had no reply."

"Do we have any idea where Russell is now?"

"Not the faintest." The commissioner paused, stroking his mustache for a brief moment. "Does the king know anything of this?"

"No."

"Perhaps he should be told."

"I think not. For the moment it's better to let sleeping dogs lie."

The king sat in a large, partially upholstered Adirondack chair on the open porch of the small cabin smoking another of his never-ending supply of Players. There was a large tin ashtray built into one arm and a holder for a glass built into the other—which he thought was a fine idea—and which now held a double gin and tonic, even though it was only just past noon. In the meadow below the cabin Buffy and one of her ladies-in-waiting, the Lady Nunburnholme, were busy gathering up bouquets of wildflowers and laughing together.

On the king's lap was a copy of one of Grey Owl's books, given to him as a gift by some dimly remembered official at a whistle-stop in the north of Ontario. He smiled, remembering how the leathery old fraud, whose real name was Archie Belaney, had visited Buckingham Palace two years before and how he and Buffy had tiptoed into the nursery unannounced as the soft-spoken man with a feather in his braided hair instructed the two enthralled and wide-eyed little princesses in the secrets of woodcraft. For days afterward none of the Corgis was safe from Lilibet and Margaret Rose with their makeshift bows and arrows, war-whooping up and down the corridors and terrorizing the little creatures, insisting that they were wolverines whose pelts would fetch "big dollar" at the Hudson's Bay Post.

The king lit another cigarette from the hot end of the previous one—a habit Buffy found "perfectly disgusting"—and then took a small sip of his drink. He was supposed to be working on the breathing and relaxation exercises he'd been taught by Logue, his Harley Street speech therapist, but today he just couldn't be bothered. The techniques were tedious, most of them involving endless repetitions of convoluted, childish sentences like "Peter Piper picked a peck of pickled peppers" and learning how to breathe with his diaphragm rather than his throat. Since he wouldn't be giving any long-winded speeches for a little while yet, he'd decided to abandon the exercises, at least for today. Logue had been very insistent that he give up smoking as an aid to his breathing, if not his general health—not an untoward suggestion since his father, George V, had died of respiratory complications—but Bertie had refused, insisting that other than Logue's exercises, the only thing that calmed him enough to speak without too much of a stammer was the cigarettes. And the gin.

The king picked up the book in his lap and stared at the cover. On it an Indian—Archie, no doubt—was paddling a birchbark canoe along the margin of a lake, tall pines rising in the background, and high above in a cloudless sky a hawk or eagle circled. If you looked very closely and carefully you could see the shy, sleek head of a young deer looking out from between the trees. Archie, born into some ghastly slum in Birmingham or Manchester or wherever it was, transformed himself into an Indian, and a famous one at that, and was now a famous fraud with his secret made public.

Both of them frauds. The king for the fact that he knew nothing of kingship and wanted to know nothing, for his petrifying fear of women, even his own dear Buffy, his secret left-handedness, virtually beaten out of him by his father and his tutors as a child, but secretly indulged whenever he could manage it, like a child sucking at his thumb. He stared at the cover of the book and felt the first sting of angry tears. A street urchin like Archie Belaney could come and go as he pleased, glide over lakes and rivers, live off the land, *be* something for himself, entertain, do good works even if that good work was nothing more than putting a gleam of another world into his daughters' eyes. And yet a king, an emperor could do nothing, be nothing. Nothing at all. Talent, desire, want and need, all of it was nothing, the bloodline was all, a proper heir the object. When you came right down to it all the King of England could do well was hit a tennis ball and shoot grouse. Hardly a reason for existence, and less of a reason for being on what was beginning to feel like an endless tour of this gigantic country that only served to make him feel smaller and more useless than he usually did.

Buffy came up the steps in one of her blue dresses, her arms laden with flowers. Lady Nunburnholme was still in the meadow. "Have we been doing our exercises?" asked the queen.

The king managed a smile and a nod. He stubbed out his cigarette. "Just getting to them now."

Chapter 16

Friday, June 2, 1939
Chicago, Illinois

Thomas Barry stood at the window of the eleventh-story suite he had been sharing with Sheila Connelly for the previous three days and looked across Michigan Avenue to the immense pewter-tinted lake that ran out to the horizon. A few sailboats had ventured out beyond the harbor breakwater, but the gray waters, the spume-edged chop and a stiff onshore breeze didn't make the thought of a day on the lake very inviting. It was only three in the afternoon but the overcast skies and an intermittent gusting rain made it seem like dusk.

Barry turned away from the window and looked across to the couch where the Connelly woman was sitting reading *Time,* a cigarette in her other hand and a cup of tea on the coffee table in front of her. She was dressed in tweed slacks, a white blouse and a pair of soft leather slippers, all new since her arrival in the United States. Beyond her, on a broad shelf below a large mirror by the door, Barry could see the copy of *The Mask of Dimitrios* she'd been given by Ridder. The ammonia-induced writing had faded weeks ago, but would come up again without any adverse effect; the FBI lab had made sure of that before they left New York.

It had taken the first week with Sheila Connelly to get her to even talk to him and another week after that to grant him the most limited kind of trust. By the third week they'd come to understand each other well enough, but only for their own alienation from the rest of the world. Barry was a British policeman born and raised in Catholic Ireland, fated never to be fully accepted by either country, and Connelly was a woman who fought for a cause she'd long since lost her passion for and belief in. By standing apart from the world at large they stood together for themselves, at least in some small way, although even now, Barry still saw himself as her minder as much as her companion. Compounding that was the shoulder rig and holster for the Smith and Wesson .38 Special Sam Foxworth had insisted that he wear while he was with her.

"She's bait," the FBI man had reminded him before they left New York. "Try to remember that, Barry. She's not some heroic figure fighting for her beliefs no matter what she says or what you think. She's a piece of tail we're using to snare Sean Russell with."

The woman dropped her copy of *Time* onto the coffee table, took a sip from her teacup and puffed on her cigarette. "All very domestic, aren't we? The happily married couple on a visit to Chicago." Barry could feel himself blushing. They'd been living in close proximity for the better part of a month now and she was forever reminding him of it, just to see him squirm. She smiled up at him from the couch. "Isn't that how it's supposed to be? Except that you're pacing up and down like an expectant father and you've got that great bloody gun hanging off you. Russell sees that and he'll do a runner, you can be sure of that."

"You just do your part and I'll do mine."

"You don't have a part," she answered. "It's been made up, and that's going to make him suspicious enough."

"Not if you calm him down." He pushed his hands into his pockets to keep from fidgeting. "You remember the story we agreed on?"

"Your name's Tom Sullivan and you're from the New York City branch of Clan na Gael." Clan na Gael was a semi-secret society of American Irish who supported the IRA, Isolationism and the fascist America First organization.

"And what do I do for a living in New York?"

"You're a New York City policeman."

"Which should explain the revolver, especially since I've taken leave to act as your bodyguard while you're in America."

"I told you and your FBI friends from the beginning: that was never part of the plan, and for a man like Russell if it's not part of the plan, it's not to be trusted."

"That's a chance we'll have to take."

"I still don't see the point of this."

"You know exactly what the point is. The contact name you were carrying lives in Detroit, this Dr. Doyle, whoever he is. In a few days from now the royal train arrives in Windsor, Ontario, just across the Detroit River. If Russell is going to make an attempt either in Windsor or a few miles along the way at Niagara Falls, he has to be caught red-handed with bombs or bomb-making materials in his possession. According to Foxworth it's the only way to make any charges stick."

"You really think he'll be stupid enough to let us come along?"

"He won't know where to go at all until you give him the book, will he?"

"I still think it's all foolishness."

"Perhaps, but what do you have to lose?"

"My life, for one thing."

"That's what I'm here for."

"No. You're here to see that I keep my side of the bargain. I give you Sean Russell and I get a new life here in America." That was the bait Foxworth had dangled in front of her—a way out, a new life without the organization. Freedom.

"Seems a fair trade to me."

She lit another cigarette and sat back against the cushions, making Barry uneasily aware of the roundness of her breasts against the fabric of her blouse. "Fair trade? You really think your friends are going to give me a new life in the Holy Land here? Don't be daft, Thomas. Once they have what they want they'll let the organization take care of me, and you know they'll do just that. They'll find me eventually and when they do they'll put a bullet in my brain, just like they've done with all the other traitors who've gone before."

"A traitor being anyone who doesn't believe in the Republican ideal—is that it?"

"We're arguing like a pair of Irishmen." She smiled.

"That we are." He laughed, feeling the tension ease slightly in one direction and increase in another. He reached down to take a cigarette from the package on the coffee table and she sat forward, her hand wrapping around his wrist.

"You've not much experience with women, have you? Political or otherwise."

"Experience enough." He eased out of her grip and lit the cigarette. He walked back toward the window and stood there, looking out at the squalling lake again.

"You're a liar, Thomas Barry. What would the monks say about a sin like that?" He could feel her standing just behind him and to one side, the side away from the revolver in its holster.

"Really," he said. "And how would you know that?"

"A woman knows these things, Thomas." She put her hand up onto his shoulder, and even though she wore no scent he could smell her faintly—soap and talc and something else beneath it all.

She was right, of course. For him women were a mystery—the brothers in Cork had seen to that. Later, in the army, the only recourse for unmarried men were prostitutes, a direction also tainted by graphic tales of horror from Brother Emmett and his brown-robed, rope-belted colleagues.

Living in a succession of police station section houses for bachelor coppers eventually turned circumstance into habit, and no matter how often his married friends at the Yard like Morris Black or Bob Fabian tried to set him up, nothing ever seemed to really take. The few times anything had gone much farther than a good-night kiss had been fumbling, red-faced disasters.

The woman moved a little closer and now he could feel the firm curve of her breast pushing into his arm. He tried to move an inch or two away but she kept her hand on his shoulder, keeping him where he was.

"What are you afraid of?" she asked. "Some Jesuit bastard in a collar who caught you with your hands inside the blanket? Told you all women except your mother and the Holy Virgin were riddled with disease?" It was close enough to the truth to make him blush again. He managed to pull himself away.

"They were Dominicans and I was the bastard," he answered, keeping his eyes fixed on the great gray expanse of the lake. "They sent my mother to the laundries. I never knew who my father was."

"Jesus," she whispered. She came and stood in front of him, reached up and laid one hand flat against his chest. "I'm sorry."

"So am I." She left her hand where it was, against his heart, and came up on her toes to kiss him softly on the lips. Her mouth tasted of smoke and of sugar from the tea. "Why are you doing this?" he asked when she moved her mouth away.

"It's all a plot to convert you to the Cause." She smiled. "Or perhaps I'm seducing you to get my hands on that revolver of yours."

"No. Tell me."

She kissed him again, her lips softer now, one hand remaining on his heart, the other coming up to brush against his cheek. "I'm lonely," she said softly. "And so are you."

"That's reason enough?"

"For people like us, I think so, yes."

"We've a rendezvous with Sean Russell in the park."

"Not for more than an hour yet. We have time."

They lay in bed together when they were done, the Scotland Yard detective simultaneously embarrassed and excited by being nude in bed with a woman, bemused by it all, especially since even the nakedness of the locker room in a public swimming bath had always been cause for acute self-consciousness. At the orphanage in Cork, in the showers, Father Emmett had noted that he'd begun to develop hair on his body and had beaten him soundly for it on the off chance he'd begun seriously to abuse himself.

Sheila Connelly appeared not to be even slightly disconcerted by the situation, lying on one hip, sharing a cigarette with him, rolling away from time to time, flicking the ash into her tea saucer on the bedside table, and that was almost as exciting as the act itself, though not as dramatic in its consequences.

"You probably think I'm some kind of slut, don't you?"

"I don't know what to think."

She smiled. "At least you're honest about it."

"Most men aren't?"

"There haven't been that many."

"I didn't mean to suggest . . ."

She smiled again. "No offense taken. Not really."

"I'm sorry."

"Nothing to be sorry for. To answer your question, the men I've known have generally been more concerned with themselves than anything else, and when they have wanted my opinion it's generally been questions about the size of their organ and their virility."

"And what do you tell them?" Barry asked, taking the cigarette from her again and drawing on it.

"Always the same," she answered, and this time the smile broadened. "You're the biggest and the best I've ever had."

"I'll wager that I'm neither."

"And I'll wager that it doesn't make the slightest bit of difference to me or to most." She reached down and touched him gently. "It's not this thing of yours that matters so much as the man it's attached to, and most women would agree with me." She rolled away and butted the cigarette out. "I think it's time we were on our way," she said, rolling back toward him.

He reached out and touched her. "In a minute."

* * *

Shortly after four-thirty they reached the stepped crescent ellipse of the granite platform holding the brooding statue of Abraham Lincoln at the far end of the long, narrow park. To the left was Michigan Avenue with its row of hotels and lofty office buildings, to the right, through the trees, were the ornate formal gardens of Grant Park and then the lake. The rain had stopped, at least for the moment, but it still dripped from the trees around the statue and wetly glazed the tall bronze figure standing eternally, head down in front of a huge bronze chair.

Russell was there before them, sitting on the granite bench jutting from the surrounding wall of the podium, his trousers protected by a folded newspaper. Sheila Connelly had the Eric Ambler book in her right hand, while Thomas Barry walked on her left. Seeing the book in the woman's hand, Russell stood and stepped forward. There was no one else on the podium. Behind them the park was empty except for a small black dog in the distance, chasing a ball for its master.

To Barry he looked much rougher than the pictures he'd been shown by Holland back in London. In those photographs, taken surreptitiously from a car parked across the road from Kelly's Hotel on Great George Street in Dublin, Russell had been bright-faced and cheerful, clean-shaven, his hair brushed back and bow tie straight at his neck. Now, rising from the bench, he looked less like a leader of men than one hunted, which of course was the truth.

The hair was red, rising in a widow's peak off a broad forehead, the eyes small and black as sin. His white shirt was going gray and stood open at the collar. The coat he wore was a size too small, tight across the broad, powerful-looking chest and shoulders. He had the hands of a butcher.

He stopped on the top step of the podium as Connelly and Barry reached the first. "Enjoy the book then?" Russell asked. Even with those few words the accent was there, thick and heavy as the hands. Brought up in the

Phibsborough slums a short spit from Mountjoy Prison, poverty and anger his bread and butter.

"Not so much as the one before," replied Sheila Connelly. According to her, this was the proper answer to his question.

"Which would that be?" The countersign.

"Epitaph for a Spy."

"Right then, that's you, love. Who's the lag?"

"A friend. His name is Thomas Sullivan."

"I've heard no mention of any friend."

Barry interrupted. "Things have changed."

"I don't like it when things change."

"Neither do we."

"Which means?"

"Which means we've taken risks enough to have you here and we don't like press conferences with you as the center of attention."

Russell's face broke into a broad grin. "You've heard then."

"Who hasn't?" Barry answered. Which was true. The news report about Alfred Dinsley, British agent, filed by T. J. Devlin of the *Los Angeles Times* two weeks earlier had set people on their ear both in New York and in Washington. It had almost been enough to shut down the whole operation surrounding Russell, but Foxworth bucked the tide and convinced Hoover that it was worth pursuing.

"There was too much talk going about," said Russell, still smiling. "The press conference was our German friend's idea." Presumably the German in question was Fritz Weidemann, the playboy Nazi consul in San Francisco; the consulate was already being wiretapped by the Bureau and they'd picked up a conversation between Weidemann, Russell and a man named Hermann Schwinn, *Gauleiter,* or leader, of the West Coast American Nazi Bund.

"It was your idea?" Barry asked.

"His and mine," Russell said. He came down a step closer. "We knew our man would be exposed and the whole thing would be put down as a hoax. Like letting air out of a tire. Gets me off the hook, so to speak." Russell's right hand slipped into the pocket of his overcoat and stayed there. He smiled in Barry's direction but there was no mirth in his expression. "Now then, 'friend,' it's time you told me just who you are."

"I'm an agent of your benefactors."

"Who would be?"

"The Clan, as you well know."

"It's not who I am, Mr. Sullivan. It's who you might be."

"I told you, a friend. I was sent along with Miss Connelly to see her safely home, and you as well if needs be. Your face is on bulletin boards in half the precinct houses in the country."

"And how would you be knowing that?" Russell said, his right hand still in his pocket.

"Because I work in one."

"You're a copper?"

"A cop," Barry said, using the word carefully. "New York City Police."

"Now isn't that grand? A copper to tend to the needs of a wanted fugitive such as myself. Will wonders never cease." Russell paused and Barry saw the hand clenching in his pocket. "That would go a long way toward explaining that gun you're wearing under yon jacket."

"It would. And what good would I be to you if I didn't have such a thing on my person?"

"True enough." Russell paused again, the muscles in his thick jaw working, his eyes skipping around the park, looking for anything out of place. "With that shite culchie accent of yours you're not long off the boat."

"Two years this July," Barry answered.

"Left from Cork City then, did you?"

"Cobh, yes," Barry answered, putting a Gaelic twist on the name to make it sound more like Cove.

"Friends on the force to get you a job so quickly."

"Friends of yours as well," Barry answered.

"Their names then."

"You'll not get them from me."

"Good lad," Russell said, coming down a third step,

standing directly over Barry now. "Never give a name other than your own, no matter who it is you're talking to." The hand came out of his pocket and landed like a stone on Barry's shoulder. "Would you be having some identification about, Mr. Sullivan? Something I can see with my own eyes."

Barry took out his wallet and handed Russell a New York driver's license and a New York City police identification card in the name of Thomas Sullivan. There really was such a man on the New York police force, his identification and administrative leave arranged for by Lewis Valentine himself, the New York police commissioner.

The IRA chief of staff examined the documents carefully, then nodded. "Seems right enough." He handed the cards back and Barry replaced them in the wallet. "What I don't understand is why the Clan didn't contact me directly. They know where I am."

"Your New York contact's telephone line is being tapped and he's been under surveillance since you arrived on the *Stavangerfjord*," Barry answered, using the name of the ship to further establish his bona fides.

"Fuck me for an idjit," Russell breathed, his accent rising. "They're like fucking rats on fucking cheese." He shook his head. "We were sure the press conference would put them off."

"It did," said Barry. "But not enough." He tried to keep his face impassive. If Russell knew just how little attention was being given to him by the American authorities he'd be ecstatic. The only thing keeping any interest in him alive was Foxworth's network of personal friendships within the Bureau's far-flung offices, and even that had its limitations. If word got out to Russell's friends in the American Congress and Senate there'd be hell to pay. The Catholic vote was a large one and not to be provoked at almost any cost.

The big Irishman turned to Sheila Connelly, studying her carefully. "You don't have much to say about all this."

"It's not my place then, is it?" She lifted her shoulders. "I'm just the messenger."

"Have you any idea what the message is?"

"No," she answered. "Nor do I want to know."

"Good," he said, "since it's none of your business." He nodded toward Barry. "You and your policeman getting a leg over, are you?"

"That's none of *your* business."

Russell let out a booming laugh and a half dozen crows jerked nervously up out of the trees behind Lincoln. "True enough, dear. Just wanted to know if you were taken or if you'd give a man such as myself a tumble."

Barry went up a step, putting himself level with Russell and shaking off Sheila Connelly's warning hand on his arm. "I think you should apologize to Miss Connelly for your rudeness."

Russell's big hand went back into his pocket. "Your chivalry is noted, Officer Sullivan, but believe me, your ladyfriend knows her place within my organization. It's just as she said. She's nothing more than a messenger, and she'll follow orders from a superior no matter what those orders are. You understand?" He moved forward, close enough that Barry could smell whiskey on his sour breath. "I don't give a shit if you're fucking her ten times a day, man. She's under my authority, not yours."

Barry stared at him for a long moment, then turned away, went back down a step and took Sheila Connelly's arm. "Come on. We're leaving the bastard on his own."

She shook him off. "No," she said flatly. "He's right. I'd whore for him if he ordered me to, because that's the way of it." She stared up at Russell. "But I'd not agree to enjoy it."

"And I'd not expect it." Russell laughed. He lumbered down the steps and took his empty hand out of the coat pocket. He poked a thick index finger into Barry's chest. "You take life too seriously, Officer Sullivan. You should try and enjoy it, especially in the company of a woman as pretty as your Miss Connelly here."

"I thought we had serious business," Barry responded.

"We do," Russell said, almost absently, "that's true."

"Then shouldn't we be getting on with it?" Above everything else Barry was surprised at Russell's lack of tension. If their information was correct Russell was going to be making an assassination attempt against the king and queen within the next few days, and here he was with whiskey on his breath. "There can't be much time left."

Russell cocked a bushy eyebrow. "Less time than I'd hoped for, Officer Sullivan, but more than I need."

Chapter 17

Saturday, June 3, 1939
New York City

Beyond the simple acquisition of the target John Bone knew that the two most important things involved in the successful completion of an assignment were the choice of the weapon and the hunter's lie. With time and experience he'd come to the conclusion that the more important of the two was the lie. Weapons could be abandoned at the last minute and replaced, but without the correct positioning the job was easily put at risk. On more than one occasion he'd found his own life in jeopardy because he'd poorly judged his escape route.

In the present situation there was a great deal of opportunity for an assassin willing to give up his own life, but after a careful examination of both the security measures being undertaken to protect the royal couple and the nature of their itinerary, Bone eventually narrowed his choice to six possible sites: a location somewhere in the upper structure of Washington, D.C.'s, Union Station; St. John's Church or the Hay Adams Hotel, taking his shot when Their Royal Highnesses either entered or exited the White House; a small office building next to the South African Embassy and directly across Massachusetts Avenue from the British Embassy, where the royal couple would be attending a reception; from the opposite shore as the presidential yacht *Potomac* arrived at Mount Vernon for a tour; from the grounds of the

George Washington estate itself after the yacht arrived; and finally, a multitude of possibilities for a concealed lie on the grounds of the New York World's Fair in Flushing Meadow Park. A seventh possibility was the grounds of Roosevelt's estate on the Hudson, where the royal couple would be spending the last two days of their tour. Bone preferred urban opportunities since they offered so many escape routes, but it was a simple enough thing to purchase maps of the area, which he did for the sake of prudence.

Twice since their arrival, Bone had traveled to cities about to be visited by the king and queen to observe the general security precautions being taken. In Ottawa, Canada's capital city, the couple, having arrived two days previously, were to dedicate a new memorial to the dead of the Great War. The tall, archlike monument sat in the center of the city's version of a Grand Plaza, Confederation Square.

On one side was the post office and other attendant buildings, on another side the heavy, columned, neoclassical bulk of the Union Railway Station, and directly across from it the Chateau Laurier Hotel, a spired, copper-roofed monstrosity looking as though it had been built by some overweight Bavarian prince with a passion for fairy tales. Occupying one of the turret rooms he'd reserved almost two weeks previously, Bone used a recently purchased Leica, a pair of binoculars and his notebook to record prearrival activities in the open square.

On the early morning of the royals' arrival at the memorial, security appeared to be minimal—nothing more than the erection of a few wooden barricades and the appearance of a few uniformed local policemen. Then, an hour or so after daylight broke, a large busload of red-uniformed RCMP officers appeared and took up an assortment of positions around the square, followed in turn by six or seven unmarked radio cars, identifiable by their large curving antennae, and fifteen or twenty plainclothesmen who began to mingle with the growing crowds behind the barricades. Using his binoculars he saw that more plainclothesmen were appearing on the rooftops of the post office and the buildings beside it, as well as on the roof of the railway station. Bone had no doubt that there were an equal number of men on the roof of his own hotel and, following the mimeographed instruction sheet slipped under his door by the hotel management, he was keeping his small window closed as per the order given by the chief of the Ottawa Police Department and the commissioner of the Royal Canadian Mounted Police.

As Bone well knew, the truth of it was that anyone intent on killing the king and queen would have no difficulty doing so, despite their bulletproof limousines, the concentration of policemen around them and all the other security measures. In 1901 an anarchist with a four-dollar Iver Johnson revolver purchased through the Sears-Roebuck catalogue assassinated United States president McKinley, and the same thing could easily happen here. For his own part, a glass cutter to take out a four-inch square of his window and an angled bench rest in the shadows could do the trick with none the wiser, but once again it came down to escaping after the fact.

By nine that morning the crowds around the war memorial were dense, a large number of them veterans in their tilted berets. The rooftops and balconies all around the square were filled, and behind the closed windows of the buildings pale faces were pressed close to the glass to catch a glimpse of the royal pair. At eleven, to the fanfare of trumpets, the royal limousine appeared, the value of its bulletproofing nullified by the fact that the top was down. Behind them came the cars bearing the prime minister, the governor general and the rest of the royal entourage.

There was a song or two played by the attending Scots pipe band, a brief service followed by an even briefer speech from the king and then the laying of a wreath. In terms of direct security Bone counted eleven uniformed bodyguards, eight men in plainclothes who were probably from Scotland Yard's Special Branch, and two very tall men who were never more than two or three yards from their royal charges.

The service and the speech concluded, the royals moved along a line of selected veterans, pausing to exchange a few words, then moving on. Then, in a moment of inspired madness, the queen stepped off the long red carpet leading to their waiting car and moved into the crowds of veterans around the memorial. Almost instantly both the king and queen were lost to view, although Bone could occasionally see the queen's broad white hat bobbing here and there among the maroon berets worn by the aging soldiers.

The security detail, uniformed and otherwise, were thrown into chaos. Bone watched as they struggled to elbow aside the crowd in an effort to move forward. Nothing seemed to work and for the better part of half an hour both the king and queen mingled with the enclosing crowd, shaking hands, pausing for a word or a wave until finally the queen's personal bodyguard and several of the plainclothes Special Branch men managed to bundle the royal couple and their entourage into the cars.

That evening Bone left the Chateau Laurier, took a taxicab south of the city to Ottawa Airport, then boarded a Trans Canada Airlines flight to Toronto, arriving just after midnight. Once again, following the detailed itinerary he'd been given, he waited in a south-facing room at the Royal York Hotel and watched as the king, essentially without protection, inspected the Queen's Own Rifles, and with his powder-blue, ever-beaming wife did another walkabout in the crowd around Union Station just prior to reboarding the royal train and setting out for the West.

Bone returned to New York the following day and continued to keep track of the tour through the daily news reports filed by the pilot train reporters. From their descriptions it appeared that the informality he'd seen around the war memorial in Ottawa had now become a habit. This new familiarity with the public could potentially be of use, but Bone knew that it was also almost certainly making their security people more nervous, and thus more vigilant than ever.

Bone spent the next ten days going through his options, eliminating them one by one. Architecturally, the Washington, D.C., railway station offered dozens of hidden areas high above the concourse where a man could easily secrete himself with a weapon, but the shot would inevitably be very high angled, which meant a very small target and almost no time at all to take the shot.

It would also be impossible to escape after the deed was done. According to Bone's information there would be fourteen thousand soldiers guarding the station and the parade route, twice that many Washington, D.C., policemen and Virginia State Troopers, not to mention several thousand Secret Service agents brought in from all over the country, the presidential detail, the White House police and several hundred State Department investigators. The same security difficulties were presented by the British Embassy; not only would a shot be difficult, but escape would be impossible.

Initially the available lie from the Hay-Adams Hotel seemed promising. The range was slightly less than three hundred yards and immediate escape, while not simple, was at least possible, although he knew there would be very little time between the moment he took the shot and the time any egress from the city was blocked by the massive security forces on hand. He did come up with a possible escape plan that would take him down to the river and a hidden boat, but in the end he abandoned the hotel. The terrain of the White House grounds was so heavily treed it afforded him only the briefest moment for the attempt, catching the president and the royal couple in the few seconds during which they stepped down from their vehicles, or climbed into them.

Bone, unlike the majority of the American public, had been informed of the extent of President Roosevelt's physical infirmity and knew that time would be taken up getting him into his wheelchair and up the temporary ramps installed under the White House portico, but even so it was unlikely that he would have more than a ten- or fifteen-second window of opportunity when his view wasn't blocked by trees. Beyond that, the Hay-Adams, the Willard and the Mayflower—any hotel within reasonable range of the White House—would be watched carefully, perhaps constantly during the visit.

The king, queen and President Roosevelt were scheduled to use the presidential yacht *Potomac* to travel down to Mount Vernon to visit George Washington's estate, but on close inspection Bone quickly abandoned it. The estate itself was too isolated to offer an escape route, and taking a shot from the shore to the yacht would be extremely difficult, the distance from the far shore to the wharf at the foot of the Mount Vernon estate more than a thousand yards with virtually no cover on Bone's side of the Potomac. To further complicate matters it was being rumored that the highways on both sides of the river would be closed on the day of the Mount Vernon trip to avoid congestion and accidents caused by rubbernecking sightseers. In the end Bone was left with what he knew almost from the beginning was the most logical place to make his attempt—the grounds of the New York World's Fair.

The New York World's Fair 1939 Incorporated was formed in October 1935 by a group of one hundred wealthy New York businessmen led by Grover A. Whalen, a man of independent means who had been a public official in New York for decades, filling roles as diverse as being an acting New York police commissioner to heading FDR's New Recovery Administration.

Whalen, his business friends and Mayor La Guardia were all acutely aware of Chicago's great success with their Century of Progress Exposition of 1933–1934 and wanted to reproduce the same kind of relative prosperity and prestige. It was also a way to rid the city of a 1,216.5-acre combination bog and garbage dump delicately named Flushing Meadows but popularly known as the Corona Dumps.

In the distant past Flushing Meadows had actually been a salt marsh fed by a tidal river leading to Flushing Bay. Once home to a peaceful agrarian band of Indians known as the Matinecocks, progress and expansion of the city saw the stagnation of the river and the extinction of the Matinecocks. With rail lines leading farther and farther out from the city, Flushing Meadows, with its Mount Corona, named for the hundred-foot-high pile of ashes, quickly became a grotesque wasteland, F. Scott Fitzgerald's "Valley of Ash."

Whalen, sometimes allied with and sometimes at odds with Robert Moses, La Guardia's power-hungry parks commissioner, quickly moved to level the mountain, fill in the swamps with six million cubic yards of ashes, and spread hundreds of thousands of cubic yards of top soil over everything.

On the surface the site looked attractive enough, especially after the Flushing River was rerouted and several artificial lagoons and lakes controlled by a massive dam and tide gate were created, but one of the city architects working on the fair was heard to comment that it was a good thing the buildings only had to last for two years, because they certainly wouldn't remain standing for a third. Regardless of doom-filled predictions, design and construction continued at a breakneck pace, including construction of the nine-million-pound Perisphere, a two-hundred-foot-diameter aluminum ball resting on eight steel columns rammed into the subsoil atop six hundred timber piles, and its seven-hundred-foot-tall triangular companion, the Trylon, both of which were created as both the futuristic centerpiece and gigantic visual trademark of the fair.

Three years and 170 million dollars later the New York World's Fair opened. In all, Grover Whalen had convinced sixty countries, thirty-eight states, Puerto Rico, the League of Nations, the federal government of the United States and every major corporation in the nation to build exhibits and pavilions on what had once been an evil-smelling swatch of swampland and which would now become a killing ground for a king.

Dressed in a suit and tie like every other adult male around him and with a camera on a strap around his neck, Bone's first impression after paying his seventy-five cents at the western entrance to the fair had been a surprising and overwhelming sense of *gaudiness* on a stupefying scale. From what he could see, the design theme had consisted of three words: *Simple, Big* and *Colorful.* Entering the fair was like stepping into a child's nursery, the floor covered with a scattering of brightly colored building blocks in every shape and size—an Art Deco–Bauhaus symphony.

Walking down a broad, overscaled concrete ramp with several hundred other visitors he was confronted by an enormous empty plaza with an iridescent gushing fountain at its center. On the left was the huge gold-toned curvilinear Home Building Center, visibly shaped like a massive, jutting, erect male organ, even from the ramp's low vantage point.

To the right, rising like a pair of hundred-foot-tall pale green bobby pins were the double arches of the Hall of Special Events, while directly ahead, bright gold and spread like a wedge-shaped fan, was the Home Furnishings Building.

Looking down at what he later discovered was Rainbow Avenue, it seemed that each of the cheek-by-jowl pavilions had been painted a different color, from lurid green to blood red, from a childish sea blue to banana yellow and back again in every possible shade, accent and combination.

Here and there along the broad processional avenues and asphalt plazas there were wedges and rectangles of grass and trees, but much of the site not covered by large, colorful buildings was taken up by architecturally created vistas designed to sweep the visitors' eyes in one direction or the other, but almost inevitably drawing their view to the monumental, dead white shapes of the Trylon and Perisphere located in the center of the fair. Taken all together it was comparable to looking at the oversized models of a set design for a film like *Things to Come,* which Bone had seen in London several years before.

Ignoring the two giant structures, he purchased an official guide book for twenty-five cents from a young, blue-uniformed girl in a pith helmet. Following the map printed inside, he went down Rainbow Avenue past the redwood plank facade of the Contemporary Arts Building, turned left between the Electrified Farm and the deeply louvered slab of the Brazilian pavilion, then crossed a low, arched bridge over the artificial river that burbled along a hundred yards or so to the spurting fountains of the Lagoon of Nations.

Just to the right on the far side of the bridge was the British pavilion, a modern though ordinary building that by choice or by chance was done in pale pink concrete of almost the exact same hue as Queen Elizabeth's favorite Betty Prior roses.

Bone lifted the Leica on its strap and began playing the visiting tourist, taking snapshots. The royal couple were scheduled to spend a little more than four hours at the fair, but this was the one place Bone could be certain they'd come. Trying not to appear overly serious about it he quickly took a dozen exposures, raking from left to right, beginning with the gold-roofed cupola of the long horticultural exhibit surrounding Gardens on Parade on three sides, then across the lawn that stood in front of the British pavilion's blushing pink wall—three gold Lions Rampant bolted to it in a staggered row—and finally the bridge at the second-story level connecting the British pavilion to the Australia and New Zealand building next door.

Turning around, Bone took another twelve shots facing away from the pavilion, looking across the sixty-foot-wide river to the opposite shore. Left to right were the dozen or more fountains of the Lagoon of Nations, the glass-walled bulk of the French pavilion with its elegant tiered restaurant overlooking the water, the Brazilian pavilion, the Electrified Farm again, and past that the compound of full-sized houses that marked the Town of Tomorrow.

Pictures taken, Bone moved on, skirting the lagoon then turning north down the long rectangle of parkland leading to the austere U.S. Government Building at the far end. Squatting like a pale yellow twin-towered Egyptian temple, it closed off the long mall that began almost a mile away at the Trylon and Perisphere. He bought a hot dog and a Coca-Cola from a pushcart vendor, then found a bench in the sparse shade offered by a young tree, where he sat down to eat his lunch and look over the guide book.

According to the map, as he'd already noted, the fair was divided into a dozen major zones, those fanning out from the theme center of the Trylon and Perisphere, color coded in shades of yellow, red and blue. The fair was effectively bisected north to south by Constitution Mall, which ran from the theme center to the so-called Court of Peace where he was now sitting. Most but not all of the foreign pavilions were located on the north side of the concrete-lined re-creation of the Flushing River.

To the west was the Administration Zone, the Communications Zone and the gates for the jointly operated IRT/BMT subway line and the Long Island Railroad station where he'd entered the fair. Due south of the Perisphere were the two main gates at Corona Avenue, and to the east, on the far side of World's Fair Boulevard, was the Amusement Area, not officially a zone but clearly an integral part of the fair with its own gate and IND subway station. There was an artificial lake as well as freak shows, carny games and girlie shows, not to mention Billy Rose's Aquacade starring Johnny Weissmuller, who played Tarzan in the movies, and a nightly fireworks display.

Bone counted eight official entrances into the fair and three or four unofficial exits, like the pathway leading around the U.S. Government Building to the semipermanent Boy Scout Camp on the open field behind it. The whole northeastern flank of the fair faced the Flushing neighborhoods along Lawrence and Rodman Streets, and Bone had no doubt that an hour or two spent watching the tall chain-link fences would provide him with everything he needed to know about slipping onto the grounds without paying the twenty-five-cent children's admission price.

Bone swallowed the last bite of his hot dog, wiped his lips with a paper napkin and drank his Coca-Cola slowly through a straw, remaining on the bench, watching the passing parade of visitors to the fair as it moved steadily back and forth around him. The extra-wide asphalt walkways and the complete lack of automobiles, with the exception of a few maintenance vehicles, meant that there was no sense of overcrowding, but a sample count for a minute or two proved the fact that at any given time the fair was playing host to an enormous number of people. This backed up a recent article he'd read in *Time* stating that the fair was admitting between seventy-five and a hundred thousand people each day.

According to Bone's information the fair would not close while the king and queen were in attendance. Presumably there would be more than the usual number of people there to see them. Based on previous experience, particularly the chaos resulting from the affair in Marseilles five years before, Bone knew that he had no better ally to ensure his escape than a panicked crowd after the first shots were fired.

He'd seen the pandemonium brought on by the queen's unscheduled contact with the veterans around the war memorial in Ottawa, where he'd estimated the throng in Confederation Square at no more than three or four thousand. Here, like the fair itself, the scale of the effect would be astronomical by comparison. A crush of a hundred thousand frightened fairgoers to melt into, a dozen or more exits to choose from, and beyond that the anonymous safety of a city of eight million people.

Bone returned his empty bottle to the pushcart vendor, dropped his crumpled napkin into a nearby wastebasket and moved on again. For the rest of the day he wandered over the grounds, taking three more rolls of photographs to document the approaches to the various exit points and the exits themselves.

He left the fair at dusk, and just before heading across the overpass leading to the IRT he heard the strong, mournful wail of a hunting horn nearby, loud enough to rise above the noises of the crowd and the constant rushing patter of the fountains. It was strange enough to touch what was left of the Irish in him, raising the short hairs on his neck. The eerie sound ended abruptly, breaking on an unblown note. Because he'd read the guide book Bone knew what he was hearing. It was the *Hejnal,* blown from the top of the Polish pavilion's golden tower each night, commemorating the death of a Cracow watchman who, centuries before, had saved the city from invaders with his call, the unfinished warning ending on a broken, jarring note as the watchman fell dead, an arrow in his throat.

In the ten days between May 25 and June 3, John Bone paid four more visits to the New York World's Fair. On the second occasion it was to gather more detailed information, on the third it was to refine his plan, and on the fourth it was to check his original findings. He knew that the fifth and final visit was an indulgence, but he was a careful man and more than anything else he believed in his own continued existence. Even so, returning to the Gramercy Park Hotel after his final trip to the fair he knew without a doubt that he'd found the perfect lie and that his escape was assured as well as it could be. All that he needed now was the proper weapon. He had just the thing in mind. To celebrate the completion of his research he went into the Gramercy bar, located just to the left of the brass revolving doors, where he had a double shot of Jameson Irish Whiskey, neat, in a water glass. Finishing the drink he made enquiries to the bartender about the availability of women in the neighborhood. Bone placed two ten-dollar bills on the oak surface in front of him and the bartender said he would take care of it, asking for nothing more than his room number and the required time the woman should be made available.

Chapter 18

Sunday, June 4, 1939
New York City

"I've been in this goddamn room for a month now. I'm getting sick of it."

"A month at the Plaza," said Dan Hennessy, perched at the end of the bed. "Most of us wouldn't be complaining."

Jane Todd shifted against the pillows behind her, trying to get comfortable. The plaster cast that ran from her left wrist up to her shoulder was itching terribly, the fresh scar under her right eye was burning and she still had pain in the badly fractured baby finger of her right hand. The worst of it was the god-awful pale pink quilted bedjacket Hennessy had picked up for her. After a month her other, less serious wounds had healed, most of them cuts and burns caused by the explosion.

"This isn't the Plaza," Jane grumbled. "It's a prison cell." Pelay the bellman had put Jane in one of the almost unrentable turret rooms in what amounted to the attic above the eighteenth floor. It was small, dusty, only a few yards from the groaning cable reels of the elevator machinery, and from all appearances the plumbing hadn't been upgraded since the venerable hotel's construction more than thirty years before.

Hennessy lit a cigarette, adding to the haze. "Quit carping," he said. "It's better than being dead."

Jane reached out with her bandaged right hand and

tapped the folded newspaper on the bedside table. "According to Buschy's creative little obit in the *News* that's exactly what I am."

"Busch thought it was a good idea and so did I." Hennessy shrugged. "You know what they say about discretion, Jane." He paused, tapping his cigarette into the big crystal ashtray in his lap. "Someone tried to kill you. Better they think they succeeded." The detective shook his head. "Just be glad you got friends in all sorts of low places."

Somehow Jane had managed to crawl halfway to the elevator after the explosion. Even so she came very close to being consumed by the fire that raged outward into the hallway from her office. The firemen called an ambulance and had Jane transported to the nearest hospital, which happened to be Bellevue, a stroke of luck since it was easy to get lost in the massive twelve-square-block facility even at the best of times.

Hennessy's card was in the burned remains of the shoulder bag she'd managed to hang on to and he was the first person notified following Jane's admission. After finding out from the firemen exactly what had happened at Jane's office, Hennessy cautioned the attending physician about discussing Jane's case with anyone, then had her file sent down to a lady friend of his in the medical examiner's office in the Pathology Building where, at Hennessy's request, she promptly lost it. With twenty thousand bodies a year passing through the morgue, almost half of which were never claimed, Hennessy knew that the chance of anyone finding out that Jane wasn't actually dead was slim.

With the help of another friend, this one in the mortuary trade, Jane was taken to the rear of the Plaza in a funeral home meat wagon. With Pelay's help, as well as that of Bill Hartery, the Plaza house dick, she was whisked up one of the service elevators to the turret room with none the wiser. Hennessy then quietly put out the word and the small news stories that appeared documenting the explosion and fire all said that Jane had died as a result of the incident, the fault presumably stemming from her darkroom chemicals.

"Still no word about the bomb?" Jane asked.

"No," Hennessy answered. "Except for the fact that it *was* a bomb, and a fairly sophisticated one." The policeman frowned. "You know I can't nag the arson boys too much about this thing, Jane. They know you and I are friends but I don't want to get anyone suspicious by asking too many questions. I'm in Safe and Loft now, remember, not the murder squad."

Jane grinned. "Not interested in avenging my untimely death?"

"I'm just being careful," Hennessy responded. "Someone did try to kill you, remember? The doc is coming in tomorrow morning to take off your cast and look at your finger. All of your poker pals chipped in, me included, and after the doctor gives you a clean bill we're sending you on vacation. Far, far away, like L.A. maybe. I already talked to Birdwell and he's going to set you up with one of his friends out there."

"You trying to get rid of me?" She grinned. "Does this mean you don't want to get into my pants anymore?"

"Quit being a smart-ass broad. I'm trying to keep you alive."

"I want to find out who wants to see me dead."

"For Christ's sake, Jane! What does it matter?" He stubbed out his cigarette, leaned forward and banged the ashtray on the bedside table. "They blew up your whole fucking office! There's nothing left. No cameras, no pictures, and from what I can tell, no insurance either."

"They murdered Ponce de Leon."

"He was a parrot."

"Still, he was my parrot."

"This isn't a joke, pal."

"Light me a cigarette."

"The doctor said you shouldn't smoke for a while yet."

"To hell with the doctor." Hennessy did as he was asked, leaning forward again to poke the Lucky between Jane's bandaged fingers. The photographer dropped back against her pillows, took a deep drag and closed her eyes, resting for a few moments, gathering her thoughts. "Look," she said finally. "You put your finger on it. I'm tapped. I don't even have the tools of the trade anymore and there's a good chance these people would try again if they knew I was still alive and kicking. Until I figure this thing out, until I find out who tried to kill me, I might just as well be dead just like the obituary says."

She paused and drew on the cigarette again, wincing as the tip of her plaster-covered baby finger grazed her cheek. "They murdered Howie for no good reason except expediency, they put the squeeze on your own boss and God only knows who else and they tried to blow me to bits because they figured I was getting too close to whatever it is they're trying to hide. You really think sending me to L.A. is going to do any good? Sooner or later word would get out that I was who I was and they'd plant another bomb, and the chances are good they'd pull it off the second time." She shook her head "Besides, I'm not leaving Annie again. Bad enough I haven't been to see her all this time."

"I can take care of Annie."

"She's my sister, Dan, and I told you I'm not going to leave her again."

"You won't do her any good dead."

"I barely do her any good alive," Jane answered. "I pay a little extra on the side so the nurses will keep her cleaned up and her hair brushed, but that's not what I mean and you know it."

"Yeah, I guess I do."

"So if I'm not going to L.A., I'd better find out who's put the button on me. You said so yourself. It's big. A story like that could make me forever in this town, not to mention the fact that I'm a little pissed about the whole thing."

There was a long pause. Finally Hennessy spoke. "I think they're watching me."

"What are you talking about?"

"Ever since the bombing."

"*They* as in other cops, or *they* as in the people who tried to snuff me?"

"Maybe both. It's nothing I can really draw a bead on, just a funny feeling. Cars in front of my building. Seeing a stranger on the street I'm sure I've seen before."

"They ever follow you here?"

"Once or twice. When I get the feeling I just go into the Oak Bar for a shot or I spend five minutes gabbing with Pelay."

"He know what's going on?"

"Not everything, but enough."

"Hartery?"

"Yeah, but just him, not his people." Hartery had a score of junior dicks under him, all but a few of whom were probably bribable.

"There was a movie that came out, eight, nine years ago. Scared me half to death. An old lady who had a bell hooked up to her crypt. I swear, I almost peed my pants."

"I remember that." Hennessy nodded. "Creepy as hell. *Murder by the Clock,* I think it was called."

"That's the one, and that's how I feel right now. Maybe I'm not dead but it feels like I've been buried alive." She took a final puff on the cigarette then held out her hand so Hennessy could pull it out from between her fingers before the bandage started smoldering. She twisted against the pillows again, still trying to find a position that was even remotely comfortable.

Hennessy put out the Lucky. "Okay, you won't run away like anybody with a brain in her head, so what is it you want to do?"

"Like I said, find out who's behind all this."

"Forget it. I told you that a couple of hours before you got blown out of your shoes. Nothing's changed, pal o' mine. It's a stone wall."

"Maybe," said Jane. "But I've had quite a bit of time to think about it all."

"You've come to some kind of brilliant conclusion?"

Jane shrugged.

"Spill."

"Try this on and see if it fits." Jane paused, looking briefly up at the low, cracked plaster of the ceiling above her head. "The only conclusion I came to is this—someone wanted Howie Raines dead, either for what he knew or what he heard or what he saw."

"This is news?"

"No. The news part is the fact that they *knew* they were going to kill him before he even left New York for Havana. He was a dead man before he got onto that plane, except he was the only one who didn't know it. It was all part of the plan, right from the start."

"How do you figure that?"

"The claim check from the queer baths at the Ariston and the bar receipt from Gloria's. Evidence on him that was supposed to convince us he was a flit."

"I still don't see it."

"They didn't pump a few pills into him and then try to cover with the claim check and the receipt. There wasn't enough time between when he got back from Cuba and when this Frankie Satin kid saw the body being dumped. They knew ahead of time they were going to need the stuff to plant on him. They were ready and waiting—car, the three torpedoes and the place to drop the body."

"So what do you think this means?"

"I think it means he was sent down to Havana by the same people who dimmed his headlights. He ran some kind of errand, reported back, and after they found out what they needed to know they snuffed him to make sure, that was the end of the trail."

"What kind of an errand?"

"He was a lawyer, a small-time one. What kind of errands does a small-time, expendable lawyer run?"

"He do de Stepin Fetchit," Hennessy answered, doing a bad imitation of the well-known black actor.

"Okay, what's in Havana for a guy like that?"

"Havana's the Mob. I can't think of anything else." He lifted his shoulders. "Costello and Lansky." Two years before, at the request of Fulgencio Batista, Cuba's young dictator, the two New York gangsters had been asked to come south and run the military-controlled gambling operations in Havana with the proviso that they be allowed to set up their own casinos and bookie operations. Within twelve months Meyer Lansky and Frank Costello had millions of dollars flowing into both Batista's coffers and their own.

"But it's not the Mob, we already figured that," said Jane. "Too many outsiders, like this thing with Kennedy."

"Maybe it wasn't directly the Mob, but they must have been involved."

"How? Prohibition's over."

"Gambling?" offered Hennessy. "La Guardia forced Costello out. Maybe it's got something to do with that."

Jane shook her head. "That was all showboating. Costello just set up again in Jersey and Louisiana, not to mention Havana. And Costello's already established in Cuba, so why would he send a flunky like Howie down there? It doesn't make any sense."

"None of it does."

"You were the one who told me a crime was only a puzzle because pieces were missing. We find the missing pieces and we figure out the puzzle." Jane reached up with her bandaged hand and gently probed the fresh, puffy scar under her eye. "Lawyers," she said a few moments later. "It always comes back to the lawyers. Fallon and McGee, Shalleck, Howie."

"All Mob related."

"And according to Noel, all connected to the Democratic Party."

"You think this is political?"

"If it's not the Mob then that's the only answer. Who else has the scratch and the weight to get to your boss Valentine?"

"This is crazy."

"Maybe. But it makes sense."

"What sense? Why would they send your friend Raines down to Havana? Why would they kill him? What does the Mob have in Havana that the Democrats want? And which Democrats?"

"Good questions. You sound like a reporter."

"No, I sound like a frustrated cop. We're talking in circles here."

"So let's stop talking and start doing something," said Jane.

"Such as?"

"Who's Frank Costello's mouthpiece?"

"His lawyer? A guy named George Wolf. Why?"

"Because maybe this Wolf character can tell me something about what Howie was doing in Havana."

"Why would he talk to you? Did you ever consider that maybe Costello might have something to do with blowing you up? That maybe Wolf knows about this?"

"I need to start somewhere."

"You ever hear of Johnny Torrio?"

"Sure," said Jane. "Big-shot hoodlum from Chicago."

"Born in Brooklyn, and he's back. An old, old friend of Costello's. Al Capone's mentor, Torrio was famous for getting rid of his enemies by sliding pipe bombs up the exhaust pipes of their cars. Sound familiar?"

"I still don't think it was the Mob. I think someone's trying to make it look that way, and I think that maybe Costello might be a little angry about being set up to take the fall for some political scheme."

"And what if you think wrong?"

"You have any other suggestion? I can't stay in here forever."

"You know what my suggestion is. Get on the Twentieth Century and go to Los Angeles. I'll keep digging here on the Q.T. If I find out something, I'll let you know and then you can decide what to do."

"Nice and logical."

"I like to think so."

"I was never the logical type. Set it up for me with Wolf." Jane stared at her friend. "As soon as you can."

Tommy Lascelles sat in the open lounge area of his railway car and gazed out the window at the rushing scenery; an hour outside of Winnipeg and already there was no sign of the seemingly endless prairie they had been traveling through. Nothing now but endless forests of stunted cedar, huge, striated outcroppings of granite and thousands of pond-size lakes reflecting the steel-gray overcast. Lascelles stroked his mustache, lit a Senior Service and tried to put his thoughts into some kind of useful order.

Once upon a time he'd had a promising career in the military, and even after the death of King George's father there had been the possibility of a respectable future in the Foreign Office. But, as though possessed by some disease that robbed him of good sense, he'd given it all up for the House of Windsor, particularly its men, and their wretched choice in women.

Today Her Royal Eructation was complaining that the food on the train was giving her gas, that her royal bath was lukewarm and that her tea, brewed from London water carried with the entourage in kegs, was likewise never hot enough. This morning she had also grumbled for the hundredth time that every time she tried to reach her precious babies on the telephone they were asleep.

Although both Lascelles and the king had tried to explain the idea of time zones, the concept continued to escape her and she appeared convinced that Greenwich Mean Time followed her about like the Corgi dogs she kept as pets, and who spent most of their day eating tidbits from the hand of their royal mistress, then shitting throughout Buckingham Palace with impunity. Thank God for small mercies, thought Lascelles. She'd tried to travel abroad with the wretched creatures once, only to find that they were grotesquely seasick and insisted on climbing into her lap and vomiting.

The woman was incredibly provincial, with barely enough education to fill one of the idiotic china thimbles she collected. Throughout the tour Lascelles had been waiting for her to make some kind of ghastly gaffe. This was a woman who regularly referred to people from Africa and India as "nig-nogs," the Chinese and Japanese indiscriminately as "chinks" and Jews as "kikes." Stopping in front of a portrait of Benjamin Disraeli on a private visit to the Tate Gallery, it had come out that the famous prime minister had been Jewish. Her response was to inquire whether there had since been some law enacted to prevent such a thing from happening again.

The rocks and trees and lakes continued flashing by the window and Lascelles bitterly consoled himself with an image of the royal Capon lowering her pale, porridgy plumpness into the narrow confines of the ceramic bathtub in the railway carriage behind him. As secretary to Bertie's brother Edward before the abdication he'd been positive that there could be no more dangerous woman on the planet than Wallis Simpson. Now he wasn't quite so sure.

The heavy door leading to the forward carriages pushed open noisily and the squat, roly-poly figure of Mackenzie King stepped into the car. Lascelles stood, making a short, stiff bow in the man's direction. "Mr. Prime Minister."

The balding little man waved a pudgy hand as he came down the aisle. "Sit down, sit down," he said. Lascelles did so and a few seconds later, after wobbling down the lurching car, the Canadian prime minister joined him. Lascelles smiled pleasantly. King had a grating, twanging voice, was profoundly irritating, and was a self-aggrandizing, sometimes pompous ass, but he was also extremely intelligent, a shrewd politician and the man who had engineered the entire tour in the first place. Given the precarious state of the world he was also potentially one of England's most useful allies. He appeared to be quite agitated, his hands clasped in his lap, fingers twitching around each other.

"Is there a problem?" asked Lascelles.

"No, no," King responded. He glanced out the window. "Feeling a little bit at a loose end."

Lascelles almost laughed out loud. Over the past weeks he'd been astounded at the Canadian's boundless energy. Now, with virtually nothing to do as they rattled through a thousand miles of granite wilderness, he was clearly very frustrated. "Maybe you should try to get some rest," Lascelles suggested. "I have a suspicion

America will be quite draining." The tall, thin man reached into the inside pocket of his tweed jacket and brought out a yellow rectangle of paper—a telegraph tear off. "The weather in Washington is in the high eighties and low nineties. New York isn't much better."

"I did want to talk about the American part of the tour," said King. "But not the weather."

"What then?"

"The president's infirmity, for one."

"The infantile paralysis."

King nodded. "Polio, that's right."

"It doesn't seem to slow him down from what I've seen in the newsreels."

"Bunkum," said King. "In the pictures, you ever see him walking across a lawn or getting in and out of a car?" King shook his head. "No, you've never seen it, because he can't. It's all show. Always got some guy in a white uniform on his left, taking his arm. Mostly his chauffeur lifts him in and out of the car, and when you see him driving, all cocky with that cigarette holder of his, he's in a special Ford with the gas and brake controls on the steering wheel. Got ramps everywhere, I've seen it for myself."

"I wouldn't have known," said Lascelles, trying to act surprised. It wasn't true, of course; he'd been fully briefed long before leaving England and both the king and queen knew exactly what to expect.

"That's the idea," said King. "It wasn't so bad when he was governor of New York, but it's been getting worse and worse. He got together with the press boys and they agreed not to show him in a wheelchair. Doesn't think it looks good to Hitler and his pals if the president comes off looking like a cripple." The Canadian made a little snorting sound. "Or maybe he doesn't think the American people would elect one."

King put his hands up on the table between himself and Lascelles. "Just thought you should know in case it all came as a surprise. Throws protocol out the window sometimes, the ramps and the wheelchair and the special things he has to do." He paused, pursing his lips. "That's one of the reasons he's not coming to Niagara Falls to welcome Their Royal Highnesses onto American soil—too out in the open for his taste."

"I don't think it will be a problem," Lascelles soothed. "Or at least not one that we can't deal with." He gave King a small, formal nod. "However, I shall apprise their Majesties of your concerns and your kind advice." It was exactly the kind of overblown comment the little man loved. Lascelles had a sneaking suspicion King jotted them down somewhere for posterity.

"Excellent," said King. He beamed, then frowned, almost in the same moment. "I've also been talking with Commissioner Wood."

"Yes?"

"He doesn't seem to be getting very much cooperation from the FBI."

"You're speaking of Sean Russell, presumably."

"That's right," said King. "Has me a little worried."

"Do we know his whereabouts yet?"

"That's what I'm talking about. There was a rumor he went from San Francisco to somewhere in Montana."

"Why would he go to Montana?" Lascelles asked. "It seems an unlikely spot for fund-raising."

"Be surprised," King answered. "Lot of Irish went to the copper mines in Butte. More Sullivans in the telephone directory than there are Smiths."

"What a strange bit of knowledge." This time Lascelles did laugh.

"I collect them." King grinned. "Ripley's got nothing on me."

"So Russell *could* have been there—is that what you're saying?"

"What I'm saying is, Commissioner Wood asked one of his CID inspectors in Ottawa to check the rumor out. Fellow named Carnak. He got in touch with an FBI man named Bannister who told him Russell had never been in Butte and wasn't expected."

"Seems cooperative enough."

"Sure, except that today Wood gets told that the post office inspector in Butte confirmed that Russell was staying there openly, entertaining guests in his hotel room."

"Odd."

"Very," King said. "Question is, what are we going to do about it?"

"I don't see that there's much we can do," Lascelles answered. "But I must say this would seem to confirm my original opinion—entertaining guests in one's hotel room doesn't sound like something an assassin would do."

"Well," said King, "I can't say I've known too many assassins in my time, but the whole thing's got me worried, I can tell you."

"What does Commissioner Wood say?"

King snorted again. "He's a policeman, Tommy. If he had his way Their Highnesses would make the tour in bulletproof boiler suits, or even better, not make the tour at all."

Lascelles grimaced slightly at the prime minister's use of his first name but didn't make an issue of it. He lit another cigarette instead. "Well, we all know there'll be no boiler suits, bulletproof or not, and the king and queen will be continuing the tour, so the whole thing is moot, don't you think?"

"No," King answered. "What I think is we should put some pressure on the Americans to find Russell and have him thrown in jail before he can do any harm."

"On what charge? The man can't be arrested on the basis of a rumor."

"Who cares what charge? I'm sure the FBI can find something. To hell with due process, Tommy, we're talking about the safety of the King and Queen of England."

"It's not quite that simple, Prime Minister. The large security contingent traveling with Their Highnesses has already been noted in the press, and not in flattering terms. They can't be surrounded by a wall of policemen. It tends to put a damper on things."

"We can't just sit around twiddling our thumbs," said King. He looked down at his hands and realized he was doing exactly that. He stuffed his hands in his jacket pockets, flushing angrily. "We have to do something."

"I think what we'll have to do," soothed Lascelles, "is assume that whatever security measures are seen to be sufficient for President Roosevelt's safety will be sufficient for Their Majesties."

The Canadian prime minister nodded gloomily. "Let's hope you're right, Tommy. God help us if you're not."

The king-emperor of the British Empire sat in his private drawing room and stared out the window as the car swayed back and forth, carrying them around endless curves through an infinity of bright small lakes, spiny outcrops of rust-stained stone and trees enough, it seemed, to build a house for everyone on the planet.

He'd been watching for the better part of an hour, ever since the prairie had so abruptly given way to these rocks and trees, and so far he'd seen no sign of civilization anywhere except the lines of telegraph poles on this side of the track, some leaning drunkenly, dark with pitch, others green and true and straight, freshly planted into the hard gravel of the trackbed, spaced, by his rough measure, approximately a hundred feet apart.

He was glad for a moment to be away from Buffy and all the rest, supposedly to spend time on the journal he so often referred to but wasn't really writing at all, if truth be known. He lit a Players and dragged the smoke deep into his lungs, expelling it with a grateful sigh. The trip was almost half over now and each of the telegraph poles whizzing by outside meant they were a hundred feet closer to home, but every passing mile seemed to add to Buffy's irritation. No matter how he tried to give her solace he invariably failed.

Publicly and even to her friends, Buffy often said that being queen was a terrible burden and responsibility she'd never expected to have put upon her, but the king knew that secretly she reveled in it, even if his own position dimmed slightly beside her energy and radiance. He was more than happy to have her take the lion's share of the limelight, if truth be told, but she was clearly tiring under the constant strain of it.

Although he'd never tell her so, the king knew that what she was feeling was fear, an emotion she purportedly did not know the meaning of. It wasn't a lack of courage that failed her now, it was the fear, much like his own, that now, with the American part of the tour coming closer, she'd make a cock-up of it all.

On their visit to France she'd charmed the French premier and the French people in general with her smiles and those thinning frocks designed for her by Hartnell, but would the Americans take to her the same way they'd taken to David when he was Prince of Wales, or would they see her for what she always saw herself as—the plump little commoner from the north who had no business being a queen of any kind at all?

The king inhaled again and sighed again. It was fine for him to depend on her compassion for his faults and frailties, but there was no way on earth she would accept his commiseration in return. He finished his cigarette and lit another.

At least she wouldn't have to give any speeches while they were in America. By his count he'd be giving more than a dozen, and from all reports, giving them in hideously hot weather, beginning coincidentally in Niagara Falls, where years before his brother had dedicated the bridge they'd use to cross from Canada into the United States.

He stared out the window, a king surveying a small part of his kingdom, wishing more than anything else to be at home with his two little daughters, playing the fool for them, knowing that to them he was as good as any other man, and even better because to them he was simply "Father Dearest" and not "His Royal Highness." He let his eyes go out of focus and concentrated on the regular rhythm of the wheels as they chattered over the rails, matching first his breathing to the sound, and then his words:

Peter Piper picked a peck of pickled peppers.
Peter Piper picked a peck of pickled peppers. . . .

Chapter 19

Monday, June 5, 1939
Detroit, Michigan

Acting on Sean Russell's orders, Barry and Sheila Connelly gave the IRA leader a two-minute lead as they left their small hotel on Congress Street, separating themselves by half a block or so, but never letting the tall, striking figure out of their sight. According to Connelly this was standard IRA procedure, the watcher behind able to see if the figure in front was under police surveillance of any kind.

At some point along the way Russell would stop to look in a shop window, light a cigarette or stoop to tie his shoelace, giving Barry and Connelly a chance to pass him. If there was anyone following, Barry would walk on the inside, away from the curb, with Connelly on the outside. If it had been Connelly alone doing the job, she would have switched her purse, or a folded newspaper, from one hand to the other.

For the next hundred yards it would be Russell looking for a tail, and then if distance warranted, they would switch again. So far Barry hadn't noticed anything, either anyone following on the sidewalk or in a vehicle. Either Foxworth's FBI agents were very good at keeping themselves hidden or Russell had managed to give them the slip somewhere along the way.

Ahead of them, the IRA chief seemed entirely unconcerned, walking slowly, smoking a cigarette as he went, a hearty, powerful-looking man out for a stroll, enjoying the sun-filled afternoon. They'd left Chicago at midnight the night before, taking a slow-rolling overnight train to Detroit on the Wabash Line, arriving at the Union Depot on Third Avenue shortly after 1 P.M. All the berths on the train had been sold and they were forced to travel by coach.

Barry was bleary-eyed from lack of sleep and desperate for a bath, but somehow Russell looked fresh and alert, without a care in the world, even though he'd nipped steadily at the pint bottle he kept in his jacket pocket throughout the trip. He'd even stopped to replenish his supply on their way from the train station to their hotel.

Barry watched as Russell reached into his pocket yet again and took a quick drink from his bottle. "He's a drunk."

"He's Irish," answered Sheila Connelly, poking her arm through the crook of his elbow and pressing herself lightly against him.

"I'm Irish and I don't drink like that."

She laughed lightly. "You seem to have come over all terribly moral, Mr. Barry, considering our situation together since we were in Chicago."

The policeman flushed brightly but he made no move to pull away from the touch of her arm in his. "What I meant was, he seems to be drinking a great deal for a man who's about to go slinging bombs about at the King and Queen of England."

"Now that's true enough."

They continued to follow the big, red-haired man, Barry's fluxing thoughts giving him a case of mental vertigo that was almost enough to make him physically nauseous. What mad fate was it that had carried him across the seas to find himself falling into what he thought could well be love with a woman who was as much his prisoner as his lover? How was it that he was in this alien city, following a drunkard assassin down God only knew what terrible path?

He expressed none of this to the woman beside him.

"He seems to know his way around well enough," he said.

"It's not the first time he's been to America."

They turned down Brush Street, walking toward the railyards and the river. In the distance, on the Canadian side, Barry could see freight cars being loaded onto huge flat-bottomed ferries for the short trip across to the United States. Reaching the rail depot at the foot of Brush Street they followed Russell onto one of the cream-colored electric trolley trains, seating themselves in the rear car, with Russell in the car ahead.

They rattled northward, weaving their way through a dozen or more clattering switchpoints as they maneuvered through the Grand Trunk Railyard, eventually gaining speed as they cleared the yards and headed north along the river on a single, one-way track. Five minutes later they passed the sprawling Marine Hospital and turned west, slowing as they pulled into Beaufait Station.

They stopped for a moment, the drone of the electric motors fading to a hum, waiting to take on passengers. The motorman in the front car blew his whistle, and just as the doors began to close, Barry saw Russell jump up and push through the doors. He and Connelly barely had time to do the same before the little train surged off again.

Russell walked up half a block to the corner of Bellvue and climbed in beside the driver of a humpback dark green Dodge sedan that stood by the curb, its engine idling. "Now what?" said Barry.

"We get in as well, I supppose."

"The tram ride was just another way of making sure he wasn't followed?"

"Something like that." She smiled. He'd spent three years in the trenches of France and Belgium, always frightened, waiting for that last, sick moment to come when the hammer was about to fall. She'd been living with that same terror for more years than that. That was the horror of it—she was *used* to this.

Reaching the automobile, Barry pulled open the rear door and let Sheila in first, then climbed in beside her, sitting directly behind the driver. The car smelled of cigarettes, Russell's whiskey breath and the sweet lavender scent of the driver's glistening pomade. The man was young, no more than twenty-two or twenty-three. He was dressed in an off-the-rack blue suit and there was a great deal of dandruff on the fabric at the shoulders.

Russell turned and looked back over the seat, smiling broadly. "This is Michael," he said, indicating the driver. "He'll be our guide and chauffeur for today."

"Where are we going?" Barry asked.

"Never you mind for the moment, Tom Sullivan. You'll know soon enough." He turned to the driver. "Off we go then, Michael, m'dear."

They headed northwest, Barry trying to remember the streets they turned onto and failing, Russell smoking cigarettes and drinking steadily from his new pint of Bushmills.

"They call this a Mickey bottle here in America—did you know that? But at home if you ask for a Mickey of Bushmills or, God help you, Jameson, they look at you terrible strange. Isn't that the oddest thing? Like the word *nigger* being used by all the top people and no one taking offense, least of all the coons." He let out a long harsh laugh.

Michael, the driver, said nothing at all, but every few seconds Barry saw him glance into his rearview mirror, eyeing his passengers. "Tell your friend Michael that it's not polite to stare," said Barry. "He's offending the lady."

Russell smiled. "He means nothing by it." The big man looked toward the driver. "Do you, Michael?" The young man continued to drive and to say nothing. Russell kept on talking. "Now did you know, Michael, that Mr. Sullivan here is a New York City policeman?" He took out his package of Old Golds and lit a fresh one from the butt of the one before it. "Fancy that, to have a policeman of my own, just like His Majesty." Russell dragged deeply on the cigarette, letting the smoke spurt out from his nose in two strong streams.

"Did you know that, Mr. Policeman Sullivan from New

York City? That the king has his own policeman and the queen as well?"

"You learn something new every day," said Barry, trying to stay calm.

Russell picked a fleck of tobacco from the tip of his tongue, examining it closely before he turned and flicked it out the open vent window. For some reason Barry found the gesture particularly obscene and turned away, staring out the window rather than continuing to look at the man's face. Tall, broad-shouldered and charismatic though Russell was, the policeman suddenly realized that the other man was somehow very small.

As they moved toward the city limits Barry saw that they were moving in a zigzag pattern through broad, tree-lined streets. The houses, mostly brick or stone, were large and set well back from the sidewalk. The neighborhood was an affluent one. "Where are we?" he asked without turning away from the window.

"Some people'd like to think it was Grosse Point, but it ain't," said Michael, speaking for the first time. His voice was flat and plain with no trace of an Irish lilt. "Good side of Hamtramck maybe, or Harper Woods—I'd give it that."

"Wouldn't mean a thing to these dear folk," Russell said. "Doesn't mean a thing to me, as a matter of fact."

"We're where the rich people live," Michael said. "Doctors and dentists and the like." He nodded to the left. "Other side of Gratiot and it's all Polacks and Wops and Kikes and such."

They turned to the right and Barry saw the street sign: FOREST. The street was like a half dozen he'd already seen on the ride—wide, with more than enough room to park on both sides, the trees in front of the houses large and mature. The numbers on the doors went up rather than down as they continued along. Eventually Michael pulled in to the curb and parked, but left the engine running.

"Home sweet home," said Russell. He turned the handle on the car door and opened it. Barry looked out.

The house they'd parked in front of was a large, two-storied affair of brick and stone, much like the others around it. There were a pair of white Georgian columns flanking a black door with a large brass knocker and the number 1142 in brass along the broad lintel. There was a small brass plaque on the left-hand column but Barry was too far away to read it. He closed his eyes briefly, memorizing the address, 1142 Forest Street.

Russell turned to Michael again. "Back here in an hour," he commanded. Michael nodded. He stepped out of the car and pulled open the rear door. "Come along you two." Sheila exited first, followed by Barry. Russell slapped the roof of the car and it moved away. Russell headed up the shrub-lined walkway leading to the front door of the house.

Climbing up the low steps to the front door, Barry read the brass plaque—*Dr. David Doyle, Physician*. The Scotland Yard policeman watched as Russell rapped lightly on the knocker, two short, short long short, short long. The letters IRA in Morse Code. Barry pretended not to notice, his eyes on a flicker of movement behind the curtains of a narrow window on his left.

Without waiting for anyone to answer the knock, Russell thumbed the door handle and went inside the house, Sheila and Barry close behind. They were in a small vestibule, stairs turning sharply upward to the left, open pocket doors leading to a wood-beamed dining room on the right. The door shut behind them. Turning, Barry saw a young man in a pair of flannels, a white shirt and a sleeveless knit vest, one hand on the door handle and the other holding the pistol grip of a drum magazine Thompson submachine gun, just like the ones Barry had seen in half a dozen gangster pictures.

"Is that really necessary?" he asked.

Russell smiled. "Oh, well, you never know who's going to be coming through the door. Better to be safe than sorry."

"This Dr. Doyle. A friend, presumably?"

"Indeed so. On a long vacation he is. Around the world with his wife, something of a second honeymoon, you might say. Allowed us the use of his house while he was gone." Allowed it, or had it demanded of him as a true Son of Erin?

"Kind of him."

"The Cause touches many of us." Russell put a pious hand to his chest, lifted his eyes to heaven briefly, then laughed again. He turned up the stairway to the second floor. As they climbed Barry picked up several strong odors that seemed to be coming from below them. Vinegar, cleaning bleach, mothballs and something that might have been corn syrup.

At the head of the stairs Barry found himself in another, wider hall. Directly in front of him there was an open door. If the wallpaper on the room within was any indicator he was looking into a nursery. To his left another pair of open pocket doors looked into what appeared to be a living room laid out with couches, comfortable chairs and several tall cases filled with books.

The walls were pale yellow and the dominant color of the furniture was green. As they entered the living room a tall, brown-suited man stood up. His dark hair was thinning into a widow's peak and small thin lips were overshadowed by the man's formidable nose. He had eyes as dark as the hair, and small.

"Joseph!" Russell boomed heartily. "Our friends Mr. Thomas Sullivan of the New York City Police Department and a young lady from the old sod, Miss Sheila Connelly. According to Mr. Sullivan the Clan is thinking that I need protection while I'm here so they've sent him along, and Miss Connelly brought much-needed intelligence from home." Russell then introduced the dark-haired man as Mr. Joseph McGarrity of Philadelphia. "Mr. McGarrity is a great good friend of mine from years past."

"Pleased to meet you," said McGarrity, "I'm sure." He shook hands with both of them. The grip was bony, but firm enough. From the sounds of it McGarrity had been in the United States for some time, but there was still a strong accent behind the flattened vowels of New World English.

"Sit down, sit down," said Russell, waving Barry and

Sheila Connelly to club chairs set across from the couch where McGarrity had been sitting. Russell crossed the room to an antique escritoire that was doing duty as an ornate bar, bottles and glasses gleaming, a filled sterling ice bucket and tongs set to one side. Murphy's, Jameson and Bushmills, all Irish, and a single bottle of gin. Fleischmann's, not Gilbey's.

Russell doled himself out four fingers of Bushmills, neat, then dropped down onto the couch beside McGarrity. The thin man glanced at the glass gripped in Russell's hand, his lip curling slightly, but he said nothing.

Russell caught the look. "You're thinking that I drink too much, aren't you then, Joseph?"

"I was."

"There's no such thing as drinking too much."

"This is serious business we're about, Sean."

"Very serious indeed by the smell of it," Russell answered, tasting the air with his nose raised. "What is it we're brewing up today?"

McGarrity gave Barry and Sheila Connelly a long look, then turned back to Russell. "The lot. Nitrated sawdust and nitroglycerin mostly."

"Blasting gelatin," said Barry. Now he knew why there was such a mixture of odors in the house.

"That's right." McGarrity looked at him. "What do you know about it?"

"Only what I learned in the army."

"And what army would that have been?"

"Irish Grenadiers."

McGarrity sneered openly. "The Royal Army then. The king's man."

"My own man," Barry answered, working to hold his temper. "As good as an orphan bastard from Cork could do in those days."

"You could have joined us instead of the army."

"What would you have given me for pay, a bullet in the head?" Barry asked. "You know as well as I do that there was no agreement between any of the factions then. You killed as many of yourselves as you did anyone else."

"So why are you with us now?"

"Because now I can do the organization some good."

McGarrity looked as though he was going to argue further but Russell clambered to his feet and raised a glass before his companion could speak. "*Whisht!* Enough blather." He cleared his throat and spoke in Gaelic. "*Go maire sib bhur saol nua.* May you enjoy your new life in America, Thomas Sullivan. Long life, a wet mouth and death in Ireland!" Russell took a long swallow of his whiskey, almost emptying the glass.

"You're the only one with a drink in his hand, Sean, and your mouth is never dry from what I've seen," McGarrity said.

"Ah, you're a hard man, Joseph." He finished off the last of the whiskey and let the glass drop onto the small table at the end of the couch. "Up now and show us your bombs!"

They went down to the main floor again, McGarrity in the lead. At the bottom of the stairs Russell's colleague turned to the left. Barry saw that this part of the house had been given over to Dr. Doyle's medical practice. There were two small waiting rooms, an office, two treatment rooms, a kitchen and a laboratory. In the ten-by-sixteen lab three men were working at a large table, while a fourth man brought in a large porcelain bowl of ice cubes.

All four men were wearing shoulder rigs that carried flat automatic pistols. The men also had large handkerchiefs over the lower part of their faces but Barry could see that their eyes were red and swollen from the fumes. The stench was enough to make his own eyes water and he could feel a burning sensation at the back of his throat.

At the table one of the men began drawing off the nitroglycerin from one cooling beaker with an eye dropper, moving it to a second beaker filled with water. Barry watched as the oily nitroglycerin, heavier than the water, dropped to the bottom of the second container. When all the explosive had been transferred the man began adding bicarbonate of soda to absorb the excess acid in the beaker.

After watching for a few moments McGarrity turned on his heel and left the room without a word. He went through a narrow door. Following him, Russell, and Sheila, Barry found himself standing in what was obviously a very ordinary kitchen, complete with a gas cooker and a refrigerator. At a table in the middle of the room another man with his face obscured was adding a number of household ingredients together to make a stiff, gray-brown paste. Barry saw a jug of Sledge Hammer ammonia, a large jar of Vaseline petroleum jelly and a box of Boraxo brand saltpeter. Like the others, this man was also armed.

"He's mixing together the stabilizer," McGarrity explained. "Like pie dough. You add in the gun cotton, some nitrated sawdust and then the nitroglycerin. You end up with a sticky sort of dynamite you can mold into any shape you want."

Russell put a beefy hand on Barry's shoulder. "A dangerous fellow, Joe is. Spoons the fecking stuff into tins of corned beef and sends them to England as gifts with a friend of ours who works as a cabin steward on the *Queen Mary*. A certain irony there, don't you think, Mr. Sullivan?"

"I suppose you could say that," Barry answered, looking at the mixing bowl and its contents. Scientists at the Hendon Police Laboratory just outside of London had examined the remains of the last few bombs exploded in Birmingham and Manchester and had come to the conclusion that the explosive itself and some of the bombs' component parts were definitely of American origin. Probably from an explosives factory just like this one.

"You don't seem terribly impressed by all of this, Mr. Sullivan," said McGarrity.

"I'm not here to be impressed, Mr. McGarrity. I'm here to see that Chief of Staff Russell completes his work and then returns to Ireland safely." He paused, wondering how much he dared aggravate Russell's mysterious colleague. "What I'd like to know is why Chief of Staff Russell is here."

McGarrity glanced at the young man with the mixing bowl. "Are you done now, Archie?"

"Yes."

"Then leave us." Young Archie scraped the spoon on the edge of the bowl and carried it out of the room. McGarrity turned to Barry. "You know why Sean is here."

"According to him it's to greet Their Majesties."

"According to him?"

"I bought the latest *Time* magazine in Chicago," said Barry, which was true enough; he'd picked it up at the railway station. "There was a detailed itinerary of the royal visit. Nothing was mentioned about Detroit. They're crossing the border at Niagara Falls."

"True enough," said Russell, "but they *are* coming to Windsor on the Canadian side of the river. We'll just have to nip across the bridge to deliver our gift to the young couple, God rot their royal hearts."

"The Canadian police must have your photograph, not to mention the Americans. They're sure to be looking for you."

"Half the Detroit Police Department is Irish, Mr. Sullivan."

"And the other half isn't, Mr. McGarrity, and it's likely that most of the Royal Canadian Mounted Police in attendance won't be Irish either."

"Life is full of risks, Mr. Sullivan."

"I don't deny it. Some are more calculated than others, however." Barry shook his head. "Bad enough that the chief of staff is so well known, but to carry a bomb across the border with so much security in place? Madness."

"It's not for you to say what's mad and what's not," said Russell, "and it's me that'll be taking the risk, boyo."

"And me that's supposed to keep you safe," said Barry.

"We don't need you to tell us how to do our jobs, Mr.

Sullivan, and we don't need you to keep Sean safe." McGarrity offered up a thin-lipped smile. "Why don't you go back to New York and save us all a great deal of trouble?" He glanced at Sheila Connelly, his expression souring. "Take the *striapach* with you," he added, using the Gaelic word for whore. "And put her on the boat for home."

The R, or research division, of Military Intelligence occupied two small rooms under the eaves of 55 Broadway Buildings. The closet-size outer office was for the typist, while the slightly larger inner office was occupied by the division's only employee, Lieutenant Colonel Joseph Holland.

His desk, as usual, was a mess, piled high with files and papers, with more of the same hanging from the shelves of his two high bookcases. Most of the files contained correspondence and references to irregular and guerrilla warfare tactics, past and present, which was Holland's special interest and the focus of his work with Military Intelligence.

Holland sat with his back to the desk and his feet up on the windowsill. Since his summary return to England the month before Holland had sent half a dozen memoranda to his own superiors as well as Kendal at Special Branch and Douglas-Home at the P.M.'s. None of them had been very forthcoming, and none had expressed any opinion at all on paper.

From what Holland had been able to dig up through his own contacts, the order to have him returned to England seemed to have come from somewhere within the Foreign Office, transmitted through Douglas-Home. Officially it had been put out that Holland was needed at home and that there had been a duplication of services regarding royal security that made his presence in the United States redundant.

The truth, of course, was a great deal simpler than that. Politically, Russell had become as dangerous as one of the pressure-detonated booby traps Holland liked to design in his spare time. Since the royals had left England the bombing incidents had almost ceased. To have Russell arrested without real cause during the royal visit to the U.S. would generate an enormous amount of negative publicity, and worse, would almost certainly cost Roosevelt at least part of the Irish vote in the following year's election.

Holland ran one hand over his bald scalp and kept staring thoughtfully out the narrow window, barely aware of the spires of Westminster peeking over the roofs and chimney pots on the buildings across from his own aerie under the eaves. Once upon a time it had all been a gentleman's game, but no longer.

He smiled to himself, turning slightly to grab his cigarettes from the desk. He lit one and went back to looking out the window. Was Russell's zealotry for the cause of Irish Independence any more or less insane than leaping out of a trench at Ypres or Vimy for God and Country? Was it madness to attempt the assassination of a king and queen if you thought your cause was just?

There he found himself stuck in the mire, sucking mud holding him in place, oozing up over his bloody gumboots. He remembered Thomas Barry's words at their first meeting at Downing Street. *Cui bono?* Who benefits? Russell was many things, but he was no fool. He had to know the consequences of killing George and Elizabeth. An Irish assassin would be the end of Ireland.

The bald man sat forward in his chair, his feet hitting the floor. He pushed his glasses back up onto his nose and dropped ash all over his shirtfront as the mosaic of his thinking suddenly became a single, seamless design. Perhaps not an Irish assassin at all. Perhaps, instead, an Irish martyr. Poor Sean Russell, in America to attract interest in his cause, vilified by the press in Los Angeles, turned into a scapegoat without rhyme or reason.

The Irish-American vote, presently split between Republican and revolutionary, would be welded together as one in a united front. Roosevelt would suffer, perhaps even lose the election as a result, and America would stay out of the war that much longer. Long enough at least to ensure England's invasion by the Nazis, leaving Ireland a free state on the far side of the Irish Sea with a German satrapy as its closest neighbor, a thousand years of oppression expunged at long last. They'd build a fifty-foot statue of Russell in bronze and drop it down into the middle of St. Stephen's Green and toast his name with Guinness until the end of time.

"May the enemies of Ireland never find a friend," Holland grumbled, remembering the old blessing he'd heard for the first time long ago. He stood up, jamming his hands into his pockets, and went to the window. It sounded good enough, but there was something not quite right about it all. It was an elaborate construct, a design as detailed as the blueprints for a building.

Perhaps a building that didn't exist.

Holland closed his eyes for a moment, thinking hard, finally remembering what it was that Stephen Hayes had said in that lonely windblown cottage on Friar's Hill, overlooking the steel-gray sea. He turned away from the window, went back to his chair and, coughing, lit another cigarette from the butt of the first. He pushed away the mountain of files in front of him, dragged the telephone forward and dialed for directory. They gave him the number he wanted, and ringing off, he dialed again.

"Quaritch's." It was the old man himself, his voice as thin as parchment but with all his wits about him.

"I wonder if you have any books on fencing."

"We have books on everything, young man," Quaritch answered tartly, assuming that anyone he was speaking to would be younger. "What sort of fencing do you mean? Fencing as in encircling a property or fencing as in swordplay."

"Fencing as in swordplay."

"Several," said the old man.

"Excellent," Holland answered.

Michael the young chauffeur took Sheila Connelly and Thomas Barry all the way to their hotel off Congress Street, dropped them at the front door and sped away in a cloud of dust. Connelly and Barry went up to their one small room with its sagging bed and small stained carpet.

"The bastards!" said Sheila Connelly, dropping down on the bed, her small fists pounding her knees. Barry sat down on a straight wooden chair that had been placed under the room's narrow window.

"Why do you call them that?"

"Because that's what they are," she said furiously. "You heard McGarrity. To him a woman is nothing but a whore. You can bet that Sean doesn't keep an opinion that's much higher."

"Then they're fools," said Thomas quietly. He stood, took the few short steps necessary to bring him to the bed, then knelt, putting his own hands over the woman's. "Fools, and blind fools to boot."

"Ach, you're the fool," she answered. "And a romantic one at that." She shook her head. "There's no place for romance with this lot, Thomas. Their only love is for bullets and bombs."

"We can have it, even if they can't," he said.

"What? Love?"

"Yes."

She squeezed his hands in hers and looked down at him. "We can have it for a moment, Thomas. No more than that."

"Then that's what I'll take."

He stood, lifting her with him, taking her into his arms and holding her, but the soft moment and the silence only lasted for an instant. As their mouths touched she began to tear at his clothes and at her own, muttering and crying to herself, eventually pulling him down onto the bed on top of her, her fingers working at the buttons of his fly, then bringing his already stiffening organ into her grip, moaning for him, her thighs parting as she lifted her hips and pulled her plain cotton underpants aside with her free hand, guiding him into her, then letting go of him, her fingers clawing at his back as she thrust upward, impaling herself on him, screaming out his name as the tears rolled down her cheeks, squeezed from her tightly closed eyes, repeating his name like a battle cry with each movement either of them made until there was no sound or movement left except their ragged breathing and the rising and falling of their chests.

Sheila Connelly must have slept because the next thing she remembered was Thomas coming back into the room, closing the door softly behind him. He had two paper cups of coffee with him and a brown bag so translucent with grease and sugar she could see the shape of the doughnuts inside.

"Been shopping, have you?"

He set the coffee and the bag of doughnuts down on the bedside table. She sat up, drawing the sheet around her breasts. He sat down on the bed beside her. "I made a telephone call as well."

"To our friends in New York?"

"Yes."

"You look full of gloom and doom, Thomas Barry. What did they tell you?"

"Russell called his Clan contact in New York just before we left Chicago last night. Foxworth's man intercepted the call and vouched for you, but there must have been some kind of countersign Foxworth's man didn't know and Russell rang off immediately. Which means he knew I wasn't from the Clan."

"Yet he leads us straight to his bomb-making factory, tells us his plans. It makes no sense at all," said Sheila Connelly. "A bullet in the brain and then tipped into the boot of young Michael's car would be more likely."

"Which means Russell showed us and told us exactly what he wanted," Barry answered.

"I think we should get out of here before Russell or McGarrity change their minds." She threw back the sheet and swung her legs out over the edge of the bed. "It's not safe to stay here."

"Foxworth wants us back in New York as quickly as possible," said Barry, standing. "I checked with the air terminal. There's a flight in two hours." He wrapped his arms around his naked companion as she rose off the bed. "So we have a little time yet."

By the time they were done, the coffee had gone cold. They ate the doughnuts on the airplane to New York.

Acting on what was later announced to be an anonymous tip, George Messersmith, onetime U.S. consul in Berlin and presently an interregnum official at the State Department in Washington, ordered the arrest of Sean Russell based on technicalities within the Immigration Act and certain passport inconsistencies.

At 7:10 P.M. on June 5, less than twenty-four hours before the arrival of the royal train in Windsor, Ontario, Russell and his associate, Joseph McGarrity, were picked up at the Michigan Central Railway Depot. They had been preparing to board a boxcar about to be shunted onto one of the transfer barges that would take the boxcar and its passengers over to the Canadian side of the Detroit River, depositing them at the Michigan Central yards on the outskirts of Windsor.

Both Russell and McGarrity were taken to the county jail on Gratiot Street, where they were searched. No explosives, weapons or other incriminating material was found on either man and McGarrity was released almost immediately. Later that night Russell was transferred under guard from the jail to the larger House of Correction on Alfred Street. A further search of Russell and McGarrity's hotel rooms also disclosed nothing of a suspicious nature.

In the early hours of the following morning, acting on a second tip, the local office of the Federal Bureau of Investigation under the direction of Assistant Director W. W. Bannister raided a large house at 1142 Forest Street in the affluent northeastern section of Detroit, slightly more than a block from the house where Charles Lindbergh had been born.

The raided house turned out to be the residence and office of Dr. David Andrew Doyle and his wife, Sarah, both of whom were out of the country on an extended vacation. According to the warrant issued by Federal Judge Warren C. Masters, it had been granted to search for "*weapons, explosives, chemicals for the making of ex-*

plosives and other bomb-making material of a potentially dangerous nature." The search, meticulous and exhaustive though it was, turned up no such items, nor any sign that such items had ever been in the house beyond the strong lingering odor of ammonia still present within the building.

By 9:30 A.M. on the morning of Tuesday, June 6, less than twelve hours after Russell's arrest, three congressmen—James P. McGranery of Pennsylvania, J. Joseph Smith of Connecticut and Martin L. Sweeney of Ohio, all Democrats—drummed up the support of seventy other Irish members of the House, calling for action at a press conference on the Capitol steps. By noon, the three leading congressmen, led by McGranery, were on the way to the White House to present their protest and petition in person. The petition was in the form of an ultimatum. Release Sean Russell immediately or look forward to a boycott of the royal visit to Washington by every Irish congressman and senator on Capitol Hill.

Chapter 20

Tuesday, June 6, 1939
New York City

Dan Hennessy had arranged for Jane to be picked up on neutral ground in front of the Stork Club on East Fifty-third. The car showed up right on time at 9:00 P.M., a black, nondescript Ford Deluxe. With Hennessy watching from the front steps of the club, Jane stepped into the back of the car, which then eased out into traffic, heading east first then north on Park Avenue.

A bull-faced man in his late twenties was sitting in the backseat. He was dressed in a suit but the thick-necked muscular body stuffed into it would have looked better in a stevedore's overall. "Put this over your head and get down low," said the man, handing Jane a dark blue wool blanket. Jane did as she was told, lifting her freshly healed arm with care to cover herself, then sliding off the seat to half crouch in the space between the seats.

A few minutes later they made a right turn and a minute or two after that Jane felt a lifting lurch and then heard the familiar, hollow humming sound of automobile tires on a bridge. The only bridge that close to the Stork Club was the Queensborough. By Jane's estimate the rest of the trip took approximately half an hour. As far as she could tell they'd headed south after leaving the bridge, which meant she was probably somewhere in Brooklyn.

Eventually the car came to a stop. Still wearing the blanket, Jane was bundled out onto the sidewalk and then into a building. For a few seconds after being taken out of the Ford she'd smelled a faint salt breeze and she was sure she'd heard the lapping sounds of water and the distant echoing toot of a tugboat. The East River. Either the Atlantic or the Erie Basin.

The bull-faced man led her up a long flight of stairs then opened up a door and guided Jane by the arm to a wooden chair with arms. Coming up the stairs Jane had smelled rotten fruit and vegetables. A produce warehouse. The bull-faced man took the blanket off Jane's head and waited for a moment until Jane's eyes adjusted to the light.

She was sitting in a large, elevated office with windows on three sides that looked down into a dark warehouse at piles of wooden crates resting on pallets. In addition to the chair she was sitting in there were two others like it and a dark wooden office desk. Behind the desk a door led into a back room of some kind, maybe a toilet.

Next to the door was a wooden filing cabinet and on top of it a caged fan was turning, ticking as it reached the end of its arc, then starting back again. There was an overhead pan light with a dangling string and a gray, goosenecked lamp on the desk. The only other thing on the desk was a green blotter, a telephone and a flat tin ashtray.

The bull-necked man poked a finger in the air in front of Jane's face. "You stay here until I come and get you, understand?"

"Sure," said Jane. The man nodded, turned around and left the office, closing the door quietly behind him, then thumped down the long flight of stairs and into the warehouse. Jane moved uneasily in the chair; her arm and shoulder were still giving her a fair amount of pain, even though she'd swallowed a handful of aspirin with a seltzer back at the Stork.

A minute passed and then another. Down on the warehouse floor she could hear the ordinary sounds of dark places—small animal scutterings, a muffled bang, the scratching of pigeons on the metal roof over her head. After five minutes Jane started thinking about getting up and leaving, but then she thought about the bull-necked man and stayed where she was. A moment later she heard a floorboard creaking and then the door behind the desk opened and a man appeared.

He was of medium height and build with short, steel-gray hair, an oval face, lightly jowled and wearing round, steel-framed spectacles across a strong patrician nose. He had a wide chin and a small mouth showing small gray teeth. Late fifties or early sixties, wearing a very expensive-looking dark, single-breasted three-piece suit, both the vest and the jacket buttoned. The small-knotted tie was dark blue with small red flecks. None of Frankie Satin's Mob flash. He sat down behind the desk. As he did so, Jane noted that he'd left the door slightly ajar behind him. No light leaked out. The back room was dark.

"My name is George Wolf. I am an attorney. You are Miss Jane Todd, the unfortunate young woman who was killed in an office explosion. For a dead woman you look extremely attractive. Particularly the shoes. I am a great lover of shoes." Jane was wearing a pair of pug-toed Walkovers that she wouldn't have really called the height of fashion, but everyone had their kinks. "I understand that you wished to see me," Wolf said. His voice was clipped and efficient with no obvious inflection or emotion.

"Someone tried to kill me," Jane answered and left it at that.

"Most people are of the opinion that someone succeeded."

"I'd like to keep it that way. I'd also like to find out who did it."

"Give me a dollar," said Wolf.

"I beg your pardon?"

"Give me a dollar. You do have a dollar, don't you, Miss Todd?"

"Sure, I've got a dollar."

Jane reached into her new suede shoulder bag and pulled out her change purse, one of the few possessions that hadn't been destroyed by the fire. She opened the little purse, took out a single and slid it across the table to Wolf. The lawyer folded the bill in half, then in half again, then stowed it in the watch pocket of his vest.

"You have now retained my services as a lawyer. I represent you. Therefore anything you say to me, or I say to you, is privileged information, protected under the law. I cannot be forced to divulge anything said at this meeting."

"Neat trick."

"Useful."

"How does it get me to finding out who tried to kill me?"

"I wouldn't know anything about that, Miss Todd."

"I'd also like to know why."

"I wouldn't know anything about that, either."

"Then why am I here? And why did you go through that rigamarole with the dollar?" Jane said. "And more important, Mr. Wolf, why are you giving up your valuable time to see me in some produce warehouse on a pier in Brooklyn?"

"I am a chivalrous man, Miss Todd. I always like to accommodate the wishes of an attractive woman." He paused. "Has anyone ever mentioned to you that you bear a remarkable resemblance to Glenda Farrell, the actress? She appears in the—"

"Torchy Blane movies." Jane nodded. "I have been told that." She smiled. "She also appeared in *Little Caesar,* the Mob picture, but that was almost ten years back." Jane paused, watching what passed for a smile flicker on and off the lawyer's face. "I'd still like to know why you went to all the trouble to bring me here."

"I like to know who my friends are, and my enemies."

"I didn't think I was either."

"That remains to be seen," Wolf murmured. "I deal in information, Miss Todd. To me it is a commodity of value."

"My stock in trade too," Jane answered. She pulled out her cigarettes and lit one. Wolf leaned forward and poked the tin ashtray forward.

"That being the case, we might well be able to make an exchange," Wolf suggested.

"Who asks who?"

"Who asks whom," Wolf said with a smile.

"I'm a photographer, not a reporter." Jane breathed in a double lungful of smoke and let it out slowly. "So who asks the questions?"

"Ladies first."

"Have you ever heard of a man named Howard Raines?"

"I knew Mr. Raines to see him. A young factotum at Fallon and McGee. What was he to you?"

"An old friend."

"He must have been more than that, Miss Todd. Old friends don't go to such lengths as you have recently, including the risking of your life."

"We went back a long way. He's part of who I am. Let's just leave it at that."

"All right. Do you know why he was killed?"

"Are you going to tell me?"

"I said an exchange of information, Miss Todd, not a gift of it."

"Do you know a man named Joseph Shalleck?"

"Certainly. A well-known trial lawyer."

"Mob lawyer."

Wolf smiled thinly. "According to Mr. Hoover of the FBI there is no such thing as the Mob."

"Dewey would disagree with you. So would I."

"Mr. Dewey disagrees with everyone."

"Shalleck got Howie to run an errand for him. In Havana."

"Yes?"

"Did that errand have anything to do with Frank Costello?"

"No."

"You seem very sure."

"Mr. Costello is a client. Any information regarding Mr. Costello's affairs as they relate to the law are sacrosanct, protected by attorney-client privilege, just as this conversation is. Thus, should I give you an unequivocal answer regarding Mr. Raines's connection with Mr. Costello, you can assume that I *am* very sure and that there *is* no such connection. Am I making myself clear?"

As clear as a lawyer ever gets, Jane thought. "Do you know what the errand was?"

"Probably."

"What was it?"

"We'll get to that later." Wolf raised one hand and adjusted his spectacles slightly. For the first time Jane was aware that Wolf's ears protruded slightly. They were also barely without lobes at the bottom. The kind of thing Sherlock Holmes set such great store by.

"How is Joe Kennedy involved in all this?"

"Joe Kennedy?"

"The ambassador to the Court of St. James."

"Ah, that Joe Kennedy."

"Yeah. 'Ah, that Joe Kennedy.' "

"Why do you think Ambassador Kennedy is involved in Mr. Raines's death?"

"The guys who dumped Howard Raines's body used a car registered to a company Kennedy owns."

"That hardly rates as a connection to murder, in a legal sense, anyway. Hypothetically these people could have stolen the vehicle."

"We're not talking about legal here, Mr. Wolf, or hypothetical. We're talking putting a bomb in my office and putting me into a cast for a month. We're talking about murder and attempted murder."

"You must have some theory of your own about all this."

"Shalleck is a Mob lawyer. He used to represent your guy Frank at trial. He was Rothstein's lawyer and he also had Dutch Schultz and Dandy Phil Kastel as clients."

"I fail to see your point."

"He was also Farley's bagman during the last election campaign and he's friendly with Hague over in Jersey City. From what I can find out, Hague went out of his way to cover up my friend's murder, or at least deflect attention away from it."

"I still don't see what you're getting at," said Wolf.

"Kennedy, Shalleck and Hague. All Democrats, all with Mob tie-ins."

"A coincidence?"

"I don't know. You tell me."

"Is that all you know?"

"No."

"What else do you know?"

"Your turn," said Jane.

Wolf stared at her for a moment, then nodded. "All right. The man Howard Raines was going to see in Havana is a professional assassin. The best."

"What's his name?"

"He uses different names. I don't think it matters."

"Humor me."

"In Havana he is known by the name Bone, John Bone. In this instance I believe he is calling himself Mr. Green."

"Is he American?"

"No."

"He's not German, is he?"

"No."

"Do you know his nationality?"

"Yes. It's moot."

"Humor me again."

"He was born in Ireland and received his early training there. He has not lived in Ireland for many years and has no connection with it."

"Howie wouldn't have known a professional assassin if one came to the door and introduced himself. He wasn't the type."

Wolf nodded. "I would say you're right."

"So how did Howie find the man?"

"The assassin was recommended."

"By who?"

"Whom," said Wolf.

"Who recommended him?"

"A client."

"No names?"

"A friend of Frank Hague's."

The Democrat overlord of Jersey City. "Who else is involved?"

"Your turn to answer questions."

"Shoot."

"I asked before if you had a theory about what was going on. You didn't really answer the question."

"I still don't have enough information."

The door behind Wolf opened wide and a short, very thin figure appeared. He looked to be around fifty with a hatchet face and iron-gray, short-cut hair. Jane had seen his picture in the newspapers a hundred times. She had even taken one or two. The man stepping into the room was Edward J. Flynn, head of the Bronx Democratic machine, a lawyer and onetime sheriff of Bronx County. Some people said he even had the president's ear, and he'd had it since Roosevelt was governor of New York. "You're Ed Flynn."

"You know my name. Good for you, lady," said Flynn. The face had the narrow, foxlike features of an Irishman but the accent was Bronx through and through. "I usually don't do business with working girls."

"Working girls sell their bodies for sex," Jane answered. "I work, but I'm a woman."

"Women should make babies and casseroles."

"I prefer making money."

"Most women like that who aren't sec'etaries are bull-daggers. You one of those?"

"You're being crude, Mr. Flynn. I'd expected you to be a little more charming."

"Just having a bit of fun with you. Seeing what you were made of."

"Sugar and spice," Jane said dryly.

"Your presence here is ill-advised," warned Wolf.

"Fuck ill-advised." Flynn turned to Jane. "Your assassin was supposed to have a meeting in New Orleans a couple of days after Raines talked to him. You know who was going to be at this meeting?"

"No."

"Joe Shalleck, for one. Another lawyer named Davis.

A senator named Ernest Lundeen and a congressman named Lyndon Johnson. A bunch of hoods from the New Orleans Mob." Flynn paused. "The killer never showed. Canceled the meeting because he said there were too many people going to be there. He was right. Security would have been compromised. He met with a much smaller group the following day."

"Who was in this smaller group?"

"I'm not at liberty to say."

"What did they meet about?"

"A job for the killer."

"What job?"

"Tell Mr. Flynn what else it is you know," Wolf interrupted.

"They knew they were going to kill Howie right from the start."

"Why would they want to do that?"

"To shut him up. Because he knew who the assassin was, had seen his face, knew who was hiring him."

"Anything else?"

"Whoever these people are, they've got the cops in their pocket, including Commissioner Valentine." Jane paused. "And it's big. Very big."

"Why do you say that?"

"Because you're here," Jane responded. "You're . . . Ed Flynn." She paused, her eyes flickering to Wolf. "And he represents the Mob. Neither one of you would be talking to me if it wasn't something important."

"Maybe we just wanted to feast our eyes on you," said Flynn. "Before we decided where to bury your lovely corpse."

"Did it ever occur to you that maybe you wouldn't be leaving here alive?" said Wolf.

Jane smiled with a confidence she didn't feel at all. "Sure," she said. "I thought about that, and then I thought that if you were going to kill me you wouldn't be sitting here talking to me. What would be the point? You'd just have the guy who drove me here put a pill in my ear and dump me like Howie Raines." Christ, Howie, you sweet dumb cluck, what you started here! Jane thought wearily.

"Very thin logic," Wolf suggested. "Perhaps we simply wanted to find out the extent of your knowledge." His lips twitched briefly. "And then kill you."

"I doubt that. I don't know enough to be worth the trouble." She turned and looked Flynn right in the eye. "Who tried to have me killed?"

"A group of people."

"Including a couple of senators and some hitters from New Orleans?"

"A like-minded group of people who would rather Mr. Roosevelt not be president any longer than is absolutely necessary. Who would rather Mr. Roosevelt didn't take us into another world war. They have their own program regarding the United States and its relationship with Mr. Hitler."

Jane was stunned. "They're going to have Roosevelt *assassinated*?"

Flynn shook his head. "The president is not the target."

"Well who the hell is?" Then Jane saw it, saw how it would work, saw how it would succeed. "Jesus!" she whispered. "They're going to kill the king and queen."

"That would appear to be a logical assumption," said Wolf.

"Appear?" said Jane. "You mean you don't know for sure?"

"No."

"So this is all guesswork?"

"Not that either," said Wolf. "Most of it is fact, some of it is supposition. We know about the assassin. We know about the people in New Orleans."

"We also know about the sons of bitches in my own party who are up to their ears in this . . . filth," said Flynn, spitting out the last word. "Friends of Caesar, conspiring to ruin him!"

"How close are these . . . friends of Caesar?" Jane asked.

"As close as I am myself," said Flynn bitterly. "Some even closer." He paused. "At least for the moment."

Jane ground out her cigarette in the ashtray and immediately lit another one. She puffed on it for a moment, thinking hard, then asked the obvious question. "Why are you telling me this? Why don't you just spill the beans to Roosevelt?"

Flynn leaned over the desk, his hawk features stark in the light from the goosenecked lamp. "Because they didn't tell me," he said quietly. "Because they went behind the back of Edward J. Flynn, the bastards, because they knew what I'd do to them, especially that self-serving cocksucker Farley." He paused and took a deep, snorting breath. "Because they're cowards without the courage of their own convictions and I want to see them brought down. Do you understand me, Miss Todd? What they intend is not what this country was made for, not what it stands for. And if I told the president he'd cancel the whole royal tour on the spot, and how would that look? We'd be shamed. That's how it would look, and there's a lot more than that at stake, believe me."

Jane stared at him. Flynn wasn't outraged at the thought of the king and queen being murdered. He was pissed because they hadn't brought him in on it. And he'd just mentioned the name Farley, which had to be James A. Farley, postmaster general, Democratic National as well as State Party Chairman and a rumored presidential candidate himself. Friends of Caesar indeed—Farley was Roosevelt's Mark Antony, the man who'd run Roosevelt's campaigns since the beginning. And Flynn had just called him a cocksucker.

"Given our relative social positions, neither Mr. Flynn nor I am in a position to reveal this information," said Wolf.

"You want me to blow the whistle on this thing? I'm supposed to be the messenger? Like Howie Raines? No, thanks."

"It's the news story of the century, Miss Todd."

"It's not a news story," said Jane. "It's an ax waiting to fall. They've tried to kill me once, they'll try again."

"Go to the newspapers then!" said Flynn angrily. "Tell the world."

"With what evidence?" Jane asked bluntly. "I'd get laughed out of every city room in New York."

"Go to the authorities," said Wolf. "We'll give you what you need to convince them."

"Which authorities would that be?" Jane asked skeptically. "Not the New York City Police Department." She shook her head. "And not Dewey. He sure as hell wouldn't believe anything Mr. Wolf had to tell him."

"The FBI," Wolf answered calmly.

"You said it yourself. Hoover doesn't even think you people exist. He thinks Winchell made the Mob up on a napkin at the Stork. Not to mention the fact that he likes workingwomen less than you do."

Wolf smiled thinly again. "Mr. Hoover is well aware that we exist," he said quietly. "There's just nothing he can do about it." He paused. "And I wasn't thinking about Mr. Hoover anyway." Wolf reached into the inside pocket of his jacket, took out his wallet and removed a business card from it. He flipped it over, took out a pen and scribbled a few words on the blank side. He handed the card to Jane. The photographer flipped it over:

Sam Foxworth
Believe what she says.
G.W.

"The head of the FBI New York office isn't Sam Foxworth. It's Percy," said Jane.

"His friends call him Sam." The implication was clear. Wolf leaned forward. "Hurry, Miss Todd. I don't think we have very much time left."

At 9:30 that evening, after an informal dinner at the Brantford Hotel on the Canadian side of the border at Niagara Falls, the king and queen rejoined the royal train, which then moved slowly and majestically across the International Bridge and into the United States of America, the first English monarchs ever to enter that great nation.

Joining the train on the American side was a welcoming delegation from Washington that included Sir Ronald Lindsay, the British ambassador, and Mr. Cordell Hull, the tall, silver-haired U.S. secretary of state.

Security provided by the RCMP was now no longer in evidence; the four-man contingent that had accompanied the royals ever since arriving in Quebec had been left behind in Canada and was now replaced by a much larger group of New York state troopers, an even dozen plainclothes Secret Service agents and, at least between Niagara Falls and Buffalo, troops spaced at hundred-yard intervals along both sides of the track, bayonets fixed.

Although nothing was said, it was clear that the special security was a response to the arrest of Sean Russell the previous day. For the first time weapons were in evidence on the train, which made some of the attending staff extremely nervous. The four-man group of Special Branch officers as well as both the king and the queen's policemen had always been coy when asked questions concerning their own weapons, but if they were armed, at least they were discreet about it. The Americans seemed to take the opposite approach, assuming that a show of power and strength would provide a deterrence against violence.

The train arrived in Buffalo shortly after 11:00 P.M., and after the king and queen made a brief appearance on the observation platform the train moved off again. The queen retired for the night, as did the rest of the welcoming delegation, with the exception of Lindsay, the British ambassador, Cordell Hull and Tommy Lascelles, who adjourned to the lounge area of the royal rail car. It was here, after some brief, relaxing conversation and a cigar that the king, using a ceremonial sword and with Lindsay and Hull as witnesses, tapped Lascelles on each shoulder and bid him rise as Sir Alan Lascelles, Knight Commander of the Victorian Order.

An hour later, as the train thundered through the dark forests and river valleys of upstate New York, the newly invested knight retired to his own bedroom, changed into his favorite gray silk pajamas and poured himself a small celebratory tot of single malt from his private flask. He lit a cigarette, took out his pen and began to write in his green morocco-bound diary.

With Russell in jail the immediate danger to Their Majesties had been dealt with, but Lascelles was haunted by the possibility that over the next few days something would happen to destroy what he had worked so hard to achieve—the forging of a bond between England and the United States strong enough to withstand the coming war. He was well aware that any perceived slight or minor indiscretion might turn everything into a shambles.

Lascelles had already had a brief, private conversation with Lindsay, who confirmed that both FDR and Hull agreed that war was now almost a certainty. On the other hand, this was most certainly not a belief held by the majority of Americans, who were deeply skeptical of British motives.

Two days before the *New York Times* had run an editorial with the comment: *"The British are never polite to us except when they want something."* The general sense in America was that they were safely insulated from any European war by the vastness of the Atlantic Ocean; clearly they knew very little of the range of German U-boats.

The whole thing, Lascelles knew, was a very tricky and delicate business. Lindbergh, Father Coughlin and the America Firsters talked long and loud about isolationism, but in the end it was the perception of the average American that held the key. Thus, the foreign secretary had not accompanied the king and queen, and even the redcoat RCMP had been left behind for the sake of appearances. That was only the tip of the iceberg.

Lascelles was well aware that a great many Americans still considered the Duke of Windsor the rightful owner of the British throne and that George, if the Americans thought about him at all, thought of him as a stuttering, colorless, weak personality, in thrall to an overbearing, plump little commoner. The king's assistant private secretary sighed over the words he'd just written, knowing how accurate they were. He poured himself another finger of Scotch and lit another cigarette.

Even though the American part of the tour was supposed to be a side excursion, it was far and away the most important few days of the entire trip. If anything, the Canadian portion had been a tedious beard to cover the real meaning of events. If the king and queen, with Roosevelt's help, could convince the American public that the royals were friendly folk, just like them, they might be worthy of their sympathy, their financial support and, if necessary, their arms.

A careful balance had to be struck between dignified regal reserve and democratic friendliness—not the easiest thing to do after Chamberlain's groveling at Munich, not to mention the matter of the Duke of Windsor and Mrs. Simpson. The Americans had always liked Edward, and to abdicate the throne of England for the love of a woman, and an American woman at that, struck a popular, romantic chord. And Wallis Simpson had a much better figure than Her Royal Plumpness.

Lascelles sighed again, stroked out the last three words he'd written and replaced it with the single word *Elizabeth.* He screwed the top back on his pen and closed his diary and his eyes, leaning back against the seat, listening to the constant hammer of the steel wheels on the endless rails. This was not the world he'd been born into and not one that he really understood.

In his time the royal family had been sacrosanct, the image of vast power and the perfect symbol of an empire that spanned the globe. Over the years he'd watched the family and indeed the empire steadily decline following the death of Victoria, until it reached its present, sad state.

A week before leaving England he'd overheard the Duchess of Kent refer to Elizabeth, her sister-in-law, as "that common Scottish girl," and tonight, with his own pen, he'd called her Her Royal Plumpness. It was true. She was a plump, common Scottish girl who resembled nothing so much as the female caddies he often used when he golfed at Pitlochcry or Royal St. Andrews.

Plump or not, common or not and Scottish or not, in America she would be the focus of as much if not more attention than her husband, the king. His Highness at least had been coached for weeks before the tour began concerning his possible conversations with Roosevelt and the other notables he would find himself being introduced to. Elizabeth, on the other hand, would have to rely on the endless frocks she'd brought with her, cut and colored to disguise the thickness of her waist and thighs and the muscular heaviness of those very common calves, better suited to striding over the moors looking out for grouse than dancing in the ballroom at the White House.

Lascelles, using every diplomatic skill he'd acquired over his career, had managed it so that she never gave a single speech, addressed no crowds, and God forbid, never talked to the reporters of the press corps that traveled with them. Lascelles had cared for kings and queens before, and knew just how easily a small gaffe could become a crumbling disaster or how one simple, innocent mistake could be transformed into outright catastrophe.

Sir Alan Lascelles, newly minted knight, opened his eyes and looked at the etched silver flask and its companion cup on the small table in front of him. Just one more tot to help him sleep and then he'd go to bed. A good night's rest to gird his loins and then tomorrow—Washington and heartfelt prayers that this time the invading English would be welcomed there.

Chapter 21

Wednesday, June 7, 1939
New York City

Shortly before noon John Bone left the Gramercy Park Hotel and walked to a public telephone booth on the corner of Lexington Avenue and Twenty-first Street. Once inside the booth he placed a telephone call to the contact number he had been given at Antoine's Restaurant in the French Quarter by the man he knew only as Uncle Charles. After speaking to the voice on the other end of the line for a few moments Bone left the booth and walked to the Twenty-third Street subway entrance, where he took a downtown Lexington Avenue local south to Canal Street. He climbed up into the bright, hot sunlight, putting on his Cool Rays against the glare.

Bone walked west for several blocks, pausing to look in shop windows, ignoring the hum and rush of traffic heading for the Holland Tunnel and Jersey in one direction and the Manhattan Bridge in the other. He also checked for any kind of surveillance and found none. Eventually he reached Mott Street and turned north, strolling into Little Italy and feeling very much at home there among the pushcarts selling olives and artichokes and goat cheese and sweet-smelling *finochio*.

He bought himself a piping-hot wedge of pizza topped with thinly sliced tomatoes and a sprinkling of cheese, then continued on. Around him the neighborhood was brilliantly alive, the streets crowded, every fire escape landing and windowsill filled with pots of flowers or herbs, the sound of music everywhere, either sung aloud in the streets or rising from crackling gramophones within the gloomy tenement rooms. Bone had spent a fair bit of time in Italy over the years and had always enjoyed himself there, but Little Italy in New York was a nation of its own, more vibrant and full of energetic life than anything he'd ever seen in Milan or Florence or even Rome.

At Grand Street he turned west again, crossing Mulberry and Baxter and then Centre Street, passing the baroque bulk of police headquarters at No. 240. From his reading Bone knew that the present commissioner of police, Lewis Valentine, commanded twenty thousand police officers in eighty-three precinct houses operating out of all five boroughs. Detectives, patrolmen, an enormous fleet of radio cars controlled by three short-wave radio stations, three motorcycle divisions, twenty emergency squads, two mounted squads, fifteen traffic units including two bridge units and a fleet of river launches—it was a colossal force, all connected by an intricate system of telephone, telegraph, teletype and radio. In a few days that force would be fully focused on him.

He crossed Centre, then Lafayette, finally turning up Crosby Street and reaching the address he was looking for. Suspended over the front door on a steel strut was a giant revolver, carved in some soft wood, the barrel and the brightwork painted gray, the grip, checkered like the real thing, painted glossy black. Hanging below the barrel was a smaller sign that said: FRANZ LAVAN, GUNSMITH. To the left there was a company that made willow-strip furniture, while to the right there was a National Beauty Parlor outlet, complete with the familiar sign of two naked women holding up a large clock, the words LADY BE BEAUTIFUL flowing in red neon beneath the women's feet.

Bone stepped into Lavan's shop, taking off the sunglasses as he entered, the movement of the door ringing a clattering little brass bell on the frame. The store was long and narrow, the floor surfaced in broad unvarnished planks, scuffed to dirty gray and lit by three pan lights dangling overhead. The walls were racked with rifles and shotguns in glass-front cases. Long glass-topped counters ran around three sides of the room displaying dozens of revolvers and automatic pistols.

Lavan appeared, coming out from behind a curtain at the far end of the store. He was wearing dark pants held up by leather braces over a slightly grimy, short-sleeved white shirt. Instead of shoes he was wearing slippers that made a swishing sound as he shuffled down the narrow aisle that ran behind the display counters.

He reached the brown enameled cash register at the front of the store and stood behind it as though it was a shield. The gunsmith was in his sixties with a round face, small wet lips and thinning white hair, with small pale eyes blinking out from behind a pair of black-rimmed eyeglasses. He was potbellied and on the short side. There were perspiration stains in the armpits of his shirt and he smelled faintly of garlic and cigars.

"What can I do for you?" he said.

"You are Franz Lavan?"

"Yes." There was a faint accent even in the single word—European, but not German. He looked at Bone closely. "I have seen you before, yes?"

"No," Bone lied. He had been in the shop almost two weeks before, looking quite different than he did now.

"I could have sworn," said Lavan, shaking his head. "I am good with faces."

Bone ignored the comment. "I understand that you are a quality gunsmith."

"How do you understand that?"

"You have a reputation."

"With some people I do."

"I require a rifle."

Lavan waved a hand around the walls. "Take your choice."

"Show me that one," said Bone, pointing to the racked item he had seen on his first visit.

"Show me two hundred dollars," said Lavan, his small

pouched lips turning up wetly in what for him was probably a smile.

Bone took out his wallet and did just that, placing four fifty-dollar bills on the glass counter. Beneath the bills in the cabinet was a trio of well-worn Spanish Astra automatic pistols, tagged at five dollars each. "Well?" Bone asked. Lavan peered myopically down at the bills then turned and shuffled off down the aisle, pausing in front of one of the tall cabinets. He brought a long chain key ring out of his pocket, unlocked the cabinet and eased the weapon down. He brought it back to where Bone was still standing. Bone took it out of Lavan's hands.

"Careful," said Lavan.

Bone checked the weapon with care. "Custom work," he said after a moment then handed the rifle back to Lavan. "Chambered like an elephant gun. I'd say a .375 Holland and Holland Magnum."

"You would be quite correct, sir," Lavan answered, glancing down at the bills on the counter. "You know your weapons, sir."

"You retooled the barrel yourself?"

"Ah, no. I'm afraid my eyes are no longer good enough for such things. The barrel is from Harry Pope's shop in New Jersey."

Pope, Bone knew, was one of the half dozen true master gunsmiths living in the United States. "You have others?"

"With Pope barrels? Unfortunately not."

"Griffin and Howe?"

"You do know your rifles, don't you, sir?"

"Do you have any?"

"I have a dozen or so of their barrels, yes."

"I'd like to see them."

"They're in the shop," said Lavan. He looked down at the fifty-dollar bills. "In the basement."

"Is there a problem with me seeing them?"

"No, no, of course not, but I will have to close the shop while we are down below. The niggers would steal me blind if I gave them half a chance."

"Then close the shop," said Bone.

"It will take some time for me to show them to you. I of course have no objection as long as you are seriously interested. . . ."

"Take the money," Bone answered, nodding at the currency on the counter. "We'll call it a deposit."

"Very good, very good!" Lavan scooped up the money, came around the end of the counter and threw the bolt, locking the door, then pulled down a dark green roller shade. "There we are, sir! If you will follow me." He went in behind the counter and Bone went with him, following the man down to the far end of the store and through the curtains. There was a doorway leading down to the basement and an open arch to the left that opened into what appeared to be a small kitchen. Bone could smell soured coffee.

"You live here?" Bone asked.

"Yes. We had an apartment when Frieda was alive, but when she died I moved here. A kitchen, a bath, a room at the back. It is all I need."

"Frieda was your wife?"

Lavan shook his head. "My sister."

"I'm sorry."

"Don't be. She fell in love with some Jew and when he left her she drank herself into the grave."

Lavan opened the door leading down to the basement, flipping on a light switch as he went down the steps. "How long have you lived in America?" Bone asked.

"From 1920," the gunsmith answered, looking back over his shoulder. "There was very little need for gunsmiths such as myself in Graz after the war."

"Then you are Austrian?"

"Yes." The wet little smile. "You know Graz?"

"I've been there, yes."

"You know the Leugg House? Very beautiful."

Bone nodded. "At the corner of the Sporgasse. Yes." Some kind of silly test.

They reached the bottom of the stairs and Lavan stepped into the shop with Bone close behind him. Like the store upstairs the space was narrow, and even longer, with a single-lane firing range stretching out under the rear of the building.

The shop itself was rectangular, lit from above by a series of dangling lights, individual machines lit by their own gooseneck lamps. Overhead pulleys running off a single large motor operated a trio of old, cast-iron barrel lathes. Behind the lathes were racks of barrel blanks, waiting to be bored out. Farther down the shop was the woodworking area with more pulleys operating several mechanical saws, another, smaller lathe and a drill press. A large table running down the center of the room was littered with parts for several different types of handguns.

"You sell a lot of revolvers to the police department?" Bone asked.

"Some," the man answered, his hands stuffed into his trouser pockets, pulling on the braces. "They come here only because I am close and their own Equipment Bureau is too dear. They must purchase their own weapons and uniforms so they bring me old *sheisse* pistols they have found in the Jew market on Orchard Street and expect miracles from me for two dollars." He shrugged. "Often I cannot do anything for them. *Sheisse ist sheisse, ja?*"

Bone looked down to the end of the shop and saw an enormous safe, almost as high as the ceiling, its heavy door slightly ajar. "A safe?"

"There was a jewelry store here before I took the place over," Lavan said with a laugh. "I use it to keep my beer cool when I am working." He waved Bone back to the foot of the stairs. "Come, try the range," he said.

The firing range was brightly lit and at the far end of the tunnellike alley Bone could make out three targets pegged to a makeshift clothesline return mechanism. One target showed an unflattering caricature of a rabbi complete with long greasy hair, hooked nose and faintly Asian eyes. The second target was a Russian in a fur hat, charging forward with teeth bared, a rifle in his hand, and the third target was FDR, a cigarette holder cocked between his lips.

Lavan picked up a handgun that was lying on a small

wooden loading table at the head of the firing range. He handed it to Bone. "Would you like to try?"

Bone looked at the gun. It was a battered old Hopkins & Allen .32 revolver. "Which target?" he asked.

"Your choice." Lavan shrugged. "A lot of people like the Jew. I get them from a printer friend of mine in Germantown. The communist and Franklin Delano Rosenfeldt as well."

"You don't like Jews?" asked Bone.

"We lost the last war because of them."

"How is that?"

"All that communist talk. Marx, he was a Jew, you know."

"Yes, I knew that."

"They are all the same: the Jews, the niggers, the communists. Stealing money and jobs away from the real workingman. It won't happen again, believe me. We won't let it."

"We?"

"America First. You know them?"

"Heard of them."

"Lindbergh spoke to us once. It was very inspiring. He should be president here. If he was, there would be no talk of fighting another war in Europe, believe me." He nodded. "A perfect world. Hitler in Europe, Lindbergh here, no Jews anywhere."

Bone lifted the handgun, checked the cylinder to make sure that it was fully loaded and then shot Lavan through the left eye, knowing that the caliber was low and there would be very little blood. The eye disintegrated wetly and the bullet continued on through the orbit and into the brain, where it then dug a ragged channel toward the back of the man's head, eventually coming to rest at the top of the brain stem. Lavan was dead before his ruined brain had a chance to process the fact that he'd been shot.

Bone dropped the pistol on the firing range counter and managed to catch the dead gunsmith under the armpits before he hit the floor. He dragged Lavan back down through the machine shop, managed to ease the door of the safe open with a cocked elbow and then proceeded to place Lavan inside the steel vault, tucking up his knees and bending down the head to make him fit. When Lavan was completely inside Bone pushed the heavy door closed, turned the locking handle and spun the combination dial. The vault was made out of steel that was at least two inches thick, and unless someone had the combination it was going to be a long time before Lavan was released from his makeshift tomb.

The gunsmith's shop was now Bone's, to do with as he pleased.

The Claremont Inn was a well-preserved green-trimmed mansion located on a sloping greensward overlooking the Hudson River at Riverside Drive and 124th Street close to Grant's Tomb. The Claremont, in business as a restaurant and hostelry since before the Civil War, was a popular summer resort that had been owned and operated by the City of New York for many years. Usually closed until the Fourth of July, the Claremont was sometimes used by city officials for important functions or meetings that had to be held out of the public eye, such as the Dewey vice sweep two years prior when the Claremont had been used as an interrogation facility for more than seventy men and women involved in the New York numbers racket. A discreet word in the parks commissioner's ear had given Sam Foxworth access to the inn for as long as he needed. Within hours of meeting Jane Todd, Foxworth had installed the photographer in a room there, along with Thomas Barry and Sheila Connelly, already in residence since their return from Detroit and the Sean Russell disaster.

On the evening of June 7 Jane, Barry and Sheila Connelly were eating a make-do dinner in the main dining room when Sam Foxworth appeared carrying a briefcase and accompanied by a small, dark-haired man in his mid-thirties. The two men sat down at the table, Foxworth introducing his companion as Avra Warren, special assistant to George Messersmith, the man at the State Department who had been instrumental in seeing Sean Russell arrested.

"Apparently we've all been played for fools, right from the start," said Foxworth. "The conversation Miss Todd here had with Wolf and Ed Flynn would seem to confirm it." The FBI man opened up the briefcase in his lap and took out a pale yellow cablegram form. He held it up, nodding toward Thomas Barry, seated across the table. "This came in from your Colonel Holland this afternoon. He remembered something that was said when you interrogated this Hayes character in Ireland. Hayes said something about Russell telling a joke. It was all a 'case of foils,' according to him. Hayes didn't know what he meant.

"I remember that. I didn't know what it meant either. It didn't seem very important."

"Well," Foxworth drawled, "the phrase popped into Colonel Holland's head so he decided to find out what it meant." Foxworth cleared his throat. "This is a quote from a book he dug up called *Foil and Sabre, the Grammar of Fencing,* written by someone named Louis Rondelle and published in 1852. *'A Case of Foils, an archaic variation on the sport in which a foil is used in each hand. The use of two foils in a match.'* "

There was silence around the table as the meaning of the phrase began to sink in. "Shit," whispered Barry. "There's two of them. A second assassin."

"That about sums it up." Foxworth nodded. "Holland did some more checking and found out that a foil is also the word they use in foxhunting for laying a false scent. That fits too."

"Fencing?" said Sheila Connelly. "What in the name of God would Sean Russell know about such a thing?" She snorted. "Bit of wood with a nail in it maybe, but a sword? I don't think so."

"He spent some time in Germany in 1936, just before he came here for the first time," said Foxworth. "While he was there he had an affair with a woman named Helene Mayer. She was the Nazi silver-medal winner for fencing in the Olympics that year."

Avra Warren spoke for the first time. "We also found out that the man arrested with Russell in Detroit was Joseph McGarrity, head of Clan na Gael in New York. They knew Inspector Barry was no New York cop and they certainly knew he wasn't there on behalf of the Clan, and that means they also knew Miss Connelly had been compromised. As you surmised, Detective Barry, you were supposed to see and hear what you did. It was bait, and we all swallowed it, I'm afraid."

"And now we've got the makings of an international incident on our hands," said Foxworth. "Every Irish congressman and senator is screaming for Russell's release or they'll boycott the reception for the king and queen."

"To hell with that," said Jane hotly. "There's another assassin out there. The second foil. What about him?"

"Officially our hands are tied," said Warren, the man from the State Department. "Attorney General Biddle is so angry about all of this he denied our request for an FBI investigation into anything to do with Russell or the king and queen."

"Unofficially?" Jane asked.

"That's why I convened this meeting," said Foxworth. "To see if we could come up with an answer before it's too late."

"What about some pressure from the Yard?" Barry asked.

"Already tried it," said Foxworth, shaking his head. "Your man Kendal wired Hoover and the director had to turn him down because Biddle refused to authorize it. Politics."

"What is the politics of having the King and Queen of England murdered on our front doorstep?" Jane asked. "These people are serious."

"Do we know exactly who 'these people' are?" Barry asked.

"According to Miss Todd, Flynn named Farley," said Foxworth.

Warren sighed and lifted his shoulders. "There are a lot of people out there who don't want the president running for a third term and even more people who don't want him to take us into another war." He nodded in Barry's direction. "Your king and queen represent exactly that."

"There has to be something we can do," said Jane.

"Such as?" Foxworth asked, a note of bitterness creeping into his voice. "Director Hoover isn't about to defy the attorney general and I for one am not going to defy Director Hoover. Mr. Messersmith and Mr. Warren here played out their hand with Russell. They won't get a second chance." He shook his head. "According to you we can't even approach Commissioner Valentine for help."

Sheila Connelly spoke up. "Could it be that it's all a hoax, like Sean and his tempest in a teapot? Something to get everyone in a lather and bring attention to the Cause?"

"Tell that to Howie Raines," said Jane. "They didn't put two in his ear or blow me out of my shoes just to get people into a lather." She looked at Sheila coldly. "Who knows if your people weren't involved in this somehow as well?"

"They're not her people," said Barry. "Not anymore."

"You taking her word for that?" asked Jane. "Pardon me, guys, but I'm from Manhattan. Think about it. She led you to Russell and McGarrity and now they've been turned into holy innocents and caused all hell to break loose in Congress."

"We were set up," said Barry.

"And maybe she was part of that as well," Jane offered.

Avra Warren put up a placating hand. "I think we should all calm down a little. Recriminations and accusations will get us nowhere."

"None of it matters anyway," said Foxworth. "I've been told specifically not to investigate anything having to do with plots to assassinate Their Royal Highnesses."

There was a long silence, finally broken by Thomas

Barry. "I seem to remember you have something called the Lindbergh Law in America?"

Foxworth frowned. "That's right, but I don't see how it applies here."

"Well, when Jane told us her story she mentioned that this Howard Raines fellow lived in New York, yes?"

"Right," Jane said.

Barry turned slightly in his chair and gestured out the window. "But his body was found on the other side of the river, in New Jersey. I doubt that Mr. Raines went with his killers of his own free will, so that would constitute kidnapping, would it not?"

Foxworth stared across the table at the Scotland Yard detective. "By God, Inspector, you really are a piece of work. A Limey telling me the law." He slapped the table hard with the palm of his hand. "I'll be double damned!"

"I'm not quite sure I understand," said Avra Warren.

Foxworth quickly sketched an explanation. "If Howard Raines was kidnapped, transported out of New York and into New Jersey and then killed, his murder becomes a federal crime that I'm authorized to investigate without any other authority. Officially we won't be looking for Russell's second foil. We'll be looking for the people who kidnapped and then shot Howard Raines to death. A simple case of murder."

"I wouldn't call it that," said Jane. "I'd call it looking for a needle in the biggest haystack in the world."

Chapter 22

Thursday, June 8, 1939
Washington, D.C.

At 10:30 A.M. the royal train backed into Washington, D.C.'s, Union Station, arriving on track twenty, which offered the shortest walking distance from the rear of the train's first car to the president's blue-and-gold reception room one floor above. The queen muttered something sharpish about President Roosevelt not coming down to the train to greet them formally, which was the norm in England and Europe, but the only ones other than the king and Lascelles who heard her were Lindsay, the British ambassador, and Cordell Hull, the American secretary of state, both of whom had the good grace to ignore the comment. Abiding by the protocols set down by the president's office, Lindsay and the Canadian prime minister accompanied the king, and the queen was escorted by Cordell Hull.

While relieved that Sean Russell was safely behind bars, Lascelles was still acutely aware that the honor guard on either side of the red carpet leading to the president's reception room was all armed U.S. marines and that the four plainclothes Secret Service agents who'd boarded the train in Niagara Falls were never more than a few yards away.

In the main floor reception room the king, dressed that day as Admiral of the Fleet, and the queen, wearing a frothy pale mauve confection and matching hat, were greeted heartily by Roosevelt and his entire cabinet, all of them dressed in formal cutaways and almost visibly melting away in the hot, soupy air. Roosevelt, standing, was wearing heavy steel braces beneath his overlong trousers, his left arm hooked through the bent arm of a dress-uniformed aide-de-camp chosen specifically for his powerful heavyset body. Roosevelt leaned on a cane in his right hand, transferring it smoothly to his left when he shook hands with the king and queen, beaming widely as he did so.

With the formal introductions over, Roosevelt was lowered into a waiting collapsible wheelchair by Gus and Earl, his two longtime bodyguards. Roosevelt used the wheelchair until they reached the main entrance to the station, then stood up once again. With his ADC and the cane supporting him the president stepped out into the open air between the massive columns of the portico with the king on his right hand. A crowd of almost seventy thousand people filled the square in front of the station, and as Roosevelt and the king appeared, they broke out into a massive, rousing cheer. A military band struck up "God Save the King." The king paused to take the salute and then they moved down the broad flight of marble steps to the waiting cars.

Lascelles, trailing along behind the cabinet and the other members of the entourage, was astounded by Roosevelt's elan and the sheer physical strength required to carry off his grand deception. Here was a man paralyzed from the waist down who had the audacity to act as though he could walk in front of an enormous crowd of his constituents.

The king, doing as Lascelles had coached him earlier that morning, stood aside to let Roosevelt go up the almost invisible ramp that had been put in place after the cars arrived, allowing the president to step directly into the back of the open limousine. As he stepped forward, away from the attending ADC, his two bodyguards moved discreetly around to the opposite side of the car and eased him down into his seat. The queen and Mrs. Roosevelt entered the car behind and the rest of the entourage climbed into their waiting cars in order. Finally, the procession moved off around the square and headed down Delaware Avenue toward the Capitol. Seated beside Mackenzie King in the car directly behind the queen's, Lascelles winced. He could see that the woman had almost immediately put up one of her parasols to shade herself, completely ignoring Mrs. Roosevelt, sitting right beside her.

The motorcade suddenly became a thundering military procession as a contingent of sixty horse guards and thirty light tanks took up their positions behind the cars and a hundred motorcycle riders of the Virginia State Police took up positions at the head of the parade. Overhead a flight of forty-odd fighter planes and ten heavy bombers roared above the procession, the wall of sound almost completely blotting out the rousing cheers of the huge crowd lining Delaware Avenue. The hot, moist air made the stifling fumes of the grinding tanks almost intolerable.

In an attempt to give more people a chance to see the royal couple, especially those who paid for seats on specially built bleachers, the motorcade crossed Constitution Avenue and drove onto Capitol Hill, passing in front of the Capitol itself as radio entertainer Kate Smith led the other assembled dignitaries on the marble steps of the building in yet another rendition of "God Save the King." The slow-moving procession of automobiles, horses and tanks then circled behind the large-domed building, passing the U.S. Botanic Garden and the Ulysses S. Grant Memorial on First Street before turning left onto Constitution Avenue, all the while flanked by rows of soldiers, sailors and marines, all with bayonets fixed as they held back the screaming, frantic crowds on either side of the roadway.

By this time even the usually calm Lascelles was beginning to feel nervous. The crowds in Canada had been voluble and enthusiastic but here, even in the face of incredible heat and humidity, the huge assembly of humanity was almost frenzied. He saw one man in a bleacher seat pounding the top hat resting on his knees into a pulp, and two women screaming and tearing at each other's frocks for a better view as the royals passed by.

Out of the corner of his eye Lascelles spotted two other women who seemed to be engaged in a face-slapping contest and several more who simply fainted dead away, either from the heat or the excitement of seeing English royalty for the first time. For his own part Lascelles was uncomfortably aware of the sheets of perspiration dripping down his body under his heavy wool suit and prayed that he didn't look as bad as the beet-red Canadian prime minister seated beside him in the open car.

"Ninety-seven damn degrees," muttered Mackenzie King. "And me wearing serge. Who would have thought?" The bald little man dug a forefinger in between neck and collar for relief and then thought better of it.

"We'll be at the White House soon," Lascelles answered, raising his voice over the din. "Perhaps it'll be cooler there."

The prime minister nodded. "At least we'll be able to get a drink."

Hot as it was, any questions Lascelles had about the American reception of the king and queen evaporated as they made their way up Pennsylvania Avenue toward the White House. The sharpshooters poised on the roof of every building and the G-men in their dark suits and straw boaters running along beside the cars were a slightly ominous note, but everywhere else there was nothing but unfettered enthusiasm with hooted calls of "Hi ya, King!" and "Hey there, Mrs. Queen!" and some loud wag gleefully yelling out, "The British are coming! The British are coming!" as the motorcade passed by.

Just as important, from where Lascelles was sitting it looked as though the king and the president had struck up an immediate friendship. The two men seemed to be talking together like old friends, turning aside every few moments to give the crowd a wave and a smile and, in Roosevelt's case, a tip of his top hat.

Whatever relationship was struck between the two

men was of vital importance, hopefully forming the core of a long-term political, military and financial alliance, augmented by the thirty-million-pound bullion shipment secretly transferred by the *Empress of Australia*'s two escort ships, H.M.S. *Southampton* and H.M.S. *Glasgow*. The shipment, the first of forty-six to be delivered between May of 1939 and April 1941 totaling 470 million pounds, would be used as collateral surety for any possible war debts incurred by Great Britain in the United States.

To accept such a bond was in direct contravention of the U.S. Constitution and the Neutrality Act. To sidestep any real and legal objections by isolationist senators and congressmen it was agreed that the bullion would remain in the vaults of the Royal Bank of Canada in Ottawa for the time being, although everyone involved knew exactly who controlled the purse strings.

Forty minutes after leaving Union Station the motorcade finally made its way through the main gates of the White House and came to a halt there. Roosevelt, discreetly screened from view, was transferred into a wheelchair and taken through the kitchen and whisked up to the diplomatic reception room. Both the king and Roosevelt immediately and gratefully lit their first cigarettes in an hour. After another very brief reception the royal couple were shown to their private quarters and everyone not actually staying at the White House was provided with transportation to nearby hotels, notably the Hay-Adams.

Following a brief rest and a chance to change clothing, the royal couple and a small retinue that included Lascelles met with the Roosevelts for what was referred to as a family luncheon. Included among the guests were various Roosevelt relatives and Mackenzie King. One of the Roosevelt sons inadvertently brought up the subject of the liner *St. Louis* with its 937 Jewish refugees fleeing from Germany, at that moment close off the eastern seaboard of the United States.

Lascelles held his breath, praying that the queen wouldn't make some terrible gaffe, perhaps involving the word *kike,* but thankfully she seemed more concerned with the overwhelming heat and sat glassy-eyed and silent, sipping the mint julep she had been given and listening as Roosevelt trotted out a complicated explanation of the American immigration laws that prevented him from allowing the ship to venture into U.S. waters.

With the meal over, the president, Mrs. Roosevelt and the royal couple set out on a brief sightseeing tour of the capital city. The first car held the king and the president, the second car held the queen and Mrs. Roosevelt, and the third car held an assortment of policemen, including Chief Constable Canning, Their Majesties' personal detectives and Colonel Edmund Starling, head of the White House Secret Service Detail.

A half dozen more Secret Service men followed in a fourth car, armed with several Thompson submachine guns, assorted revolvers and three shotguns. State troopers formed both head and tail for the column, and more Secret Service men clung to the running boards of each of the royal automobiles. An hour and a half later, greeted by three thousand cheering, flag-waving Boy Scouts and Girl Scouts assembled on the presidential lawns, the royal couple returned to the White House to prepare for their upcoming garden party and reception at the British Embassy later that evening.

Jane Todd switched off the big radio in the smoking room of the Claremont, then did a reasonably good imitation of the ponderous, overblown commentator singing the praises of the royal couple as they left the White House for their garden party at the British Embassy. "The queen, looking exquisite in a lovely white crinoline gown of Empress Eugenie style with alternating bands of frilled and stiffened lace and tuck marquisette, was carrying a parasol of white lace and wearing a hat with a large gardenia in front and long white gloves . . . Jeez! It's a fashion show! Anybody know what 'tuck marquisette' is?"

"Well, I think now we can assume that our man isn't in Washington," said Thomas Barry. He dropped a thick, ringed notebook on the glass-topped table in front of his club chair—the full royal itinerary for the United States portion of the tour, provided by Avra Warren from the State Department.

"What makes you say that?" asked Jane, easing herself down into her own chair, careful not to put too much strain on her healing arm and shoulder.

"Too much security in plain sight," Barry answered. "This fellow won't be taking any unnecessary risks."

"You seem awfully sure of yourself."

Warren and Sam Foxworth came into the room, followed by Sheila Connelly, who was carrying a coffee tray. Jane noticed the attention Barry was giving her legs and she bristled slightly.

"I've just gotten off the phone with Ambassador Messersmith," said Warren. "We tried to delay it but Clan na Gael put up a five-thousand-dollar bond. Russell will be released tomorrow morning. Apparently they're going to throw a party for him at the Irish Embassy in Washington."

"Bloody hell!" Barry said.

"It's irrelevant now," Warren said with a shrug. "He did his job, deflected our attention away from the real threat."

"Our invisible killer," said the Scotland Yard man. "The professional."

"Inspector Barry is right on the mark," said Foxworth. "The man we're looking for is a professional assassin, hired to do a job. He's no madman with a cheap revolver."

"I still wish I knew who was doing the hiring," said Jane. Sheila handed her a cup, which she balanced on the wide arm of the chair.

"Avra and I have been working on that," said Foxworth. "We've got a few promising leads." Sheila poured for the others in the room, then took a cup for herself and went to stand close to the fireplace, just behind Barry. There was a small fire crackling cheerfully in the grate, taking the evening chill out of the air.

"Actually, it's rather a good thing that he's a professional," mused Barry. "A killer he may be, most likely the best that money can buy, but a man who also knows that the money is of no use to him if he's dead."

"Which in itself gives us something to work with," said Avra Warren. He took out a battered old Kaywoodie and a flat green tin of Holiday Pipe Mixture, loaded up and put a match to the bowl. He drew several long puffs to give himself a good light, then blew a cloud of aromatic smoke toward the ceiling. "We've had six assassination attempts on presidents, starting with Andy Jackson and ending with that Zangara fellow in Miami who wound up shooting Mayor Cermak of Chicago instead. With the exception of John Wilkes Booth, who thought he was a hero of the Confederacy, all of the assassins and would-be assassins were crazy as bedbugs and none of them was a professional killer." He blew another smoke signal toward the ceiling. "It's hard to defend against a lunatic, but a killer like ours is going to have a set of rules he goes by. If we figure out the rules, perhaps we figure out the man."

"We don't need to figure out either," said Jane abruptly. "If he's going to make an attempt it's going to be here, in New York, and it's going to be at the World's Fair."

"Why?" Foxworth asked.

"I must say you do seem awfully sure of yourself," said Barry, intrigued.

"Go on," said Foxworth, "why the fair?"

"Because it's what they're looking for, a big splash, and the symbolism is perfect. All the nations of the world gathered around to watch England take it in the neck." She gave Barry a broad wink. "Not to mention that it all started here. Howard Raines was a New York lawyer, the connection was through the New York Mob. These people have got their fingers in all the pies, including the cops, which they can't say about Washington."

"A nice story, Miss Todd, but that's all it is," said Avra Warren. "The attempt could come anywhere."

"I'm afraid I have to agree with Jane," Barry offered quietly. "I've read the itinerary carefully. Except for the fair the king and queen will be constantly moving targets. Odds for success would be almost impossibly low and there's nowhere on that itinerary that offers a proper lie."

"Lie?" asked Warren.

"Place to shoot from," said Foxworth. He nodded thoughtfully. "I'd tend to agree," he said. "What exactly do they have on their agenda?"

Jane reached out and picked the book up off the table and flipped to the appropriate pages. "A visit to the Capitol, trip down the Potomac River on the presidential yacht for a visit to Mount Vernon with a stop at a conservation camp on the way back, laying a wreath at Arlington, tea with some Girl Scouts at the White House, a formal dinner at the British Embassy, then back onto the train for the trip to New York."

"Behind closed doors, in automobiles or on the yacht," said Barry. "I really don't see much opportunity."

"But why the World's Fair?" asked Warren.

"They only stop three times in New York—Battery Park when they get off the U.S.S. *Warrington,* the fair, and Columbia University."

"Why not Battery Park?"

"Not a chance," said Jane. "They're not getting off at the park anyway. The only place they can arrive is the Battery Marine Building. Check it out yourself—the closest building the killer could take a shot from is at least three hundred yards away, and he'd need to be up on a high floor to get past the trees."

"No one is allowed into any of the buildings unless they have an office there and can prove it," said Foxworth. "And no one is allowed on any of the rooftops except police sharpshooters and observers. According to La Guardia there're going to be fifteen thousand cops along the route."

"Led by a man whose loyalty has been called into question," said Avra Warren. "We've been watching him as well. In the last two weeks the commissioner has had secret meetings with every one of the Holy Name societies and a two-hour meeting with our newly anointed cardinal."

"And Spellman is Joe Kennedy's old friend," said Jane.

"That's assuming there's a connection," Foxworth put in. "Which I'm not entirely convinced of. Valentine's a cop, for Christ's sake!"

"And an old friend of Ed Flynn's," added Warren.

"Forget the politics. Look at the facts." Jane tapped the cover of the book. "According to this, after the Battery it's fifty-five miles an hour all the way to the fair. I don't care how good this guy is. He isn't shooting anyone traveling at that speed."

"She *is* right," said Barry. "The fair site is the most logical."

"A few hundred acres is a hell of a lot better than all of New York City," said Foxworth. "But it's still a few hundred acres. A lot of ground to cover."

Jane shrugged. "So what? You fill the place up with agents, put them everywhere."

"Not as easy as it sounds," Foxworth responded. "In the first place, the fair is New York City jurisdiction. We'd be stepping on Valentine's toes." He paused. "Playing with the Lindbergh Law is okay as far as it goes, but the Bureau has no authority to act as a security force for foreign dignitaries. Not to mention the fact that we still don't know how far up the ladder this conspiracy goes." He shook his head. "A small group investigating the murder of Howard Raines must be the extent of the Bureau's involvement."

Jane made a grimacing face. "Sounds like you're worried about your job more than keeping the king and queen from getting killed, Foxy old man."

Foxworth scowled. "You're here at my pleasure, Miss Todd. You have no official status here whatsoever. Don't wear out your welcome."

"That's a load of manure and you know it," Jane answered. "I'm here because I know too damn much and you don't want me going to the papers with it." She waved a hand at Sheila Connelly and Thomas Barry. "Just like our two lovebirds here." Barry blushed furiously and the Connelly woman gave her a look that would melt stone.

"Without some kind of proof no one would believe you."

"Try me."

Avra Warren held up his hands, palms outward. "Gentlemen, ladies, please. We need answers here, not arguments."

"You can probably narrow the territory somewhat," said Barry.

"How?" Avra Warren asked.

"In my limited experience professional killers always look for a sure thing. They leave as little to chance as possible."

"Your point being?" asked Foxworth.

"According to the itinerary there is only one place at the fair which it is certain Their Majesties will visit—the British pavilion. There is a reception and the king is to inspect an Honor Guard of ex-servicemen on the side lawn."

"Is this common knowledge?" Warren asked.

Barry shrugged. "I think we can assume the killer knows it."

Warren frowned, puffing on his pipe. "You think that's when he'll make the attempt?"

"He'll be somewhere within two hundred yards of the pavilion," said Barry.

"Why two hundred yards?" Foxworth asked.

"I was a sniper's observer during the last war," said Barry, his voice flat and unemotional. "Two hundred yards is the optimum range for a flat trajectory. You don't have to worry about wind age and the heat of the surrounding air. If the opportunity presents itself he might shoot from closer than that, but not farther, I'm sure of it."

Sheila Connelly spoke up for the first time. "How is this man supposed to bring a high-powered rifle into the fair grounds without being noticed?"

"He'll find a way," said Jane. "You can bet on it, Irish."

John Bone sat at the kitchen table in the rear of the gun store and examined the prints he'd picked up that afternoon from the Kodak dealer. They were mostly standard tourist snaps of the various pavilions at the fair so the ones he was really interested in wouldn't look out of place. He separated out the useful ones, then picked up the magnifying glass he'd found in Lavan's workshop in the basement, jotting down the occasional note in his ringed binder. When he was done he took the binder to the front of the store, picked up the telephone receiver beside the cash register and dialed. The call was picked up on the third ring.

"I'd like names and addresses to go with the following license plate numbers," he said politely. "A green Dodge, 2V 32 90, a brown Ford, 9K 51 80 and a green Buick, 8A 36 73." He listened for a moment as the numbers were repeated back to him. "I'll call again in an hour." Bone hung up the receiver, gathered up his notebook and went back down to the basement shop to complete his other chores. Precisely an hour later he made the second telephone call and was given three names and three addresses.

Chapter 23

Friday, June 9, 1939
New York City

Although the Communications Act of 1934 had banned wiretapping, virtually every FBI field office in the United States had long-standing relationships with the telephone company, allowing them to bridge local line pairs right in the exchange used by the tapped subscriber. When the tapping was done this way even the most suspicious or the most concerned telephone user could never prove that the line was tapped, and an expert could check the line minutely without discovering anything, since there is no actual, physical tap anywhere near the premises under electronic surveillance.

In the case of the New York field office the bridged lines led from the New York Telephone Company's massive skyscraper headquarters on West Street to the basement of the Federal Courts Building on Foley Square. Bypassing the regular switchboard entirely, the bridged lines led through the basement to a locked room in the rear of the building officially designated as Records Storage for the FBI offices high above.

In fact the room contained more than twenty automatically monitored Western Electric Presto Disc Recorders, which recorded all conversations held on the tapped lines on lacquer-covered aluminum discs. At regular intervals the discs would be removed and replaced, the used disks then transcribed and the transcriptions sent to the special agent in charge who had asked for the tap in the first place.

Since the recordings and the transcriptions were illegal a Do Not File designation was invented. The recordings, transcriptions and any records relating to them were given the DNF heading, which meant that instead of being sent into the Bureau's Central Records system, the files remained within the field office and were regularly destroyed, usually immediately preceding internal Bureau Inspection Audits. In the case of the bridge taps requested by Sam Foxworth, both the approvals for the tap and any resulting information came directly to him, effectively closing the circle.

With as many as twenty different taps in progress at any given time, active cases tended to be transcribed first by the special secretarial staff used for the purpose. Since Sam Foxworth wanted to draw as little attention as possible to his activities he did not give his tap requests any special urgency, and thus they were at the bottom of the transcription list. This seemed reasonable since there had been no activity on the line at all since the tap had been ordered.

The two calls made by John Bone to the New York number he had been given were recorded on disk at 5:16 P.M. and 6:17 P.M. the previous day. The preceding shift had ended slightly more than an hour before the first call and the disks weren't checked again until after midnight. Seeing that there had been some activity during the 4:00-P.M.-to-midnight time period the disk was removed and taken up to the transcription office on the fifth floor, where it remained until 9:00 A.M. With its low priority the disk wasn't transcribed until almost 3:30 in the afternoon, at which point it was sent to Sam Foxworth's office.

Once again, since there was no priority assigned to the case, the envelope with the transcription of the telephone conversations was not given a red URGENT tab. Not that it would have made a great deal of difference since, by a stroke of bad luck, Sam Foxworth's secretary, Alice Spencer, had gone to a dentist's appointment earlier that afternoon for the removal of an abscessed molar.

Still in great pain after the removal of the tooth Miss Spencer went home after the appointment and never returned to the office that day. Thus it was that the first Sam Foxworth knew of the calls from John Bone to the location of the tap was on his return from the Claremont Inn at 6:30 on Friday evening, less than twenty-four hours before the king and queen were scheduled to arrive at the New York World's Fair.

Of the three addresses received by John Bone the previous day, two were in Queens and the third in Brooklyn. It was the Brooklyn address that interested Bone the most since it belonged to a night-shift maintenance worker at the fair named Leo Hamner. Of the three people he'd subsequently photographed, Hamner was the only one who was roughly the right size. He certainly had the right occupation.

When he had telephoned earlier in the day, disguising his voice and posing as a clerk from the Brooklyn Water Department, Bone learned from Hamner's mother that the house on Adelphi Street belonged to her, that Leo slept during the day and didn't leave for work until at least 7:30 P.M. and that the water pressure in her toilet was sometimes embarrassingly inadequate and could they send someone around to fix it as soon as possible. Bone promised to see what he could do.

Using Lavan's automobile, a ten-year-old panel truck, Bone picked up the last of his supplies and returned to the gun shop a little after 3:00 in the afternoon. By 5:00 he had erased any evidence of his presence at the shop and had burned the notebook in which he had compiled his research over the previous weeks. By 5:30, now fully committed to his plan, John Bone loaded the last of his equipment into Lavan's truck and headed for the Brooklyn Bridge.

Hamner's home on Adelphi Street was a two-story green-and-white federal-style house three doors in from the corner of Lafayette Street in the Fort Greene district of Brooklyn, less than a dozen blocks from the Brooklyn Navy Yard. Bone went once around the block, identifying Leo Hamner's Dodge, then parked on DeKalb Avenue and walked back to the house. He paused in front of Hamner's vehicle, checking the cardboard World's Fair entry pass taped to the inside of the windshield, then went down the short brick walk and up the wooden steps to the front porch.

The front door of the house was open to let in the cooling evening breeze, Bone's way barred only by a flimsy screen. He used the ignition key from Lavan's truck to slice open the copper mesh; then he reached in, flipped up the latch, and pulled open the lightly framed door. He stood silently in the small vestibule for a few seconds, listening. He could smell bacon frying and hear the sound of shuffling footsteps. He could also faintly make out a softly pitched falsetto singing "Carry me back to old Virginny." Hamner's mother cooking breakfast for her son just as darkness was beginning to fall. Bone took two steps forward, gently easing the front door closed behind him.

In front and to the left a steep flight of stairs covered with a Persian patterned rug runner led up to the darkened second floor. In front and to the right a long hallway led back to the kitchen. There were two entries on the left: one a narrow door open but covered by a green curtain hanging from a bar that probably led into a sitting room, and farther down the hallway a pair of pocket doors leading into what had to be the dining room. Halfway down the hall between the two doors was a small shelf unit for the telephone and a straight-backed kitchen chair. A stub of pencil hung on a string thumbtacked to the side of the telephone shelf.

Bone took another step forward, carefully keeping to the side of the passage. He flipped back a corner of the curtain and saw the dark sitting room. Empty. He reached into the left pocket of his jacket and took out the Browning Automatic he'd removed from Lavan's showcase, then reached into his right pocket for the crude silencer he'd manufactured with the material and equipment he found in the gunsmith's basement shop.

The silencer was really nothing more than a steel tube bored with a row of holes on each side to reduce velocity, one end tapped to screw onto the barrel of the automatic, and filled with washers made from screening much like that used in Hamner's front entrance. Bone paused, screwed the silencer onto the end of the gun barrel and then took seven silent steps, bringing him to the open doorway leading into the kitchen.

The cupboards were pale yellow, the counters green and the floor covered in linoleum the color of dry slate. There was a farmhouse table in the middle of the room and four chairs around it. On the table was an open newspaper, a large glass ashtray and a red-and-black tin of Target cigarette tobacco.

Mrs. Hamner was standing in front of the stove, a cigarette dangling from her mouth, wearing a long flannel dressing gown belted around the waist. She was in her late sixties or early seventies, her face crumpled in on itself, leathery and seamed from a lifetime of smoking, her gray hair done up in a ragged bun held together by a string net. The upper lip pursed around the wet end of the cigarette was sprinkled with short gray bristles that matched her hair.

The woman had a spatula in her right hand that she was using to stir both a cast-iron frying pan full of scrambled eggs and a second pan of bacon. On a warming shelf above the stove was an enamel plate covered in newspaper being used to drain the fat from bacon already cooked.

Mrs. Hamner looked up as Bone stepped into the kitchen. "I guess I left the door off the hook," she said. The old woman went back to stirring her eggs. A long ash fell from her cigarette onto the front of her dressing gown. "Shit," she said and tried to brush it off with her free hand. She looked at Bone again. "You got here quick enough."

"Traffic was light," Bone answered, confused. The woman

didn't seem even slightly upset by having a strange man with a gun in her kitchen.

"Still don't know what the FBI wants with Leo. He's just a janitor, for Christ's sake. A goddamn sewer cleaner." She slid the spatula under several strips of bacon and hoisted them up onto the warming shelf. "Mind you, he'll tell you that he's really a sanitary engineer, but he never engineers nothing I can see." She pushed both frying pans off their burners, then turned away from the stove and put out her cigarette in the ashtray. She sat down, popped open the tobacco tin and took out a packet of rolling papers.

"Do you know who it was who called you?" Bone asked. Somehow the FBI had found out about him and played it logically, covering anyone with access to the fairgrounds.

"Said his name was Foxworth. Said he was sending an agent around for protection." She pinched tobacco out of the tin, dropped it onto one of the gummed papers and quickly rolled herself a cigarette. She reached into the pocket of the dressing gown, pulled out a box of matches and lit up. "Protection from what—that's what I'd like to know."

"Probably from me," said Bone. He lifted the pistol and fired once, the bullet taking the old woman in the chest and knocking her back out of the chair, the cigarette flying out of her hand. Blood pumped quickly from the wound, soaked up by the flannel dressing gown. Looking around the room Bone spotted a doorway. He opened it and looked down into darkness.

He smelled the musty-sweet scent of basement. Putting the silenced Browning down on the table he grabbed Mrs. Hamner by her slippered feet and dragged her over to the top of the basement steps, making sure that no blood oozed out onto the linoleum. When he had her lined up he lifted her under the shoulders and toppled her forward down the stairs. She disappeared into the basement with a series of thumps. Bone closed the door, spent a moment locating the dead woman's still-burning cigarette and put it out in the ashtray. He looked around the room. There was nothing obviously out of order except for the abundance of food on the stove.

Locating a garbage can lined with a paper shopping bag under the sink Bone used the spatula to scrape the eggs out of the frying pan and dumped the bacon and the greasy sheet of newspaper as well. He drained the grease from the bacon frying pan into a tin can on the warming shelf then put both frying pans and the enamel plate in the sink.

With those details taken care of he picked up the revolver and went back down the hall to the stairs. He listened for a moment and, hearing nothing, climbed to the second floor of the house.

He found Leo Hamner still asleep in his narrow bed in the small back bedroom of the house. He was sleeping on his stomach, his face buried in his pillow. Draped over a chair at the end of the bed were dark blue coveralls with the words *1939 New York World's Fair Inc.* stitched over the left breast pocket and *Leo* on a rectangular patch over the right. Under the chair was a pair of tall gumboots and a rolled-up pair of thick socks.

Bone stepped up to the bed, leaned over and fired twice into the base of Leo Hamner's neck, angling the barrel slightly up and forward. The man's body twitched several times, the legs jerking spasmodically under the covers, and then he was still. Bone put the gun down on the bed and quickly stripped off his own outer clothing, redressing in the blue coveralls. It was an almost perfect fit except for the sleeves, which were an inch or so short.

He found a half-filled laundry bag in Hamner's closet, emptied it, and refilled it with his own clothes. Leaving the silencer on his weapon he carried the bag of clothing downstairs and left it in the front hall, close to the door. When that was done he went back into the kitchen, started up a pot of coffee and waited. Fifteen minutes later the doorbell rang.

Bone went down the hall and answered the ring, quickly opening the screen door so the man wouldn't spot the slit in the screening beside the latch.

The man was tall, in his mid-thirties, wearing a brown

suit and brown hat with a white shirt. "You're Leo Hamner?" the man asked, eyeing the coveralls.

"That's right," Bone said. "You'll be the FBI fellow my mother said was coming around."

"Yeah," the man said. "Special Agent Neil Gordon." He took a small leather ID wallet out of his jacket and flipped it open for Bone. He looked over Bone's shoulder and down the hall. "Where is your mother?"

"Went to her bridge club," said Bone. "Why? Was she supposed to wait?"

"No. Not really."

"Why don't you come in?" Bone said. He stood aside and let the FBI man into the house. "Come on back into the kitchen and we can have some coffee."

"All right," said Gordon. He followed Bone back into the kitchen.

Bone nodded toward the pile of dishes in the sink. "We just ate or I would have fixed you some eggs."

"I'm fine," said Gordon, seating himself at the table. Bone made up two cups of coffee, asked how Gordon liked it and added milk and sugar. He put a cup down in front of Gordon and then sat down himself in the seat recently vacated by Leo's mother.

"Maybe you can tell me what this is all about," said Bone.

"I'm really not at liberty to discuss it," said Gordon. "But I can tell you that the Bureau thinks your life might be in danger."

"Can I go to work?"

"I'm afraid not."

"Who's going to square it with my boss?"

"I'll do that myself." He paused, frowning.

"Something the matter?"

"You've got a bit of an accent. Faint, but it's there. Irish, isn't it?"

"That's right."

"Funny. Hamner doesn't sound like an Irish name."

"It's not." Bone got to his feet, pulled out the silenced Browning and leaned over the table, placing the end of the silencer just above the bridge of Gordon's nose. He fired once, the sound no louder than a pair of hands clapping sharply. The FBI man died without a sound, his head snapping back, his chin in the air. There was very little blood.

Bone stared at the dead agent and considered his options. Bone knew who Sam Foxworth of the FBI was, and the telephone call to Mrs. Hamner and the resulting presence of Special Agent Gordon meant that his contact's telephone had been tapped. That in turn meant the other two addresses he had considered as backup possibilities were now useless. Worst of all it meant that the entire project had been jeopardized. Not only did the FBI know of his existence, they also knew that he was going to strike at the fair.

After his first reconnaissance of the Flushing Meadows site Bone had given himself a ninety-percent chance of accomplishing his objective and an eighty-percent chance of escaping cleanly. Now, even with the enemy forewarned, he still considered that he had at least a seventy-five-percent chance of killing both the king and the queen and a sixty-percent to seventy-percent chance of escape.

Not good odds, but an acceptable risk considering the payment. He knew that it would take weeks or perhaps even months to unravel the conspiracy that had led to his being hired in the first place, and by then he would be long gone. Bone knew that the prudent choice would be to abandon the project right now. To go forward, however, meant that there would have to be some alterations made to his original plan.

Avra Warren hung up the telephone in the Claremont manager's office and leaned back in the wooden swivel chair.

"News?" asked Thomas Barry.

"Assistant Director Foxworth managed to get through to all three phone numbers. He's sent agents to each residence. They've also arrested the man who answered the telephone when the killer called. He's being brought in for interrogation."

"Who is he?" asked Barry.

"A law clerk," Warren answered. "He works at a company called Sullivan and Cromwell."

Jane was impressed. "Oil companies, right? Remington Typewriters?"

"Among others," Warren answered dryly, "including the government of Panama, I believe."

"So who was he clerking for?"

"One of the junior partners. A man named Allen Dulles."

"Make any sense to you?"

"On the surface, no," Warren said. "Sullivan and Cromwell is definitely a Republican firm."

"But?" Jane prodded.

"The company represents large business interests that might be hurt if the United States becomes involved in a foreign war. Several of the larger oil concerns have contracts with Germany, as does International Telephone and Telegraph."

"Is this man Dulles directly involved himself?" asked Barry.

"We won't know until we talk to the clerk."

"Well," Jane said, "at least it confirms that the killer is going to make his attempt at the fair."

"Was going to," answered Warren. "I doubt he'll even make the attempt now. He'll know he's been compromised. We've got the contact, it won't be long before we have him." Warren smiled confidently. "That is, if he's foolish enough to remain in New York."

"So what are you going to do?" asked Jane. "Call off the dogs? This guy's a professional killer. What makes you think he's going to give up so easily?"

"Common sense," said Warren, lighting his pipe. "A fox doesn't run toward the hounds, he runs away."

"This is no foxhunt," said Jane. "I don't see what's changed. He had to know the security around the king and queen was going to be tight from the minute he took on the job, but that didn't seem to stop him. How much tighter can you make it?"

"I'm afraid I agree with Miss Todd," said Barry. "We

may have deflected his method of getting into the fair but that's all. The only thing we know about him is his name, and that's probably phoney as well."

"That's not quite true," said Jane. "According to Foxworth all three of the cars mentioned in that telephone call belong to night-shift workers at the fair. The Hamner guy is a janitor with the fair administration office, Wurts is a watchman at the National Cash Register exhibit and Benuki has some kind of job sterilizing the equipment in the Borden Building, the one where the cows go around in a circle all day."

"Not much to go on," said Warren.

"Better than nothing," Jane replied.

"Do they have anything in common other than being night workers?" Barry asked.

"Not that we can tell," said Warren, shaking his head. "Two live in Queens, the other lives in Brooklyn."

"Cars," said Jane, snapping her fingers. "It's the cars."

"What do you mean?" Warren asked.

"All three of them have cars. Our killer had their plate numbers."

"I still don't see what you're getting at."

"Think about it. This guy isn't wandering around New York idly jotting down the license plate numbers of random cars. He saw those plates at the fair. That means all three of them drive to work and park on the grounds. They don't take the subway."

"So what?" asked Warren, obviously irritated.

Barry nodded to himself. "He needs an automobile because he's taking something into the fair too large or too heavy to bring with him on the Tube."

"A weapon," said Jane. "It has to be." She turned to Warren. "Get Foxworth on the horn. We have to get out to the fair now."

"Even if what you say is true Their Royal Highnesses won't arrive until noon tomorrow."

"You're missing the point," said Jane.

"Which is?"

"The guys he was interested in are night workers. One way or the other he's going to be on the grounds tonight.

He's not going to be going through the turnstiles with all the rubes tomorrow."

"He's setting up a hide," offered Barry. "We used to do it all the time in the trenches. Find your vantage point the night before, dig yourself in, wait for the target to appear in daylight."

"These aren't the trenches, Inspector Barry. This is New York City."

"The same rules apply," Jane insisted. "We've got to get out there, find out where he's lying up."

Warren stood up from behind the desk. "The same rules do *not* apply, Miss Todd, and no one is going out to the fair tonight. You in particular."

"You're out of your mind."

"No," said Warren bluntly. "I'm following procedure. Inspector Barry and Miss Connelly have already put us into a terribly embarrassing position regarding Sean Russell—we're not about to make the same mistake twice. Not you, Inspector Barry or Miss Connelly has any official status at all. Assistant Director Foxworth and I are in agreement. You will remain here until the king and queen are safely back on their train and leaving the country, is that clear?"

"If we don't have any official status you don't have any jurisdiction," said Jane.

"I really wouldn't try and test that hypothesis if I were you, Miss Todd." The dark-haired diplomat came out from behind the desk. "Now if you'll excuse me."

Jane moved back a step and let Warren go past and leave the room.

"Well," said Barry, "that would appear to be that." He slumped down into a chair in the corner of the office.

"Like hell it is," Jane said. She went around behind the desk and picked up the telephone. "Let me make a call and see what I can do."

Chapter 24

Friday, June 9, 1939
New York World's Fair

With the coming of darkness the fair became something more than the gaudy, primary-colored exhibition of the daylight hours. As night fell the crowds thinned dramatically, the broad walkways and avenues almost empty, the soaring architecture of the buildings and exotic temples becoming more like the strangely lit and oddly serene ruins of some future age mysteriously brought back into the past. Strangely, for a fair that presumed to encompass the entire world, there was a sameness to it all, as though it came from the vision of a single mind, colors seen by a single eye.

Nothing seemed real. Fountains lit from within turned water into white, liquid marble; trees were bathed with light from invisible miniature spotlights at the base of their trunks that turned their bottoms rich green, their leaves and branches deep blue. Aircraft warning lights blinked on the Trylon, four on each face and one at the summit. Strangest of all, cloudscapes projected on the face of the Perisphere slowly revolved while ethereal otherworldly music played, a single amplified length of piano wire vibrating in an almost ominous cosmic wind.

From one side of the fair to the other it was the same: Big Joe, the stainless-steel worker on a seventy-nine-foot-high tower in front of the tomblike Soviet pavilion, was bathed in light as red as blood; the zigzag lightning bolt spire of the General Electric Building flashed hugely in yellow and white, while the flared, venetian blind fins of the triangular Petroleum Building glowed sapphire blue in the deepening night. The scale of everything was overwhelming; the human visitors were reduced to small strolling shadows in the darkness.

It was the darkness John Bone craved. Dressed in the dead FBI agent's suit and driving his Ford instead of Leo Hamner's Dodge, the assassin drove north through Brooklyn and then east along Horace Harding Boulevard to the fair. Turning off Horace Harding at the newly built cloverleaf he drove a few hundred yards along the Grand Central Parkway extension, following the amber lights that took him to the entrance gate at Fountain Lake. He showed Agent Gordon's badge and identification to the guard, explaining that he was on official business.

"This king thing tomorrow, right?" said the young man, smiling.

"Can't really talk about it," Bone answered, but he smiled and gave the guard a wink.

"Gotcha," the kid said and winked back, holding up his thumb and index finger like a gun and clicking his tongue. He waved Bone on through the gate. The assassin turned left onto Orange Blossom Lane, dark and deserted now, then turned right into the small parking lot to one side of the Florida Exhibit a hundred yards farther on. The Spanish-style building with its palm trees and carillon tower was one of the fair's orphans, an exhibit placed out of its theme area, in this case a state exhibit in the Entertainment Zone rather than with its sister states on Rainbow Avenue or Lincoln Square.

Working swiftly in the darkness, Bone stripped off the FBI agent's clothes, revealing Leo Hamner's dark blue coveralls underneath. He reached back behind the driver's seat, pulled out Leo's tall gumboots and slipped them on. Changed, he climbed out of the car, unlocked the trunk and took out the canvas duffel bag from Lavan's gunshop. He locked the car, pocketed the keys, then headed back along the wide sidewalk to the maintenance workers' dock at the edge of Fountain Lake. There were a half dozen wooden flatboats tied up, each one powered by a small Electrol twelve-volt outboard.

There was a security guard dozing in a canvas deck chair at the end of the dock, a thermos and a lunchbox beside him. "Who's that?" he called out without bothering to get out of his chair.

"Leo," Bone answered, keeping his voice low.

"You're early," said the guard.

"Yeah," Bone answered, and that was all there was to it. The guard slumped back into his chair and Bone eased the canvas bag down into the nearest boat, undid the line, then stepped down into the boat, positioning himself in the transom seat. Using Leo's keys he found the one with the Electrol lightning bolt, turned it in the ignition slot of the motor and headed out into the lake. Had the guard questioned him more closely Bone would have used the silenced Browning again and taken the body with him across the lake to be disposed of later.

Three hundred yards ahead of him were the glittering lights of the amusement area midway, with everything from the gigantic roller coaster screening Frank Buck's Jungleland with its chicken-wire-and-stucco volcano to girlie shows designed by Salvador Dali and bare-naked ladies frozen in giant blocks of ice. Even from the far side of the lake Bone could hear the rumble and roar of the roller coaster and the raucous come-hither music from the sideshows.

As he neared the middle of the artificial lake he veered slightly to avoid the jutting pipes of the fountain jets and the fireworks barges waiting for the midnight show. To his left, on the western shore, he could see the amphitheater of the Billy Rose Aquacade, dark now until the 8:30 performance, while to his far right there was only darkness. Somewhere over there was the fair's end, vacant spoiled ground, old drainage pipes and construction materials, a tall fence, and beyond that the real world and streets of Queens County. He was getting close to the opposite shore of the lake and he made some small adjustments with the rudder lever, aiming the blunt prow of the flatboat at a rectangle of darkness that marked the entrance to the lake's outlet into the concrete floodway of the Flushing River. Letting the boat find its own way for a few moments he pulled open the drawstring of the duffel and took out the shapeless U.S. Rubber raincape he'd purchased at Macy's sporting goods department after choosing the lie. He dropped it over his head, pulled up the hood, then took hold of the engine tiller once again.

Silently the flatboat slipped under the bridge that led from the concert hall to the amusement area and Bone found himself gliding down the narrow waterway, music and screams from the roller coaster and parachute jump on the right mixing with the chatter and bang of the chained rifles in the shooting galleries on the left. A shadow on the water loomed and he steered around it—the permanently moored canal boat beside the outdoor Heineken beer garden with its electrically operated windmill and its clog-footed waitresses in full Dutch dress. No one seemed to notice as he passed by on the dark water. Another hundred feet and he reached the second bridge spanning the river.

"I gotta be out of my mind doing this," said Dan Hennessy, pulling away from the rear entrance to the Plaza. He was driving an unmarked police department Chevrolet instead of his own car, with Jane Todd and Thomas Barry sitting beside him on the wide front seat.

"Out of your mind if you don't," Jane answered. "I'm going to make you into a hero, Danny boy."

"I don't want to be a hero. I just want to get my pension, and I'm about to lose it because of a weird broad who wears pants half the time." The New York cop checked the traffic, then swung up Fifth Avenue. Reaching Fifty-ninth Street he turned right and headed for the Queensborough Bridge approaches. "What about the Irish dame we left back at the hotel? She going to run out on us? Leave us in the lurch?"

"I don't think so," said Barry. "She could have done that any number of times over the past days."

Jane lit up a Lucky and handed the pack to the Scotland Yard man. "She's our hole card, Dan. But it's a good thing you got a man on her. Our British friend here thinks the world of her, but he's thinking with something other than his brains, if you know what I mean."

Barry shifted in his seat but Jane could feel the heat coming off him. She knew she'd taken one step too far and could have kicked herself.

"You have no idea what you're talking about," said Barry quietly.

"She'd better hang on to the affidavit you all signed," Hennessy warned. "If things screw up, that's all we've got." It had taken the New York detective the better part of an hour to get things organized and drive up to the Claremont. In that time Jane had banged out a ten-page affidavit on the battered old Royal typewriter in the Claremont office. She, Barry and Sheila Connelly had all signed it; then Jane had sealed it in an envelope and dripped red candle wax over the flap for good measure. In the event that they were arrested or otherwise detained over the next thirty-six hours, Sheila, with the help of Pelay and Bill Hartery, the Plaza house dick, was to see that the affidavit was put into the hands of Noel Busch at *Newsweek*. As extra security Hennessy had left a cop with her in the room.

It was a rough document without a lot of detail, but what detail Jane had written down was damning. In effect it said that there was a high-level conspiracy to assassinate the king and queen, involving people in business as well as government, and that for various reasons the conspiracy was being not only ignored, but covered up for the sake of political expediency.

"Who knows?" Hennessy said and shrugged. "Maybe she's already torn the stupid affidavit up and is setting sail for the old sod even as we speak."

"I seriously doubt that," said Barry, holding his temper. They hit the bridge, the wheels thrumming noisily. "She'll never go home again. There's nothing for her there now except a bullet in the head."

"Unless she was part of it right from the beginning.

Christ, they'll give her a medal for leading you people around by the nose like she did."

"You're wrong," Barry answered flatly.

"You think that just because you're dizzy for her."

"What?"

"He means you're infatuated with her and she's maybe pulling the wool over your baby blues," said Jane. "Think that could make some sense? Any other ideas on why someone who looks as good as her would fall for someone like you?" They were passing over Welfare Island, the asylum dark below them, its central tower darker than the air around it, like a black hole in the night. She still hadn't gone to see Annie since the bombing, telling herself there hadn't been any time, knowing it was a lie, knowing she was more concerned with herself and her fears than with her sister. She knew she was a complete mess because she'd also been wondering about what Wolf the lawyer had said. How much of this was really for her memories of Howie and how much was for the brass ring she'd grab if she managed to get an exclusive on the story unfolding around her?

They reached the end of the bridge and drove through the bright lights and bustle of Queens Plaza before heading down Northern Boulevard into the deeper darkness of the semirural area, their headlights grazing the sides of tumbledown farm buildings and roughly made greenhouses.

"I thought I saw a sign back there written in Chinese," said Barry, looking back over his shoulder. "Is that possible?"

Hennessy laughed. "This is New York, pally, Anything's possible."

"There's a lot of Chinese farmers out here," Jane explained. "They grow special vegetables for the restaurants on Pell Street."

"I still don't know what it is we're going to accomplish with this little jaunt," said Hennessy a moment later. "Other than me losing my job, that is." He shook his head wearily. "Every cop on the force is going to be lining the parade route tomorrow, you have to get a special ticket to go into your own building if it's on the way and they're putting shooters on every roof. On top of that the feds have everything else covered while this king guy and his wife are there." He turned to Jane. "You said yourself that Foxworth put a plug in the guy's plans with that phone tap."

"That's the problem," said Jane. "Warren from the State Department and Foxworth think they've scared our man off."

"And you don't believe it, right?"

"No. He's supposed to be the best in the world. He's got to have some other plan to go to if one doesn't work out."

"And you don't have the slightest idea what that plan would be, do you?"

"We know he needed to get in there at night. All three of the people he asked about were night workers."

"What else?"

Jane nodded toward Barry. "Our Limey friend says he'll be within a couple of hundred yards of the British pavilion."

"Because you figure that's where he'll make the hit?"

"Yes," said Barry. "From what I understand there are no speeches or presentations planned, nothing out in the open anyway. The only time he'll have a stationary target is outside the pavilion."

"If the killer is there at all."

"Yes," said Barry, "if the killer is there at all."

"*Is* he going to be there?"

"I think so." The Scotland Yard man nodded. "He may assume that Foxworth and Warren will do exactly what they have done—stand down their alert." He shrugged. "As far as they're concerned, Russell has been dealt with and the second assassin's plan has been compromised. From the killer's point of view it may be a very different story. Presumably there is a great deal of money at stake. He won't give up if he thinks he stands a reasonable chance of completing his assignment and getting paid."

"Which he does," said Jane hotly, "especially considering the way things have gone so far." She glanced at

Barry. "Your people left you out on a limb so you could be the scapegoat in case anything went wrong with the Russell situation. Now Foxworth and Warren can't run fast enough to get away from the idea of a second assassin. All this stuff I brought them about Flynn and Kennedy must be scaring the pants off them. If this gets out somehow it's going to raise some serious hell."

"Which," said Hennessy, a sour note in his voice, "is no doubt why the people behind this tried to blow you into little tiny pieces." He shook his head, both hands gripping the wheel tightly. "Just remember I told you so, pally, okay?"

"Why don't you sit on your thumb and just drive the car, Dan?"

"Sure thing, Jane," said the cop with a grin. "But has anyone given any serious thought to exactly what we're going to do when we get to the damn fair?"

"Do what Foxworth and his friends won't," Jane answered promptly. "Find the son of a bitch and kill him."

By 8:30 Bone had piloted the flatboat along the concrete river to the back side of the Court of States just beyond the overpass for World's Fair Boulevard, the four-lane thoroughfare that acted as a convenient divider between the serious sections of the fair and the amusement area around Fountain Lake.

The Court of States, representing twenty-three states and Puerto Rico, was a multibuilding exhibit shaped like a long horseshoe around a shallow, rectangular pool, all of which straddled the Flushing River from the boulevard overpass to the Japanese and Czechoslovakian pavilions a hundred yards or so to the northwest. At first glance it appeared as though the artificial river simply vanished under the base of the Jeffersonian-style Virginia exhibit, but in fact the flow out of Fountain Lake was diverted through a wide concrete culvert, fitted with a trash rack for catching refuse thrown into the stream and just big enough to allow the flatboat to pass through.

Among other things it had been Leo Hamner's responsibility to travel the length of the river from the lake to the spillway, clearing the accumulated garbage tossed into the river each day that wound up being trapped in the trash racks, then taking his nightly haul downstream to the Flushing Bay Piers, where it would be pitchforked onto a barge and taken to a landfill in New Jersey.

Keeping to Leo's schedule Bone killed the engine, tilted it up on the transom and then used a long-handled wooden rake from the bottom of the boat to clear the garbage from the wide mesh of the trash rack. There was an extraordinary amount of it: food wrappers, dozens of copies of *Today at the Fair,* copies of various real newspapers, several soggy hats, both men's and women's, diapers, stuffed toys and other smaller prizes from the midway, at least a dozen unrolled, bloated prophylactics, a shoebox that turned out to hold one red child's shoe and a perfectly modeled birchbark canoe eight inches long and fitted with a carved cork Indian seated in the middle. Etched into the side of the canoe with some kind of burning tool was the word *Opemigon.*

Trash dumped into the bottom of the boat, Bone moved the flatboat forward by bracing his hands flat against the rough concrete of the culvert and pulling. Within a few seconds the boat had been completely swallowed by the culvert and Bone found himself moving through complete darkness, sweating hard now under the raincape. Halfway along his right hand grabbed empty air and he knew he'd reached the side passage that fed the pool that ran the length of the Court of States. The side passage and everything else about the intricacy of the site's waterworks had been shown on the blueprints the clerk in the administration building had proudly shown him on his second visit to the fair.

He reached the far end of the culvert and paused, using both hands to keep the flatboat from being pulled out into the open by the current. He glanced up at the radium dial of his wristwatch. It was 8:41. From this point on, timing would be critical. The exit point of the culvert was directly under the south end of the Pennsylvania pavilion, a three-quarter-size reproduction of Independence Hall, complete with its own copy of the Liberty

Bell, with appropriately placed crack, a carillon tower like the original and a recording of a bell that rang out every hour on the hour from opening in the morning to closing at night.

Two hundred feet away along the watercourse was the main floodway entrance to the Lagoon of Nations. Along the left bank was a shrub-covered slope at the rear of the Missouri, Washington, D.C., and Belgian pavilions, while on the right bank there was the looming, featureless slabs of marble marking the Soviet pavilion and its centerpiece, the floodlit statue of Big Joe at the summit of his tower, striding over everything, the red star of communism held high in his strong right hand.

On his last two visits to the fair, Bone had paced off distances along the length of the river and clocked the speed of its current. Although the speed varied depending on the time of day and width of the river, he knew that between his present position and the entrance to the lagoon the river flowed at an average of a little more than seven miles per hour, or 616 feet per minute. At that rate, unpowered, it would take the flatboat roughly twenty seconds to go from the culvert to the lagoon.

At 8:45 Bone began to notice a steady increase in the number of people moving along the walkway beside the shrub-covered slope on his left and the sidewalk in front of the Soviet pavilion, all of them moving in the direction of the lagoon. It was almost time.

"It really is quite amazing," said Detective Inspector Thomas Barry as they made their way along tree-lined Constitution Mall. "I've never seen anything remotely like it." He smiled. "It's very . . . American."

"We're not here to sightsee, pally," Hennessy grumbled.

"Quit complaining," said Jane. "You were the one who started me off on this whole thing, and this is where it led."

"No," said Hennessy. "This is where you took it, and it's going to get us in deep trouble before the night is over." He looked back over his shoulder. "You notice no one gave us a second look coming in here with my badge? All those plain black Chevys parked around the New York City building inside the main gate? This place is already swarming with dicks. This place closes down they're going to be welding all the manhole covers shut and putting their best shooters on all the roofs. By the time the sun comes up the whole fair's going to be locked down tighter than my aunt Fannie's fanny."

"Our guy knows that as well as you do," Jane answered. "He's figured it out. He's got a way around all that."

"And a way out as well?" Hennessy shook his head. "You're dreaming, Jane. Your guy, if he ever existed, is waiting for the midnight sailings from the West Street piers. He's gone. I should have known better. This whole thing is a wild-goose chase."

"No," said Barry, "Jane's right. He's here."

"Yeah, well last I heard everyone thought Sean Russell was the assassin and he was going to blow everyone up in Detroit. Now it's somebody else and he's going to do his dirty work here."

"Russell was nothing more than a distraction to keep us occupied while the real assassin got on with it."

"Look," said Jane, "we've been over this a hundred times. The voice on the telephone Foxworth tapped isn't a figment of anyone's imagination. He's real."

"All right," said Hennessy. "So now that we're here, what do we do to catch him?"

"Try and think like he does," said Barry. He dropped down on a bench in front of the Heinz exhibit, a white, slightly pointed dome that looked just like the hat Harpo wore in all the Marx Brothers films with a giant, floodlit 57 standing above the entranceway.

Jane glanced through the glass doorway. Inside there was a tall, bright blue column in the center of the exhibit, covered with entwined figures and golden vines. Halfway up the column was a giant glass saucer with water spilling over the edges, and on top of the column was a golden nude woman crouched like a monkey holding up a crystal sphere with one hand, while the other arm crossed discreetly over her private area. Jane wasn't quite sure what it all had to do with pickles and ketchup. She sat down beside Barry on the bench and lit a cigarette. Hennessy stalked back and forth in front of them, his hands jammed into his jacket pockets. All around them the remaining people at the fair seemed to be moving toward the perimeter of the Lagoon of Nations.

"Think like a professional murderer," said the detective, lighting a cigarette of his own. "Shouldn't be too difficult for a homicide dick."

"The king and queen will be surrounded by police," said Jane. "Secret Service, New York State troopers, New York City police."

"Plus a dozen or so from Special Branch," Barry added.

"Shooters on the rooftops, don't forget," said Hennessy.

"What about crowds?" Jane asked. "They're not shutting down the fair for the visit, are they?"

Hennessy shook his head. "Nah. They're just going to cordon off the areas the king and queen will be going to for a few hours, cops every twenty feet or so."

"That's good for the killer," said Barry.

Hennessy looked skeptical. "You think he's going to shoot from the crowd?"

"No, but when he does shoot the crowds are going to panic. The cordons won't hold them back. It'll give him cover."

"How long between the shots being fired to the gates all being sealed?"

"No more than a minute or two," said Hennessy. "It's just like when the president opened the fair in April. Radio cars at all the exits and observers everywhere with army field telephones." He grimaced. "Like I said, Aunt Fannie's fanny." He paused. "Russell may have been nothing but a distraction but he sure put the fear of God in everyone. I heard they even have minesweepers out in the harbor in case someone tries to blow up the ship they're using to come across from New Jersey." He made a snorting sound. "Like no one would notice New York Harbor being mined."

"Don't be so sure." Jane laughed. "No one noticed the krauts sabotaging all those freight cars full of dynamite on Black Tom Island on the Jersey side during the war. I was sixteen years old. Woke me up out of a dead sleep ten miles away, broke windows on Park Avenue."

"This guy's not going to be using a freight car full of dynamite."

"We've been assuming he's going to use a rifle," said Barry. "Perhaps he has some other weapon in mind."

"Like what?" Hennessy asked. "Can't be a pistol, not if he figures on getting away with it. Explosives are probably out as well."

"Why?" Jane asked. She nodded toward Barry, seated on the bench beside her. "Tom here actually saw Russell's bomb factory."

The Scotland Yard man was shaking his head. "I agree with the detective," he said. "It leaves too much to chance. According to the newspaper articles the king and queen have rarely been on schedule. A minute or two early or late and the bomb goes off without doing any harm to them."

"Not to mention the fact that we've got a whole squad of guys to take care of that kind of thing," Hennessy put in.

Jane pulled out the guide book she'd bought at a booth just inside the main gate. She flipped it open, turning to the map, squinting at it closely. She looked up, comparing the view and the map, pointing across Constitution Mall and Rainbow Avenue. "French pavilion, Brazil pavilion. Both high enough and close enough. The All Electric Farm is out because even the silo isn't as tall as the side wall of the Brazil building." She turned slightly, pointing to the right of the mall. "You might have a shot from the top of the Heinz building here, but people would see you from a mile off."

"Nothing else?" asked Hennessy.

"There's a building in the Gardens on Parade exhibit, but it's awfully close and they're sure to have it covered.

The only other thing I can see is maybe one of the houses in the Town of Tomorrow."

"What exactly is that?" Barry asked.

"Just what it says," Jane answered. She looked down at the book. "Fifteen model homes of varying styles and materials. They've got a brick house, a redwood house, plywood, glass, Celotex—whatever that is—even a motor home."

She shrugged. "Some of them have got two stories. Maybe he found an attic to hide in. I did a photo feature for *Life* about it. The houses are ready to move into."

"What about the range?" asked Barry.

"You'd have to pace it off, I guess, but some of the closer ones are within two hundred yards, easy."

"That has to be it," said Hennessy. "He hides out in one of the houses overnight, seals himself in or something so a search won't find him, takes his shot, then slips into the crowd and walks away."

"Let's go and look," said Jane, getting up from the bench.

"Or tell Foxworth," said Hennessy. "That's what we *should* do."

"I don't really think Assistant Director Foxworth is really very interested in any theories about our second assassin," said Barry, rising from the bench himself. "Director Hoover has done everything he can to limit his participation in events thus far, and I think Foxworth has seen the wisdom of his master's ways."

Hennessy moaned. "For Christ's sake, Jane! You mean to say we have to run this bastard to ground ourselves?"

"Let's go and take a look at these houses," Jane answered. "Then we can decide."

They headed up the mall, following the crowds to the Lagoon of Nations, reaching the immense pool just as the 9:00 show was about to begin. Without warning the two main fountains in the center of the lagoon dropped away to nothing and the lights snapped out.

"What's this?" asked Barry.

"Watch," Hennessy answered, grinning. "It's a pip, believe me."

There was a brief moment of silence, the recorded bell sounded in the tower of the Pennsylvania exhibit, and then, as suddenly as darkness had fallen across the lagoon, its waters suddenly began to glow, brighter and brighter. A dense mist began to rise from the surface of the still water and then, abruptly, a hissing cloud of bright blue steam roared up from nozzles around the edges of the pool, forcing people away from the guardrails before they were soaked.

The fountains in the center of the lagoon began to rise again, climbing higher and higher, the wall of mist around the entire pool now changing colors as spotlights played across the suspended curtain of droplets, first rose, then amber, then blue. Music began to swell, great powerful gusts of strings and blaring, triumphant horns, the sound seeming to come from within the lagoon itself. As the music became louder, the fountains rose with it. Then, twin pillars of flame roared up a hundred feet and more, drawing a collective gasp from the assembled crowd. A dozen hidden searchlights made an arching roof of brilliant beams overhead as the music climbed even higher and the blazing tongues of flame rose into the sky again. Then the fireworks began.

As the recorded ringing of the bell boomed out overhead Bone released his restraining hands from the edge of the culvert and the flatboat rushed silently forward in the current, guided by the tiller arm. A quick check confirmed that the walkways on both sides of the river were empty. Everyone was gathered around the lagoon.

The boat reached the floodway entrance and slid into the narrow opening. Once again Bone ducked low and lifted a hand to stop the flatboat, waiting for the exact moment when the music began to swell and the curtain of mist began to rise at the edges of the lagoon. He counted off the seconds in his head, listening to the music and waiting for the loud gasp from the crowd announcing the first flaring of the massive gas jets. As the flames roared upward into the sky Bone released the boat and simultaneously twisted the key in the outboard's ignition.

Seconds later he slipped out through the lagoon opening of the floodway and headed for the other side.

According to the information Bone had gathered the lagoon show used more than a thousand water nozzles capable of throwing twenty tons of water into the air at any given moment, four hundred gas jets, sixty searchlights, 350 noiseless fireworks cannons and three million watts of brilliant light. A live band played in the concert hall, the music broadcast to the crowd around the lagoon from huge, theater-style speakers that poked up just above the surface of the water. The show was controlled by three technicians from inside the United States Building at the far end of the Court of Peace, all three men seated at a vast console like an organ's, fitted out with the dozens of switches and buttons controlling the water nozzles, the fireworks and the gas jets. The whole extravaganza, fireworks included, lasted for exactly six minutes.

Right from the start John Bone had realized that getting his equipment to his chosen lie would be the most difficult challenge confronting him. The necessary apparatus was large, cumbersome and impossible to explain away. Bringing it to the lie could not be accomplished during the daylight hours. Bone also quickly came to the conclusion that coming in by water was far and away the safest and most expedient path to the lie and his best escape route as well.

During daylight, the paths along the meandering course of the river were filled with strolling visitors to the fair, and the grassy, lightly sloping banks on either side were a favorite picnicking spot, but during the evening hours, especially after dusk, the walkways were virtually empty. The lagoon was a different story. The four-hundred-foot-wide, eight-hundred-foot-long basin was one of the fair's focal points and there were always groups of people leaning on the guardrails or sitting on the benches, resting or waiting for friends.

Leo Hamner regularly made his rounds along the water course, and just as regularly he must have crossed the lagoon, but Bone wanted no one to remember his passage—too much depended on his remaining invisible.

Ironically, he came to the conclusion that the only time to cross the lagoon was when the most people were focusing their attention on it. For the six-minute duration of the show the fine nozzles around the edge of the basin effectively screened the surface of the water, and the spurting fountains, floodlights, gas jets and pyrotechnics saw to it that everyone's eyes were looking upward for that brief space of time.

With the hood of the raincape tight across his neck and forehead, Bone crouched in the bottom of the boat, his legs curled around the duffel bag, his hand gripping the tiller of the electric outboard as he piloted it across the lagoon, trying to keep an equal distance between the curtains of spray around the perimeter and the potential disaster of the boat being silhouetted against the gas jets and the colored sprays of water.

According to his calculations, at full throttle it would take the little motor three minutes to run the length of the lake, but Bone knew it could easily take another minute or even two at the half throttle necessary for the last part of the traverse. Although fewer people watched the show from the wide span across the river at the western edge of the lagoon, there would be some, and he had to guide the flatboat into the egress floodway on the first try. If he missed he would be seen, and if he was seen he would be remembered, or worse, reported to one of the fifty or so policemen who patrolled the grounds.

Still counting the seconds off in his head, Bone looked up briefly and was startled to see how close he was to the west-side floodway. He twisted the tiller handle sharply, cutting almost all the power, sliced through the misty curtain at almost the precise spot he'd aimed for and vanished into the darkness under the bridge. Less than ninety seconds later the thundering music reached its crescendo, timed to the blazing firework canopy high above.

Then everything vanished in a single instant, the twinkling sparks of the fireworks winking out, the music falling silent, the roaring water from the fountains crashing down, all twenty tons of it slamming into the lagoon like a massive ocean breaker crashing against a cliff. Strangely, the sudden silence and the darkness was the most dramatic moment of the show, and for a few seconds the crowd around the lagoon stood in stunned amazement and then burst into wild applause.

As the people began to clap, Jane Todd felt a hand drop down onto the shoulder of her jacket. She turned to find herself staring at a dark-faced Sam Foxworth. Behind him was a quartet of clean-shaven, earnest-looking young men in dark, expensive hats and dark, expensive suits, and behind them was a pair of bulky, wide-shouldered men with harder faces and cheaper suits. The two larger men stepped forward.

"Michael," said Hennessy, grinning coldly. "Come to arrest me, have you?"

"You know this guy?" Jane asked.

"Michael Murphy," Hennessy explained. "Head of the commissioner's Confidential Squad. Time was, we were pals."

"You've been suspended pending an investigation," said Murphy.

"Investigation of what?"

"Who's to say?" Murphy shrugged. "I was just told to bring you along." He poked a thumb in the direction of his burly companion. "Billy's here to lend a hand if you get edgy."

"Not edgy," said Hennessy. "Just a little disappointed."

"I do as I'm told," said Murphy. "Are you coming along?"

"Sure," said Hennessy. He turned to Barry. "My best to your lady friend," he said and went off with the two New York City detectives without a backward glance.

"Speaking of your lady friend, where is she?" Foxworth asked Barry.

"Who?"

"Miss Connelly."

"I have no idea."

"Miss Todd? Do you know where she is?"

She nodded at Barry. "Like he says."

Foxworth turned to one of his men. "Is there a jail here?"

"There's a lockup in the administration building."

"Put them in it," said Foxworth.

"What are you charging us with?" asked Jane.

"You're not under arrest," said Foxworth. "I'm taking you into protective custody. If I think of something to charge you with later, I'll let you know."

Chapter 25

Saturday, June 10, 1939
Red Bank, New Jersey

Sir Alan Lascelles, Knight Commander of the Victorian Order, assistant private secretary to His Royal Majesty and English gentleman, stepped across the wooden railway ties, smoking a cigarette, enjoying the silence and the early-morning mist, wondering at the vicissitudes of life that could take you from Buckingham Palace and the corridors of power to a railway siding on the outskirts of the seaside resort town of Red Bank, New Jersey. Somehow it didn't seem the sort of thing that would be included in your obituary in the *Times*.

A tall figure wearing cavalry boots and a flat-brimmed cavalry hat stepped out of the fog in front of him, a rifle at port arms across his barrel chest and a holstered revolver on the hip of his dark blue motorcycle jodhpurs. He was a New Jersey State Police trooper, one of the swarm that had surrounded the train when it pulled onto the siding just before dawn. Lascelles had clearly reached the edge of whatever safety zone had been laid out by the local authorities. The trooper stared at Lascelles and Lascelles stared back, wondering how the man would react if he decided to continue his walk and go around him. Instead, Lascelles deferred to the very large policeman, dropped his cigarette end on the cinders on the side of the road, ground it out with the toe of his shoe, then turned and headed back to the train.

The last official day of the tour was clearly going to be arduous. Foggy or not, it promised to be another day of wilting heat. Even so Lascelles couldn't help but feel relieved. The queen had managed to get in and out of Washington without offending anyone and the king had managed several private talks with President Roosevelt and a number of other key people, including J. P. Morgan of the Morgan Bank, several Vanderbilts and John D. Rockefeller Jr., head of the Chase National Bank and Equitable Trust.

There had been another important meeting at the embassy dinner the night before, which the king and Roosevelt attended but which the queen, thankfully, did not. His Majesty had asked the advice of Lindsay, the ambassador, and the president regarding the possibility of the royal family going into exile, perhaps in Canada, in the event of war. Lascelles had kept his own counsel on the subject but Lindsay was quite blunt and so was Roosevelt. Even though His Majesty considered himself both ill-fitted and ill-prepared to be a king in wartime, the idea of him abandoning his people in their darkest hour would almost certainly be perceived as cowardice. To affect any lasting alliances he would have to remain in England until flight was the only option.

Ambassador Lindsay quietly reminded His Majesty that the last English king to face invasion had been Harold II, who died at the Battle of Hastings in 1066, surrounded by a few of his loyal men. Roosevelt then graciously offered to give the queen and the two princesses, Elizabeth and Margaret, asylum should hostilities break out. The king just as graciously declined, knowing perfectly well that if he didn't cut and run, then neither would the queen nor the little princesses.

The subject was dropped, the guests at the embassy were rejoined for a final cocktail and then, just before midnight, the Roosevelts and the Lindsays accompanied the king and queen to their waiting train, which left the station a few minutes later, heading north toward New York. At 4:30 A.M. they reached the railway siding outside Red Bank and paused, waiting for daylight and their trip by automobile to the waiting warship docked at Fort Hancock on Sandy Hook, some twelve to fifteen miles distant.

The observation platform at the rear of the royal train appeared out of the mist. Lascelles stepped around it and continued forward until he reached his own car. Another uniformed New Jersey trooper was waiting beside the metal stepping stool leading up into the car, this one without a rifle but with the same stern, automatonlike expression on his face. Lascelles found himself wondering if the men were chosen for the width of their jaws and the thickness of their necks. The trooper saluted and Lascelles climbed up into the car, looking forward to coffee and another cigarette or two before the king awoke and the day began.

At five minutes to nine the royal train lumbered slowly across the train bridge spanning the Navesink River and pulled into the gaily decorated railway station in the little town of Red Bank. The entire town had come out to see the train and its occupants. A great roar of applause broke out as the king and queen stepped out on the observation platform of their car. The queen, predictably enough, was wearing a blue ensemble complete with matching parasol against the threatening sun, while the king had chosen a dark gray morning suit and a gray top hat rather than a uniform since today's festivities were relatively unofficial.

The Red Bank Volunteer Fireman's Band struck up "God Save the King" and the royal couple stepped down from the train. The governor of New Jersey and his wife were introduced, followed by the mayor of Red Bank and his wife. After a few minutes of posing for the photographers, the king and queen were handed into the large Packard limousine awaiting them and the procession set off for Sandy Hook and Fort Hancock.

As the lead car pulled away the king noticed a plump, well-dressed older woman at the edge of the greeting party arguing angrily with the Red Hook mayor and was informed that she was Mrs. Charles English, the wife of the mayor of Asbury Park, a neighboring town. The woman had apparently purchased an enormously expensive bouquet of flowers that were to be presented to the queen, but the bouquet had somehow been waylaid and sent to the Red Bank police station.

Driving along beside the widening river the procession of cars passed more cheering crowds on either side of the highway, once again held back by New Jersey state troopers, all of them armed with rifles, bayonets affixed. Even the strong police presence couldn't detract from the scenery, much of it reminiscent of English countryside—rich green fields broken by darker patches of forest, parts of the roadway overhung by towering, ancient elms, their trunks and lower branches gnarled by time.

Crowds lined the streets of every town and village, most of the spectators frantically waving handmade Union Jacks and cheering, some of them trying to sing "God Save the King" and inadvertently switching to "My Country 'Tis of Thee," which clearly startled the king and queen, who had no idea that there was another song sharing the same tune as the English National Anthem. Little girls scattered flowers on the roadway in front of the advancing cars and everybody waved, including the inmates of a small country nursing home, most of them in wheeled chairs or cots assembled on the lawns.

At the little village of Rumson they turned toward the sea and the landscape changed again, the narrow twisting roadway between the fields and trees giving way to a wide road and esplanade with a wide sand beach sweeping down to the sea on the right. The beach was crowded with morning bathers, who sprinted up to the edge of the road as the royal tourists swept by, the young men and women in their bathing costumes, sunburned and tanned, still dripping wet, contrasting wildly with the formal dresses, morning suits and top hats of the entourage. In the far distance, but visible now rising above the mists, lay the hazy New York skyline, a forest of slender towers like a city of ghosts on the horizon.

The procession passed through the town of Sea Bright and continued northward up the Sandy Hook Peninsula to Fort Hancock, once part of the fortifications around

New York and now a coast guard station. Warped into the pier was the destroyer *Warrington,* its entire crew turned out in dress whites around the decks, saluting as the king, the queen and the rest of the entourage were shrilly piped aboard. A neighboring escort cruiser, already waiting in the bay, let out a roaring royal salute of guns, and at that same instant the royal standard broke from the *Warrington*'s yardarm, the first occasion in the history of the United States that the king's flag had ever flown from any of its ships' standards.

As the *Warrington* moved out into open water pandemonium broke out over all of Lower New York Harbor. Liners, ferries, tugs and tramp steamers thundered and screamed their welcomes on horns and sirens. Ahead of the *Warrington* a pair of navy minesweepers cleared a path while astern and on either side an escort of thirty coast guard vessels fanned out across the wide expanse of water. Overhead a dozen army air corps planes swung lazily back and forth in the brightening haze as the fog finally began to lift.

Lascelles was summoned to join the king and queen, who stood side by side on the bridge, gazing ahead as they approached Manhattan. In the distance an overloaded tour boat chugged across their bows, the crowds of well-wishers on its upper decks causing a perceptible list even from almost a mile away. As it swung out of the *Warrington*'s path, hundreds of balloons were released into the sky, each one printed with the Union Jack.

"Quite the we-welcome, don't you think, Alan?"

"Yes, sir," Lascelles said. "Quite exuberant."

"Exhausting is more like it," said the queen. "And this insufferable heat!"

"Ba-bad luck, Buffy, I'm afraid."

"I think we should have been warned," the queen responded, giving Lascelles a pouting look, as though he should have had better control over the weather. "I don't know why we have to go to this dreadful exhibition or whatever it is. We should have gone with the president and his wife to the country for the weekend or we should have started for home." She let out a long-suffering sigh and gripped her pale blue hat with one gloved hand as a gust of wind threatened to blow it off.

"It's a World's Fair, ma'am, and attending it was Ambassador Lindsay's suggestion some months ago."

"I've been to enough church fetes in my time," said the queen. "I don't need to see another, particularly an American one."

"This is something more than a fete, ma'am, if you don't mind me saying. Considering the times the ambassador thought attending an international exhibition of this sort might do something in the way of fostering good relations between England and a number of other countries."

"Well, bugger Lindsay and his suggestions."

"I-I really don't mind, dear," said the king. "And I've always ra-rather wanted to see New York. David used to say it was quite wonderful."

At the mention of her brother-in-law's name the queen turned away, her expression cold. Any mention of the Duke and Duchess of Windsor was anathema to her, and the king's jaw tightened as he realized his mistake. "Sorry, Buffy," he said.

"Quite all right," she answered, turning back to him and glancing at her husband's secretary. She put on a small martyred smile, looking over the king's shoulder at Lascelles. "It's just that in my condition I'm liable to faint, and I wouldn't want to embarrass anyone." Lascelles turned away, flushing. Dear God, he thought, she's having her Visitor or she's with child. Either event was a daunting state of affairs, especially since he was more than reasonably sure that a royal pregnancy would not have been the result of relations between husband and wife. Lascelles closed his eyes for a moment and gripped the rail, wishing desperately for a cigarette. The woman would be the death of him.

At 11:15, already half an hour behind schedule, the U.S.S. *Warrington* eased gently up against the bunting-covered Department of Docks pier and dropped anchor. As the chains rumbled down a dozen bands struck up

"God Save the King," all in different tempos and with variations depending on their sheet music, but it didn't matter in the least since no one could hear them over the din of New York's welcome to the royal couple. Car horns blared, another cannonade salute blasted out from the guns at Fort Jay on Governor's Island, factory whistles screamed and bugles tooted—all of that in turn swallowed up by the thundering cheers from the immense crowd assembled in Battery Park and beyond.

As the king and queen came down the gangplank and reached the three-hundred-foot-long red carpet laid out before them, Herbert Lehman, the governor of New York, stepped forward with an outstretched hand, followed by the squat, toadlike figure of Fiorello La Guardia, the mayor of New York City, a procession of other notables on his heels. The welcoming ceremony took precisely two minutes and the king and queen, the governor and the mayor walked slowly to the open car that was to convey them to the fair in Flushing Meadows. Behind the lead car, fourteen other limousines, all of them closed, waited for Lascelles and the other members of the royal retinue, traffic duty being attended to by a fully uniformed Lewis J. Valentine, commissioner of police. At his signal the whole parade of vehicles moved off, turning sharply north onto West Street and the elevated highway that ran along beside the Hudson River piers, rather than take the somewhat unsightly East River route.

Special Branch, the Secret Service and the New York police had all agreed that other than the threat from Russell in Detroit the king and queen would be most vulnerable on the ten-mile route from Battery Park to the World's Fair site in Queens. La Guardia had estimated a crowd of more than two million, Commissioner Valentine had predicted three million and, in the end, there were more than four million New Yorkers crowded along the route. Thirteen thousand uniformed policemen, more than half the entire force, had been enlisted to man the wooden barricades to keep back the crowds. For the sake of security a speed of fifty-five miles per hour had been set for the motorcade and the attending squad of motorcycle outriders.

The high rate of speed along the West Side Highway lasted for less than five minutes. La Guardia, making conversation from the small, uncomfortable jump seat facing the queen, informed her that a million people alone, many of them children, were assembled in Central Park. Hearing this, the queen, had a brief conversation with her husband, who in turn relayed a message to the driver of their car. The driver, Mayor La Guardia's own chauffeur, immediately slowed to a more sedate, and visible, twenty-five miles per hour.

Eventually, after wending their way up to Fifty-ninth Street and driving sedately through the throngs in Central Park, the motorcade turned east onto 122nd Street and headed for the Triborough Bridge. Twenty minutes later and almost a full hour late, the royal procession of automobiles reached the North Corona Gate and drove onto the site of the New York World's Fair at last.

Chapter 26

Saturday, June 10, 1939
New York World's Fair

Even through the walls of the windowless detention cell in the administration building Jane Todd could hear the resounding cheers of the crowds assembled around the main gate and a twenty-one-gun salute from the New York Police Rifle Team. "They're here," she said, turning to Thomas Barry. The Scotland Yard detective nodded almost absently, sitting on the bunk against the side wall of the narrow cell, smoking another cigarette and staring up at the ceiling. There was another bunk against the opposite wall, an open toilet but no sink, and a heavy metal door painted dark yellow. The floor was painted concrete.

"What time is it?" Barry asked.

Jane checked her little Bulova, squinting in the pale light. "Twelve forty-five."

"They're late then."

"So's our lunch."

Since being taken to the cell the night before, the two had seen no one except a silent, uniformed policeman, who'd brought them a simple breakfast of toast and coffee earlier in the morning. Jane got up from her own bunk, walked to the door and smacked it hard with the palm of her hand. "We can't just sit here and let this happen."

"We don't seem to have much choice in the matter," said Barry.

Jane went back to her bunk and sat down. "How much of the itinerary do you remember?" she asked.

"There's a welcoming ceremony at the New York pavilion just inside the gate. Then they do the rounds of the exhibits and go to the British Empire pavilion for some kind of lunch."

"And then they do their inspection of the British Honor Guard on the side lawn?"

"Right," Barry said.

"Then we still have time."

"Hope springs eternal?" said the detective.

"Something like that," Jane answered. "I think Foxworth may yet see the light."

"What makes you think so?" Barry asked.

"Something you said a while back," said Jane. "About this guy not leaving anything to chance."

"I'm not sure I see what you mean."

"Neither am I . . . yet." She got up and went to the door again, pounding on it with her fist this time. "Goddamn it! Open up!"

The weapon John Bone had chosen was a bastard, constructed from a half dozen guns he'd found at Lavan's shop, but based on the original Lancaster rifle he'd spotted in the gunsmith's racks when he first visited the store. Most Lancasters Bone had seen were classic double-barreled side-by-side shotguns, but he had occasionally seen twin-barreled rifles, usually built in express calibers as African elephant guns.

The Lancaster he'd seen in Lavan's was something different: a four-chambered rifle in a massive .500 caliber with British Whitworth Fluid steel barrels and a complicated lockwork designed like a double-action revolver. A single, flat mainspring mounted at the rear of the action drove a striking rod so that with each trigger pull the rod drew back and then flew forward, striking the firing pin.

The pin was arranged in a square formation to match

the barrels, and as the firing pin shot forward a small, spring-loaded stud engaged a helical gear, turning the striking plate ninety degrees, the pin striking each of the four barrels in turn as fast as the trigger was pulled.

The advantage to Bone was immediately clear. Any self-loading rifle available to him, such as the Mauser, the Krag or Springfield, had relatively slow bolt actions. Automatic weapons like the Browning or the Thompson were gas-blowback operated, only good for short range, and depended on rate of fire to take out a target rather than accuracy. The Lancaster action, although more than forty years old, gave Bone four shots available almost instantly. By his calculation the weapon could be emptied in slightly less than three seconds.

By replacing the heavy-caliber express barrels with a carefully spot-welded quartet of lightweight twenty-six-inch Winchesters cut down from Lavan's collection of "sportified" military model 70s, Bone created a dead accurate .30-.06-caliber rifle that would give him four shots with an almost perfectly flat trajectory over two hundred yards—more than he needed.

By stripping off the heavy walnut stock and replacing it with a simple piece of tube steel tapped at one end and fitted with a leather-padded butt at the other, he dropped the weight from twelve and a half pounds to seven, even with the added bulk of a telescopic sight. With barrels, action, butt and sight broken down into their component parts, the weapon easily fit into his duffel bag, as did the modified Graflex tripod he was using as a targeting rest.

As the first volley of the salute rang out Bone began to put his exotic weapon together, keeping well out of sight, deep in the shadows. With the four-barreled device assembled and loaded, he snapped the action closed, automatically cocking the rifle. He then dropped it into the padded rest on the tripod, tightened the clamp and put his eye to the sight, swiveling the floating mount on the tripod until the podium in front of the British pavilion came into view.

Glancing away from the sight he noted the faint fluttering of the half dozen Union Jacks on the roof of the building. Putting his eye back to the sight he adjusted it by a single click to take in windage and the stifling heat, both of which could throw off his aim if he wasn't careful, even at such a relatively close range.

He touched the guide arm of the tripod with the tips of his fingers, bringing the crosshairs up a fraction of an inch. The first two shots for the king, chest high, crushing his heart, the second volley for the queen, striking her a little higher, somewhere close to the base of the throat, the explosive power of the soft-nose bullets probably enough to decapitate her. Stepping away from the weapon Bone stood back in the shadows and waited. He smiled. Even over the roaring of the crowd he could hear one of the bands nearby doing a brassy rendition of "The Bluebells of Scotland," Her Majesty's favorite song.

More than anything else in the world Bobby Zwicker, twelve years old, wanted to be a professional baseball player, preferably shortstop for the Brooklyn Dodgers, not so much because he liked the team, but because Ebbets Field was only a mile or so away down the Kingston Avenue trolley line, making it close to home. To him, baseball was the most manly thing in the world, even better than sneaking peeks through the basement windows at Pratt and watching the naked models standing there looking so bored even though they had everything showing you could ever hope to see. Dolph Camilli and Cookie Lavagetto, Babe Phelps, and Fat Freddie Fitzsimmons were the names of his current heroes and Goodie Rosen, pug-nosed and mean, was the essence of the underdog and a Jew to boot. They were saying the team was going to be better this season with Leo Durocher managing, but he didn't care. It wasn't who played, really. The game was the thing.

Except general admission was an out-of-this-world $1.10, a decent seat on Saturday was even more and the only other way to see the game was from the roof of a garage on Bedford Avenue or by lying prone on the sidewalk by the exit gate in the deepest corner of right center field. The big steel doors didn't quite fit flush against the ground, and if you looked through the crack, twice as wide as an eyeball, you could see most of center field, left field and two-thirds of the infield, but the only way to tell if someone was safe or out at first was by the reaction of the crowd. On top of that you had to worry about a cop poking a shoe in your ribs and telling you to move along.

All of which was why Bobby Zwicker rose each day before dawn, picked up his forty-four copies of the *Brooklyn Eagle* and rode his bicycle up and down the streets of Bedford, pretending that the folded projectiles he tossed up onto his customers' porches were serving as good practice for his future career as a big leaguer.

Today the headlines were screaming about the King and Queen of England visiting New York and the fair but Bobby wasn't even mildly interested. Six days dragging himself out of bed and delivering papers was buying him a blissful afternoon at Ebbets, two hot dogs, a Coke and a half-decent view of Rosen hitting at least a little *bingle* or two if everybody prayed hard enough.

At 6:30 A.M. he started on his tour of the neighborhood, and at ten past seven he flipped a paper up onto the Hamners' front porch at 331 Adelphi and rode on, vaguely surprised that the old bag's front door was still closed. In his experience it was usually open by now, with the woman in her dressing gown waiting for the paper with a cup of coffee in one hand and a smoke in the other.

At 7:45, his route complete, Bobby bicycled up Adelphi again on his way home. The Hamners' paper was still on the porch and the door was still closed. At the time Bobby assumed that she'd either had too much to drink the night before and was sleeping in, or she'd coughed herself to death. Reaching home he said as much to his mother, who smacked him across the rear end with her own copy of the *Eagle* and told him to have more respect for his elders, even though she was smiling as she said it.

At 9:30, on her way to the butcher shop on DeKalb,

Bobby's mother also noticed the paper still on the porch. It was still there when she came back in the opposite direction fifteen minutes later. Concluding that it was really none of her business she went home, had a brief discussion about the situation with her husband and then took things in hand by calling Mrs. Hamner on the telephone. There was no reply. An hour went by and she called again. Still no answer. Frustrated, she argued with her husband, sure now that there was something wrong.

Silently cursing his son's powers of observation at seven in the morning, Arnold Zwicker, who had intended spending the Sabbath doing absolutely nothing, which included attending services at the synagogue, walked down Adelphi to 331 and hammered on the Hamners' front door. Getting no response after repeated knocks he went around to the rear of the house, climbed the rickety back porch and knocked again. Like the front door, the rear door was closed and locked.

Leaning outward and cupping one hand over his eyes against the glare, Arnold Zwicker peered into the dark kitchen. At first it looked as though everything was in order, but then he noticed a dark streak of color on the floor, leading to the basement doorway. For some reason he could not really fathom at the time, or even many years later, he knew exactly what he was seeing, even though his initial suspicion was that Leo had finally become fed up with his mother and beat her to death with one of her frying pans. Feeling bile rising sourly in his throat, Bobby Zwicker's father backed away from the window, tiptoed down the porch steps and then ran like hell back to his own home, where he telephoned the police.

By then it was 11:00 in the morning. The police, short-staffed by the security measures for the royal visit, took almost an hour to respond. Leo Hamner was found, shot to death in his bed, and his mother and Agent Gordon were found in the basement. Special Agent Gordon remained unidentified until 2:30 in the afternoon when his relief, an agent named Breur, appeared. Foxworth, coordinating FBI security measures for the royal tour from his office, was informed of Gordon's murder at ten minutes to three.

By midafternoon Lascelles could see that both the king and queen were finally succumbing to the strain of the day's events. Visiting the United States pavilion at the far end of the fair site they were faced with a receiving line consisting of more than three hundred local dignitaries. Lascelles himself had a brief discussion with Grover Whalen, the fair's chairman. Whalen had the presentation cut short, changing it to allow the royal couple to simply move along the line, bowing to the guests, occasionally shaking a hand or having a brief conversation.

Visits were made to a number of the governmental pavilions, including several of the state exhibits, the Japanese pavilion and the Irish Free State pavilion, where Lascelles listened to the queen asking a little too ingenuously about the granite monument dedicated to Padriac Pearse and the men executed by the British army during the 1916 Rebellion. Traveling with Whalen, La Guardia and other notables in one of the absurd Greyhound motor trains the king and queen were exposed to the tremendous heat of the day, worsened by the heat-absorbing asphalt roadways, the massed crowds behind the wooden barricades and the diesel fumes of the motor train itself. Once again Lascelles had a word with Whalen, and once again the itinerary was shortened. By 3:00 P.M. the royal couple still hadn't been given lunch, the king was beginning to mutter about his need for a cigarette and a restorative glass of whiskey and the queen was looking quite ill.

After a flying visit to the Italian pavilion, where the Italian commissioner general gave them the fascist salute, and a brief pose for photographers in front of the Mounties and totem poles outside the Canadian pavilion, the king and queen were finally escorted into the British Empire exhibit, where the queen was given a couch to lie down on and the king was given a Players and a double shot of Dewar's, neat.

Jack Lait, reporter for the *Daily Mirror,* observed the

proceedings from a telephone booth, where he called in his story for the late edition, bucking the trend and referring to the somewhat wilted queen as a "cute, cuddly, homely-looking girl in a blue ensemble that was becoming enough but wouldn't have rated a second glance in a Broadway theater lobby."

As the royal entourage disappeared inside the air-conditioned pavilion, the crowd, held back as far as the Lagoon of Nations, began to slowly disperse. By 3:45, somewhat revived, the king and queen were enjoying a light, informal lunch of cold chicken and salad while outside in the adjacent Court of Peace a military band played a medley of light music to aid their digestion, including—as a special gesture to the Queen—yet another rendition of "The Bluebells of Scotland."

The door to the detention cell swung open and Assistant Director Sam Foxworth stepped into the narrow room, closing the door behind him. His face was chalk-white and the hand holding his cigarette was shaking slightly.

"Trouble?" asked Jane.

"Last night we sent agents to the houses of all three people your second assassin was interested in. This morning we found one of those agents dead. Shot once in the head. The man he was sent to protect is dead as well and so is the man's mother."

"Which one was it?" Jane asked.

"Hamner. The janitor," said Foxworth. "You were right. The son of a bitch is here."

"I thought he'd be the one," Jane said. "The Borden's guy and the other one were too specific. Hamner was a janitor—probably had all sorts of pass keys. Now the killer has them."

"It looks as though he used my own agent's car and his identification to get into the fair last night," Foxworth said. "We're checking with the gate guards now to see if anyone remembers him." He shook his head. "At least then we'll know what he looks like."

"I don't think that matters now," said Barry. "Where are the king and queen?"

"Having lunch in the British pavilion." Foxworth checked his wristwatch. "They're running behind schedule."

"How long until they do their inspection of the Honor Guard?" asked the Scotland Yard man.

"Ten minutes. Fifteen at the most."

"We know where the killer's going to be," said Jane. "We figured it out last night."

"*Where,* goddamn it?!"

"And have you leave us here? Forget it, Foxworth. Open that door and we'll lead the way. And I want my bag back. It's got my new camera in it."

"I'll arrest you!"

"No, you won't. You're not that stupid. Now open the goddamn door."

The houses of the Town of Tomorrow were designed to look like a small section of a futuristic subdivision, the dwellings arranged on three winding streets that led absolutely nowhere. The town was located on a two-and-a-half-acre site nestled in behind the Contemporary Arts pavilion, flanked by the Electrified Farm on one side and the curving shape of the Home Building Center. The fourth side of the exhibit faced a narrow strip of parkway that led down to the river. Beyond that, on the opposite bank, was the Gardens on Parade exhibit and the British Empire pavilion.

The lawns of the town were sodded and trimmed, looking a little burned in the heat wave. Saplings had been planted and shrubs banked along driveways; the fantasy community had even borrowed a scattering of next year's automobile models from the Chrysler, Ford and General Motors buildings, parking them on the streets and in the opened garages for a more lived-in, authentic look. Of the fourteen houses being displayed, nine were two-storied but only three had reasonable lines of sight from their second floors to the side lawn of the British pavilion.

By the time Jane, Barry, Foxworth and four of his agents battled their way through the crowds on Rainbow Avenue to the futuristic town site, another crowd had begun to assemble on the Spillway Bridge and the bank of the river all the way along to the French pavilion and the Lagoon of Nations. The first few bars of "Rule Britannia" rang out and the people began to cheer again. Everyone's attention was on the British pavilion as the uniformed Honor Guard marched into view and took up their positions on the side lawn. This was to be the royal couple's last official function at the fair. For the time being the Town of Tomorrow was deserted.

"Which house?" yelled Foxworth, standing in the middle of the central street, his heavy pistol drawn and in his hand.

"I'm not sure!" Jane yelled back. She took a small Contax camera out of her bag and started shooting.

"Take a guess!" Foxworth bellowed. "We're running out of time!" He glared at Jane. "And put that damn camera away!" Jane smiled and stuck out her tongue at the man. She kept on shooting.

Barry swung around on his heel, squinting in the hammering sunlight, trying to remember what he'd been told during his training in the army more than twenty years before. In this case the elevation was already there—the Town of Tomorrow was built on an artificial hill twelve to fifteen feet higher than the river. The three houses on the river slope side of the road and closest to the All Electric Farm would give clear views of the side lawn. Two others, at the farthest end of the curving road, were also in a direct line, but at least another hundred yards away. Not an impossible shot, but considerably more difficult. "Those three," said Barry at last, pointing at the last three houses on the street. Foxworth waved his men into the houses, one after the other.

"You'd better be right about this," said the FBI man.

Jane laughed coldly. "Little bit late to be shifting responsibility. You guys have screwed this up from the beginning."

"Just so long as they don't screw it up now," said

Barry, still scanning the houses. Something wasn't right and he felt a strange flush of cold sweat at the back of his neck.

Jane picked up the look and questioned it. "What's the matter?"

"He's not here," Barry whispered. "This is wrong."

"It's the only place that works," Jane insisted.

"No," said Barry, shaking his head. "It's not safe enough."

"Why not?" said Foxworth. "All he has to do is melt into the crowds back on Rainbow Avenue."

"It fits," said Jane. "Leo Hamner probably had keys to all these places! It has to be here!"

"It's not." "Rule Britannia" had swung into "Pomp and Circumstance." The appearance of the royal couple was imminent now, barely seconds away. Thomas Barry moved away from his companions, walking down between the white clapboard Cape Cod and its ultramodern concrete-and-steel neighbor, pausing at the top of the dry grass slope, peering over the heads of the massed crowds across the dark line of the river to the side lawn of the British pavilion. Two dozen old men stood there at rigid, arthritic attention, expatriates all, wearing the wounds and medals and uniforms of a war that had almost been forgotten. His war. A gust of hot wind blew across the fair, snapping the flags and rippling the water and taking him back.

In 1915 Barry had been in a place called Kut-el-Amara, an ancient stronghold on the road to Baghdad. He and fifteen thousand other men had been brought there under the command of a foolish young officer named Townsend to take a meaningless piece of the desert named Ctesiphon. A wind like this had been blowing that day when they finally met the forces of Nur-ud-Din, a madman in league with the Turks and the Germans. Almost no one had survived the battle, yet the policeman, once a soldier, was sure that not one man in ten thousand could find Ctesiphon on a map or the name of Nur-ud-Din in the history books. History was as fleeting as the hot wind on his face and both would pass away no matter what happened here this day.

In fifty years no one will remember this any more than Ctesiphon.

Jane watched as the four FBI men came out of each of the houses, shaking their heads. "The son of a bitch isn't in any of them," said Foxworth.

"Then where the hell is he?"

"You tell me."

Jane turned and stared at Barry, still standing between the houses at the top of the slope. She looked back at Foxworth. "Hamner was a janitor?"

"That's right."

"Did he do anything else?"

"He was a janitor, damn it! He did what janitors do."

"*Nothing* special?" Jane prodded.

Foxworth shrugged. "One of things he did was clean out the trash that collected in the river."

"When?"

"Every night. He used a boat."

Jane whirled around. From where she stood she could see down to the wooden Tree of Life statue and just beyond it to the Spillway Bridge, crowded for its entire span with hundreds of spectators waiting for the king and queen to appear. The bridge was concrete, fitted with a high guardrail set with flagpoles and created from four low main arches in the center of the river and two much smaller circular openings close to either bank.

"Oh Jesus!" Jane whispered. With a single movement she reached out, grabbed Foxworth's pistol from his hand and raced off toward Barry. "It's the bridge!" she yelled. "It's the bridge!" On the other side of the river there was a roar of applause as the royal couple appeared in the sunlight and "God Save the King" began for one last time that day.

As the anthem began John Bone made the final adjustments to the gun, watching through the reticle as the slim man in the gray suit and topper climbed up on the podium with his blue-frocked wife beside him. With the powerful lens of the sight he could see the powder caking a little around the creases of her neck and the flanges of her nostrils. There was a faint dark perspiration line just under the rim of her powder-blue hat. She was clearly feeling quite uncomfortable. Bone twisted the knob of the scope, bringing the crosshairs into perfect focus, watching for even the faintest heat mirage that might interfere with his aim. There was none.

Bone shifted slightly, putting himself directly behind the tripod now, the shallow water from the stream eight inches up his gumboots, the concrete bottom of the spillway conduit giving a strong, firm footing. The tunnel under the bridge and the water would absorb most of the sound when it came. What remained would be drowned out by the cheering crowds.

Behind Bone, the flatboat, bow-first in the water, was nudging the trash rack set halfway down the length of the spillway pipe, riding easily on the light current. It would take Bone no more than five seconds to climb into the boat, release the trash rack and head downstream, first gliding solely on the current and then with the motor brought into play. All the attention of the people on the bridge above him and the ones lining the banks of the river would be on the spectacle of the king and queen and then the horror of their brutal assassinations.

He turned his attention back to the rifle, easing his shoulder into the leather-padded butt piece, his long, powerful finger slipping into the circular trigger guard, taking up the slow pull until the ring was tight against the curl of his flesh. No more adjustments now, or even thinking, letting the mind empty, the eye filling with nothing but the target and the last exhalation before the primary shot.

"Hamner used some kind of boat to clean up trash," Jane panted as she ran up to Barry at the top of the slope. "Our man's in the culvert under the bridge! He has to be!" She thrust the pistol toward the Scotland Yard man.

Grabbing the pistol from Jane's outstretched hand, Thomas Barry raced down the slope leading to the walkway, elbowing the crowd out of his way as he ran, his shoulders working now as he threw himself forward like a battering ram, desperately pushing ahead until finally he reached the water's edge and ran forward through the shallows. The pistol lifted in his hand, pointing into the shadows of the nearest bridge tunnel as the first in the crowd saw his gun and screamed, their frightened outcry and pointing fingers lost in the surrounding clamor.

Under the bridge the assassin was lost in the process of his art. His targets both stood together on the podium now, the king raising his hand to tip his top hat toward the crowd, the queen raising her own gloved hand in that small cupped gesture she'd created to ease the pain of too much waving. Bone's finger had fully reduced the pull, now needing only the pressure of a whispered breath to move it. Then he heard the splash. He looked away from the eyepiece of the sight in time to see the silhouette of a man standing a few feet outside the mouth of the bridge tunnel, a large handgun pointing in his direction. Almost without conscious thought Bone smacked the lever on the floating head of the tripod and spun the rifle around in the direction of the silhouetted man, who was still standing there, gun in hand, apparently frozen in place.

As the barrel swung around, Bone took up the pressure on the trigger again, squeezing back just as the man with the pistol dropped down onto one knee in the shallow water and fired at the same moment. Bone whispered something almost inaudibly an instant before. The single shot fired from the four-barreled, remodeled Lancaster traveled two hundred and fifty yards, the trajectory almost perfectly flat as Bone had predicted. The shot buried itself in the concrete of the narrow footbridge that led across the river in front of the Brazil pavilion, missing the left, open-toed sandal of a well-to-do young woman taking movies with her father's Bell & Howell Filmo by less than an inch, sending out a spray of concrete chips. For a moment the young woman thought she'd been stung by a bee and wrote about it as such that night in her diary, the only known record of the single shot fired from John Bone's weapon.

Three out of five of the shots fired from Foxworth's military-style S&W Model 1917 struck Bone, the .45-caliber bullets hitting him in the chest, blowing him back into the flatboat and sending it crashing through the trash rack, where it then dropped over the slight lip of the spillway and headed downriver, unnoted by anyone except Detective Inspector Thomas Barry of Scotland Yard.

The second assassin was gone.

After a rigorous debriefing by Sam Foxworth back at the FBI offices, Hennessy, Jane Todd and Thomas Barry returned to the Plaza. Jane Todd's gloomy prediction turned out to be correct. There was no sign of Sheila Connelly anywhere. Hartery the Plaza house dick, Pelay the bellman and the cop Hennessy had left as insurance had been playing bridge with the Connelly woman as a fourth. At some point during the late evening she had excused herself and gone into the bedroom of the suite, which also contained the bathroom. She picked the lock of the door leading to the adjoining suite and disappeared. It was later learned through Foxworth's contacts that she had been smuggled aboard the North German Lloyd ocean liner *Bremen* and worked her way across to Le Havre as a chambermaid. From Le Havre she took a ferry to Rosslare, then a train from there to Dublin, and finally reached Belfast.

Barry was devastated, especially since she had apparently taken the signed and sealed affidavit with her.

"She took us, Tommy. She took us all," said Jane, easing herself down onto the arm of her upholstered chair.

"I feel like such a fool." He shook his head. "I'm not very good with women when you get right down to it."

"None of us is," Hennessy snorted. Pelay appeared with a tray of drinks and set them down on the card table.

"He is not kidding," said Pelay. "I have had the pleasure of meeting his wife."

"Watch it, runt. She's a fine woman, in her own way."

"As was Medusa. You know, the one with the snakes for hair. Turned men to stone with a single look I think I heard."

Jane took a bottle of beer from Pelay's tray for Barry and one for herself. She handed one down to the Scotland Yard man. "I ever tell you about my sister?"

"No."

"Her name is Annie. She's what some people call feeble, or more like a vegetable. Never moves, never talks, never really does anything."

"I'm sorry."

"Don't be." Jane shrugged. "It's not like she knows what she is. I go and visit her sometimes. She's in the asylum on Welfare Island. We crossed right over it on the way to the fair."

"I didn't know," said Barry. He took a sip of the beer, wincing at its frosty coldness. The Americans' penchant for cold beer and ice in their drinks was something he'd never get used to.

"What I mean to say is, sometimes I have dreams about her," Jane continued. "Not dreams like in sleep, but visions, or an idea of what it would be like if she came into a room, dressed nicely, carrying a purse, her hair all brushed neatly and said something like, 'Hey, Jane, let's go shopping,' or 'Let's go to Coney Island for the day.' You know it's never going to happen, you know it can't happen, but that doesn't stop you from thinking about it. I think that's what happened with you and your Irish. She's a mirror and she lets you see what you want to see when you're with her. It's her . . . talent . . . I guess you'd call it." She shrugged and took a swallow of her own beer. "Who knows? Maybe she even believed it herself when she was with you. Believed that it was possible to escape the terrible place she was in, the terrible past she came from."

"She as much as told me so," said Thomas Barry quietly. "We were in Detroit. She said the organization had no time for romance; they were only interested in bullets and bombs. She said, 'We can have it for a moment,

Thomas, no more than that.' I believed her, and she knew I would."

"It is like anything good in life, kiddo. We only have those things for a fleeting moment and then they are gone." She smiled broadly. "All the more reason to enjoy them while you have them." She leaned down and gave Barry a soft, lingering kiss on the cheek. "Lesson learned. Just because a lady's nice and pretty doesn't mean she's pretty nice."

"I wonder who the killer really was?" Hennessy mused from a couch on the other side of the room. "And who he was really working for?"

"The assassin was Irish," said Thomas Barry, his voice barely above a whisper. "Although I'm willing to wager we'll never know for sure who hired him."

"How could you possibly know he was Irish?" Hennessy scoffed.

"Because he spoke to me, just before I killed him. Spoke in the Old Language to me as though he knew I'd understand."

"What did he say?" asked Jane.

"Three words only. *'Slan, mo cara!'* Good-bye, my friend! And then he died."

"Maybe he meant he was about to kill you," Hennessy offered.

Barry shook his head. "No. He knew I'd be faster. He knew he was going to die. He looked like death itself standing there, part of him already a shadow."

"How do you say, 'It's over' in Gaelic?" Hennessy asked.

"Ta se thar," Barry answered.

"Then that's what it is then. *Ta se thar*!" he said and smiled. He leaned forward and tapped his cold bottle against Thomas Barry's and both men laughed.

"But what if it's not?" Jane said.

"What are you talking about, you foolish girl?"

"Tom here shot him, but did he kill him?"

"I shot him in the chest. From twenty feet away. He's dead enough."

"No body."

"What are you trying to say?"

"They haven't found his body yet. And it will be a waste of time to drag the river. I'm trying to say that this John Bone, or Mr. Green, or the Devil himself might have thought of everything."

"What everything?"

"A bulletproof vest." She nodded to herself. "He killed that FBI man, stole his car and his clothes. Why not his bulletproof vest as well? They all have them."

"No," Hennessy whispered, shaking his head. "That would mean . . ."

"That would mean he let the current take him all the way down the river. That would mean he's still on the loose."

Barry nodded coldly. "And that he'll make one last attempt on Their Majesties."

"With not a soul looking for him," said Hennessy.

Chapter 27

Saturday, June 10, 1939
New York City

Hennessy hung up the telephone and swiveled in his seat to face Jane and Thomas Barry. "There were three cars stolen from the parking lot at the Flushing Bay Pier this afternoon. A green '35 Nash, a '37 Ford Coupé in blue and a white '39 Dodge. They picked up a bunch of joyriders in the Ford, so we can scratch that one. The Nash and the Dodge haven't been recovered. The Nash is plated 2V 32 90, the Dodge is 3J 20 86. Both of them are New York." The policeman shrugged. "On the other hand the IRT station was just as close."

"He wouldn't have taken the chance," said Jane, shaking her head. She was sitting on the couch across from Barry now. "Easier to watch people getting onto the trains than it is to watch ten or fifteen acres of parking lot."

"The real question is, where's he going?" said Hennessy.

Barry gingerly took a crumpled piece of carbon paper out of the inside of his jacket pocket. He laid it out flat on the coffee table. "I found this in the wastebasket in Mr. Foxworth's secretary's office. It's the last page of Their Majesties' itinerary for their stay in America."

"I'll be damned," said Hennessy. "I didn't know Limeys were so sneaky."

"I wonder what other talents he's keeping from us."

Jane grinned. Barry flushed and used two fingers to straighten out the sheet of carbon paper.

He leaned forward, peering down at the artifact. "According to this, the royal couple will be dining at President Roosevelt's home in Hyde Park tonight at approximately eight. Sunday's agenda begins with breakfast at nine, church in the village at eleven, back to the house at Hyde Park to change into casual clothing, and then at noon they go off with the president et al to a picnic lunch on the estate. At two they are scheduled to go to Mrs. Roosevelt's cottage at Val Kill to go swimming, followed by tea, and then back to the president's home. Dinner at six, followed by farewells at the Hyde Park Railway Station as they board the royal train for their return to Canada at ten. In parentheses for both the church and the railway station it says to expect crowds."

"No kidding," muttered Hennessy. "You'd think they were Gable and Lombard the way people swarm around them."

Jane looked at her watch. It was ten after seven, the light outside only just beginning to fail. "We rule out the train station and the church, too many people and too many cops."

"Same with anything to do at the president's house," put in Hennessy. "Cops all over the place, Limeys as well as our guys."

"The picnic or the swimming thing," said Jane. "Those are the only private events that aren't at the house."

Barry stared down at the sheet of carbon paper. "What's the terrain like at this Val Kill spot? And what exactly is a kill? Sounds a bit ominous."

"It's Dutch for brook, or stream," Jane answered. "I did a photo feature on Val Kill for *Life* a few years ago. It's Eleanor's private little spot away from the big house. It's on the wooded side of the estate, west of the Albany Post Road and Route 9G farther east. They widened the stream to make a swimming hole and put up a big fieldstone-and-clapboard cottage. Pretty place. She's got some kind of factory out there in the woods too, making furniture."

"How many ways in or out?" Hennessy asked.

"There's lots of trails through the bush, but as far as I know there's only one actual road."

"He'll find an out-of-the-way spot to park his automobile and then he'll walk in," said Barry.

"But the king and queen won't be alone," Hennessy offered. "They'll have cops all over the place at Val Kill as well."

"He'll be there hours ahead of time, long before Their Majesties appear."

"Which means he'll have to go to ground somewhere not too far away," said Jane. "Tonight. A hotel or a motor lodge."

"Why? He might go directly to his hide," Barry suggested.

Jane shook her head. "Not likely. He's off his home turf. It'll be dark soon. Some guy stumbling over the Roosevelt estate shining a flashlight around is going to be pretty obvious."

"How many hotels do you think there are in the vicinity?" asked Hennessy with a sigh.

"Why don't we find out?" Jane said. "Get hold of Pelay and have him bring us up a Red Book."

"What's a Red Book?" Barry asked.

"The Hotel Association puts it out every year. It's like a telephone directory for hotels all over the country."

"Like an RAC Guide." The Scotland Yard detective nodded. When Jane looked confused, he explained, "Royal Automobile Club."

Hennessy made the call, the bell captain brought up the thick red-covered book and Jane flipped to the alphabetically listed section for New York. "It's got to be Poughkeepsie," said Hennessy, looking over her shoulder. "It's the only place within reach." There were three major and one minor hotel listed for the Hudson River town of forty thousand—Earles, with 55 rooms, the Kings Court with 150, Nelson House with 160 and the Poughkeepsie Inn with 120 rooms.

Jane jotted down the names and addresses on a sheet of hotel stationery, then walked Pelay back to the door.

"Can you bring us up some sandwiches?" she asked. "Corned beef, ham and cheese, that kind of thing? Put 'em in lunch bags. I think we're going to be eating on the road." She led Pelay out the door and into the hall.

"You want more beer too?" he asked.

"No. Maybe a few sodas."

"Sodas, okay. Coca-Cola."

"Great," Jane said, speaking quietly. "And one more thing."

"Sure, you bet."

"A gun."

Pelay looked shocked. "A gun, Janey? What for are you wanting such a thing?" He was beginning to look very nervous.

"I need a gun, to protect myself."

"When?"

"Now. I'll pick it up from you on the way out of the hotel."

"What kind of gun you want?"

"Whatever you've got handy." She patted him on the cheek. "Just so long as it's got bullets in it."

"Anything else while I'm at it?" Pelay said, curling his lip. "You want maybe I get you a Tommy gun or something?"

"No, but I will be needing a car."

"Whose car?"

"Yours would do." Jane gave the little man her best smile. Pelay drove a brand-new, bright yellow Plymouth Roadking convertible coupé complete with whitewalls. It might as well have been a Lincoln or a Caddie for all the care and attention he gave it.

"You want *my* car?"

"It's life or death. Otherwise I wouldn't ask." She paused. "And I need that little camera I saw in Bill Hartery's office." The house detective's diminutive camera was a cheap little Univex Mercury, but it had a self-synchronizing flash unit.

"You want me to steal Mr. Hartery's camera? Janey, you are stretching our friendship to its very limits."

"I told you, Pelay, it's life or death." She grabbed a

bit of cheek between her thumb and forefinger, tugging affectionately. "Do this for me and I won't tell the guys at our next poker game about what the so-called countess from Montevideo said to me."

The blood drained from his face. "You know about that?"

"All about it."

"I will fetch what you need."

"Good man." She pushed him gently down the hall and went back into the room, closing the door behind her.

"What was that all about?" Hennessy asked.

"Pelay's bringing us up some more sandwiches."

"Well that's all fine and good," said Barry, "but I really think we have to address the situation at hand."

"Address it how?" Hennessy asked. "Take it to Foxworth?" The policeman snorted. "He wouldn't give us the time of day. As far as he's concerned our man's floating out in the Flushing Bay somewhere, getting nibbled on by the fish."

"What about the bulletproof vest? The stolen cars?" Barry asked.

Hennessy shook his head. "Not enough. We can't be absolutely sure of the vest and there's no way to tie the stolen cars to our killer."

"I think the two of you should go up to Hyde Park tonight," said Jane. "Tommy here still has some clout. Maybe he can convince his Special Branch colleagues that we've got a problem. Maybe you can do the same with the Secret Service."

"What about you?"

"I'll go check out the parking lots of the hotels in Poughkeepsie. It's a long shot, but it's worth a try. If I strike out at the hotels I'll check out as many of the motor lodges as I can heading north. If I find one of the stolen numbers I'll get word to you."

Hennessy's eyebrows furled. "How?"

"Call in to the Plaza every half hour. I'll leave a number with the front desk if there's any news."

"I don't like the idea of you running into the fellow on your own," said Barry.

"I'm a big girl, Tommy. I can take care of myself." She offered up her best smile. "I promise I won't do anything stupid."

"That'll be the day," Hennessy grunted. He chewed on his lip for a moment. "Maybe the Limey's right. Maybe one of us should go with you."

"I need a white knight to protect me. Is that it? And you're nominating yourself?"

"It's a good idea, Jane, and you know it."

"No, Dan, it's a bad idea. You wouldn't get five yards into Hyde Park without Tommy's Scotland Yard identification."

"Then why doesn't he go by himself?"

"I doubt he can drive one of our cars. For him it's the wrong side of the road."

"Actually, both sides are the wrong side for me," Barry answered. "I never learned how to drive at all." He shrugged. "Not much point, living in London."

"Maybe I'll teach you when this is all over," said Jane.

"I'd like that." Barry smiled.

"If you two've finished batting eyelashes at each other, maybe we can get this show on the road."

"Absolutely," said Jane. "Just as soon as Pelay brings the sandwiches."

John Bone stood bare-chested, looking into the mirror in the rear of the gunsmith's shop. The quilted canvas-and-lead-plate FBI vest he'd worn was draped over the toilet seat a few feet away. Gently prodding with his fingers Bone tested the pain from the three dark bruises on his chest. One of the bullets had struck the vest just beneath the heart. The second had taken him in the left upper ribs, knocking the wind out of him, and the third struck in the upper right chest dangerously close to the neckline of the vest. Had it struck flesh it would have wounded him badly, if not killed him outright.

To the good, however, the shots had served to blow him off his feet and into the boat, sending it over the weir and downstream to safety. It had been a near thing, and after he had stolen the automobile from the parking lot by the pier, it had occurred to him that perhaps discretion really was the better part of valor in this particular case, and the project should be abandoned. It would have been an easy enough thing to make a change of clothing, abandon the car he'd stolen and take the next train to Florida. Within twenty-four hours he could be back in Havana, or in Nassau, and from either destination he could vanish almost instantly, reappearing in any part of the world he chose.

But instead, he had decided to stay and complete his assignment, in which case he would collect the rest of his payment. He had known almost from the beginning that this would likely be his last major operation. Not only did he want to go into retirement on a successful note; he also wanted to go into retirement with as much money as possible. Moving through the gunsmith's shop, gathering up what he needed to finish things, he decided that while the odds had swung slightly against him, they had not changed radically.

By his calculations they now stood at approximately sixty-forty against. The element of surprise was gone, and from this point on, the royal couple would be even more closely protected. The time element had now been reduced, and because of that, so had the possible targeting opportunities. On the other hand, if it was assumed that he had been killed under the bridge, then the odds would swing tremendously in his favor, since there was no sense in taking precautions against an adversary who no longer existed.

He checked the wristwatch he'd discovered in the bedside table in the back room upstairs. Seven-thirty. The luggage he'd retrieved from the Gramercy the day following his takeover of Lavan's shop was already in the trunk of the stolen Dodge, as were his small bag containing the handgun he'd decided on, an Austrian Steyr automatic, and detailed maps of the area around the Roosevelt estate he'd picked up in Washington in the event there was a problem at the fair. The silenced British DeLisle carbine, complete with a Leupold scope, was packed in a rifle case, leaning up against one of the display cases by the front door.

Bone decided against taping the bruise on his side, even though he was reasonably sure at least one rib was cracked. The tape would restrict his movements, and the pain was easier to endure than failing his mission tomorrow. He slipped on a fresh shirt, eased himself carefully into his suit jacket and out into the shop, turning off the light in the back room as he left.

He scooped up the screwdriver he'd brought up from the shop, slipped it into the pocket of his jacket and then picked up the rifle case. He went out onto the deserted street, used Lavan's ring of keys to lock the door behind him, then poked the keys back through the mail slot in the door.

That done, he took the rifle case to the car, put it into the trunk with the rest of his gear, then closed and locked the trunk. Stooping down, he took the screwdriver out of his pocket and used it to remove first the rear and then the front license plates, which he then slipped into his jacket. Bone checked his watch again and then began strolling south down Crosby Street. He turned right on Canal, heading west, and eventually turned north again and into the Village, a man out for an evening stroll, enjoying the first cool breezes of the day.

Bone found what he was looking for in a narrow passage between a shoe factory and a warehouse just off Le Roy Street: an old stake-sided delivery truck, obviously parked there for the night and completely out of sight. He went down the alley and within five minutes he'd removed the plates from the old truck and replaced them with the ones from the stolen Dodge. A half hour after that, with the truck license plates on the car in front of Lavan's, John Bone headed out of the city.

Chapter 28

Saturday, June 10, 1939
Hyde Park, New York

Sir Alan Lascelles sat in the wing chair beside the window in the well-named Pink Room on the second floor of Springwood, President Roosevelt's estate in the Hudson River Valley, and smoked a cigarette. Her Royal Highness had carried herself off to bed shortly following the disastrous and disastrously late dinner during which an entire service of Limoges china had been shattered when a serving table collapsed. The king was off with the Canadian prime minister chatting away happily about events of state. When Lascelles had left Roosevelt's smoking room twenty minutes before they had been discussing their mutual distaste for the Russians, and Lascelles, neither a diplomat nor a member of the Foreign Office, tactfully withdrew.

In the royal household, overhearing some conversations was decidedly unwise and could easily lead to banishment to some god-awful corner of the empire where it either never stopped raining or never rained at all. As the eldest daughter of the late viceroy of India, Lord Chelmsford, Lascelles's poor wife, Joannie, had spent enough time in awful climates. At their age neither of them were up to a stint in someplace like British Guyana or the Ivory Coast. A chill ran down his spine at the very thought of it.

He finished his cigarette and sat back in the comfortable chair, allowing himself to relax a little. There were only three events scheduled for tomorrow: church, a picnic, and tea at the First Lady's cottage at Val Kill. Roosevelt, bless his shrewd heart, had seen to it that their leave-taking from the United States would be without too much in the way of pomp and circumstance, sending them on their way with a minimum of fuss. Another few days and they'd be back aboard ship and on the way home. He smiled at that. Home—now didn't that have a nice ring to it. A week or so of leave with Joan and the children at their country house in Dorset, without a single royal in sight—what a treat that would be!

A knock at the door brought him out of his reverie.

"Come in."

The door opened and Hugh Cameron, the king's policeman, stepped into the room. "Sorry to interrupt you, sir, but there're two men who'd like to see someone in authority."

Lascelles glanced at his wristwatch. It was almost ten. "Who are they and what do they want at this time of night?"

"They're policemen, sir. One of theirs and one of ours, so to speak. They say it's extremely important."

"Where are they?"

"Two Secret Service men are detaining them in the main hall downstairs, sir."

"I'll come down," said Lascelles. Picking up his cigarette case and lighter he followed Cameron out of the room.

Jane was tired and she was running out of hotels. She'd checked the first three on the list, first looking through the parking lots and on the street, then going in and buttonholing the hotel night clerks, paving the way with a ten-spot each time. No white Dodge and no late check-ins that even came close to the description of the elusive Mr. Green, or whatever his name was.

She turned off Main onto Market Street, then turned again onto Cannon, finding the Poughkeepsie Inn just a little off the corner. She parked the bright yellow Plymouth across from the hotel entrance, then climbed out of the car and went across the street. The parking area filled up the corner lot beside the six-story brick hotel, lit by a pair of streetlights. She felt her heart jump in her chest as she spotted a ghostly white Dodge parked at the back of the lot. Threading her way between the other vehicles she saw that it was a '39, brand-new, just like the one stolen from the World's Fair site. Reaching the car her spirits fell as she saw that the plates were all wrong. Instead of 3J 20 86 the plate on this car was T9 33 47. She let out a long breath and turned away. Time to start hitting the smaller places along 9A and State 9 itself, the old Post Road highway that was the main road to Hyde Park and Albany.

She stopped in her tracks and turned back to the big coupé as the realization hit her. The Dodge couldn't have that plate number because all license plates in New York State had a number-letter pair at the beginning except for trucks, which always started with the letter *T*. She walked back to the Dodge, took a careful look around to make sure no one was watching her and bent down to check the plate. Sure enough there were fresh scratches around the screw holes on the rear plate. She didn't even bother with the front plate. She knew she'd hit pay dirt. Tom Barry was sure the killer was Irish, and it was a pretty sure bet that only someone from New York would know about that small peculiarity with the license plates. If he'd chosen a car instead of a truck she would have missed it.

Standing up, Jane headed back to the sidewalk, feeling the weight of the small Brazilian copy of a German Walther that Pelay had given her along with the car. She had no idea where he'd got it from and the little man had offered up no explanations. Reaching the sidewalk Jane stopped, adjusting the heavy bag on her shoulder. She checked her watch. It was just past ten.

The smart money said she should go into the lobby of the hotel, get a bunch of change from the night clerk and use a pay phone to make a trunk call to the Plaza and leave a message at the desk there. She had no business bearding lions in their dens and even less business getting too close to a man who'd already killed several people, including an FBI agent, and by her definition was at least partly the reason her first true love had been murdered and then dumped in a New Jersey ditch like so much garbage.

"Well, screw the smart money," she whispered angrily under her breath. This was her fight and her story as much as it was any man's and she was goddamned if she was going to give it all up now with a pretty little curtsey and go stand on the sidelines while the men played the Green Hornet and Kato from the serials. One way or the other she was going to put the finger on this guy and make him real instead of some sort of ghost. Ghost or not, according to Tommy he'd taken three shots to the chest. Even though he'd had a bulletproof vest on, he would definitely have a bruise or two.

She looked down at herself. Blue cardigan over a pleated white silk dress, blue linen shoes and no hat. She looked more like she was going off to play a round of golf than hunting down a killer, but at least she didn't look like a broad on the make. She adjusted the heavy bag on her shoulder and went into the hotel. The lobby was long and narrow, leading to the elevators, the carpet inevitably red. The reservation desk was on the left and a pair of double doors led into the restaurant-bar. The sign over the doors read The Henry Hudson Room and a sandwich board on the floor announced the piano stylings of "Gloves" McGinty. The fuzzy eight-by-ten pasted onto the poster showed a leering man in his seventies holding up a pair of long-fingered hands encased in white gloves. What a gimmick. Jane headed for the reservation desk and a young clerk with a poor complexion who reminded her of Ricky, the soda jerk back at Walgreens.

"I wonder if you can help me," she asked.

"You want a room?"

"Maybe later. Right now I want information."

"Like what?" He frowned and his whole face wrinkled up like a raisin. "You're not a pro, are you? My uncle hates pros coming in here."

"Do I look like a pro?"

"I don't know what a pro's supposed to look like. I don't think we get a lot here. All I know is my uncle hates them and he owns the hotel and he says don't let any single woman into the hotel unless she's got a phoned-in reservation and luggage. You got any luggage?" Ricky the soda jerk was a Don Juan compared to this kid. He had the personality of an earthworm and a brain to match.

"I'm not a pro, I promise."

"So what kind of information you want?"

"Information about the guy with the white Dodge in your parking lot."

"What about him?"

"Is he registered here?"

The kid smiled. "I can't remember."

Jane reached into her bag, took out her wallet and dropped a sawbuck on the counter. The kid swept up the ten-spot and slipped it into the pocket of his red uniform jacket.

"The white Dodge."

"He's registered here."

"When?"

" 'Bout an hour ago, little less."

"Under what name?"

"I can't remember." The kid smiled.

Jane offered up another ten. "Now can you remember?"

"Green."

"What room?"

"509."

"That's the fifth floor?"

"Yup. But he's not there."

"How do you know?"

"I saw him go into the bar about ten minutes ago and he hasn't come out, so I guess he's in there."

"How do I recognize him?"

"Tall, thin, a little on the pale side, like he doesn't get a lot of sun. Real dark hair."

"Black hair."

"Yeah. A bit long."

"Clean-shaven?"

"Yeah."

"Thanks," said Jane, "you're a peach."

"You got any more questions, lady? I could use the dough."

"Maybe later," said Jane.

John Bone sat in the end booth of the Henry Hudson Bar and sipped his double shot of ice-free Jameson. Thankfully the bald, white-gloved piano player had taken his leave a half hour before, so at least he could drink in peace. Almost eight hours had passed since the incident under the bridge at the World's Fair and the initial burning pain of the bullets' impact had dulled to a deep ache now. By morning, when it came time to play out the final act of this game, his muscles would be stiff, but not enough to influence his aim. Everything else seemed to be in order as well.

Bone had heard about Sterling's development of the DeLisle, but somehow Lavan, the late gunsmith, had managed to get his hands on a prototype. The carbine seemed to be based on a Lee-Enfield bolt action but was fitted with an integral silencer all the way along the barrel and was chambered for the U.S. .45 pistol cartridge, itself subsonic. Bone had fired off a dozen shots in Lavan's basement and it was almost completely soundless. He had also taken care of the matter of transportation. Coming in to Poughkeepsie he'd stopped at a service station to use their toilet facilities, and he'd noticed an old Harley-Davidson WJ Sport chain-locked to a pipe behind the station with a cardboard FOR SALE sign hanging on a string from the handlebars. The padlock on the chain would be easy enough to pick and the motorcycle would give him exactly the same kind of advantage the 500cc Dresch had given him in Marseille.

The Sport was known to be a very quiet machine, which would make his approach to Val Kill safer. Afterward the Harley-Davidson could take him where no automobile could follow. Looking over the maps he saw that he could use back roads to get out of New York State and into Connecticut within twenty minutes with no chance of being followed. He could be in Danbury within an hour and from there it would be a simple thing to take a Greyhound north into Boston. From there he could either sail or fly out of the country without any difficulty.

Bone caught a hint of movement out of the corner of his eye and looked up from his drink. The restaurant-bar was a long rectangular room set with booths on either wall, tables running down the middle and the bar built against the short wall nearest the door. A small riser and the piano took up the back wall. A woman with a large bag over her shoulder was standing by the door, letting her eyes adjust to the dim light. She appeared to be in her mid-thirties, blond, wearing a white dress with a blue cardigan. She was startlingly beautiful, her eyes large and intelligent, her cheekbones high and her mouth just a little too wide, which made her all the more attractive. She said something to the man behind the bar, who nodded and disappeared through a door that led back into the kitchen.

The woman came down the length of the restaurant and stopped at the table directly opposite his booth. She took the bag off her shoulder and dropped down into the chair facing Bone. She let out a long sigh, then turned to her bag, rummaging around in it until she came up with a package of Lucky Strikes. Apparently she had no matches or lighter to go with the cigarettes.

"Shit," she said. She looked across at Bone and smiled. "You wouldn't happen to have a light, would you?"

Bone slid out of the booth, took two steps, then reached down and plucked the book of matches out of the spring clip of the metal ashtray on her table. There was one exactly like it in his own booth and at every other booth and table in the restaurant. He opened the book of matches, tore one out, struck it and held the flame toward the woman. She shook out one of her cigarettes and lit it without making the slightest attempt to seem surprised that the matches had been in front of her all the time.

"May I join you?" Bone asked. The woman certainly wasn't a prostitute, and that made the situation even more interesting to him.

"Sure," said the woman. "Ships that pass in the night and all that." Bone turned away for a moment and retrieved his drink, then came back to her table and sat down. "My name's Jane," said the woman. "What's yours?"

"John," he answered.

"John and Jane, now that's convenient."

"Convenient?"

"For ships passing in the night."

The barman came out of the kitchen with a sandwich on a tray. He paused to draw a glass of beer from one of his taps, then went down to the table. He put both the sandwich and the beer in front of Jane. She took three singles out of her bag and waved away the change. She pinched out her cigarette and left it in the ashtray.

"Egg salad," she said, lifting half the sandwich. She took a healthy bite, wiped her lips with a paper napkin and sipped her beer, wondering just what the hell she was doing. She'd called the Plaza and left a message, complete with hotel name and room number. Then, like an idiot, she'd stepped into the bar and sat herself down ten feet away from the man. The trick with the matches was the kind of thing you saw Myrna Loy doing to sucker a suspect in a Thin Man movie. On the other hand, it had worked.

She saw the man across from her open his mouth to speak and she stopped him with a wave of the hand. "You're about to ask a really dumb question."

"I am?"

"You were about to ask me what a girl like me was doing in a place like this."

"It had crossed my mind," he answered. "One doesn't often meet an attractive woman alone in a bar in Poughkeepsie."

Jane smiled and took another sip of beer. There was something just a tiny bit wrong with the way he pronounced Poughkeepsie. There was also something horribly wrong with the things she was finding herself thinking about. He was handsome as hell, in a ghostly sort of way, but it wasn't so much that as the look in those cold gray eyes of his. Violence and some kind of terrible hunger. It was making her weak in the knees. If she'd been forced to stand up at that instant she knew she would have fallen down. She took another bite of sandwich and washed it down with another slug of beer.

"So what is a girl like you doing in a place like this?" he said.

"I'm a reporter," Jane answered. "Doing a society piece on their royal personages when they go to church tomorrow. Couldn't find a hotel room left in Hyde Park, so I came down here." It made sense and she could back up the reporter part of it without much trouble. "How about you?"

"On holiday," he said. "Taking in the sights."

"Been to the fair?" Jane asked, cursing herself silently the instant the words were out of her mouth. You didn't play word games with a killer.

"Several times," Bone answered.

"Exciting, isn't it?"

"I found it a little too . . . enthusiastic," he said, looking for the right word.

Jane took a long swallow of beer, relit her cigarette and forgot about the rest of her sandwich. "So what *do* you do for excitement?" she said quietly, knowing exactly what she was doing now. She had to see him without his shirt. She saw the night in front of her as clearly as a photograph appearing in the developing tray. Wish me luck, Annie, she thought and sent up a little prayer.

"I meet beautiful women reporters who like egg salad sandwiches and beer and can't see a book of matches a foot away from them on the table."

"I'm farsighted."

"You're very lovely," he answered.

"I bet you say that to all the girls." But of course he

didn't, because he didn't have to. The terrible attraction of a snake about to strike and the looks of a lothario—any woman's secret dream.

"I don't meet many girls like you."

"Like me?"

"You're not afraid."

"Of what, you?"

"A stranger in a strange land. Most women would be."

"Should I be? Afraid, that is?"

He smiled and in the movement of his lips and the small softening of his eyes Jane saw something of his past, a shadow of his youth. "Some women enjoy fear," he said at last. "It makes life more exciting for them,"

"What makes life exciting for you?"

"Nothing," he answered. "Excitement can cause you to make mistakes. It's something to be avoided."

"Even when it comes to women?"

"Every rule should have one exception." He smiled again, and she was lost.

They undressed on opposite sides of the bed in his room and for the first time in a long time Jane felt no shyness or embarrassment at revealing her body to a man. He stared at her frankly and she did the same, studying the play of muscles in his arms and chest, the spray of thick dark hair between his nipples and the heavy swelling pulse of his organ as it lifted out of the thicker black hair thatching his groin.

She stepped out of her panties and laid herself on the pale sheet, her legs falling open like a gift as he covered her, his biceps corded and palms flat just below her armpits, the skin of his wrists just touching her breasts, hard with the ache she felt. She was wet and ready to take him, but even so, it was a shock as he slid into her inch by inch and then began to move in a steady rhythm that seemed to go on forever.

She lost track of time as he changed his motion and her position beneath him and finally, after some endless length of time, he lifted her legs over his shoulders and began to pound into her almost savagely. At the same time he moved his hands, cupping them under her shoulders in a small, gentle motion that made her hips arch upward and said everything about the man he might once have been and made her think, just for an instant, that perhaps she was wrong.

But she knew, had known from the instant he'd taken off his shirt and she'd seen the bruises put on him by Thomas Barry—the man she should have felt this way for. The man with Tommy's mark on him exploded inside her so hugely that she thought he'd torn something inside her, burned her up, destroyed her soul. Even when he was donc he stayed hard and in her for a long time, not moving, staring down at her until at last, with exquisite slowness, he withdrew inch by tender inch until he was gone and lay beside her, his breath barely louder with his exertions. She turned half on her side and put her hand flat on his chest and felt no heartbeat.

"It's true," she whispered.

"What is?"

"Nothing. Just something someone once said to me." He was a ghost, just like Thomas had said. She let her hand lie there for a moment longer and then she roused herself. "I've got to use the bathroom. Be right back."

"Don't you hurry on my account then," he answered, his voice in a soft lilt she thought might be the voice he was born with, so much the same as Tommy's and two such different men. "I'll just smoke one of those cigarettes you have such a hard time lighting."

"Sure," she said, her heart thumping hard. "As long as I can borrow your shirt." She shivered, but not from any cool breeze. "It's a bit chilly in here."

"Of course." He leaned over the side of the bed and brought up the shirt. She shrugged into it then stood and went to her bag and tossed him the Luckys, the book of matches tucked in between the package and the cellophane. He caught the package one-handed, and while he worked the matches out and lit his cigarette she crossed the room, hands crossed under her breasts, and opened the bathroom door and shut it behind her.

Once inside the bathroom she sagged back against the door and struggled hard to keep from sobbing aloud. She'd just made love to a killer and had never been so aroused in her entire life. She'd just betrayed a man she'd begun to fall for and here she was standing half naked in a bathroom, wondering what in God's name she should do next. She eased her left hand out from under the shirt and gently put the automatic pistol Pelay had given her on the toilet tank.

If John, or Mr. Green, or whoever he really was had gone looking for her cigarettes on his own he would have found the gun and that would have been the end of it. A bullet to the head, just like Howie. She felt tears forming and wiped them away quickly. She wasn't crying for poor old Howie. She was crying for herself, baffled by herself, terrified of the man who lay naked on the other side of the door, but still feeling the stolen heat from him like a hot coal just below her stomach.

Jane squeezed her eyes tightly shut and tried to put herself in the man's mind. If you were a guy who was going off to kill the King and Queen of England the next day you might want to take a woman to bed, but you'd probably hire a professional, of which there were undoubtedly a few, even in Poughkeepsie. What would you think when you were given the come-on by a woman at ten o'clock at night in the hotel bar, and she told you she was doing an article on the king and queen and had he been to see the New York World's Fair?

You might get a little suspicious, so what would you do then? You'd go through my bag, you murderous son of a bitch. That's what you'd do. You'd start going through my bag the minute the bathroom door closed.

And what would you find? Oh Jesus, you'd find all the names and telephone numbers written down on all those scraps of paper, Howie's itinerary coming back from Florida and his name, the name of the clerk at the law firm, and the name of the law firm itself. Hennessy's name and rank, Tommy's name with Scotland Yard scribbled beside it. Doodles of little crowns on stick people and a stick person firing a gun done on a paper napkin from the Claremont.

Enough to charge, convict, sentence and execute you for being a fool. Stupidly, the only thing she could think of was that her bare feet were cold on the bare white-tile floor, and in her reflection half seen in the medicine cabinet mirror she had a serious case of what her high school friends used to call bed hair. Then she had a split-second vision of rosettes of blood spreading across the white shirt she was wearing, the spreading stains over the same place where Tommy's shots had struck before.

She leaned away from the door and picked up the pistol. Turn the button on the barrel down, pull the side back to insert a shell into the chamber and then squeeze the trigger. Eight shots. She put her ear to the door but she couldn't hear a thing. She grabbed a towel off the rack beside her and wrapped the gun in it, using her thumb to twist the safety button down. Then with the towel muffling the sound she pulled back the slide, wincing at the heavy click. She put her ear to the door again but still heard nothing. Maybe he hadn't moved at all and was still lying in bed smoking and staring up at the ceiling with that big, thick cock of his lying across his thigh, waiting for her to come out of the bathroom so they could start all over again. She would look stupid coming out the door in his shirt with a gun pointing at him, saying, "Hands up. I'm making a citizen's arrest!"

But he wouldn't be in bed, covered in the streetlight glow spilling through the window. He was waiting outside to kill her. Suffocate her with a pillow, strangle her with his belt, a quick snap of her neck with those strong hands. It would be quick and it would be silent and she knew she'd never have the nerve to actually point the stupid gun at him and squeeze the trigger because that's what cops and killers did and she wasn't either of those. She was the one in the pictures she sometimes took for Hennessy. She was about to be Howie Raines, lying in a ditch with some cop photographer using a little wooden compass to show which way her head was lying.

"Like hell," she whispered. She ground her teeth together, opened the door and stepped out into the room, her right hand bringing up the Walther. The next day, a week, a month, a dozen years later and it was always as though time stood still. She saw her lover at the end of the bed, the sheets littered with the contents of her shoulder bag. He had his trousers on and was leaning over his own suitcase on the little bench at the end of the bed, his hands sliding a fat-barreled rifle of some kind out of a gun case, working the sliding bolt with a single slap of the ball of his thumb, bringing the weapon up, aiming at her. Just then there was a crash of splintering wood as the door to the room smashed inward, both Dan Hennessy and Tommy surging through the doorway, guns drawn, but too late because her lover had swung the rifle in his hands around at the first sound of the door opening and was already firing.

But so was she, her finger squeezing the trigger, the pistol jumping in her hand, striking with all eight shots, stitching holes in him from his thigh to his jaw, blood spurting in great arcs from his femoral artery, one shot under his arm going through both lungs and heart, the seventh and eighth bullets blowing pieces of his face against the far wall, bits of bone rattling across the wallpaper like tossed dice before they tumbled to the floor. He dropped to his knees, the DeLisle falling from his hands, and then fell forward on the ruins of his face.

"No vest this time," said Dan, sliding his pistol back into its holster. "Nice shooting, Janey."

She stood stock-still, the empty gun still dangling from her hand, the smell of gunpowder and blood filling the room, her ears ringing from the shots she'd fired. She turned and saw Tommy looking at her from a few feet away, looking at her in the dead man's shirt, knowing what it meant, the smile of relief on his face faltering for a small moment, and then he stepped forward and took her, weeping, into his arms.

AFTERWORD

Over the weekend several meetings were held between Roosevelt, His Royal Highness and Cordell Hull at the president's Hyde Park estate on the Hudson River. The meetings were held in the late afternoon and evening and their content was never discussed openly. In point of fact, the meetings outlined the American strategy that would eventually become Lend Lease, and while Roosevelt made no direct commitment to fighting in a European war, he did tell the king that he would intercede should Hitler actually invade England. At the end of the weekend the king and his queen consort boarded their train again, returned to Canada and eventually went back to England. The identity of the dead man in room 509 of the Poughkeepsie Inn was never discovered. His killing by Jane Todd, a newspaper photographer from New York City, was deemed to be justifiable, and after a hearing in the Dutchess County Superior Court the file was closed, although it is public information and can be viewed at any time if there is sufficient reason for doing so.

John Bone's body was cremated and the remains dispersed without ceremony or record.

Although FDR was personally advised of both the assassination attempt by Bone and the conspiracy that led to it, he dealt with the situation internally rather than by hanging the Democratic Party's seditious dirty laundry out in public, both for his own political good and also for the good of a country poised on the edge of war, something FDR was even more aware of after the royal visit.

Within twelve months of the events at the World's Fair, Postmaster General Farley had been removed from office as a cabinet member and as both national and New York State chairman of the Democratic Party. Those jobs were then taken over by Ed Flynn. Prior to the 1940 elections and without warning, Roosevelt summarily dropped Cactus Jack Garner as his running mate, replacing him with Henry Wallace. As soon as it became diplomatically possible, Joseph P. Kennedy was removed from office as ambassador to the Court of St. James. He never held any kind of public office again.

Considered at the time to be one of the most dangerous men involved in the complex plot to see Roosevelt unseated, Allen Dulles, a lawyer with the firm of Sullivan and Cromwell, was given a straightforward choice: go to jail or come and work for us. Roosevelt, always a man to keep his enemies close where he could see them, offered Dulles a job with another lawyer acquaintance of his, Bill Donovan, who would go on to form the Office of Strategic Services, an Ivy League intelligence service that was tailor-made for Dulles's personality. Following the war and after Roosevelt's death, Dulles became head of the Central Intelligence Agency while his older brother, also a lawyer at S&C, became secretary of state. Cardinal Spellman was never directly implicated in the plot, although the FBI file on Joe Kennedy noted Farley's visit to the cardinal who was in residence at Kennedy's Palm Beach house earlier that year.

Percival "Sam" Foxworth was shot down and killed in North Africa while on a secret mission during the war.

Sean Russell died of a ruptured appendix on board a German submarine that was returning him to Ireland after a meeting in Berlin in 1941. He was buried at sea, and a statue of him stands in a Dublin park to this day.

Jane Todd's sister died of influenza less than a year after the events depicted here. Unable to join any of the women's branches of the armed forces as a result of the wounds she received during the bomb attack on her office, Jane headed for Hollywood, eventually becoming a well-known publicity agent there. In 1972 she wrote her autobiography, *Hot Toddy,* but mentioned nothing about her connection to the royal visit of 1939.

Sheila Connelly remained with the IRA for the rest of her life, acting as a courier and occasionally as a driver. During the war she married another IRA member named O'Toole and bore him two children, Eamon and Sean. Her husband was convicted of murder in 1947 and was executed for his crime. She outlived both her children, seeing Eamon into the ground after a skirmish with the RUC during the marching season of 1958, and burying the remains of her son Sean in 1964 after an accident involving a shipment of Czechoslovakian-made Semtex plastic explosive.

Sheila Connelly herself died in a similar accident while shipping 250 pounds of the explosive to an IRA weapons depot in Clonmany by Malin Head. Fortunately the accident occurred in the early morning on a deserted road and no one else was injured, although the blast was said to have been heard as far as Buncranna, more than twenty miles away.

Thomas Barry returned to England immediately following the events outlined here, resigned from Scotland Yard a few weeks before the outbreak of war and joined a military intelligence unit. Eventually becoming a high-ranking officer in MI5, Barry retired in 1965 and was seen on the Civil List the following year in recognition of his long service to the Crown. He was prevented from writing his own memoirs under the conditions of the Official Secrets Act, although it is doubtful that he would have done so anyway. He returned to Ireland on only one occasion—the memorial service for Sheila Connelly held in the churchyard of St. Patrick's Cathedral in Armagh on July 12, 1974. His presence at the memorial service in the Ulster city was noted and photographed, and he was questioned about the event by his onetime colleagues at MI5, but he refused to say anything. The matter was not pursued. Sir Thomas Barry never married and died in 1980 at his small country estate in Herefordshire, the Glory. As requested in his will, several hundred letters written to him by Jane Todd between 1940 and her death in 1978 were interred with him.

Queen Elizabeth, the Queen Mother, once known as Buffy by her husband and John Bone's second target on that day, is still alive as of this writing and still has a definite preference for powder-blue dresses and Pink Betty Prior Roses.

—Christopher Hyde
Dublin, Republic of Ireland, 1999
Nassau, the Bahamas, 2001

AUTHOR'S NOTE

Contrary to the disclaimers usually provided in novels, the vast majority of the characters and events depicted here are entirely real. The visit of King George VI and Elizabeth, his queen consort, to North America during the late spring and early summer of 1939 has been portrayed in absolutely accurate, minute-by-minute detail, from the clothes they wore and the food they ate to the composition of their security detail. More important, the efforts of Scotland Yard's Special Branch, the FBI and other federal and state agencies to track down and apprehend an Irish assassin intent on killing the king, the queen and Franklin Delano Roosevelt on American soil have been included, much of the information culled from newly declassified State Department and Royal Canadian Mounted Police documents.

How close that assassin came to achieving his goal has never been described until now, although for many years there have been a number of vague rumors, most of them relating to the involvement of the Irish Republican Army and of one man in particular, Sean Russell, IRA chief of staff at the time.

In fact, neither Russell nor the IRA had anything at all to do with the plot. The real conspirators were all Americans and included several senators, a Catholic archbishop, a lawyer who would go on to become head of the Central Intelligence Agency, Roosevelt's own vice president, and a man who, following another assassination, would himself become president of the United States more than twenty years later.

While several hundred books have been consulted in an effort to give a socially and politically accurate picture of that tumultuous time in America, I am greatly indebted to the grandson of one of the key participants in the story, who gave me free access to his grandfather's private diaries. Without those diaries, especially the entries between Thursday, February 18 and Monday, June 12, 1939, the truth might never have come to light.

For the skeptical among you who read this story and say, "Pure fiction," I urge you to telephone M. Georges Colbert of the Hotel Louvre et Paix (DRagone 35.37) in Marseille and ask him to describe what he discovered under the floorboards of room 506 on a July afternoon in 1964 when he was redecorating. He'll be happy to tell you, and for a small fee he'll even send you a postcard.